PENGUIN BOOKS

LIES WE TELL ABOUT THE STARS

SUSIE NADLER

PENGUIN BOOKS

PENGUIN BOOKS

UK | USA | Canada | Ireland | Australia
India | New Zealand | South Africa

Penguin Books is part of the Penguin Random House group of companies
whose addresses can be found at global.penguinrandomhouse.com.

www.penguin.co.uk   www.puffin.co.uk   www.ladybird.co.uk

First published in the USA by Dutton Books, an imprint of Penguin Random House LLC
2026
First published in Great Britain by Penguin Books, 2026

001

Copyright © Susie Nadler, 2026

The moral right of the author has been asserted

Penguin Random House values and supports copyright. Copyright fuels creativity, encourages diverse voices, promotes freedom of expression and supports a vibrant culture. Thank you for purchasing an authorized edition of this book and for respecting intellectual property laws by not reproducing, scanning or distributing any part of it by any means without permission. You are supporting authors and enabling Penguin Random House to continue to publish books for everyone. No part of this book may be used or reproduced in any manner for the purpose of training artificial intelligence technologies or systems. In accordance with Article 4(3) of the DSM Directive 2019/790, Penguin Random House expressly reserves this work from the text and data mining exception.

Design by Anna Booth

Printed and bound in Great Britain by Clays Ltd, Elcograf S.p.A.

The authorized representative in the EEA is Penguin Random House Ireland,
Morrison Chambers, 32 Nassau Street, Dublin D02 YH68

A CIP catalogue record for this book is available from the British Library

ISBN: 978–0–241–79956–7

All correspondence to:
Penguin Books
Penguin Random House Children's
One Embassy Gardens, 8 Viaduct Gardens, London SW11 7BW

Penguin Random House is committed to a sustainable future for our business, our readers and our planet. This book is made from Forest Stewardship Council® certified paper.

For Iris and Jonah, my Gemini

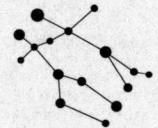

Day 1

Nobody will ever believe Celeste when she tells them, much later, that she was thinking about earthquakes at the moment when the Big One finally came. Specifically, she's thinking about the word *terremoto*, which she learned just this week in AP Spanish, and which is so much better and scarier than the English word, sounding almost like the thing itself as it trembles your tongue. This is the kind of stuff Celeste thinks about all the time, only ever speaking the thoughts to her mom, who appreciates nerdy things, and to Nicky, who appreciates everything.

There's an attic room at the top of Celeste's family's house that's almost too small to stand in. Technically it's storage, but Celeste claimed it last year to get some space from her parents, wedging her stuff in the corners, making it cute with piles of thrift-store pillows. Ursa takes up half the floor space lying down, wiry quills of her black fur stuck in the rug for good, since nobody ever wants to drag the vacuum upstairs. The two of them are alone up there—Celeste doing Spanish homework, Ursa lying in her usual watchful mound—when the shaking starts. Right before, the house was so quiet that they could hear the kitchen clock ticking all the way downstairs. No wind, which is strange up here on the hill, where the wind can tear up trees and Pride flags.

This one isn't at all like the quakes Celeste has felt before, little bumps that woke her up, no more consequential than if they'd happened in a dream. Instead there's a tangible stillness, then a weird second or two of faint vibration in her skin. The dog lifts her head sharply, as if alert to some intruder—and then a jolt, the slap of a giant hand, and the house seems to slide across the street and back again. Celeste is knocked back onto the pillows. Then the bed lurches, dumping her on the floor the instant she starts to scream. Everything blurs, but she scrambles to her knees, gasping "Fuck fuck fuck," clutching the carpet, her mouth filling with blood. Ursa's barking her head off, her huge body swaying. Above them, the bookcase starts to lean and rattle. Some old advice pops into Celeste's brain, and she drags the dog under the desk just as the photos and records and books start cascading off the shelves. Her Jupiter lamp pinballs across the room and bursts into shards. Downstairs, there's a terrible chorus of clanging and pounding, shattering glass—then a long, blistery shriek that will turn out to be the noise of a seam splitting open down the center of the stairs.

Celeste squeezes her eyes shut and buries her face in Ursa's fur. She tries to think of what to do, how to save their lives, but instead she can't stop thinking about how pissed she is at Nicky. If he'd showed up at the library after school like they'd planned, she'd be there with him instead of here, alone. But he stood her up again—in fact, she didn't even see him at lunch, and he hasn't returned her texts all day. Celeste knows why he's acting this way, but that doesn't make it easier.

Finally the house stops shaking, but Celeste's body doesn't. Her eyes burn; her heart's a hammer. Her tongue swells and bleeds.

The air is thick with white dust, and there's a gravelly sifting noise and the sound of something heavy tumbling down the stairs. Ursa's panting, soaked with drool, her claws sunk in the rug. Celeste forces her trembling hand to stroke the dog's head. She's afraid to move— maybe the house could crumble with one wrong step—but she's suffered through enough drills, as mandatory as math at San Francisco schools, to know that it's better to get outside for the aftershocks. She manages to find her feet, Ursa scrambling to her side.

They tiptoe through the mess. Celeste grips Ursa's collar and steadies herself on the wall. At least the little box of her room seems basically intact, if not the precious stuff inside. Amazing garage sale turntable smashed flat in the corner. Big geode from Joshua Tree pulverized in sparkly bits. And her gorgeous *Mars Pioneer*—a delicate, painstakingly half-built model of the shuttle that will launch in May. It'd been perched carefully on her otherwise messy desk, a project started with Nicky that languished in recent weeks, since everything with him got so weird. Today there was a test flight of the *Pioneer* heat-shield system—they were supposed to watch it together at the library, but Nicky ghosted her. Now all Celeste can see of the model is a cracked wing pinned under a pile of books. She feels desperate to rescue it, maybe to gather a bag of stuff, or even check the rest of the house, but then there's another little jolt— *We have to get out NOW.*

Her backpack's by the door with her diabetes bag inside, Ursa's harness tangled on top, so she clips the dog in, grabs the backpack, and runs. At the stairs, they recoil: A jagged maw runs all the way from top to bottom, the wood and plaster split open. The dust in the air is heavier now, and there's a chemical smell, maybe the stinking guts of the stairs or something worse. Celeste covers her mouth with her sweater and tightens the leash. Ursa's too big and clumsy for this, but she'd jump through fire for Celeste, so they climb down as fast as they can, the dog clambering ahead, her paw pads catching on the splintered wood.

Outside, Celeste gasps for breath with a feeling of relief that lasts about a millisecond. She's always thought the shaking itself would be the freakiest part of a big quake, but it turns out the sounds are worse: car alarms blaring, terrified shouts hanging in the sky. Sirens already wail in the distance, too, and they won't go away for days, endlessly approaching and retreating. Ursa wildly sniffs the air, her black eyes wide and wet. There's a weird yellow haze, but at least it feels slightly safer out here, with neighbors trickling onto the street. Mrs. Toy stumbles out of the house next door in tears. She hugs Celeste, babbling about her parents, and says when it's safe, she'll go inside for some almond cookies, which Celeste remembers eating with tea, eons ago, on Mrs. Toy's plastic-covered couch. One of the neighbor nannies rushes up to them clutching a baby, distracting Mrs. Toy long enough for Celeste to sneak away and plant herself on the curb.

Her head's a little swimmy, her mouth still tasting of metal. She fumbles in her bag for her phone. No service. She stares at the useless screen. Her mom and dad are both at work, or maybe heading home already, stuck on the road? A car is one of the safer places, Celeste remembers from some YouTube video, but then she also remembers a video from the '89 quake—those cars tumbling into the broken gulf of the freeway in Oakland. Thinking of that makes her want to vomit into the gutter, so instead she thinks about Nicky.

Where could he be? The fact that she doesn't know is infuriating and strange. Not very long ago, the likelihood of the two of them being apart after school was basically zero. The few hours before dinner were always theirs together. They did homework, hung out reading in coffee shops, pretended to shop for shoes, listened to music at Celeste's—rarely at Nicky's, not since he moved in with his grandparents last year. Ever since the move, things haven't been the same, but it's only in the past couple of weeks, with Nicky stuck in such a shitty mess, that Celeste has started to worry about losing him altogether. Each time it takes him longer than a minute to text her back, she starts to panic. Now she scrolls through her photos just to look at him for a second, their goofy selfies with his wild grin, the thick brows she helps him wax into perfect crescent moons. She figures if there had to be a giant earthquake, at least one upside is that everyone might be too distracted to bother with Nicky's shitty mess anymore. Maybe it will all just slip away in the chaos.

Some shouting up the block yanks her away from her phone. The couple from the yellow house, both named Dave, come striding down the hill in hard hats and neon vests, calling out names to check in with the neighbors. Celeste's pretty sure the Daves are some kind of fire department volunteers. (They're old, but also totally ripped; you can see the weight machine in their living room from the street.) They're heading her way, but she can't imagine opening her mouth to speak—it's getting harder not to cry or throw up or otherwise lose it in some horribly public way—so she grabs her backpack and takes off with Ursa, charging around the corner and up toward Tank Hill. That's where she and Nicky always said they'd meet up in case of a quake or zombie attack, on the off chance that they weren't already together when the shit went down. She has a feeling he isn't there, a hollow feeling left over from the library this afternoon, but at least she can get a look at the rest of the city from the top.

Her chest tightens as they climb the steep sidewalk. There's a joint in her diabetes bag, but she doesn't want to smoke it, not when she might be alone until dark, or who knows how long? People are already clustered crying in the street. Others pour out of their houses carrying cats, and Ursa dutifully strives to ignore them. Tree limbs dangle from curls of bark or lie where they've fallen on parked cars. Most of the houses look okay—not demolished, just weirdly askew, their windows shattered, the garage doors crumpled. It's bedrock up here, her parents always said; the damage will be worse in the flatter parts of town. Celeste thinks about the crack in the stairs, a fracture in the spine of her house— do they all have wounds like that? From outside it's impossible to tell how bad things are behind the doors. She hurries past without looking too hard.

At the top of Tank Hill, there's no sign of Nicky. The hollow feeling widens and presses out on her ribs and back. Celeste keeps her face down, veiled behind the curtain of her messy dark curls, hoping nobody will ask if she's okay, because the answer isn't clear. But then she stands on a rocky ledge and looks out over the view and sees the plumes of smoke rising over the city and across the bay, spreading into a kind of black-and-yellow haze, and the frozen chains of cars all along the winding streets and down the belt of Market Street as far as the water, hears the sirens swirling into a frenzy up here in the middle of it all, and Celeste understands that there are probably lots of people *way less okay*, and she finds herself not exactly praying, because she doesn't believe in anything you can pray to, but hoping in a desperate and smoldering sort of way about her parents and Nicky. None of the usual tourists and stoners are up here today, so she digs her nails into the weave of Ursa's leash, opens her mouth, and just kind of wails for a second. The sound that comes out seems as loud as the sirens. Ursa watches carefully, her head cocked; this doesn't look like a blood sugar spike, but she's ready if it turns out to be one.

"I'm okay, girl, you awesome animal. What would I do without you?" Celeste kisses the dog's head, wraps her arms around her thick neck, and watches the view for a while, the two of them perched on a boulder. It's getting cool, leaning toward dusk (4:40, says Celeste's rapidly dying phone). She puts on the threadbare Irish fisherman sweater from her backpack. Out of habit she looks for the bright planets, but nothing peeks through the thick haze. When she and Nicky were kids, Celeste's dad used to bring them up here all the time, lugging his telescope; now they like to come by themselves to smoke weed and eat popcorn and use the star map on their phones. Pickings are usually slim in the fogbound, light-polluted SF sky, but a few of the planets are sometimes bright enough to see.

The two of them have had a plan since they were little: Space Camp, MIT, NASA training together, a mission to Mars. They shared the dream just like they shared everything else—even their birthday—a coincidence that seemed, when they met at age three, like a genuine miracle. Nicky used to joke that Celeste would never make it to NASA because it was just too corny for somebody named Celeste to become an astronaut, like their dentist, whose name was Dr. Plack. As it turned out, though, Celeste's disqualification from astronaut-hood was real. Her type 1 diabetes diagnosis came at the end of seventh grade, three weeks before they were supposed to fly to Houston for Space Camp. Nicky didn't want to go alone, but she wouldn't let him give it up, and he's been the keeper of the dream ever since. They don't talk about going to Mars together anymore, but MIT and NASA are still theoretically part of the plan. Nicky likes to scroll crappy Cambridge apartments, planning their life as roommates, the movie nights they'll throw for their friends with lots of cheap wine.

"The first queer astronaut!"

"No fucking way! What about Sally Ride?"

"Okay, fine—the first *cis gay male* astronaut."

"Probably not. A lot of those early NASA guys could've been gay for sure. It wasn't exactly cool for military dudes to come out in the seventies."

Nicky gasped, crowed with laughter. "*The Right Stuff* is the sexiest movie *ever*."

They've been having the same conversation for years, this one just a few months ago. They were sharing cherries and popcorn, dangling their legs over the side of the same rock where Celeste is huddled now with Ursa. Nicky grinned, talked into his fist: "This is Major Toniolo coming in from Ursa II, over."

Celeste rolled her eyes and studied her handful of popcorn. Lately their little NASA game had started to annoy her, making her feel inexplicably queasy, like it was something they shouldn't be caught doing.

"Come in, Ground Control, come in! Jesus Christ, Ground Control, have I lost you? Communications failure! Mayday, mayday!"

Finally, she relented. "Roger, Toniolo, how do things look up there?"

"Gorgeous, Ground Control. You ever notice how the Milky Way looks like a big smear of jizz on, like, a black sheet?"

"Gross, Nicky!" They cracked up, spilling the popcorn over

the rock. After the laughing faded, he told her how his early application to MIT was finally done, the essay a real tearjerker about his single mom. "They're gonna fucking eat it up," he said. "What about yours?"

She shrugged. She hadn't started her application yet. Even now, two weeks before the final deadline, she *still* hasn't started it. Somehow she hasn't started any applications at all, not even her safety schools. Every time she sits down to open the forms, Celeste just kind of freezes up. She tries to imagine her life elsewhere, in a new place with new people and new doctors, and her chest fills up with a wide, cold bubble, blocking her breath. She figured at least the essays would be a breeze—writing always feels like a relief—but she still hasn't even made it past two sentences of the stupid diabetes essay the college counselor told her to write.

"Slow as shit," she told Nicky after a minute. Then she admitted, "I'm actually not applying early. I guess I need more time."

She waited for him to freak out, to remind her about their future apartment and movie nights and space-to-Houston chats, but he just gazed out over the city, spitting cherry pits into the weeds. Nicky's future felt so certain to her then, vast and inevitable as an iceberg, and she always seemed to be scrambling up the slippery slope of it—that is, until his giant four-alarm blaze of a fuckup melted the ice. Celeste feels like they've been flailing in the waves ever since, drifting apart. Now the city's smashed back to Victorian times, her house is probably going to swallow itself in a sinkhole, and who the fuck knows where Nicky even is.

Somebody starts to honk like crazy out on the street, as if that's actually going to help. Celeste knows the feeling, though—like if you could just get to the other side of this jam, then everything might be okay. She thinks it must be the burning smell making her dizzy, but then Ursa places a paw on her arm and barks twice, their alert signal for when Celeste's blood sugar spikes. More people are here now gawking at the smoke, so she goes to a bench tucked away in the bushes to check her continuous glucose monitor app—shit, 300—stupid not to check it sooner. She tries to dose the insulin pen, struggling to calculate in her blurry brain. One time she and Nicky carved their names in this bench. She closes her eyes, feels the letters under her fingers, and tries to breathe. Usually the air up here is cool and tangy with eucalyptus and pine and the blowing fog, but today it feels thick and dry, like eating a mouthful of ash.

Finally, she manages to prep and prime the pen. With the needle in her belly, Celeste fails, as usual, to think about something pleasant, instead remembering that time freshman year when she fell asleep in first period and woke up in the ER—this was before Ursa, back when she was still trying to hide the diabetes at her new school—she blinked her eyes open, saw her parents and Nicky dozing in ugly hospital chairs, and found herself wondering if Jackson Beale had been in class when it happened. Did he see her body get flopped onto a gurney by hot paramedics, and if so, was he jealous? What a dumb thing to think about when you're hooked up to an IV, and even dumber now, hiding in the bushes with a needle like some kind of junkie while the world is falling apart, but Celeste can't help it. She caps the pen and sinks into a soft gray place for a minute; then, all at once, with a burst of clarity, she realizes she needs to get home. What the fuck is she doing here where nobody can find her? What if her parents came home while she was gone? She shoves the kit back in her bag and runs down to the street.

THE SIDEWALKS ARE EVEN MORE CROWDED THAN before. Celeste and Ursa hurry down the hill, weaving through stopped traffic, drivers hanging over their open doors or sitting on bumpers, murmuring to each other or staring blankly at their hopeless phones. Celeste knows she looks nuts, young and alone, running in combat boots and baggy jeans with a huge lumbering Newfoundland, but nobody tries to help or stop her, all of them wrapped up in their own cocoons of shock.

"Jesus, Celeste, where have you been? Dave, she's here!" The bald Dave meets her at the corner, clutching his heart over his neon vest. "Mrs. Toy said you ran off. Don't do that again, okay, kiddo? You gave us a scare."

Celeste apologizes vaguely, out of breath. She asks about her parents, but nobody's seen them. The Daves nuzzle Ursa with their beards and ask about her family's emergency plan. They've always been so nice: giving out full-size candy at Halloween, not snitching when they caught her rolling a joint in Sutro Forest. Nicky always called them the Care Bears, back when they were his own neighbors, too. Celeste tells them she's supposed to meet her parents at home. Bald Dave touches her arm and says he's sure they're on their way. "What about Nicky? He's not with you?" Celeste's stomach lurches. She shakes her head, coiling Ursa's leash around her palm. The Daves glance at each other. "Hey, we could use some assistance here, if you're up for it?"

In front of their house, they've set up a folding table with bottled water and protein bars, a stack of those shiny silver blankets. Celeste follows them to the table and tries to help for a while, checking off names and handing out waters, the warm bulk of Ursa drawn up close at her side. They make a safe zone in the street with some traffic cones and lawn chairs, far away from damaged trees. Most of the neighbors around at this hour are old people, plus a few nannies with babies—the nannies are new, since some of the old people died and/or sold their houses to techies for crazy money. That's what happened to Nicky and his mom: Their nice landlord died about a year ago, and his evil son jacked up the rent to get them to move so he could sell the place. Now a couple of EV-driving parents live there with their screamy kids, and Nicky lives with his grandparents way over in Vis Valley, on the other side of town.

Celeste stays with the babies in the safe zone while the nannies reluctantly dash inside for diapers and bottles. Bald Dave helps Mrs. Toy find the gas shutoff in her garage, and then they both help her rescue her terrified yellow bird in its foul cage. Everyone seems to be waiting. At last Celeste's phone buzzes in her pocket—her heart leaps, but it's just the reminder to check her sugar. Still no bars. She scrolls through old texts from Nicky as if they might contain a clue about where the fuck he is, but there's really not much of anything from him lately, just the maddening bouts of radio silence and Celeste's own long chains of question marks in reply.

An hour passes like this, maybe two. More neighbors start showing up in dusty office clothes, some walking mangled bikes or dangling high heels from their fists, a kind of twisted version of what happens at the end of every day, the tide of commuters rolling in. Celeste wanders back to her house and stands with Ursa on their brownish patch of lawn and wrings her hands. The Daves show up a minute later and ask if she's doing okay. She bites her lip, watching the ground between her boots, the weeds shoving up through a sidewalk crack. "Oh, honey," bald Dave says, crouching to wrap her in a muscly hug, and when he squeezes, it makes her cry, like wringing a sponge, a steady stream of tears and twisting sobs in her chest. He strokes her matted hair, this almost stranger she's actually known for most of her life, and tells her that everything will be all right, even though neither of them has any way of knowing if this is true.

SOON IT'S DARK, SO VERY DARK, THE BLACKEST DARKness the city has ever seen. A sliver of moon casts a ghost of light against the haze. In the distance, strange patches of orange glow drift into the sky, a morbid aurora that must be coming from the fires. Celeste is literally camped out with the Daves in their front yard; they've decided it's safer to sleep outside tonight. They set up an old-school canvas tent and feed Celeste a Cup Noodles, cheerily joking about s'mores and charades, sneaking worried looks at each other. Their kindness moves and embarrasses her, so she tries to play along, suggesting a sing-along around the little campfire in their hibachi ("Mrs. Toy, get over here for some show tunes!") and even offering the joint from her backpack, which they ruefully decline, citing their commitment to the emergency volunteer squad.

"Listen, sister, wouldn't I *love* to take you up on that," says redhead Dave, and bald Dave pats her knee and says with a wink, "You go ahead, sweet pea, we won't tell. God knows we need to self-care like crazy right now." She is just about to light it with shaking hands when one of the dark shapes beyond the firelight reveals itself as the tall, poncho-wearing, weary-shouldered silhouette of her mother.

"Celeste? Celeste! Oh my god, Shane, she's here!" And then both her parents are there swooping her up, one of her mom's many soft hand-knit ponchos enfolding her like wings, her dad's pleasantly funky-smelling beard scratching her cheek. With all the crying and hugging, she can't answer any of their rapid-fire questions (*ohhoneyareyouokay—haveyoucheckedyoursugar—wereyouherewhenithappened—howsUrsa—haveyoubeeninside*) until they are sitting around with the Daves later by the fire. Celeste's dad has gone into their house to poke around gingerly, maybe gather a few supplies, and have a look at the damage, the beam of his flashlight flickering on the windows. Celeste's mom explains that traffic is totally stopped everywhere. Eventually she abandoned the car, after wrangling it into the parking lot of the boarded-up bowling alley on Stanyan. Shane had been rehearsing at Davies Hall—he's a second violin in the symphony—and he walked all the way home in a group of musicians lugging their instruments like some kind of wayward minstrels, splintering off to their respective neighborhoods until Shane was the last one coming up over Twin Peaks, where he spotted Bonnie doggedly trudging to get to Celeste.

"I'm just so relieved you were home," Bonnie says. She wraps her arms tighter around Celeste, a kind of cuddling they don't do so much anymore. "But I'm really sorry you had to go through it alone, honey." Behind Bonnie's words Celeste can sense more words—*Where is Nicky?*—but they haven't been talking about him recently, with the big fuckup hanging in the air. Still, Bonnie looks like she might be about to ask.

"I wasn't *alone*, Mom!" Celeste lets go of her mother and snakes her arms around the dog's neck, covering her big black ears. "Ignore her, Ursa. She's in shock."

Bonnie leans over to apologize to Ursa, kissing her scruff. "Thank God for you, Ursa! And the Daves!" She blows them kisses over the flames, they pass her the can of soup they've been heating up for her, and for a moment Celeste feels so warm and loved, she almost forgets this isn't just some friendly neighborhood weenie roast. Then Shane comes back and sits close to the fire. "Jesus, Bonnie," he says, rubbing the bridge of his nose, the Irish lilt of his voice decidedly less whimsical than usual. "It's pretty bad. I mean, I think we're lucky, really, on the whole. But it's not good." He explains about the crack in the stairs.

"How do you even fix something like that?" Celeste wonders, and her dad pulls her close.

"I don't have a clue, love." Then they all sit speechless for a while. Celeste stares into the fire and tries not to think about what else is burning out there in the darkness, the acrid vapor she can taste on her tongue. She buries her nose in her dad's sleeve, listening to the crackling flames and muffled voices from neighbors' tents and the sirens, always the sirens, coming close and then trailing away.

Day 2

The next morning Celeste wakes up in a tent beaded with fog. She's alone except for Ursa, who's stretched out at her feet like a cheesy hunting lodge rug. They made a kind of "Princess and the Pea" bed with blankets and pillows from the living room, Celeste sandwiched between her parents, none of them sleeping much. There was an aftershock in the night—a small one—but still, it freaked everybody out. It took a while for Celeste to stop crying afterward. Her phone was dead, along with the CGM app, and her sugar tanked, maybe she'd dosed wrong with the noodles—so Bonnie had to feed her some juice, her own hands shaking too hard to hold the cup. Then the neighbors' babies and Mrs. Toy couldn't calm down, keeping them all awake for another hour.

Shane and Bonnie must've crept out of the tent at dawn. Celeste can hear them whispering out there now, exchanging rumors, wondering about the bridges and the massive, hideous new buildings downtown and the older homes in neighborhoods built on tidal flats, like Nicky's grandparents' house.

"She hasn't even mentioned him."

"She's probably just worried. Let's see what we can find out today."

There's a rustling, her mother's snuffly tears. Celeste presses her ear against the damp tent wall. "He's been so pissed at me," Bonnie says, her voice ragged. *Pissed*, like Nicky was just stuck in some kind of snit, a dumb teenagery mood. Like Bonnie hadn't pushed him right to the edge and watched him teeter. A spark of fury in Celeste's throat makes her scoff. Bonnie says, "I just can't bear to think—" but then Celeste's dad softly tells her everything will be fine. Why do they all keep saying that? The world is literally crumbling.

Celeste throws off the blankets, burying Ursa. She shoves on her boots and does her best to storm out of the tent, no easy feat without a door to slam. "You think I can't hear you?" she hisses at her parents. An annoyed crow shrieks from its perch in one of the broken trees. The Daves sit at their table in the safe zone, crouched with some neighbors around a hand-crank radio. Celeste blows past her parents to join them, Ursa close at her heel.

The broadcast is staticky but audible as bald Dave fiddles with the dial. Magnitude 8.1. Epicenter Bolinas. Death toll over one thousand and rapidly climbing, hospitals already past capacity. Fires getting under control, but some entire city blocks are still burning, others in ruins. Cut to a reporter shouting into a phone over the sound of maybe a river? No, Celeste realizes, it must be fire hoses, or even the roar of flames? "Michael, we think—dozens of people—collapsed, and the team can't get past—" and then a silence that also seems to roar. "Judy? Judy, are you there? We lost you, Judy. Let's try to get her back." Someone switches the radio off. Celeste's head begins to fill with inky bubbles. Her mom is suddenly at her side, pressing a yogurt into her palm.

"Eat something," Bonnie commands in her teacher voice. "And please lose the attitude. We're all doing our best." Celeste finds a seat on a lawn chair and forces herself to eat even though the yogurt's sour. Bonnie crouches in front of her and looks in her eyes, holding her wrist. "Listen," she says, "I'm worried, too, okay? They're saying we have to shelter in place, but as soon as it's safe, we'll walk down to school and see what we can find out."

Their school is a designated neighborhood community relief center. Celeste isn't sure what this means, but her mom, who's head of the language arts department, is on some kind of safety committee that made it happen. With phones and internet down, she guesses it's probably one of the few places they can go to find out what the hell is going on.

Celeste's dad hands her a paper cup of instant coffee and tells her he's heading inside to look around again. She holds the cup under her chin, feels the steam on her face. For a minute she lets herself imagine finding Nicky at school in the middle of the chaos, flopped in one of the cafeteria chairs with his dog-eared copy of *Dune*. His body always looks so out of place at school, like an undercover cop in a bad movie, tall and broad and (as of last year) sporting a real beard, the hipster-barista kind, dark and full and impeccably trimmed. He's become so good-looking, with those bright black eyes and big easy smile and his square chin like a statue's. At their public middle school, it had sucked for Nicky, being the early bloomer, the gay kid with the peach fuzz and the too-small clothes and the sick best friend, but at Golden Gate, their private high school, Nicky reinvented himself. He's the guy who can buy liquor and get into bars in the Castro, who cracks everybody up with his Italian mobster voice—*take the cannoli*. Somehow it all works—the beard and the close haircut and his infectious twirling laugh—the cute signature look he can actually afford: skinny jeans, a rainbow of Converse, a candy-pink hoodie—people love it. He's crew team captain and a fucking stellar student, too, full scholarship, always winning awards. Nicky just draws people to him—he walks around with this warm light basically shooting out of his pores. But Celeste can see behind the light; she knows the heart of him. He is terrified he will ruin things. The stakes are always so high.

"Dad, can I come?"

Shane tries to object, but she follows him anyway, leaving Ursa to wait patiently on the driveway. Her dad stands in the front hall listening intently, as if all the broken things and the rupture in the stairs might somehow be the work of a burglar still rummaging through the house. Celeste starts picking up books and straightening them on shelves, but it feels like a dumb gesture, like trying to dig a grave with a spoon.

"Can I go up to my room?"

"Not yet. I'll have to find some boards to stabilize the stairs. Don't know if we have anything lying around that'll do." He mutters to himself about taping the cracked windows, bringing the gallons of drinking water up from the garage. "Gotta get my head on straight, love, then I'll give you a job to do." Seized by a sudden urgency, he hurries down the hall, and she realizes: the basement studio, his instruments. He had his most valued violin with him at rehearsal, but downstairs he keeps his mother's Irish harp, a few guitars, and the quarter-size violin he played as a kid, which Celeste spent a lot of time squawking on in fourth grade until (with a sadness in his eyes that burned itself on her brain) her dad agreed to let her stop the lessons. Now his relieved laughter peals out from the basement: "Everything good down here!" And she is glad for him. Is there anything that Celeste holds so precious to herself, anything she feels desperate to rescue? The only thing she can think of, really, is Nicky. But even if she figures out a way to save him, there isn't any place she can count on finding him anymore.

While her dad's in the studio, she wanders around aimlessly picking things up and putting them back—crooked picture frames, plants knocked over. Their Christmas tree lies on its side on the living room rug, its beaded star tossed clear across the room. The kitchen floor sparkles with broken glass and china, the yellow cabinet doors all flung open. Another massive fissure runs the length of the tile countertop. Celeste picks her way to the broom closet and starts to sweep some shards.

It wasn't so long ago—two weeks? Every day since then has seemed so long and lonely—that Nicky was sweeping here, cleaning up an exploded bag of corn chips. Celeste sat on the edge of the counter, making a list of things Nicky could do to make money. She was trying to convince him to quit selling papers to the rich dummies at their school, a lucrative but super-risky scheme he'd been pulling for over a year.

"Prostitution?" she suggested.

"Ugh, too exhausting."

"Phone sex, then?"

"Huh! That could work, actually!"

He flicked a corn chip at her, and she caught it and ate it. So far, the list of ideas wasn't long. Nicky had already tried every legit job he could find, but none of them paid a fraction of what his brilliant essays could earn. Ever since he and his mom, Carla, were evicted, he'd been worrying on overdrive about paying for college. Carla had started working double nursing shifts just to keep up their share of the tuition at Golden Gate, and Nicky was studying his ass off, hoping he'd get into MIT and qualify for a full ride. The backup plan was never clear—what would he do if they didn't get enough aid? Probably crazy loans and work-study to make ends meet. Meanwhile, most of the other seniors at Golden Gate think a FAFSA form has something to do with pro soccer. Celeste has never blamed Nicky for seeing an opportunity there—but they both knew that if he got caught, MIT wouldn't give him a fucking cent.

The corn chips were in the trash, and so was the list, when Celeste's mom came home and found them sharing a smoothie, one of their superfood concoctions with almond butter and four kinds of leafy greens from the freezer. Usually, Bonnie would grab a straw and pull up a stool, ask about their day, or maybe even share some juicy teacher gossip, a ploy to get them to stay and hang out with her instead of retreating upstairs. But that afternoon she just stood there slumped in the doorway, her face kind of gray, messy topknot even messier than usual, with a pencil stuck through it.

"Nicky—" she said, and then, after a long pause: "First of all, I love you."

"Aw, Bonnie-Mom! I love you, too." He crossed the room to hug her, but she was stiff. He backed away a step, shrinking, his shoulders collapsing like they always did when he'd gotten in trouble when they were little. Bonnie crossed the room, opened her bag, and laid the papers out on the tile counter one by one. They were the papers Nicky had sold—not all of them, just the ones from this month's AP World Lit, Bonnie's only class for seniors—but enough to get him in deeply serious shit. Paragraphs glowing violently with highlighter and red pen: places where Nicky had fucked up and pulled stuff direct from the internet, or even from his own previous work. Celeste felt her eyes grow wide. She gripped the edge of the counter and wished for Ursa, who was asleep in the other room.

"Oh," Nicky said. "Holy shit. Holy holy—"

"Celeste, could you give us a minute alone, please?"

"Can't she stay? She knows everything."

Celeste's mother turned to her and stared. The light was shifting in the kitchen, sun behind a cloud, the afternoon waning. "You knew about this? But you didn't— I mean, you weren't *involved*—"

"*No*, Mom, I would never!"

Nicky's hand flew to his face, like she'd slapped him.

"I mean—" She lowered her eyes. "I wasn't. Involved."

Her words hung in the air like a sour smell—*I would never*— the wrong thing to say in so many ways. True, she wouldn't have done what Nicky was doing, but only because she didn't have to. Celeste's parents aren't rich, but they do get the teacher's tuition break at Golden Gate, and her grandma Mimi has been saving to help with college. Nicky's dad died when he was a baby, and Nonna and Pop can't help very much; if anything, they need Carla's support now, too.

"I don't understand," Bonnie said wearily. "How did this happen?"

Nicky folded his arms and tucked himself into the corner, picking at a peeling door frame. "It wasn't, like, a *choice*," he said. "The first time I did it for a friend, like as a favor. And then, I don't know, people just heard about it, I guess? So I just kept going." At first, he explained in a small, choked voice, he didn't even plagiarize. Somehow it felt okay if he just took the other kids' assignments and wrote them himself. He was actually doing *more* work, right? Improving himself by learning the stuff those kids were choosing *not* to learn. Setting himself up better for the future, even. And he was fucking awesome at it, better than AI; the teachers could usually spot ChatGPT, but not Nicky, a master ventriloquist for his classmates. After a while, though, he'd gotten so tired. Started pulling material from published stuff online. Got sloppy and put some of the same stuff in his own work. He told Bonnie he'd always meant to stop, but the jobs had kept coming his way, and it had been hard to turn them down.

"These are not jobs, honey." Celeste knew Bonnie's disappointed face so well, but she'd never known it to twist itself in that sad way for Nicky. "I wish you'd come to me instead," her mother said. "You understand I can't just let it slide, Nicky. I have to report this kind of thing. This is really quite a pile of shit you've got us both in."

Nicky looked like he might cry, which even Celeste hadn't seen him do in years. It felt like an emergency, like she needed to do something to stop this conversation now or they might never get over it. Was there maybe a joke she could crack? Or could she pretend to faint, get them all in a tizzy, so they could bond over her blood sugar like usual? But her mom just handed Nicky a paper towel to wipe his eyes and gave him a hug. Then she pulled away and looked him in the eye again, her own face slick with tears, too.

"I hate this, but you need to tell your mom," Bonnie said, "and she can help you figure out how to turn yourself in. Tell her, please, or tell the school. Otherwise I'll have to do it for you."

"Wait," Nicky said, his voice trembling, "you're *threatening* me?"

"I can give you a week, Nicky." She kissed his cheek and went upstairs.

The kitchen fell silent, the smoothie congealing on the counter. Ursa came in and nosed around at their heels. Nicky dropped his face, clawed at his beard. "I'm *fucked*," he said. "I am just so royally *fucked*."

"You know what? I'll just talk to her. Maybe she'll change her mind. Maybe if you promise, I don't know, never to do it again—or to go tutor kids in the Tenderloin or something—"

"Listen, don't fucking judge me, okay, Celeste?"

"I'm not!"

"Jesus—'I would *never*.'" He looked down at her with a wet glare. "It's not like you're the queen of awesome choices, okay? Where's your insulin pump, Celeste?"

"What does that have to do with this?" She knew exactly where it was, upstairs shoved under the bathroom sink next to the tampons. Nicky knew it was up there, too, and he knew what happened the last time she tried to wear it. The fucking thing was robotically connected to some app on her parents' phones, and they hounded her the whole time she wore it, freaking out every time she had the tiniest dip or spike in her levels. Finally, she ripped it out one night when she was stoned and ended up in the ER with an infection from the wound. She's been refusing to wear the pump ever since, despite the constant nagging from her parents and Dr. Pierce.

"I'm just saying, you sit there all superior, like you'd never do something as stupid as cheating."

"I didn't mean—"

"You know what? You can't fucking understand! Nobody's kicking you out of your house, Celeste! Grandma's paying your fucking tuition!" He was shouting, picking the papers up and rattling them in the air. He threw them across the kitchen, and Celeste watched them float clumsily to the floor.

Bonnie reappeared in the doorway then, her eyes wet and red. "Nicky," she said weakly, "that's enough."

"They'll expel me," he said, spitting the words. "I can forget about MIT. Forget about all of it." Then he muttered, "I gotta get out of here," and left the front door hanging open behind him.

THE DOOR IS OPEN NOW, TOO, LETTING THE SIRENS in. Celeste leans on the broom, looks at herself in the mirror that fell off the pantry door. The cracked glass splits her in two, a cleft of light slanting down through her face and chest. Absently she fingers the CGM button on her thin arm, showing through her sleeve. She hasn't been eating enough lately, and she's lost a bunch of weight, flattening her cheeks and boobs. Dr. Pierce keeps saying she needs more calories, but between the shit with Nicky and the shit with her (as yet nonexistent) college applications, she's been too stressed to bother with whole grains and healthy fats. The Gemini constellation necklace she always wears, which used to drape on her collarbone in kind of a pretty way, now sinks into the weird hollow there. Sometimes Celeste doesn't even recognize her reflection, the sharper nose and chin making her brown eyes absurdly big. (Nicky says she looks like a badass manga girl, but Celeste knows he's just being nice; 100 percent of manga girls have big boobs, and 0 percent of them have curly hair.)

She thinks of how he looked at her when she said that thing: *I would never.* So self-righteous, which is something he always accuses her of being when they fight. Was that the moment when Nicky decided he didn't need her anymore? She texted him over and over that night, but he didn't reply, and he wasn't at school the next day. Eventually he came back, but he was different, distant, and he had a plan: to disappear. Run away, maybe, but *disappear* was the word he used. He told her in secret, locked together in the third-floor gender-neutral bathroom; he was still figuring out the details of his plan.

"You can't tell," he said. "Not a single fucking soul. Promise me on Ursa's life." And she did, because at first she thought he was just being dramatic, in classic Nicky style. But as Bonnie's ultimatum approached, he started to fade out a little, bailing on plans and sending single-word replies to Celeste's epic text monologues. He started to talk about where he would stay, how much money he'd saved, even the shoes he would probably pack (not the green Docs, too conspicuous). Celeste started waking up in the mornings with a fluttery panic in her throat. She was afraid to try to talk him out of it, still stinging from the fight in the kitchen and *you can't fucking understand*. One week became two, and Bonnie still hadn't turned him in to the school, but she was stressed and curt at home, never even mentioning Nicky—this kid she'd practically raised, who'd had an assigned seat at their table since he was in diapers. All this, and then the planet decided to just rip right open along the seam.

Celeste drops the broom and runs up to her room, cracked stairs shifting under her boots. Her dad shouts, but she just has to get a notebook; writing is the one way she knows to help herself feel better. The mess is as she left it, broken bookshelf and its contents sprawled across the rug, the hanging plant disemboweled, a splatter of black soil. It takes a minute to dig out one of the cheap spiral notebooks she buys by the dozen in Japantown. She grabs a pen, picks her way to the bed, and hugs her ratty old monkey, Emperor Palpatine, who smells like Ursa's breath. Then she manages only to write

Where is Nicky?

before her phone blasts in her pocket, dinging and buzzing like crazy. Celeste yanks it out. She assumed it was dead, but now she sees the thin red line of life and a sad parade of texts from Nicky's mom unfurling on the screen: *Are you ok??? He's with you, right?? Please msg me right away! I'm so worried!!! C, please send me a msg if you can.*

More missed messages and calls: from Celeste's grandma Mimi, and her aunts in Ireland, and a few sorta-friends on group threads already miles long with drama—but no Nicky. Celeste scrolls through them all three times. And then the last one from Carla, the same three simple words Celeste has just written in her journal:

Where is Nicky?

There are different ways to be gone, of course. *Lost/gone/missing.* Celeste's pen hovers for a minute over the page in a grip so hard her hand shakes, phone clutched in the other hand. The thing is, Celeste and Nicky have always had a kind of deep telepathy, a way of just *knowing* if the other one is in trouble—it's almost chemical, like the way Ursa knows when Celeste's blood sugar drops or spikes. Celeste squeezes her eyes shut and listens to her breath. She sets down the pen and phone and presses her fingertips against the small fiery sun tattooed on her wrist, as if to take her own pulse.

And all at once she knows: Nicky might be missing, he is probably lost, he might even be gone—but not for good.

"Sweetheart, check your phone, I'm getting through to Granny and Da!"

Her dad bangs around downstairs, laughing a little with relief. Celeste picks up her own phone and opens the texts from Carla. *Where is Nicky?*

He's not here, Celeste types. *But I know he's okay.*

And then the screen goes black.

Before

They got the suns sophomore year, which feels like ancient history, even though the tattoo sometimes hurts just as much as when it was new.

It was an afternoon in the fall. Celeste remembers that physics started late, and while Nicky read to a bunch of friends from *Vanity Fair*, Celeste leaned on the windowsill, twirling a curl of her hair on a pencil, looking down at the pools of sun on the Panhandle grass, and wishing for a free period so she could take Ursa outside to frolic with her dog buddies. Finally, the principal came to the lab to announce that Ms. Vaughn had gone home sick, and she made them put their phones away and put on a science podcast. Celeste slumped in the seat next to Nicky, scrawling *BLARGH* in his notebook margin. But at least it was a new episode of *PodLab*, one of their favorites, with the host with the soothing sexy-nerdy British voice. When they settled in to listen with the lights low and Ursa snuggled between their chairs, Celeste became transfixed, and Nicky was, too—they kept exchanging wowed glances and writing exclamation points on each other's notes.

"The Sun Has a Wind," that's what the episode was called. It was about the *Voyager* space probe, and why Carl Sagan wanted to send it off into the universe, and about the Golden Record of sounds from Earth it contained, and the love story between Sagan and his research partner, which was dreamy and forbidden at first and just so beautiful. Some scientists talked about where *Voyager* is now, and how it won't be long before they'll lose track of it, and how we might never know whether it ended up in the hands of some other unfathomable beings or just kept floating in space and time without end.

So—where is it now?

In the pause.

Turns out the sun has a wind—every star has a wind, in fact—and the theory goes that this wind is what gives our solar system a shape, and beyond the edge of the solar system, past the reach of the sun's wind, lies a great stillness, a kind of pause. And scientists have figured out, based on a sudden quieting of *Voyager*'s transmissions, that the probe is there now: in the pause. Beyond the pause, *Voyager* will stop transmitting altogether.

After class, Nicky and Celeste just couldn't quit yapping about the podcast, so instead of heading down to the Panhandle with everyone else, they took Muni home and spent the afternoon up in Celeste's room with her laptop. They found a whole website for the Golden Record where you can listen to the same sounds that are out there traveling through space. The labels are strange and poetic—*Fire, Speech; Footsteps, Heartbeat, Laughter; Mud Pots; Thunder*—and the sounds themselves are haunting, layered with static, making them seem ironically alien.

They wanted to find the episode and listen all over again, so they googled the title, "The Sun Has a Wind." "Look at the crazy shit people search." Celeste laughed, showing him Google's suggestions in the search bar. "'The sun has a rainbow around it.' 'The sun has a face!'"

"Wait, look—the sun has a *twin*? For real?" They read about the theory that stars are born in pairs. "That's *dope*," Nicky declared. "Like you and me, CB!" Celeste felt warm on her skin, as she did whenever he pointed out their closeness; it's obvious which of them is the sun and which the twin in this metaphor. As kids they would always pretend they were twins, because of the birthday thing, and because neither of them had an actual sibling. They called their twin selves Belinda and Benjamin, after their real (and miraculously alliterative) middle names. The nickname CB was like a secret code from the game that carried into their older life.

Nicky had an idea that day: They would get twin suns tattooed on their arms. They went down to a place in the Haight, the one that sells the crystals, where the lady is too nice to turn down a lame fake ID. They picked a flaming golden sun no bigger than a thumbprint and presented their wrists for the needle. Nicky went first, looking pale and wobbly after. During Celeste's turn, she cycled through words in her head to try to distract herself from the pain. *Wind/twin/wind/twin. Footsteps/heartbeat/mud pots/thunder.* The pain felt like a splintering deep in her bones, but when it was over, she felt proud, wearing a permanent brand of their friendship.

Afterward, they stood outside admiring the suns. A kid they kind of knew was leaning against the crystal shop wall; they see him around the Haight sometimes, this cute, brown-skinned boy with shocking blue eyes. He hangs around the street kids but doesn't seem like one of them. Nicky always teases her about how she gets all blushy whenever he shows up. "Yo, it's Beauty and the Beasts," he hollered at them, leaning over to pet Ursa. Celeste tightened the leash. "Hey, relax, I'm not gonna hurt him. I love animals, see? You guys get some new ink?" They showed their wrists, and he laughed. "Adorable," he said, and Nicky told him to fuck off. "Love you too," the kid called after them, his sky-bright eyes flashing at Celeste as she and Nicky climbed onto the bus.

Day 9

In the pause. That's where the city seems to be drifting, too. Everything suspended. Sidewalks clogged with half-parked cars lightly coated with dust and ash. Streetcars stuck with their doors half open, aboveground and below. Tacos and bagels and delicate salads half eaten, left behind in restaurants. People are sleeping in the streetcars, even eating the abandoned meals. Voices on the emergency radio are wondering just how many more people the quake will make homeless. It's December, so the days are cool and sunny, but soon it could rain, turning the rubble into sludge, soaking the half-collapsed shelters and hospital wards. In her notebook, Celeste wonders about the blue-eyed boy; a lot of the Haight kids sleep in Buena Vista Park, but she hasn't ever seen him with a pack or a tent. Where does he go at night? She wonders about the park, the droopy tennis court and faded jungle gym, the craggly bottlebrush tree with three big knots like a face, somebody's sleeping bag curled up neatly in the crook of a branch.

Celeste thinks about all the corners of her heart that look like the corners of this town. She scrawls in her notebook, trying to imagine what they all look like right now. The little yellow rec center where she went to day care, with its tree-stump stools and tie-dyed silks hanging on the windows, teachers sweeping the terrified children under the tables. The neighborhood library where Celeste always studies with Nicky, a stately brick palace, like something stolen from a different, older city, piled high with fallen books and the crumbs of stone columns. The belowground aquarium in the park, with its indigo tunnels. Do fish feel earthquakes? Celeste has no idea. She thinks of the tank glass buckling and giving way, flooding the tunnels with eels and slippery kelp, probably still rotting there now in the dark. And down the hill, the stage is set at the opera house for a *Nutcracker* performance that won't go on. A dust of glitter snow and broken light bulbs, tulle skirts tossed from their hangers, the gilded lobby with its toppled Christmas trees.

Or maybe—and this is the part that sends Celeste into a dizzy black dive whenever she tries to write about it—those places are just *gone*, destroyed. There isn't any way to know, really, with the power still mostly out, and cell service too spotty to get the internet. The lights only came on for a few minutes last night before they blinked off again with a quiet pop. Somewhere out there, the rest of the world is watching, sending their fucking thoughts and prayers, clicking and scrolling past it all, but here in the dark there's nothing to scroll, only the whispers and worries of neighbors: the slowest news cycle ever. Even emergency radio is pretty bare-bones, directing people to shelters and evacuation centers. Motorcycle cops are constantly growling past the end of the street, watching for curfew-breakers; one of them told the Daves there's looting all over town, the roads still jammed with debris and trees and totaled cars. Until they get it under control, people who have a roof are expected to stay under it, so Celeste and her parents are living like post-apocalyptic Girl Scouts, camping in the living room, rationing their canned goods and bottled water, and shitting into a bucket, reading by flashlight at night or listening to Shane's violin. Christmas came and went. Usually they spend it with Nicky and his family, a crab feast at Nonna and Pop's on Christmas Eve. This year they lit candles and ate beans on toast and read Dylan Thomas out loud, like they used to do when Celeste was little. They sang a few carols by the hibachi with the Daves, but it made Celeste so sad that she claimed a headache and went to bed.

Whenever the phones flicker to life, she scrolls frantically for any sign of Nicky. Still nothing—only the endless coil of texts from his mom, who is wild with worry, assuming the worst. Unlike Celeste, whose parents won't let her out of their sight, Carla actually did try to go out searching, but the cops sent her home with a warning and the number for a FEMA caseworker. Now she's hunkered down with Nonna and Pop, their hundred-year-old home miraculously unscathed.

Celeste keeps telling Carla she thinks Nicky's okay, but it's so hard to text when the network keeps crapping out, and anyway Celeste isn't sure how much to say. Should she tell Carla that Nicky was planning to run away? Would it even help, since she has no idea where he's gone? At night, with the sirens keeping her awake, Celeste's imagination finds him in dark places: some abandoned storefront with the cops' lights on the windows, a tent camp in the shell of a burned-out warehouse. In the daytime, though, when she can go outside and breathe, nicer possibilities occur to her: Maybe he's at a downtown hotel—the one where they used to sneak in and steal peppermints from the front desk—using his saved-up cash to lay low in style. Or maybe he's just nestled somewhere quiet in the park, living on peanut butter and tortillas, waiting out these first days of quake craziness.

All Celeste really knows for sure is the seed of Nicky's plan. To disappear for a while, to become somebody else. It all seemed kind of hypothetical, really, until he was gone.

"So . . . where would you go?"

"CB, Cookie, stop with the fucking conditional already! Where *will* I go is the question. It's a done deal."

"Okay, fine. Where *will* you go?"

They were at China Beach, avoiding Bonnie, about a week after she had confronted him. Nicky stood with his feet in the frigid tide, looking out over the Golden Gate, only the very highest lights twinkling above the fog.

"What if I just stayed *here*? But, like, became somebody else? People do it every day. That's what SF's all about, right? That's why other people come here in the first place!" He sighed, folding his arms across his chest. "I guess it would be easier to leave town. It's just . . . I would really miss this place."

And what about me? Will you miss me?

They did talk a little bit about what she could tell everyone when he left. He knew his mom would probably find out about the cheating, but Celeste didn't want to be the one to tell her. Nicky was stressed, that's what she'd say. Stressed or maybe depressed. Both were true, anyway, and Celeste was a terrible liar. She would say she'd told him to ask for help, to see the school counselor or something, but he'd set his mind on running away. She would say she didn't know where he'd gone. And she doesn't.

There was another thing he said later that night at the beach, a thing Celeste has been trying not to think about. The foghorn was bellowing, there was a briny kelp smell in the air, and Nicky was sitting on a wet rock, shining his phone flashlight at *Dune*, rereading (as always) his favorite part: when Paul, super high on the spice, first has the vision that his destiny is basically to destroy the known universe.

"You know it still comes out the same, no matter how many times you read it," Celeste said. "He's still gonna fuck shit up."

Nicky looked down at the book with a pale frown. "Maybe it would be easier for everyone if I just died."

She didn't say anything except his name, but he must've heard the panic in her voice, because he laughed and said, "Never! Are you kidding? The world needs me." He grinned and blew her a kiss and then walked a little way down the beach, running his hands through his smooth black hair. Ursa whined after him, and Celeste's heart made a painful fist.

Lying back on her sleeping bag in the living room, she spreads her notebook over her eyes, tapping the spine with her pen. She kind of gets why Nicky would choose *now* to disappear; it fits his flair for the dramatic. This way he can vanish in style, a tragic disaster victim. Carla won't go looking for him, and she can grieve right along with everyone else. It makes sense, but a small part of Celeste's brain wonders, *How could he?* How could he put Carla through this? How could he leave Celeste alone, flailing all by herself? And another part of her brain—a quieter, darker part, like a well that she can hardly stand to stare down into, even for a second—is wondering, *What if he's actually dead?*

She won't write it down, can't even form the letters with her pen.

Her phone buzzes suddenly, so she tucks the notebook back in her sleeping bag. More texts from Carla: *I'm going to school now. Please meet me if you can.*

Celeste runs outside, poor bored Ursa eager at her heels, starved for some action. Bonnie, who's been next door helping Mrs. Toy, huddles on the sidewalk with some other neighbors. It turns out the shelter-in-place order has finally been lifted, replaced by a sunset curfew.

"When were you going to tell me?" Celeste demands, and her mother does that gritted-teeth sighing thing that she hates.

"We only just heard," Bonnie insists. "I still think it's not safe—"

"I'm walking to school. Carla's on her way there."

"Not alone, you're not. And Ursa doesn't count. Anyway, honey, it'll take her forever to get across town—"

"Dad! Dad, where are you?"

Eventually she wears her parents down, and they agree to join her, coming up with their own reasons to justify the trip. Bonnie's probably needed at school—after all, she's on the Relief Center Committee—and Shane wants to check on the car, maybe drive it home if the roads are clear enough. Nobody mentions Nicky. It isn't until they're actually headed down the hill, carrying one of the emergency backpacks from the garage, picking their way in silent awe over the sycamore limbs and fractured sidewalks, that Celeste finally says, "Don't you guys care *at all* about where he is? I mean, don't you even *want* to know if he's okay?"

"Of course we do," Bonnie tells her wearily. "We're worried sick. I just didn't think you wanted to hear from me right now. About him, I mean." She tries to touch Celeste, who pulls away. "We'll help Carla talk to the police. They'll have a system—"

"You're right, I don't want to hear from you." Celeste lets Ursa pull her ahead a few steps. She knows it's not really fair to punish her mom for any of this—if a different teacher had caught Nicky, he'd probably have already been expelled—but it feels better than letting Bonnie think she's being some kind of Good Samaritan. Celeste pops in her earbuds, even though her phone's too low on juice to play music, and walks ahead, ignoring their orders to stay close. The streets are still a mess. Cars are heaved onto the curbs or parked in the street, with just enough space for the odd ambulance or cop car to get through. People stand in their driveways talking with folded arms or sweeping aimlessly, making clouds of concrete dust. As Celeste and her parents wind down through Cole Valley and into the Haight, there's no end to the awful surprises: a row of Victorians smashed together like toppled wedding cakes, only one still standing haughtily at the corner; the shards of a stained glass cupola making a broken mosaic down the driveway of a Korean church. Celeste's parents hurry to walk tight on her heels. There aren't many people around down here, just cops and hard-hat workers waving them past the closed-off streets. No fires, but Celeste can smell them burning elsewhere on the wind.

The neighborhood is full of tents. People sleeping on sidewalks is nothing new in SF—Celeste is used to it, in a way that sometimes makes her feel like a monster—but now the tents have multiplied, springing up in their gumball colors on driveways and doorsteps, in the tiny street gardens. When they walk past Celeste's elementary school, she lets out a long breath: The old building looks shockingly okay—watercolors still hanging in the windows, even—but the schoolyard is dotted with tents and cars, like the parking lot of some alternate-universe music festival where everybody's sad instead of high.

There's something that doesn't feel real about it, as if they're on the set of a bad movie. Even though Celeste's been told her whole life that a big quake was coming, she's never exactly been worried that it would. The last really awful one was 1906, and it always seemed more fascinating than scary, because it felt so far away, the whole city burning, ladies fleeing the fires with their parasols. Celeste and Nicky are into old-timey things, and the '06 quake was always just one of those things to them, a cool relic. There was even a famous legend in Nicky's family about it: His great-great-grandfather Paolo lost his whole rich family in the quake and showed up at an orphanage by himself at age six with nothing but the fancy little-gentleman's clothes on his back, the woolen short pants embroidered with his name. Celeste and Nicky loved the story. They used to ask Nonna to tell it over and over, back when she could still remember things like that.

Celeste cringes to think of it now, but they even used to *wish* for a big quake, just so they could feel one. There was a room at the science museum where you could wait in line to go inside and feel the floor shake while grainy 1906 footage projected on the walls, horses and men in top hats gawking at the wreckage. Then 1989, the World Series, the broken bridge. Most people walked out looking horrified—or, at the very least, a little woozy—but Nicky and Celeste loved it. They would run right back to get in line again, as if it were a carnival ride.

The real quake was different. It wasn't something you waited for, giddy and laughing, steadying yourself on a rail. It occurs to Celeste that the sureness of the planet under your feet is one of those things you take for granted until it's gone. She plants her steps carefully as Ursa leads her down along the shattered asphalt slope of Clayton Street. She wishes, so desperately, that she could talk to Nicky right now. What would he say about that room at the museum? About how stupid they were to think it was anything like real life?

IT ISN'T UNTIL CELESTE AND HER PARENTS ARE STAND-ing in front of the new Golden Gate Prep building—a seemingly intact monument to seismic planning, with towering safety-glass skylights and reinforced concrete beams—when Bonnie grabs her hand and asks in a shaky voice if she's ready, that Celeste realizes that in fact she might not be ready. So much terrible news possibly waiting inside the school. Everybody asking about Nicky. Carla, hysterical and broken, wanting answers. Also—Celeste is repulsed with herself for thinking it at a time like this, but she's pretty sure she looks like crap—she hasn't showered in over a week, her fisherman sweater is grimy, and the matted brown mop of her hair smells like soup. (She was almost out of her special curl goop before the quake, and now the bottle's down to the very last drop.) "We'll be with you," her dad promises, tenderly patting her nasty hair, and for probably the hundredth time today, Celeste wills herself not to cry.

They step inside, where it's cold and dim, except for a wash of winter sun coming through the glass front wall. Everything's a mess—lockers and chairs overturned, trophy case cracked—but it still has that new-building smell, the chemical carpet smell, the pristine tinge of steel. Bonnie's wiping her eyes, and Shane tells her it's not so bad, which is true. Celeste expected worse. Still, it's hard to imagine going back to school, which makes her feel even more like she's floating in the pause, somewhere outside the real orbit of her life. Following the hum of voices, they make their way upstairs to the gym. Everything's sort of damp; the emergency sprinklers must've gone off, maybe from the smoke outside. Celeste catches herself enjoying the fact that pretentious Oona Dunne's award-winning self-portrait got soaked in its place of honor in the hall. Then she realizes she has no idea what's happened to Oona Dunne and immediately feels like a giant turd. Even though Oona always says, "That *resonates* with me," in a way that makes Celeste want to puke, she doesn't deserve to get crushed in a pile of rubble, not really.

As it turns out, Oona hasn't been crushed. Instead she's there with her mother checking people in at the door of the gym, greeting them soberly and handing them little swag bags of bottled water and protein bars, like the hostess at an awards show. Celeste sidles around the bottleneck as best she can with Ursa, pretending not to see Oona. Bonnie and Shane have stepped aside to hug Principal Reyes, but Celeste doesn't want to talk to her, either, especially not about Nicky, so she keeps moving into the gym. Noisy generators out on the blacktop, their massive cords snaking through the doors, are powering some floodlights and a big TV with a crowd around it watching CNN. Nurses in scrubs and ponytails sit at tables under the basketball hoops taking blood donations, bandaging injured people, and handing out little plastic cups of pills. Another table with crates of packaged food and drinks has drawn a crowd. Celeste doesn't see many familiar faces.

She wanders over to watch the news, expecting dire quake reports, but it's about the Mars mission, apparently still on schedule for May. Celeste feels weirdly shocked; shouldn't everything else have paused, too? Jessica Watkins, the mission geologist, is talking about radiation levels in rock samples, and the absurdly rich tech dude who's funding the research keeps interrupting her, as if he actually knows anything about geology. In the before times, Celeste was obsessed with Mars updates—especially with Dr. Watkins, who went to Stanford on scholarship, like Bonnie—but right now she can't seem to stomach it. Instead she decides to climb the bleachers to scan the floor for Carla. Sleeping bags and blankets are laid out along the varnished benches, here and there a dirty teddy bear or baby blanket.

"Celeste!"

It's Bridget, waving and leaping over the sleeping bags, then closing her in a boa-constrictor hug. Celeste isn't big on hugs, but Bridget sure is. They hooked up for a minute sophomore year, when Celeste realized suddenly that all the boys she wanted to kiss were pretty much idiots. Bridget isn't an idiot—she spends her summers wiping the floor with super-geniuses at cryptography competitions. Kissing her at parties was nice, but Celeste always chickened out when they ended up alone. Still, the hug feels good, and she's so glad Bridget's okay. Unlike most people, Bridget has always been nice to her in a real way, not in a *Hey, aren't you friends with Nicky?* way.

"This is fucking insane, right?" Bridget is tiny and cute but swears like a sailor, sometimes in the same breath in English and Cantonese, the language her parents also use to constantly scold her for swearing. She has this habit of frequently smoothing her satiny hair that Celeste still thinks is kind of sexy, even though she's pretty much over girls in general when it comes to hooking up. "Did you check in yet? Everybody's checking in on Snap. Oh wait, you don't do social, right?"

"Not anymore." Celeste knows what's about to happen, which is the rapid download of a ton of information. Bridget on a good day is the most efficient rumor mill around, so Celeste has a feeling that post-disaster Bridget is going to blow her mind.

"Right, fuck that anyway. Who gives a shit about Snap. But I mean, it's kind of helpful for stuff like this. All the seniors checked in safe except for you and Nicky and Graciela Lopez, but I know Graciela's visiting her grandma in Mexico, so she's fine. Oh my god, did you hear about Jackson's house? *Totally* burned down. Like, the whole fucking thing. I feel *so* bad for him. He posted an Insta reel and it is *all gone*. I just can't believe this shit. And Maestra Liz, her apartment building? She lives in Oakland? Just collapsed. Like, *ruins*. I just can't believe this is happening."

They're still hugging. Celeste tries to let go—her head has started to throb from the weird blue light and the mildewy smell in the air, and those horrible bits of news—Maestra Liz, the sweet Spanish teacher who goes to Burning Man and wore a crazy beaded dress one day to teach them tango—and Jackson Beale, Celeste's old crush, not that smart, but cute and friendly. She thinks of the circles of people she knows, people from school, from her other schools, her parents' friends, her cousins in Marin, just spinning along their orbits when suddenly the quake, like a blast of solar wind, sent them all careening into space.

And then, finally releasing her, Bridget says, "So where's Nicky?" It's a simple question. Everyone expects to find them together. If one of them is safe, so must be the other. Bridget's searching the crowd for his face. "I could really use a Nicky hug right the fuck about now." Celeste feels weak. Her cheeks are hot, and the generator's buzzing in her bones. Ursa eyes her closely, standing up tall on the stairs.

"Wait, there's his mom!" Bridget's waving again, and then Carla is coming up the bleacher stairs with Bonnie and Shane, looking teary and gaunt in one of Pop's plaid flannels, her hair greasy, her motorcycle helmet tucked under her arm. In an instant, Celeste finds herself squeezed in another hug.

"Celeste, baby girl, what a relief to see your face," Carla says, kissing her and crying. Her arms are so tight around Celeste's neck. "Oh, honey, what are we going to do?"

Celeste looks at the faraway ceiling and feels herself sinking, the blood pouring into her feet. Ursa barks three times, the CGM alarm starts blaring on Celeste's phone, and suddenly Bonnie's got her wrapped in those poncho wings, making her sit. Everything blurs. Sounds and smells and faces smear into a sticky paste. Someone feeds her a gummy bear. "Sweetheart," her dad is saying softly, *"eat."* He gives her another one, and she chokes it down, one after another. In a moment, her breath is back, then her vision, lines and colors emerging from the smear. Her parents kneel at her sides, and Carla's holding her hand.

"What the fuck?" Bridget is saying. "She wasn't even acting weird—"

"It's okay, she's okay," Bonnie insists, whispering it to Celeste, as if to convince her.

"I'm so sorry." Carla squeezes Celeste's thin hand, tucks a curl behind her ear. "I shocked her, didn't I."

"It's not you," Bonnie says. "The stress, it makes her blood sugar crazy. And she hasn't been eating well, none of us have." They continue to talk like she's not there, Carla kneading her hand. Celeste wants to ask them all to back off, but she can't seem to make the words. The paste still clings in her throat, and anyway, Carla looks so terrified, it doesn't seem right. She's been to the Red Cross and the police station, waited in a two-hour line to report Nicky missing.

"This is what they're saying— After a few days . . ." She shakes her head, doesn't stop shaking it, her hand tight and sweaty around Celeste's.

Bridget again: "Holy shit—Nicky's *missing*?"

Celeste digs for the words, and at last she manages to mutter, "He's gone." Carla breaks down crying, but there's more Celeste needs to say. She fumbles for her phone, but it's in her backpack, which has fallen between the seats. If only she could just call Nicky, he would tell her what to do. Through her wet eyelashes she can almost see him over there across the gym, in his favorite spot at the top of the bleachers, too far away for anyone who actually cared about whatever game or rally was going on below. The long bent legs, the pink sweatshirt, the glimmer of the Ray-Bans he's always getting yelled at for wearing in school. He waves, blows her a kiss, flashes his little sun.

"Bridget, be a love. Go and get Celeste a juice box, would you?" Shane dispatches Bridget, who wanders off, stunned, into the crowd. Bonnie kneels with Carla now, rubbing her back.

"They gave me some idiot FEMA caseworker," Carla sobs. "Her name is *Merlot*, if you can believe that. I haven't even been able to get this Merlot person to return my texts."

Bonnie shakes her head. "I'm so sorry, Carla. How can we help you?"

"They're right, aren't they? If he was in a hospital, we'd know by now. Or—I mean, if . . . he could be trapped somewhere! Celeste—" She clutches her hands again. "Honey, please—wasn't he supposed to be with you? What do you mean he's *gone*?"

Bridget turns up then with an OJ, looking sad and shrunken, hiding inside that shawl of hair. With the sips of juice, Celeste begins to feel her breath steadying, the words in her brain sorting themselves once again into thoughts. It's her turn now—time to walk the tightrope, to tell Carla the vague little bits she knows, somehow without betraying Nicky's trust. Carla's a good mom, and Celeste has always loved her. Her family's pretty old-school, but she let Nicky wear her shoes and makeup when they were little and only adored him fiercely, always. Except she also needed so much from him. His dad was gone—an army pilot, occasional boyfriend of Carla's who would come to see her when he was in town—deployed to Afghanistan when Nicky was two and never came back. That was when they moved into the house next door to Celeste's. Nicky slept on the trundle in Celeste's room while Carla did nursing school at night. When he turned out to be so brilliant, she did everything she could to send him to private school, working tons of extra shifts, going broke in the process. She needed her boy to go and do great things, so these last few years, when the money got even tighter, they were both angry all the time about needing each other. Sometimes Celeste played the go-between or the comic relief when they were fighting. So, what's she supposed to do now? Go between again.

"I didn't mean—like, *gone*," she says at last, her voice trembling. "It's just—he had this plan." And she tells Carla the stuff they talked about at the beach, only last week, but it seems like months ago. He's been depressed, she says. Under so much pressure. With MIT, the scholarship. His grades were suffering. He was going to run away. Start over somewhere. Any day now—that was the plan.

Celeste is trying not to notice her own mother's tight mouth, the raised eyebrows. She tries to send Bonnie some telepathic mother-daughter messages: *DON'T. JUST. PLEASE. DON'T.* If Bonnie spills the whole truth, Nicky will never forgive either of them.

"But—I don't understand," Carla says, pacing now, hands at her hips. "Are you saying he just . . . *ran away*? After the quake? What are you saying? Why didn't you say this before?"

"Okay, let's take a breath here." Bonnie fixes Celeste with a fiery look. "Sweetheart, of course we all wish—"

"I'm telling you, Mom, this was his plan, I swear."

"I knew he was having a hard time," Carla says. "But he wouldn't . . . How could he just *leave* us, after something like this? I mean, without even knowing we're okay—Nonna and Pop!" She turns to the blank scoreboard, as if the answer might be broadcast there in bright red pixels. "No," she says, "he wouldn't."

"Maybe he's, like, checking on you?" Bridget offers hopefully. "Online, I mean. If he's out there somewhere."

Carla gives her a puzzled look, but then she seems to settle on this idea: "That could be, I guess. I posted on Facebook as soon as I could get on." She asks Celeste some more questions, Bonnie looking increasingly nervous and pissed. When did he decide this? Where was he planning to go? I don't know, I don't know. Doesn't Celeste have any texts or emails they could see? "It's not that we don't believe you," Shane tells her gently, but she insists truthfully that there aren't any texts. Nothing since the quake, and even before that, they never texted super-private stuff to each other; even the chillest parents they know can't resist snooping.

A phone starts chiming loudly in protest, that obnoxious default ring tone, and everybody scrambles—turns out it's Carla's. "Merlot? Christ, it's about time!" She steps away to take the call.

Celeste stares down at the people milling around the gym. Has she really fucked things up for Nicky now, giving them all a reason to hope? Maybe she should have just let him disappear? The idea of answering more questions makes her sick. Her parents are talking to Bridget; Carla's on her call. Maybe Celeste will just take Ursa and go look for Nicky herself. In her mind the map of the city unfurls, all the places he could've gone glowing warmly with Nicky-light.

She stands up to leave, whispering to the dog, but then something strange startles her: It's that hot blue-eyed kid from the Haight, hovering at the food table, loading up a backpack. He looks sneaky but also scared, minus the usual swagger. She ducks behind her mom, using the poncho as a shield, but the boy's on his way out anyway, darting past Oona's table, an apple in his teeth.

"Celeste," Bonnie hisses, "can I have a minute?" They scoot down the bleachers, out of earshot of Carla, who's still on the phone, scribbling frantically on a paper towel in her lap. "Honey," Bonnie says, "listen, you know I'm desperate for Nicky to be safe—"

"I'm not lying, okay? He had a plan to run away, for real. Ever since you found out."

Bonnie's face crumples. "I just don't . . . How could he do that to Carla?"

It's hard to answer, because Celeste doesn't know. The only thing she knows is this: Nicky hasn't been himself. The Nicky-light has been fading, sometimes even flickering out, leaving her to stumble around in the dark. "He's been in bad shape, Mom. He thinks everybody's better off without him."

Bonnie covers her face with her hands, rubs the bridge of her nose. It's what she does whenever she's trying to will something to be different, as if she could just wipe away the truth and open her eyes to a new one. "Things can feel so shitty when you're a teenager," she says. "Sometimes I forget."

"This doesn't just *feel* shitty—it *is* shitty."

"All right, Celeste, Jesus," Bonnie says. "I don't think we need a semantics debate right now. Believe it or not, I'm trying to help."

Carla's off the phone, still scribbling, blinking frantically. She looks over at them and waves the paper towel in the air. "I told Merlot what you said. She gave me a plan!"

"Are you going to tell her?" Celeste asks Bonnie in a low voice. "About the cheating?"

Bonnie's eyes fill with tears again, but she erases them with her sleeve. "I don't think she needs to know right now."

Celeste grabs her mom's arm. She understands suddenly just how much she needs Bonnie to believe her. "Mom—Nicky's alive," she says, almost angrily, wanting to shake her. "I can *feel* it."

"Okay," Bonnie says with a wobbly breath, "let's find him, then."

Carla grips the paper towel, stumbles over the sleeping bags. "Celeste, I need you! Merlot says to start with the last time you saw him."

Standing outside of school in the fog, worrying the tail of his backpack strap between his teeth, like he used to do when they were little. *Bye,* he told her with a weak double-cheek kiss, and it only seemed strange later that he shouted at her through the open door, *Twins forever!*

"Wednesday morning," Celeste says. "The day of the quake. I ran into him on the way into school. We don't have class together on Wednesdays, so that was it. I couldn't find him at lunch. He was supposed to meet me at the library after school, the Sutro branch on Waller, where we always go. But he never showed up, so I went home."

"Oh my god, are you serious?" Bridget's been hovering nearby, engrossed in her phone. They all turn to her and stare. "A whole big stretch of Waller is really messed up. Somebody's gas leak set a fire. That library—it's totally gone. Collapsed."

Bonnie reaches out to fold Carla into her poncho. Celeste sinks her fingers into Ursa's black fur. She can feel the dog's heart galloping. *No,* she tells herself, *he never showed up.* The other terrible possibilities are down there at the bottom of the well, flames licking up the side of it, screams echoing faintly.

Before

Celeste can remember only one other time when she didn't speak to Nicky for days. Summer after freshman year, babysitting one night, she got inspired by a game of interplanetary house that the little girls were playing, and after they went to sleep, she wrote a story about a colony of women living on Mars, birthing girl babies with genetically modified sperm from Earth and populating the planet with females. Celeste almost never wrote fiction, and she never would've shown the story to anybody but Nicky. He loved it and proceeded to bug her about it the rest of the summer, insisting she should send it off to some contest. Finally he just went behind her back and submitted it himself.

When the email came letting Celeste know that she'd won the contest and the story was going to be published, she immediately threw up in the girls' locker room, where she'd been checking her phone during PE. She refused to see or talk to Nicky for at least a week, but when her copy of the magazine arrived in the mail, she lay in bed rereading the story in a state of nausea and wonder, touching her name on the glossy byline. In the morning, she finally showed it to her parents and texted Nicky: *Okay, thank you, but please never fucking do that again.* Probably she couldn't have held out much longer without talking to him, anyway.

That was only seven days, maybe eight or nine tops.

Day 21

By the time Celeste finally gets to start looking for Nicky in earnest—or at least for some piece of evidence, some little clue that he's out there—it's been twenty full days since she laid eyes on him. No eyes, or even words. No texts, no posts, no nothing. Three whole weeks.

Well, that's not exactly right: She's laid *her* words on *him*, sending daily texts into the ether. She even ended a yearlong social media hiatus to keep an eye on his accounts; she'd deleted all her apps junior year, when somebody had posted a photo of her passed out on a desk and labeled it *Stoner Sleeping Beauty*. Nicky stood up for her in the comments (*She's diabetic, fuckhole!*), but the thing had legs, hopping from Snap to Insta and back again like some kind of disease-bearing mosquito. It was no big deal, really—Celeste always hated social media anyway—but now she's desperate for any sign of him, thoroughly addicted to refreshing the stupid feed on Nicky's stupid page.

The paper fliers are more Celeste's style. The whole city is draped with them, weirdly festive petticoats of missing persons fliers on the telephone poles and bus stops, fluttering down the gravelly sidewalks and into the gutters. Nicky's photo is everywhere, one among the many. Now that the power's back on and roads are starting to open up, Celeste and her parents have been spending their mornings driving around in gnarly traffic with a stapler and a stack of Nicky fliers. They stop in different neighborhoods and plaster a couple of blocks with his face and a phone number and an email address, then back to the traffic again—staying within two miles of home, per the city's constantly shifting, endlessly confusing post-disaster rules.

That's the big fancy rescue plan Merlot came up with: fliers. Sometimes Celeste thinks the goal of the plan is really just to placate Carla, because there isn't anything especially smart or official-seeming about it. Merlot told Carla the police are stretched too thin after the quake to investigate each case like they normally would. Nicky's in the system, so they can keep track if anything turns up, but that's about as much as the cops can do right now.

Celeste has been desperate to go out looking for Nicky on her own—she's got some thoughts about places where he might think to crash—but her parents won't let her out of their sight, with her blood sugar still going wild from the stress. Carla's texting constantly to ask Celeste's advice, but she mostly plays dumb. The last thing she wants is for Nicky to resent her for blabbing when they finally see each other again. Ever since he started talking about this plan, she always hoped—assumed? too scared to really ask—that what he really wanted was to disappear from everyone but *her*. Like she would still be his *person*, the one connection to his old life, taking secret calls and sending him clothes or money, and maybe, eventually, helping him find his way back.

But now—three weeks, still nothing.

Finally today they lifted the two-mile rule, so Celeste and her dad are heading across town to see Carla and her parents. Shane stood in a two-hour line to buy them some groceries, stuffing and some canned yams for a Christmas do-over, and Celeste offered to come along and help put up more posters. But what she really wants is to get into Nicky's room and start combing through his shit.

Through the window of Shane's old Civic, Celeste studies the broken city and wonders about the clues Nicky might've left behind. Too risky to text, but maybe he's tried to get in touch with her in some more secret way? The whole town seems sprinkled with cryptic messages. Traffic light boards stationed at every corner, blinking in and out with their garbled warnings. Shrines piled up on fences where buildings used to be, graffiti in a sad shorthand: *Never 4get SF BKLY NPA we love U!*

They're making their slow way through the Haight when she thinks of asking her dad to drive her past the library site. Her parents made her stay home from postering that part of the neighborhood—too upsetting. They never explicitly pointed out that Nicky could be buried there, but she knew they were thinking it. She knows they still don't really believe he's alive. They cry and whisper about it at night when they think she's asleep, like when she was younger, when they'd have hushed conversations with the doctors while they sent her off to look at the fish tank. She fucking hates being humored.

"It's really bad," her dad warns when she asks, but he's already turning off Stanyan for the detour; Celeste knew that asking him alone was a good bet. Her parents are always arguing about how much she can handle, with Shane coming down on the *more* side. As they get close to the library, though, Celeste starts to wonder if her mom might've been right. She feels a dampness settling on her skin. There's a tarry smell in the air, even through the window, and the streets are carpeted with glass and clogged with debris, a narrow path for traffic drawn in police tape. Soon they can hear the roar and whine of dump trucks, workers shouting. Ursa sits up in the back, panting and pawing at the seat. Then they finally pass the library's closed-off street.

It looks like photos Celeste has seen of war zones. It never occurred to her, honestly, that she would see this kind of thing in person. What an asshole she has been, just assuming that disaster and destruction were exclusive to some other, less pretty part of the world. She's sickened by herself and by the scene in front of her, the black skeletons of cars and buildings, sometimes nothing left but chimney pillars, other times just the half-melted furniture arranged in tidy groups, sofas and coffee tables and chairs, like they're waiting for somebody to come back and play Monopoly in the vanished living room.

They can't get any closer, but from here she can see, most impossible of all, a mountain range of bricks in the spot where the library once stood. The breeze kicks up flurries of ash that roll over the tops of the mounds and disperse like powder snow. Particles of pages. Or people. Everything suddenly sounds so far away, ensconced in the muted hush of the library itself.

The librarians always loved Ursa. Whenever they spotted her, they would stop shelving and gossiping and come out from the stacks to coo and tickle her ears. Celeste never knew their names.

Workers in marshmallow suits are scaling the mountains with careful steps, scooping dust into bags in slow motion, like they're collecting samples on Mars.

Not Nicky. They will not find Nicky. Somehow Celeste feels more certain of this than ever, even as the chill weight of what's happened here settles in her chest.

Her dad clutches the wheel. She rests her forehead on the cool window.

"Why did you let me do that?"

He takes her hand. She feels his violin callus, like she used to do after a bad dream. "You're old enough to see what you want," he says. "God, I wish you weren't, though."

"Nicky isn't in there, Dad."

"I know, kiddo."

IT'S HARD TO MAKE SENSE OF IT ALL WITHOUT NICKY. For every other giant thing that's happened in Celeste's life, he's been there at the center, holding her in orbit. The stuff that's too terrible to joke about, too soul-crushing to talk about—that's the kind of stuff they've always slogged through together. Celeste's diagnosis, the hospital stays. The eviction. The summer when Nicky came out as queer to his father's parents in Missouri, and they sent him home a week early. The only reason they made it through any of that, really, was that they made it through together. But now it's like there's a conveyor belt just constantly dumping unbearable news in Celeste's lap, and Nicky's off somewhere else becoming someone else.

A week ago they got an email from school: two students confirmed dead, both freshmen, killed together in a rec center collapse in the Marina. And there were others: a recently retired basketball coach; the janitor's wife. Celeste didn't know any of them, not even the freshmen, but still the email made her weep uncontrollably. It took her parents over an hour to calm her down, and afterward she felt too guilty to sleep, because most of the tears were really, in the end, for Nicky. She launched another litany of texts into the void, then stared at her phone until Bonnie came in and made her put it away.

SHANE PUTS ON SOME QUIET PIANO MUSIC AND doesn't try to make Celeste talk about it, thank God, on the slow drive to see Carla. Finally, Nicky's grandparents' little blue clapboard house comes into view, peacefully unharmed. The window-box petunias, still brightly blooming, fill Celeste with a deep and almost sweet-tasting relief. Ursa wildly wags her tail in the back seat. Celeste wants to fall to her knees and kiss the dusty, leaf-littered steps. Instead she helps her dad gather the grocery bags and lug them to the door.

Carla is glad to see them; she's had a terrible day. Her always perfect red nails are bitten and bleeding, the polish chipped. Her skin is an oystery gray, her nose raw and pink, and she clutches wadded tissues in both fists. She's even wearing an old set of scrubs, which she hates. She's always threatening to quit nursing unless they redesign the scrubs with a more flattering butt.

"Oh you guys. Bless your hearts." And she pulls them both into a neck-wringing hug. "Come on in. Mom's in the kitchen," she says unnecessarily; Nonna is always in the kitchen. It used to be she was always cooking, but now she just sits at the table while a cup of coffee gets cold. Today she's ostensibly folding a pile of dish towels, but really she's gaping at the towels like they're a pile of snakes. Celeste sets the bags down and leans to kiss her papery cheek, even though it's been ages since Nonna recognized her.

"Hi there, Nonna."

Nonna looks up at her, blinks a few times, and says, "You're Nicky's little friend," which surprises them all.

"That's right, Mom!" Carla says brightly. Usually she obsesses about making sure Nonna gets to the hairdresser and has clean clothes on, but today her cardigan smells a little ripe, and her hair is flattened in weird places, showing her pale scalp.

"I feel so bad." Carla sinks into the chair next to her mother. "Mom's hair place is still closed, and I don't have the patience to curl it myself."

"Aw come on, she understands." Shane kisses Nonna's other cheek. "Don't you, love?"

"Charlie Sullivan, aren't you looking good!" Nonna grins at Shane, then explains to Carla, "He sat behind me in church. Once I let him get under my shirt at choir practice."

"Mom!"

Shane laughs it off and starts opening cabinets while Carla scolds her mother. Good thing Pop's out on a pharmacy run; he gets testy when Nonna starts going on about her old boyfriends. Nicky's really the only one who can carry on a conversation with her these days. Whatever she says, he just goes with it, like some kind of improv comedian. "Nicky! The monkeys are in the oven!" she might say, agitated, getting pretty pissed, but then he'll commiserate, which calms her down: "They *are*, Nonna? Again! You gotta be freakin' kidding me! How'd they get in there, anyway? What kind of crap are they trying to pull?"

Ursa settles into her favorite spot under the table, and Celeste sits with Nonna to fold the towels while her dad and Carla put the groceries away. There's a sunbeam warming her chair, and Rosemary Clooney is on the record player. It feels good to be here with Nicky's family in the house that somehow still has that pignoli cookie smell, even though Nonna hasn't made them in years. The china bowl of cherries—Celeste and Nicky's favorite—is on the table, like always; Nonna bought them religiously from the Korean grocery down the street, and now Pop must've made a special trip. Celeste pops one in her mouth, closes her eyes, and tries to conjure a better reason for being here. But it's sour and tough, a winter cherry shipped from some evil industrial farm. And Carla's misery is hard to ignore, anyway, like a window left open when the fog comes in, the cold infecting the room. She says she got a call from Merlot today.

"She's surprised we don't have at least *something* to go on. Somebody should've called the tip line by now." Carla's staring at a carton of milk as if deciding whether to put it away or hurl it through the window. "Three weeks," she adds, the frown melting deeper into her chin. Shane tries to give her a little pep talk, but there isn't much to be said, no real needle of hope in this whole shitty haystack. Celeste can't bear it.

"Hey, would it be okay if I go up to Nicky's room?"

"There's an idea," Shane says. "Look around a bit, yeah? Maybe you'll find something Carla missed." Carla agrees and offers Shane a beer, seeming faintly cheered by the tiniest hint of a stone unturned. On her way upstairs, though, Celeste feels bad for letting them think she's their foot soldier. She knows where to look, the secret spots that Carla probably missed on her own sweep of Nicky's room—but Celeste won't be sharing her findings. It's bad enough that everyone's poking through his stuff when he's not here, herself included. She stops in the doorway, the guilt staring her in the face, Nicky's presence glaring at her from the corner with folded arms. Even Ursa gives her the stink eye.

This room isn't nearly as steeped in Nicky-ness as his old one. So many months after the move, his taped-up boxes still sit defiantly in the corners. Nicky's beloved emo band posters and celestial maps are rolled up in the closet, only a bunch of favorite photos thumbtacked on the walls: glamorous gothed-out Carla outside the Fillmore in the nineties; Celeste and Nicky looking extra nerdy and cute next to their model rocket at the sixth-grade science fair, then looking extra nerdy and not as cute at the opening night of the *Dune* movie, dressed as Paul and Chani in dirty Fremen robes with tubes in their noses. ("You owe me, to a *massive* degree," she told him, but he just grinned and paid for the popcorn.) His solar system mobile is shoved in a bookcase, planets in a heap, instead of hanging over his bed like it did in the old house. But still: This place smells like him. Like weed and coconut shampoo and toothpaste. Free weights stacked in the corner. Favorite Converse in sherbet colors in a neat line under the bed. Calendar counting down to the *Mars Pioneer* launch, the days crossed off in red pen, hanging above his nightstand.

Celeste takes the calendar off the wall and runs her finger over the last three weeks, all blank. Then she flips to the launch date, May 21, which also happens to be their twin birthday. When NASA first announced the *Pioneer* mission date a few years ago, they were both so stunned that neither of them could speak. The first humans ever to travel to Mars, launching on their eighteenth birthday! Right then they started saving money for tickets to Florida, talked about camping on a Space Coast beach, maybe going to Disney World after. But that was before the eviction, the cheating. Celeste's pretty sure that Nicky's put the money he saved for the trip into his college fund by now—or maybe he's buying food or toothpaste with it, wherever he is. Still, he's drawn an elaborate sketch of a rocket over their birthday, with a border of hearts. And he didn't miss crossing off the day of the earthquake.

She tacks the calendar back on the wall. Fake Nicky's still

hanging out in the corner, but now it feels like he's looking at her expectantly, encouraging—like, *What are you waiting for??*

And then she realizes—of course he knows that she's here. He'd have planned on it. Maybe he even left clues behind for her to find, in places only she would think to look.

Celeste calls Ursa inside and shuts the door, puts on Arcade Fire, and gets to work. One thing strikes her right away as weird: His desk, always messy with books and paper, is empty. Almost finals time when the quake hit, but Nicky wasn't studying. She spends some time poking through his school laptop, but there's nothing of note, and no work for college apps, even though he planned to apply to a few backup schools. To be fair, somebody snooping in Celeste's own stuff wouldn't find much evidence of a college-bound senior, either. Most schools have extended their deadlines for Bay Area kids; after putting off her applications for months, Celeste should probably feel grateful, but she just can't bring herself to give a shit right now. The old plan—MIT, NASA—feels flimsy without Nicky, just a bunch of daydreams. If it was scary for Celeste to think about going away before, it's terrifying now. She's never even traveled anywhere on her own. Ever since the diagnosis, Nicky's always taken care of the hard stuff for the both of them: making friends, figuring out the future.

Too depressed by the empty desk, she starts on the rest of the room, digging shamefully through his drawers. Seeing all his disembodied junk makes her wonder about the Mars book, the little black notebook Nicky always carried around for doodling equations and crazy ideas about space. As far as she knows, it never leaves his back pocket unless he's writing in it, so she wouldn't expect to find it where Nicky himself is not. Still, thinking of it makes her feel the vacuum of his absence even more deeply in this room full of stuff. She does her best to resist, feeling stretched and sore as she starts on the closet, where there's a file carton with some of his little-kid artwork. At the bottom, she knows, is the shoebox where he keeps his pot. She knows he kept the cash there, too, from the counterfeit essay jobs, because he told her once that she should take it if he ever got run over by a Muni train or poisoned by Safeway sushi. She opens the carton to sift through the piles of drawings and collages, dusting her sweaty hands with glitter and oil pastel, and at last she finds the shoebox at the bottom.

But the cash is missing. Gone. Celeste's heart leaps to a sprint. Is this *PROOF*? Sure feels like it, or at least like a point on the *Nicky's alive* side of the scoreboard. Celeste reminds herself to breathe, and with each breath a new question floats into her brain. Maybe he *moved* the money? Maybe he just didn't trust her, after that day in the kitchen with Bonnie? Maybe he put it in the bank? But none of these possibilities feels quite right. It seems much more likely that he has the money with him, which *strongly suggests* he was ready to run on the day of the quake. She wonders how much he saved, in the end, and how long it could possibly last.

There's more in the box. Nicky's weed in a squat glass jar and also, oddly, a blue plastic bottle of pills. Not from a pharmacy, clearly. The pills are tiny and white, but she can't tell what they are, maybe Percocet or Oxy. She empties the bottle into her still-glittery palm. Nicky never used to take pills, but in the past few months, with everything going on, Celeste knew he'd been trying them out. She thought it was only at parties, though, when some rich kid was buying. This stash is huge—it has to be worth way more than Nicky could afford. And why would he leave them behind? Maybe he was hoping for a new start? Who knows. She zips them into her backpack. Maybe this could be a clue, too.

She finds an envelope full of receipts—no surprise there. Nicky's been obsessed with money lately, agonizing about every little expense. Celeste shuffles through the receipts, most of which are for purchases she witnessed herself—a sweater from Community Thrift, a couple of carnitas tacos from Farolito—and then there's one from the crystal shop on Haight, the one where they got their sun tattoos. It's from the day before the quake. Three items, all listed as *Misc. Spiritual Guidance*, which might be hilarious if Celeste were in a laughing mood. She tucks the receipts in her backpack next to the pills and shoves the shoebox back in its spot.

Most of his clothes are still here, as far as she can tell. There's the orange puffer jacket, his favorite—he liked to call it Pumpkin—doodled all over with silver Sharpie, stars and equations and even dumb things like the phone number for the cheapest Chinese delivery for when his mom worked night shifts. Celeste is surprised he didn't take the puffer—won't he need Pumpkin, wherever he's going? She double-checks that she's alone (except for Fake Nicky, still watching eagerly, and Ursa, of course, who snuffles her disapproval). Celeste takes Pumpkin down from the hanger and hugs it, the coat collapsing to nothing in her arms, an empty husk without his big body in it.

For a moment Celeste can feel herself leaning over the edge of the well, the dark possibilities reaching up from down there, singeing the ends of her curls. Then she gasps and yanks herself back up, remembering: *He WANTS everyone to think he's gone. Like for good*. He had to know they'd be doing an inventory of his stuff. Except for maybe his backpack and its usual contents, he wouldn't have packed anything obviously precious; he wouldn't have wanted to tip them off. Nicky's smarter than all of them put together. He's always a few light-years ahead of everyone else. *That's why he'll get to outer space someday,* Celeste thinks. *In a way, he's already up there while the rest of us are stuck down here.*

NONNA IS STILL AT THE KITCHEN TABLE WITH THE pile of towels when Celeste and Ursa finally wander back downstairs. Shane and Carla are banging around in the basement, probably cleaning up. Celeste can't imagine what it must look like down there after the quake. Nonna's basement is like the cargo hold of a pirate ship, a labyrinth of cobwebbed boxes and crates; Nicky and Celeste used to think goblins lived down there. Some of the boxes even date back to Nonna's grandpa, the mysterious Paolo, the one who was orphaned in the 1906 quake. Celeste remembers a day, when they were maybe twelve, Nonna had been telling one of their favorite Paolo stories, about how some of the other kids at the orphanage had tried to steal his expensive clothes, his only belongings. Nonna had asked them to wait while she went down the dark stairs to the basement; then, after a few torturous minutes listening only to the ominous whir of the fridge, they watched her emerge holding a pair of tiny plum-colored velvet suspenders.

Celeste wishes Nonna could tell her the story again now. The way she's smoothing the dish towel reminds Celeste of how lovingly she held those suspenders. She told them Paolo never remembered his childhood before the quake, the pampered life he must've lived. The life he'd started out with was over; he had invented the new one out of thin air.

"You're Nicky's little friend," Nonna says again, uncertainly, and Celeste smiles and agrees, "Yeah, I am." Then she gets an idea. *Maybe Nonna knows.* Nicky might've talked to her, told her about his plan. She's the only earthling Celeste can imagine, besides herself, whom he might've trusted to hear it.

"Nonna," Celeste says, leaning in for a whisper, "when was the last time you saw Nicky?"

"My boy Nicky! Such a good boy."

"Yeah." She puts her hand on Nonna's arm. "Did he tell you he was leaving? Or . . . maybe he told you where he was headed?"

Nonna laughs. "Oh yeah, sure! Promised to send me a postcard."

"Really?" Celeste pulls the chair closer, heartbeat drumming in her ears. "He did? What else did he say?" She squints into Nonna's hazy eyes, trying to figure out if this is one of those rare moments when she's lucid.

"He was leaving," Nonna says sharply, but maybe it's just that thing she does sometimes, where she ping-pongs your own words right back at you.

"Nicky told you he was leaving?"

She smiles out the window at the wispy clouds. "My good boy," she says. "Promised to buy me a rocket ship!" Celeste's heart thuds on the floor. It was dumb to think she could turn Nicky's poor demented grandma into an informant. This isn't even a real conversation; it's just the monkeys in the oven again.

But then a change seems to come over Nonna. She makes a sly little sideways smirk, and her eighty-year-old body suddenly starts to move like a little kid. She rises from her chair like she's on springs, gathers the pile of towels, and balls them at her chest. She looks straight at Celeste and says, "He told me he'd see me up there!" And then she begins to shout at the top of her voice, a slow countdown from ten. Around five, Shane and Carla appear at the basement door looking alarmed, but Celeste is transfixed. The volume of Nonna's voice seems to rattle the quiet house, making a kind of breeze that whips her skirt, as if the rocket launchers were firing at her feet.

"Three . . . two . . . one . . . BLASTOFF!" She flings the towels into the air, and they jet to the kitchen ceiling before drifting down to the floor.

"Mom, what the hell?" Carla storms around, exasperated, collecting the towels, and Shane is helping Nonna back to her chair, joking about it being a beautiful day in Cape Canaveral. But Celeste feels like something very real just happened, something she needs to understand.

Celeste can imagine Nicky packing up that morning with the purple dawn at the window: folding his money into his messenger bag, leaving behind the pills and Pumpkin, coming down to breakfast, his mom still at the hospital, Pop still in bed, only Nonna sitting there with her coffee at the table. He wouldn't have, *couldn't* have left without saying goodbye to her.

See you up there, Nonna!

Merlot doesn't know what the fuck she's talking about. Nicky is still out there, and Celeste isn't going to wait for somebody else to find him.

Day 41

The fact that people are calling it the Big One irks Celeste to no end. She complains about it at lunchtime to her mother and Ms. Tanaka. Can't they think of something that's less of a cliché? "It seems so flippant, like a name for a roller coaster or something."

"Celeste, I love how your mind works," Ms. Tanaka says, "and I'll never deny the power of words, I mean—far be it from me. But really, this isn't a great time to go around being so hard on people."

Ms. T is eating a packaged salad at her desk, Bonnie is at her own desk with a bagel, grading papers, and Celeste is hiding out (again) in the English department office at lunch, curled up on the windowsill with the spider plants. It's their second week back at school, post-quake day forty. Forty days Nickyless. Still not even so much as a text from some burner phone or a slyly coded comment on Insta. Sometimes Celeste wonders if Nicky really *has* become someone else, not just metaphorically but for real, like maybe something fell on his head in the quake and gave him amnesia, so he truly had to invent himself all over again.

"That's what I keep trying to tell you," Bonnie says. "We need to support each other now. Enough with the snark."

"I'm not the one using some silly nickname for, like, a fatal disaster. What about the people in *mourning*? It's disrespectful."

Bonnie and Ms. Tanaka glance at each other knowingly through a moment of silent chewing.

"God, really? I come in here so I *don't* have to spend the whole lunch period pretending not to notice the way people look at me."

"It's just, we were talking earlier . . ." Bonnie gets up from her desk, walks over, and tucks a curl behind Celeste's ear. Ms. T follows with a purple flier, hands it over, and retreats to her salad. Celeste folds the flier and shoves it into the pocket of her mom's dress.

"Yeah, thanks, but I'm not going. It's a *grief* group."

"Okay—but it's for kids who've experienced loss. He is *lost*, isn't he? You can't argue that."

"Point to Mom," Ms. Tanaka says. "She's playing your game now, Celeste."

"I don't care what you call it; I'm not going."

"Sweetie, we're only trying to help. You've got to start talking about this. You can't keep eating lunch in here every day."

"Fine, I'll leave."

"Celeste—"

But she's already out the door with Ursa, surfing the tide of kids in the hall with her head lowered, aiming for some other place to be semi-alone. The skylit library is out—too many fellow seniors cramming for the rescheduled finals (which is what Celeste should be doing, too, except her brain can't focus on anything but *where's Nicky*). She's always liked the back of the theater, cool and dark and humming with the low buzz of the light board, but now it's the place where the crying kids go, and Celeste isn't desperate enough to join their ranks just yet. The little alcove by the science labs, with its leafy treetop view—where she and Nicky used to go for private talks—is now equipment storage for the repair work. The school's remaining earthquake scars are being smoothed away on the weekends, which makes Celeste think of this horror movie she watched once with surgeons sneaking into people's bedrooms at night to operate. She feels like the only person in the building—maybe the world?—who isn't bending over backward to just mop the guts and move on. Already there's pretty much nothing left about the quake in national news; scroll any news app, and it's like it never happened. What the fuck became of everybody's thoughts and prayers? Did they just get shoved down inside the city's wounds, stitched over with staples and glue?

Unfortunately, Celeste has also been feeling like she'd rather endure horror movie surgery than show up for senior year. She's always been into school—she's one of those freaks who kind of likes taking tests—but she also never had to do school without Nicky before. Walking in every morning, she can't escape the panicked feeling that she's left something super important at home. Technically Celeste has other friends, but she doesn't seem to know how to be friends with them without Nicky. She feels like a monstrous dick, too, because some of them are going through terrible shit: Devin's living all the way out in Livermore with his aunt, commuting every day to the city for school, while they fix the gas lines in his neighborhood; Jordan's family is staying in some crappy hotel, and her dad is still sick from the smoke inhalation—they think he might have a tumor on his lungs that nobody knew about before. Celeste hates herself for avoiding them, but when they do hang out, she can't find anything to say. They aren't close, anyway; Celeste has never been close with anyone, really, except Nicky. And he's always been the talker of the two of them, while Celeste has a way of keeping silent that makes people want to talk. That's what always made them a good team. Without him, her own silence kind of reverberates in her head until she feels suffocated by it.

The lit-mag office is usually empty at lunch, so Celeste heads down there, taking the long way to avoid Mr. Ackerman, the college counselor, who was trying to snag her all last week. The other seniors have been practically camping out in his office, trying to figure out the new extended deadlines, but Celeste's ignoring his emails. She gets enough questions about her (as yet nonexistent) application essays at home.

At lit mag there seems to be a meeting going on, but before Celeste can disappear, Oona Dunne spots her. "Celeste, hey! I'm *so* glad you're here! We were just talking about you." Somehow Oona always manages to sound like she feels bad for you; there's this permanent pity in her voice, her brow earnestly creased. She loves to bring up the fact that she and Celeste both have Irish dads, like it's some kind of insane coincidence, as if Ireland were an alien exoplanet and not an English-speaking, Budweiser-loving nation of eager emigrants.

"Uh—talking about *me*?"

Oona and some other girls sit at a table with their lunches neatly laid out, but they don't seem to be eating (also no surprise, since they're all mantis-elbowed quinoa eaters; Nicky calls Oona and her friends the Blandorexics). They're leaning in as Oona's fingers hover over the screen of her iPad. Oona 2.0 and 3.0 start to laugh, but Oona shoots them a disapproving look. "I didn't mean we were *talking* about you, not like that, I just meant—so, we're the Memorial Planning Committee, actually? We're planning the memorial assembly? With Mr. Rosales. But he's out today, so we just went ahead with the meeting."

Nothing happens at this school without a committee—not even grief, apparently. "Yeah, good luck with that—"

"So, we were wondering if maybe you wanted to speak. At the memorial? Like, read a poem or something. Or give a little speech."

Celeste's face gets hot. Fiddling with her overall strap, she looks down at Ursa. "Um," she says, "thanks, I guess? But shouldn't you ask those kids' friends? I mean, it's really horrible, but I didn't even know them. And I think I only had PE with Janet like once freshman year." Oona bites her lip, exchanging awkward looks with 2.0 and 3.0. Suddenly Celeste understands—it hits her in the back of the throat, and she spits out, "Wait, what the fuck, Oona? Are you serious? You can't put Nicky in the memorial, for fuck's sake! He's *missing,* not *dead*!"

The mantis elbows start folding all around the table. Oona's brow collapses even more earnestly into itself, as if she's making a real effort to wring out some tears. "God, Celeste, I was just trying—"

"What do you think his mom's going to say when you invite her to the funeral for her totally *alive* son?"

"I mean, Mr. Rosales was going to talk to her, of course!" And then Oona does start to cry, and one of the Blandorexics rushes to her side, draping her in syrupy hugs.

Celeste draws a sharp breath. "You know what, I'm sorry, okay? Sorry." Then she flees the scene. Even Ursa looks disappointed, trailing at her heel. Before school started again, Celeste had hoped maybe her dad was right, that coming here would make her feel better, more "normal." But who even knows what that means anymore? She thinks of *Voyager*, drifting in the pause, carrying its memories into the blank unknown.

People whisper as she makes her way down the hall. Maybe they somehow already know that she just cursed out the Memorial Committee, but more likely it's because of Nicky. Bridget means well—at Carla's urging, she's been posting on message boards in every godforsaken corner of the internet, trying to keep a digital eye out—but she's also managed to turn the subject of his disappearance into the worst kind of tragedy porn, the gossip and speculation constantly cycling from phone to phone. Everybody, all the time, is talking about Nicky, and whenever Celeste arrives, they clam right up, so she feels like she's dumping steaming piles of awkward silence wherever she goes. They might as well keep talking, anyway, because she already knows most of them think she's batshit. The prevailing belief is that Nicky's almost definitely dead, and Celeste is in denial.

The worst is when Celeste overhears people talking about him like he's some kind of martyr, and all that's left behind is the angelic glow. It's almost like everybody *wants* to believe he's dead so they can just cry and moan and then get on with their lives. Like the crew team—they keep cornering Celeste with their weird sympathy and muscle-bound hugs and cute Nicky anecdotes, wanting to *reminisce* together, even though they've hardly ever talked to her before. And worse, kids who hardly knew Nicky, like Oona and her clones, seem almost energized by their proximity to death and suffering, like they're enjoying the drama and spectacle of it all. It's disgusting.

Simmer down, CB, Fake Nicky warns her, slinging his long arm around her neck. He keeps popping up every now and then to shock her, sometimes to say something moderately useful. She tried interrogating him, like about those fucking pills, stashed now in an old pair of roller skates in her room—why was he taking them, how many—but he gets cagey about questions, seems more interested in scolding her with his wit, as usual. *Time to remove the pole from your ass, okay?* he says now. *Everybody lost somebody here.* She reaches for his hand, but he plants a kiss on the top of her head and disappears.

Celeste can hear Bridget calling her name, but she ducks into the bathroom. Thankfully it's empty. Celeste locks herself in the disabled stall with Ursa and sits down on the closed toilet with her face in her hands. Soon Fake Nicky is back. *Oh, Cookie,* he says with a grossed-out frown, *is THIS what we've come to? What are you, the loser girl in some Disney Plus show?* "Shut the fuck up," she tells him. "This is all your fault." And then a group of loud sophomores bursts in, shutting him up for real. One of them complains about a boy she keeps failing to break up with. Celeste listens mindlessly for a minute, oddly comforted by how dumb the conversation is. She hadn't been aware that it was okay to start having dumb conversations again. She wonders if she could even have one if she tried.

"He's, like, the vein of my existence," the girl tells the others, and they groan in sympathy. *BANE,* Celeste longs to shout from behind the door of the stall. But when they're gone, it occurs to her that Nicky is the vein of her existence, in a way. And now she feels his absence like a missing beat of her pulse.

A LITTLE GOOD NEWS: THIS AFTERNOON, FOR THE first time since the quake, Celeste is out on her own. She's managed to keep her blood sugar in check and dose her insulin without fucking it up for a full week, and so she told her parents she's walking home by herself, they can't stop her, and if they try, she'll go and sleep in Nicky's room at Carla's. That's a bluff, really, and they know it; she can hardly stand to be around Carla, who's so discouraged that Celeste worries any minute she might start shopping for a casket. But Celeste just had to get her parents off her back somehow. When the bell rings at the end of the day, she texts her mom goodbye, slams her locker, and bolts for the door. Ursa's not very good at bolting, but they still get there ahead of any other seniors, which is good enough. Celeste doesn't want company.

She's heading for the crystal shop to ask about Misc. Spiritual Guidance. It feels surprisingly great to be walking by herself. Crystal Visions isn't far from school, but the burned-out library and its neighbors are in between, so Celeste takes the long way, walking along the Panhandle and up Central, then back down Haight. She doesn't love to walk on Haight Street itself—between the tourists and the street kids' dogs growling at Ursa, it's pretty much the worst—even Celeste's hippie grandma Mimi, actual former commune dweller, who likes to lecture them about the Summer of Love and how much the Haight meant to her generation, avoids it now at all costs when she visits from Mendocino. Still, because it's close, Celeste and Nicky often end up hanging out there after school despite themselves, sneaking refills at their favorite coffee shop or vintage browsing at Relic, or getting boba at the place where the grumpy owner makes Ursa wait outside.

The coffee shop's still boarded up, but the boba place is open, so Celeste stops there before Crystal Visions and ties the dog to a bench at the curb. She orders her tea unsweetened, which somehow takes forever and makes the owner even grumpier, and by the time she gets back, Ursa is not alone. The kid with the wild blue eyes, the one Celeste spotted at school cramming food in his pack after the quake, sits on the bench, petting Ursa's forehead and whispering to her in Spanish. Celeste's whole body tenses up as she reaches for the leash. The boy's so involved with Ursa that it takes him a minute to notice her struggling one-handed with the knot.

"Hey, been looking for you. Want a hand?" He reaches to hold her tea, but she turns away. "Cool, cool," he says, leaning back on the bench, "just tryna help you out. Listen, where's your friend? Haven't seen him around lately."

She gestures at Ursa's nylon vest with her chin. "She's working," she says. "You're not really supposed to pet her."

He holds up his palms. "My bad. I couldn't resist, though. Big sweet teddy bear." He smiles at Celeste still struggling with the knot. "You tie knots pretty well for a blind girl."

She shoots him a glare. "She's not a guide dog. Obviously."

"Yeah, so what's she for, then?"

She sighs instead of answering. The kid leans over his knees, gently moves her hand aside and starts working the knot himself. Celeste pulls her palm to her chest. The place where he touched her crackles with sparks. She wants to grab Ursa and run, but she doesn't know if she's actually afraid of the boy or afraid of those sparks, which surge through her body in a way that makes it hard to stand up straight. What's her deal with this guy? Whenever he turns up, it feels like she's suddenly powered by somebody else's remote control. He seems genuinely concerned with the knot, so she can safely stare at him. He's skinny but built, with big hands, like a basketball player but short, not much taller than Celeste. His skin is coppery brown, and those crazy eyes are a color that doesn't even seem earthly, like Neptune blue. He's always hanging out with the street kids, but up close, she can see that his clothes are clean: a surplus jacket, Warriors T-shirt, and stupidly giant jeans that show the waistband of his plaid boxers, the kind a mom would pick out. Celeste scolds herself: *Stop thinking about his underwear, for fuck's sake!*

He gets the knot untied and hands over the leash with a deep bow. "Your steed," he says.

"My what?"

He shrugs. "I'm into Arthurian stuff. King Arthur, you know?"

She stares at him for a second. This is Celeste's biggest weakness in the boy department: when they surprise her by liking weird books. "Well, thanks," she mumbles, walking away, keeping Ursa close. She feels his eyes on her and can't help recalling these are the same railroad overalls she's put on every day this week. At least she bothered with earrings—little red beaded hoops—and a clean T-shirt, one with a wide neck that shows off her shoulders and a black bra strap. She can't ignore the sparks again when the boy falls into step at her side.

"Thing is," he says, "I need to talk to your friend. It's like an emergency situation."

"What? Why?"

"Some people around here are looking for him. That money he owes?" He shakes his head and adds, "Not a good idea to fuck with these dudes."

All at once the sparks turn from fire to ice, and Celeste's heart skips a couple of frozen beats. "That's not him," she says, trying for extra casual. "You're thinking of someone else."

The kid frowns. "Figured he told you, the way you're all lovey-dovey and shit."

Celeste laughs too loudly in a way that makes it clear that nothing at all is funny. "Whatever, he's like my brother."

"Yeah, okay. Well, tell your *brother* he better pay his debts." It must be obvious she's confused, because the boy goes on: "He asked if I could get a few pills for him to sell." Celeste swallows a sour gasp. "I don't mess with that shit, myself. Hella racist, to be honest—just to, like, assume?" Celeste folds her arms, feels herself trying to walk a little faster. The boy is right, of course—but he shrugs, a little sheepish, showing a smooth stripe of skin above his jeans. "Anyway, I might've told him who to ask, though. Wish I never did. Now they're asking *me* to find your boy. And I don't even *know* these assholes, really." He shakes his head and laughs, a little cold. "The pills, that's what you rich kids like, right?"

"We're not rich," she says, but as soon as it leaves her mouth, she can hear how ridiculous this sounds, even before he laughs.

"The fuck you're not," he says, not exactly in a hostile way, but still she feels embarrassed, reeling about Nicky and the pills, trying to figure out what to say back. They walk for a minute in silence, past a head shop with plywood over the windows and a music store full of dusty guitars and a locked-up Thai place with broken tables heaped inside. They wade through a group of angry-looking dreadlocked white kids, one of whom is flicking cigarette butts at a parked car. Neptune boy tosses them a sharp nod.

"Friends of yours?" Celeste says.

And then it's like he's suddenly fed up with her cluelessness. He spits a sigh, hikes up his jeans, and says, in a hard voice, "Listen, I'm not playing. Where the fuck is he?"

Her chest tightens. Then she hears herself saying, "He died. In the quake." The words taste terrible. It feels like an epic mistake to have even considered uttering them.

"Aw, fuck, for real?" the kid says, but Celeste picks up the pace, trying to lose him, tugging Ursa along. The sun goes behind a cloud, and everything takes on a gray chill. "Shit, that's rough. I'm really sorry about that," the boy says, catching up to her again, his voice kind of soft now and stunned. It's a weird moment; somehow his reaction, even though it's in response to her lie, actually makes her feel better, which is more than she can say for the many excruciating conversations about Nicky she's had to endure at school. The boy's shaking his head, still talking: "Shit is wild, this earthquake? I can't believe it really happened, you know?" Finally, they're at Crystal Visions. Celeste puts her hand on the door.

"Don't follow me in here, Lancelot," she says, surprising herself again. Is she *flirting* with this kid now? Like that's going to help get rid of him? She looks at him directly for the first time. His mouth is scrunched up with what looks like worry. *Stop staring at his mouth!*

"Like I said," he says, shoving his hands in his pockets, "the money. These dealers, they're not exactly the understanding type."

"Yeah, cool, thanks for your concern." She yanks open the door and runs into the shop. It's dim inside, the windows tinted black, so she can't tell if he's gone, but who cares—this place is like a magic cave, a portal out of the icky Haight and into a secret quiet world. Celeste taps the RING FOR SERVICE bell and breathes it all in while she waits. There's a lavender mist in the air, a huge improvement over the pee-and-incense perfume outside, and the light comes almost entirely from artificial candles scattered everywhere. The walls and display cases are packed with intricate crystals and geodes, some of them giant, some tiny, all glittering in the fake candlelight, as if there's something alive inside them. Each one is like a little planet, crusted with glowing landscapes in alien shades of blue and green and copper and rose. Celeste and Nicky have always liked to come in here, and the lady never seems to mind that they hardly ever spend money.

Except Nicky apparently did. Celeste takes the receipt out of her wallet and smooths it against a glass case. She thinks again of the pills hidden inside her skates at home. She wonders how much more she could've helped if she hadn't been so eager for Nicky to just *be okay*, to get back to the way he was before. There were times in the last year when he was spiraling, for sure, and she was just too scared to watch. Once, pissed at him for taking Molly from a stranger at a club, she left him there dancing with a group of older guys. Another time she went home early from a party, and Jordan told her later that Nicky got so high he almost fell off a fire escape. Celeste never even brought it up with him. *One-time thing*, she told herself. *He's just stressed*. Now she watches Fake Nicky leaning in a corner, running his finger over the amethyst core of a geode. *Don't beat yourself up*, he whispers. *Did you really think I would never have any secrets?*

"Oh my goddess, it's you!" The shop owner floats in from the back room and collapses over Ursa with kisses. "You must know, this dog was sent from the beyond to rescue us. She has the spirit of an ancient warrior queen."

"Yeah, thanks," Celeste says while the lady feeds Ursa from a jar of dog cookies. Then she sits on one of the glass cases, layers of patchwork skirts spilling around her, and eyes Celeste keenly.

"I've been wondering when you'd arrive."

"You have?"

"Yes! I just opened again a few days ago—you can imagine the state this place was in after the tremor. Took me a whole week just for the cleansing! So much toxic energy." She draws an absurdly long breath, then finally exhales, smiling calmly. "At least it's all over, though, right? That week before was torture. Everything off balance, the vibrations getting stronger and stronger. Nothing I could do but keep my chakras in order and wait."

"You knew it was coming?"

The lady hops down from the case, begins piling her black curls into an eagle's nest on top of her head, securing it with chopsticks pulled from somewhere inside her skirt. She's wearing a long string of opalescent marbles, each of which seems to contain a wisp of swirling fog. "Of course," she says. "That's what I told your friend." She frowns a little, presses the beads against her chest. "Not a great time for a journey. Earthquakes cause *massive* energy shifts, I mean colossal. But! Also lots of opportunities for renewal. So there's that." She places her hands on Celeste's shoulders and looks straight in her eyes in a way that would probably make her flee for the hills if she weren't so riveted. "I asked him to send me a messenger, to let me know he was okay. And here you are! What's your name, anyway? I always just think of you as my two little suns."

"Celeste."

The lady throws up her arms. "Ha! Of course it is! Well, I'm Joan." She starts bustling around the shop, inspecting the cases, polishing the stones with the tail of her lacy shawl. "That one always surprises people. Why didn't I change it? Joan of Arc, of course. I could never abandon my namesake."

Celeste is bursting with questions, but she can't figure out how to jump on the runaway train of this conversation. Joan asks if Celeste knows about the stabilizing properties of jasper. "This spirit jasper shard is especially potent; see how it's crusted with smoky quartz? You could bury it in the ground in your yard, for the aftershocks."

Celeste clears her throat. "So—my friend was here? I mean, I know he was here; I have his receipt." She holds it up in the candlelight, but Joan is still peering into the rugged little landscape of the jasper.

"He came in the day before the tremor. I almost closed early, the vibrations were so intense, but then I sensed a transcendent visitor on his way." She sighs, sets the jasper back down on its velvet pillow. "How's he doing?"

"Well—actually, I'm looking for him, sort of. I haven't seen him since the quake. And I found this receipt—"

"Oh," Joan says, frowning again, "you're not the messenger, then. Interesting."

"Can you tell me what he said? Or why he came in, maybe?"

Joan is fingering her beads one by one, agitating the wisps of fog. "He said he wanted some protection for a journey. I sold him some moonstone chips—great for homesickness."

Celeste looks away, pushing back a surge of tears. Nicky's a science guy at heart, even if he thinks it's fun to read the tarot once in a while. Still, she can imagine him rattling the moonstone chips in his pockets, waiting for a bus somewhere, when the planet begins to shake.

"Oh, and he mentioned the beach, so I gave him an aquamarine." Joan rolls her eyes to the dark ceiling, throws up her hands. "I tried to tell him to wait, you know? Especially to stay away from the water. You never know what a massive energy shift is going to bring up out of the ocean."

The beach. Celeste remembers that night just before the quake, which might as well have been in another century, watching Nicky walk away along the glowing white edge of the tide in the dark.

"Sorry to say this, honey, but he also had me cloak his aura,"

Joan says. She crosses the room and puts her hand on Celeste's shoulder. "We cleared his energy, and I gave him a fluorite wand."

Celeste suddenly feels very tired. The lavender mist must be getting to her. "I have no idea what any of that means."

"It means you won't find him unless he wants to be found." Joan opens a drawer and removes a small black pyramid of stone. She places it in Celeste's palm and closes her fingers over it. "Marekanite obsidian," she says. "A gift. To heal your sorrow." Celeste runs the pad of her thumb over the rock's smooth surface. Joan places a finger under her chin to lift her face and looks into it searchingly, her eyes narrowed. "If you're not the messenger," she says, "I wonder why you're here?"

"I'm looking for my friend."

"Maybe it's not just him you're looking for." Joan raises her eyebrows. "Earthquakes are major spiritual events, Celeste. When the faults move, all kinds of energies are released. You can't escape them. It's almost like slicing open some kind of planetary vein." Celeste feels the surge of her pulse in her own wrist, veins entwined around the little sun, skirting its rays. "Nobody *really* survives an earthquake, that's what I'm saying. We're all forever altered."

"I have to go." Suddenly Celeste feels the need to escape the cave, as if there might be a dragon waking up nearby. "Thanks for your help. And for the stone."

"One more thing. He left a talisman behind. Forgot it here that day. You should probably take it." Joan disappears into the back room, loudly struggles with a squeaky drawer, then returns with a satisfied smile, holding Nicky's little black Moleskine notebook, the one with the big *N* scrawled in silver Sharpie on the front. Celeste's body goes stiff with shock. She'd just assumed he had the Mars book with him—and yet here it is, hidden in the crystal cave.

It's almost like Joan went back there and unearthed one of Nicky's body parts. The Mars book is where he keeps his notes about all things extraterrestrial: formulas and diagrams Celeste can't even pretend to understand; questions he's pondering, stuff he learns from PBS or planetarium shows; notes from journal articles about the *Pioneer* mission. It's like Nicky's idea of a diary, full of science porn, everything written in his favorite pink ink. He never exactly kept it private, but then, he never really let it out of his sight, either.

"Carry it with you. Maybe it'll help." Joan squeezes Celeste's arm. "Even lost souls are drawn to their precious belongings." She clears her throat, her smile turns a little sad, and a different voice comes out, less Joan-the-aura-cloaking-soothsayer and more Bonnie-the-concerned-mom. "Or maybe you can give it to his family?" she says. "They'll be wanting reminders of him right now."

Celeste thanks her again and zips the book into her bag while Joan gives Ursa a long hug goodbye. Then they leave the crystal womb and emerge into the painfully bright and smelly day. When Celeste's eyes adjust, she sees that the boy is still waiting nearby, talking on his phone, and also that her bus is at the corner, huffing and puffing to lower itself for a crowd to board. She runs for the bus with Ursa. The boy follows, calling to her in Spanish. He catches up with her at the Muni door and grabs her hand. Celeste pulls away, but not before a comet's worth of fiery sparks blast through her body. She looks down at his hand, expecting what, maybe a blowtorch in its place—but instead there's a tattoo she hadn't noticed before, peeking out of the cuff of his jacket: the radiant blade of a sword.

The kid says, "Wait," and, "Come on," but she's pulling herself and Ursa up the stairs. The driver knows her; this is the bus she and Nicky always take to her house from school.

"That guy bothering you?" he says.

"Sort of," she mumbles, and the driver unceremoniously shuts the door in the kid's face. Celeste falls into a seat, pulling Ursa close between her knees. She glances out the window, sees the boy still standing there, running his hands anxiously through his smooth hair.

Before

Back in the fall, their college counselor said they needed extracurriculars, so Celeste and Nicky conspired to join the debate club together. The deciding factors were these: (1) Ms. Tanaka always brought good snacks, and (2) meetings were in the fishbowl, the best classroom in the new building, a glass dome on the roof with a high-powered telescope and a view stretching out to the west (now closed until further notice, the glass webbed with cracks). Also, as it turned out, the mock debates were fun, even kind of exhilarating. Celeste liked the way they could all argue and yell at each other and at the end just forget it ever happened, no harm done.

And then one Tuesday at the end of September, Ms. Tanaka scrawled this resolution on the white board: *The Pioneer mission to Mars is a waste of taxpayer money.*

"You've got to be fucking kidding me!" Celeste grabbed Nicky by the hood of his sweatshirt. He cackled, throwing back his beard.

"Piece of cake," he said, cracking his knuckles, miming a few Rocky-style punches. "I better get *against*. I could do *against* in my deepest sleep, like cursed-by-the-wicked-witch sleep, like practically *dead* I could argue against that bullshit." He crumpled a piece of paper and chucked it hard at the resolution on the board. A couple of kids cheered, but Ms. Tanaka shot him a look.

"Can it, Nicky."

"Sorry, Ms. T," he said, casting beams of light out of that solar-powered Nicky grin. "You know how I feel about Mars, though."

Like all the teachers, Ms. Tanaka adores Nicky, so she forgave him and put him on *against*, which meant that Celeste got *for* by default. (Ms. T never put them on the same team.) Celeste was furious—and also stumped. She might as well have been asked to argue for the eradication of sunsets or puppies. She sat hunched at her desk, pouting and doodling through the silent note-taking time and the initial discussion, when kids on both teams get to just lob around their ideas. Naturally, chatterbox Oona 3.0 spoke up right away for Celeste's team, ready with an endless tirade about how there are better things we could do with the gazillions of dollars the government spends on the space program. She stood and rattled off numbers for probably three minutes straight, boring them all to tears. Only Nicky seemed to be listening, scribbling feverishly in the Mars book with his pink pen. Finally Ms. Tanaka broke in.

"Okay, maybe let's start with something more basic. Why do humans want to explore space, anyway?"

"Because it's cool?"

"Because it's beautiful?"

"You can do better than that. What else?"

Another Oona-ish girl piped up in a dreamy voice: "I mean, I think it's like this idea that, like, something *bigger* than us is out there, you know? I think that idea really *resonates* with people."

Celeste expected Nicky to snort, maybe shoot her a subtle eye roll, but instead he agreed, bouncing his leg so hard that he was practically launching out of his desk. "Yeah," he said, "it's like—everything in our lives seems so *important* and *urgent*, and then you think about the fact that our whole civilization is basically a pebble, not even a pebble, like a speck of dust floating in a universe so vast that we literally can't comprehend it . . . Well, it's sort of comforting? Or liberating, even. Like what we do every day, you know, the decisions we make, they're just totally *meaningless*, right? I like thinking about that sometimes."

Everyone silently stared at Nicky like he was an actual alien. Celeste turned away to look out over the view, the treed expanse of Golden Gate Park rolling all the way to the water, and then the endless silvery blue, the day so clear you could almost see the curve of the planet on the horizon.

"That's bleak, bro," somebody said.

"Yeah, I don't get how that's *comforting*, Nicky."

Nicky looked imploringly at Celeste. She did get it—thinking about space made her feel free, too—but she was still mad about getting stuck on *for,* so she folded her arms instead of defending him. He sighed loudly and slapped the Mars book closed. "Forget it, screw you morons."

Ms. Tanaka interrupted (she lets them curse in class but draws the line at name-calling) and sent them off in groups to write their formal arguments. That was it for Nicky, though. After all the trash-talking and paper-throwing, he didn't speak for the rest of the hour, abstained from the actual debate. Afterward, when Chris Yee joked around by shouting "Fuck NASA!" on his way downstairs from the roof, Nicky just stormed off, looking like he wanted to slam the guy against a locker.

"Hey, overreact much?" Celeste caught up with him a block

from school. His dark hair, always carefully combed in a shining wave, was out of place, but when Celeste reached up to fix it, he swatted her hand.

"I thought you were coming for dinner?" she said. "Bonnie's making pesto."

"Yeah, I'm tired, see you tomorrow." He disappeared onto the bus with Ursa gazing after him, slobbery and forlorn. Celeste texted him later: *Haters gonna hate*, and then: *Sorry I didn't back you up* and some planet and star emojis. She even found a new *PodLab* episode about Mars—about the gross billionaires who'd funded the research, and how people thought they might already be making plans to stake land-ownership claims—the kind of thing Nicky would usually eat right up. She texted the link and asked if he wanted to listen together on Zoom, like they sometimes did since he moved. But he never replied. Celeste found herself mindlessly thumbing through their texts waiting for the little gray dots to pop up, a pathetic scenario that would soon become distressingly familiar.

The next day they were fine. He'd already started selling papers by then, but he wouldn't tell her about it until a few weeks later. She forgot all about what had happened in debate club, until the Mars book emerged from the lavender mist in the crystal cave.

Day 58

She's reading through the Mars book yet again on the bus when she finds that same little speck-of-dust speech from debate club, almost verbatim, scribbled there in Nicky's pink ink, in his practically unintelligible handwriting.

Of course, she's heard Nicky talk about space in this way lots of times before. But now that he's gone, reading the words in the Mars book gives them a new shape, like she's put on a pair of 3D glasses and suddenly sees, behind the letters, another string of totally different symbols with a different meaning. With the glasses on, she understands this: Nicky was carrying more than even his huge rower's shoulders could bear, and it was the heaviest stuff. Fear of failing. Hope. A giant sandbag of expectations. That's what he was trying to say in debate club: Thinking about the cosmos helped him feel lighter. In space, at zero gravity, everything's weightless. Liberated.

You got a problem with my shoulders? Fake Nicky eyes her from his spot across the aisle of the bus. She swats at him with the Mars book, but before it can touch him, he's gone.

Celeste has had the book for a couple of weeks now, and she's spent hours scouring it for clues. Most of it might as well have been written in Martian, though, for all she can understand; Nicky's passions for vector data and probabilities are two of the maybe three things that Celeste can't claim to share with him. There's other stuff in the book, too, like pages of notes about the *Pioneer* mission, and more philosophical musings of the "humanity is a meaningless smudge of poo on the bottom of the sneaker of the cosmos" variety. Nicky's read some of it out loud to her before, so none of this feels much like clue material.

Except! In the back, after some blank pages, with no title or any other associated fanfare, there's a juicy little list. Places the two of them love in SF, some of their very favorites. Secret nooks of Golden Gate Park, the dunes at Ocean Beach, a dim sum bakery on Clement. It reads, strangely, like some kind of highlights tour of their friendship—a catalog of stops on the double-decker bus ride of their life.

Celeste has probably read the list a million times now, backward and forward, and she still doesn't know what it means. Are these just the places Nicky felt sad to leave behind? Did he visit them before he left, for old times' sake? Was he planning to visit them in his new life, as his new self?

Somehow, she's going to figure it out.

In her room Celeste has pinned up a transit map of the city, the one they put on the wall in the BART station, which, it turns out, you can get for free if you're polite to the turnstile person instead of harassing him like most assholes do. She added a sprinkling of gold pushpins to the map, stuck in all the places on Nicky's weird list (plus their favorite beaches, because of the aquamarine from Joan). The map is now the only thing left on Celeste's bedroom wall. At first she just took down a few posters to make room, but then she ended up taking everything else down, too—even the star map Nicky had brought home from Space Camp and the amazing photo of her grandma Mimi as a hot young hippie, wearing a peasant dress on the commune. Ever since Celeste tucked it all away in her closet, her room feels weirdly transitional, especially with the broken bookshelf gone and all her books just stacked against the walls. Still, she can't imagine putting all that stuff up again. Everything except the transit map feels like a distraction: white noise obscuring the voice she's aching to hear.

Each morning before school, Celeste consults the map to plot her route, and as soon as the dismissal bell rings, she gets on Muni with Ursa and rides out to one of the pins. Sometimes it takes them forever—two or three transfers, which might've seemed like a pain in the ass to Celeste in her previous life—but these days she doesn't mind riding Muni at all. In fact she almost looks forward to it, the winter sun warming the bus, Ursa kneeling at her feet. The city through the windows is still so dusty and broken, glittering with shards, but Celeste feels strangely safe inside the bus as it heaves up and down the impossible hills. Often there are wanderers muttering or shouting, but they mostly keep to themselves, or Ursa's bulk keeps them at bay.

Last week they started with Nicky's favorite beaches, since the aquamarine felt like Celeste's most promising actual clue. She brought the missing person fliers along and showed them to Muni drivers and grocery checkers and surfers; at Safeway and the surfer coffee shop, the cashiers apologized and waved her grimly toward the pinboards hanging by the doors, smothered with fliers just like hers, their edges warped from the salt air. She combed Nicky's preferred stargazing spots on the dunes, picking through the green carpet of ice plant. On the shoreline at Fort Point, in the echoing shadow of the Golden Gate Bridge, Fake Nicky made an appearance to inform Celeste that she should lay off the Netflix detective shows (an opinion her parents seem to share), but she ignored him and kept on uselessly shuffling through the sand.

Nothing turned up at any of the beaches. Celeste decided to replace the gold beach pins with silver ones to check them off the list. She doesn't know what she would do if she found anything; it occurs to her once in a while that if Nicky's really out there starting a new life, aura-cloaked and all, he might not want her snooping on his trail. Then again, the list in the Mars book seems deliberately written for her—these are *their* places, all lined up neatly on the page—the book and the receipt left behind where she would find them, like tantalizing breadcrumbs. Celeste can't help but feel like Nicky meant for her to follow them. And even if he didn't, she can't imagine spending her time any other way right now.

TODAY CELESTE AND URSA ARE RIDING THE BUS ALmost an hour to get to Fisherman's Wharf. It's a part of town that she and Nicky mostly avoid like it's pestilent, except for the awesome photo place at Pier 39 where you can try on gold rush costumes and have an old-timey picture taken by somebody wearing a fake handlebar mustache. The photo place is number one on the Mars book list. They've always loved going there, taking way too long to choose costumes while the annoyed photographer files her nails on a stool.

Celeste and Ursa get off the bus on North Point, and they don't have to wander for more than a minute before Celeste can tell that the whole area is deserted, much of it roped off with caution tape and wire fence. She heard it was bad over here, that fires along the

Wharf kept burning days after the quake, but seeing it in person is different from looking at tiny photos on her phone. The tourists have been replaced by cops in neon vests, waving Celeste away at every turn, standing guard at burned-out hotels and souvenir shops. Boats docked along the marina are topped with the fluttering, scorched remains of sails, like something out of a pirate story. *What the actual fuck am I doing here?* Celeste wonders, hoping for Fake Nicky to show up with a reply, or at least some kind of morbid joke to lighten the mood.

Celeste wanders toward Pier 39, following the barks of the sea lions, who haven't abandoned the place along with everyone else. Somebody in a hard hat yells at her to get outta here, it's no place for kids. She hurries away and loads Ursa back onto the bus.

Safely home, she replaces the Pier 39 pin with a silver one and studies the map, looking for some kind of pattern in the pins. She tries to connect them in pencil to make a shape, but every time, no matter where she starts or finishes, the lines just form a messy web, and she feels tangled up in it, more tangled by the day. Not that it's a bad feeling. Maybe it's more like a hammock than a web.

Sometimes, in low moments, Celeste lets the doubt creep in. Maybe Nicky didn't intend the list for her at all. It's so unlike him, after all, to have left the Mars book behind. Maybe he knew she'd look for comfort in the crystal cave, and maybe he did mean for her to find the book . . . but why? She has spent hours wondering—in class, on the bus, in her bed in the dark—following the spider's floss of maybes until she loses it in the air.

"Hey, sweetheart!" Bonnie bangs through the front door downstairs, dropping a bunch of bags. "Sorry I'm late! We better get going, traffic looks bad getting downtown."

Celeste groans, sinks to the floor, buries her face in Ursa's neck. "I don't get why I even need to go."

Her mom's in the doorway, red-faced, rattling her keys. Both Celeste's parents think her sleuthing is getting out of hand. She overheard them talking in the kitchen the other night, whispering about how, after so many weeks, Nicky was almost certainly gone—that's the word they used, but they meant *dead*—and how were they ever going to convince Celeste? Bonnie was sobbing, but Celeste felt only a red-hot bolt of anger. She stormed into the kitchen, muttering "Fuck this" without meeting their eyes, grabbed a diet soda, and ran upstairs, ignoring their calls to come back and talk.

Bonnie frowns at the transit map on the blank wall. "I thought you were working on your applications this afternoon."

"I was, okay? Just taking a break." In fact the almost empty essay file is open on Celeste's laptop, but the last actual sentence she wrote in it was before the quake. She's heard some kids at school talking about using the quake as an essay topic, which seems to her like a pretty gross exploitative move. "Actually, I could use some more time today," she says. "I'm getting somewhere with the essay. I should probably stay home."

"You know it's important for us to support Carla," Bonnie says. "We're all she has right now. I don't want to put you in this position—"

"Yes, you do, otherwise you just *wouldn't*."

"That's not fair. It's only an hour—you can keep working tonight."

Celeste grabs her backpack and her cozy yellow old-man sweater and edges past her mom, down the plywood stair slope, and out to the car. They told Carla they'd join her at some ludicrous meeting with the police and FEMA at a Union Square hotel, for families of people still missing after the quake. Celeste went along to one of these meetings before, thinking she might learn something valuable, or maybe even encounter the mysterious Merlot. But Merlot never turned up, and the purpose of the meeting seemed to be to dole out pep talks and donuts.

Traffic indeed sucks, with so many streets still closed, and by the time they get to Union Square, they're ten minutes late. The area, like the Wharf, is eerily empty of the usual selfie-snapping tourist hordes. A cable car rattles down the hill with just a few passengers; Celeste half expects them to be skeletons wearing I ♥ FRISCO T-shirts. There's a snowbank of trash along the curb on Powell and tent encampments lining the square, people huddled in sleeping bags next to the shuttered department stores. Celeste crosses the street with her head down. Ever since the quake broke her life into pieces, she hasn't been thinking much about how bad it's been for people whose lives were already in pieces before. A woman pushing a baby stroller piled with her belongings glares at Celeste, who says hi dumbly and hurries into the hotel.

The ballroom is packed but strangely quiet. Probably two hundred people are there, filing into folding chairs, their voices low and tired. Celeste and Bonnie find Carla just as an official-looking dude in a gray suit steps to the podium and asks everyone to please sit down so they can begin. Pop sits next to Carla, and Celeste hugs them both before she takes her chair. Pop, a construction foreman, used to be a big guy, but his body's shrunk a bit since Nonna's dementia got so bad, and even more since the quake. He tries to smile at Celeste, but it's like his mouth can't quite curve that way anymore.

"See the reporters?" Carla points out the row of them up front, a few with news cameras propped on their shoulders. What kind of show are they about to put on here? But Carla seems hopeful. She leans over Pop's lap and whispers, "Maybe we can get an interview about Nicky!" Celeste smiles robotically—she still isn't sure if Nicky's going to murder her for spamming the city with pictures of his face, so talking about him on camera feels like a bad idea—but before she can respond, a hush takes over the room, because that's the *governor* taking the podium now and clearing her throat into the mic.

"Welcome," she says as the crowd quiets down. "Good evening, and welcome."

Carla's looking even more hopeful, a pink flush rising in her cheeks, but Celeste doesn't get it. If the actual freaking governor of California showed up here to deliver a news flash, it's hard to imagine it being a positive one. Also, her face looks sort of impatient and pained, like she can't wait to get home and take off her makeup.

"On behalf of the state of California and the city of San Francisco, I want to thank you all for joining us tonight." The microphone squeals a little, and the governor covers it with her hand, hissing at the gray-suit dude, who hurries to fiddle with the dials on the podium. The governor smiles stiffly, then finally gets the thumbs-up from suit guy to proceed. "Ladies and gentlemen," she says, "first of all, let me say how very sorry I am for the ordeals you have been through as a result of this tragedy. You have been living through one of the most trying times in the history of this great city, but San Francisco has weathered trying times before, and I'm hopeful that because of the incredible spirit and goodwill of our citizenry, we, the entire state of California, will emerge stronger and more beautiful than ever."

She pauses, straightens her shoulders, stares down hard at the podium for several seconds, during which time Celeste realizes that the governor is afraid she is going to cry. Celeste watches the woman's face and can almost feel her own face forming the same expression, as it has done many times before: eyes swelling, mouth twisted at the corners. The room is gripped by a taut silence, broken only by some nervous coughs. Suddenly Celeste feels very cold, and the ballroom lights are giving everything a vile pink tinge. She sinks into her sweater, pulling the yellow cuffs over her hands, longing for Ursa, whom they left sleeping at home.

"However," the governor says grimly, "as you all know, we've suffered terrible losses, and the time has come for us to grieve. To that end, I've come here tonight to inform you that the state of California will begin issuing death certificates at this time for individuals reported missing on or around December eighteenth." Gasps and sudden sobs begin to rise from the crowd and fill the room, alive and frantic. Celeste sinks farther into the vinyl seat of her chair. "In the absence of identifiable remains, the state will legally presume these individuals dead, with the Tomales earthquake as the stated cause of death, so that families may proceed with the bereavement process and manage any legal matters involving the victims' estates."

Carla doubles over, weeping into her lap, with Pop slung over her back. Bonnie wraps Celeste in her poncho wings and holds her against her shuddering chest. They're all crying—Celeste has never heard anything so awful as a room full of people in so much pain. The governor's still talking, promising families that the search for remains will continue, more apologies and promises, grief counselors and social workers and *blah blah blah*, then she apologizes one last time and leaves the room in tears herself. Gray-suit guy gets up and drools a few minutes of instructions onto the podium, lists of resources and next steps that nobody in the room is in any shape to process; then, finally and mercifully, he shuts the fuck up.

It's probably ten minutes before Carla can stand. Even then, she needs Bonnie and Pop on either side of her, themselves barely upright. They file into an elevator full of broken zombies, the heaviest elevator in history, and ride it down to the lobby. Celeste walks behind them, dragging her boots on the carpet. She looks at Carla and thinks, *She's giving up. That's what giving up looks like.* Fake Nicky never seems to appear when his family's around, but Celeste thinks if he did, he would be totally wrecked and weeping, too. Even if he wants his mom to think he's gone, he would never want to see her so horribly fucking sad. Celeste stares at the sun on her wrist and feels it burning under the skin. She clamps her other hand around it like a claw.

BONNIE INSISTS THAT CARLA AND POP COME HOME with them for dinner. A neighbor is spending the evening watching Turner Classics with Nonna, and Shane has a chicken pot pie in the oven. "We should be together tonight," Bonnie says, so they agree in a wordless daze, their faces slack and pale. In the quiet house, Shane pours a deep glass of wine for Carla and a beer for Pop, and they sit not drinking while Celeste sets the table with trembling hands. Then they sit not eating the pot pie, either. Bonnie tries a few times to start a conversation, offering help that doesn't exactly address the reason for needing it—she could take Nonna for a day or two, or run any errands Carla can think of, or make some phone calls for her. But Carla just spins the stem of her glass, making a whirlpool in the wine. Celeste tries to keep her fork from shaking, picks at her crust and makes a little pile of peas, and says nothing at all, even though there's an asteroid belt of words violently circling in her brain.

She wants to hurl the asteroids. She wants to hurl them at their heads until they understand. They *can't* just give up. When they give up, Nicky goes from *missing* to *gone*. He goes from *lost in space* to *blown to smithereens*.

After dinner, dishes done, nobody seems to know what to do, so Shane turns on basketball for Pop. The Warriors are in all-black jerseys and shoes, which seems to Celeste like the stupidest possible tribute. At the commercial, a plug for the local news comes on. There's a bit about *Pioneer*, video of the crew in training, all of them wearing red-and-gold ribbons in honor of quake victims. Some images from the Jet Propulsion Lab, story at ten. And then, without warning, there she is again: the governor at the podium, in front of the same drab burgundy curtain, with the same pained look on her face.

Celeste's body freezes in knots. Carla is covering her mouth, shaking her head at the anchorman's voice. "Today the official death toll from the Tomales quake rises to a stunning count of *four thousand two hundred fourteen* as the city declares the *death in absentia* of the earthquake's missing victims." They cut to a scene out of a sci-fi movie, a huge open room with metal walls, like the inside of a giant fridge, with rows and rows of tables draped in white shrouds, and others where people in lab coats look to be studying piles of dust. "Meanwhile, in a temporary identification center housed at the historic flower mart, medical examiners continue to comb through the rubble in search of remains. That story tonight at ten."

Shane fumbles with the remote, muttering "Jesus Christ," and after finally managing to shut the TV off, he throws the remote at it and drops his face in his hands. But it's too late—Carla has started to weep again. The noise of her sobs makes the asteroids in Celeste's brain spin faster and harder. Pretty soon one of them is going to collide with her mouth, so she leaps to her feet, ready to run, wanting to save them all from the impact. Instead she hears herself shouting, "So that's it? You're giving up! He's dead, just like that, just because they said so?"

"Celeste!"

"No, I want to know! He's dead, right? That's what we're going with now? That's the word on the fucking street?"

Suddenly her dad's up in her face, his mouth twisted with pain. He tries to grab her arm, but she pulls away. "Celeste, enough!"

"Well, if the *governor* says he's dead—"

"Celeste, goddamn it, that's *enough*!" It's Pop, who's been silent since the hotel. His ragged voice is such a shock that it blows the asteroids clear into another galaxy. "Goddamn it," he says again. He draws a deep, rickety breath and sets his hand on Carla's back, which seems, for the moment, to calm her sobs. "You're a good girl, Celeste," he says, "like family to us. And we're going to have to face this thing together now. Our Nicky's gone. That's all there is to it."

He finds a handkerchief in his pocket and works at wiping his eyes. Carla turns away, refusing to even look at Celeste, and her parents are giving each other a weary, anxious look, a *how the hell will we ever get through this* look that Celeste already knows too well. Suddenly she feels very far away, too far for them to hear her anymore, like she's looking down at them from a rising rocket. So even though there are many more things she should probably say, she turns and flees, scrambling up the plywood slope that used to be the stairs.

She slams the door to her room and climbs into bed in her sweater and jeans, covering her face to erase the image of that horrible place with the shrouded tables. Her heart's pounding so hard that it makes her whole body shake, even her eyeballs. After a moment Ursa lumbers over and lays her heavy head on Celeste's belly. "Oh, hi," Celeste says, relief already flooding her chest. "I didn't know you were up here." The dog climbs onto the bed to join her. They have this trick where they lie next to each other and Celeste tries to make her chest rise and fall at the same time as Ursa's back, and eventually everything feels a little bit more okay. She tries it now, staring up at the web of lines on the transit map. It takes a while, but it works. Her heart calms down, and the shrouded tables fall away, and all that's left is her and Ursa and the map with its sprinkling of pins.

Then all at once she sees it. The pattern in the pins. She climbs over Ursa, digs in her desk for a ruler and pencil, and starts connecting the pins to form the shape she finally sees.

It's a constellation, of course—the best one, their favorite. Bright enough, on moonless, fogless winter nights, to view the scattered glitter of its most brilliant stars, even without a telescope. They have a game: Whoever spots it first gets the first drag off the joint. But at the dawn of summer, right around their birthday, the sun passes through it, and it disappears.

It's Gemini. The twins.

Before

"Want to know why Pollux was immortal, and Castor wasn't?"

"I'm trying to study here, but okay, sure."

"'Cause Zeus raped their mom—fucking *Zeus*!—and then she had sex with Castor's dad *on the same day*."

"Ugh, Nicky, so horrible! Is that even a thing? Twins from two different dads?"

"Actually, there were two girls, too. Quadruplets. One of them was Helen of Troy. It looks like maybe they hatched from eggs? Or just the boys did? Weird." They were whispering in the Sutro library, ostensibly studying for a calc test, but Nicky was writing a final paper on the Argonauts for world lit, and Callie Tran was going to pay him two hundred bucks to do it. It was the first week of December. In a few days, Celeste's mom would notice some fishy sentences in Callie's Argonauts essay that matched sentences in Nicky's own work; a couple of weeks after that, the library would vanish, and so would Nicky.

"Oh shit, it gets worse," he said. "Want to know why they hatched from eggs?"

"Do I have to?"

He shoved the open book across the table and stabbed the page with his pen. "It says he turned himself into a swan, and then he raped her. Like, with his *bird penis*."

"Jesus, Nicky." Celeste couldn't resist looking down at the book. Sure enough, it was a painting of a woman having sex with a swan, the beak draped over one of her breasts, the wings unfolding above them. The woman had one of those Michelangelo bodies, long-limbed and mushy, with an oddly serene look on her face. "That is so disturbing! Thank you very fucking much." She slapped the book shut and shoved it back at him.

"It's messed up, right?" He shuddered and pushed the book away with the tip of the pen, holding his nose. Celeste tried to get back to work, squinting at the numbers to get her head around them again, but Nicky was still doing his Nicky-thinking dance, bouncing in the squeaky chair.

"Bro! Do you mind? I would really like to ace this test. My grade's on the brink."

"Sorry, yeah, you gotta work. MIT doesn't love B's in math."

MIT doesn't love empty applications, either. Celeste used to daydream about shopping with Nicky to fill their campus apartment with junky furniture; now, when she tried to think about that life they'd been planning for years, she started feeling panicky, her breath coming in cold bursts. In those Cambridge fantasies now, she herself was nowhere in sight—only Nicky. Nicky rowing crew on the Charles; Nicky's long torso hunched over a microscope.

"I was just thinking, Castor and Pollux are cool, though. You know how they ended up in the sky?"

She dropped her head in her book.

"Castor got killed, 'cause, you know, he was the mortal one, and Pollux didn't want to just go off and live forever on Olympus without his twin, so he asked that fucking rapist Zeus if he could share his immortality with his brother. So Zeus put them up in the heavens together. Boom. Gemini."

"Good story," Celeste admitted, her mouth smushed on her math problems.

"What do you think, CB? Which one of us is Castor, and which one's Pollux?"

She blew a sigh into the spine of her book. "Can't I be Helen of Troy?"

"Uh, gender-biased much?"

She raised her head, pushed the curls out of her face. Nicky was looking serious now, like it really mattered how she decided to reply, so she tucked her pen in her book and thought for a minute.

"Okay, I guess I feel like you're Pollux. You know, godly and all. Ready to head to Olympus for eternity."

"Huh," he said, scratching his beard. "Well, I think the jury's still out. Maybe you'll turn out to be Pollux."

She looked at him squarely. "I'd give you half my immortality."

"Me too. Immortality sounds like a total bore anyway. I don't wanna stick around this rock any longer than I have to." He frowned into his lap, getting the distant, hopeless look Celeste had been noticing too often, his eyes blank and tired. It made her queasy to look at him. She flipped her pen across the table to snap him out of it, and he caught it and laughed. "Hanging out in the heavens with you, though," he said. "I could be down with that for sure."

A couple of days later—calc test aced, Argonauts paper forged— they borrowed Pop's ancient Buick and drove to stay with Celeste's grandma north of Mendocino for the Geminids meteor shower. Mimi lives in a shingled bungalow teetering on a rocky cliff, surrounded by giant ferns and pillowy mounds of moss. Her deck, even though it feels like it's about to break off into the ocean, is the best stargazing spot on a clear night. Plus, she keeps bees and makes this amazing honey bread and tells them stories about her days of free love and weed-growing before she had Bonnie. While Nicky set up the telescope, Mimi carried out a pile of musty afghans and a tray of honey bread with a big glass of blackberry wine for her and a taste for each of them in a jelly jar. They wrapped themselves and Ursa in the blankets and waited, watching the twins, sipping the wine, listening to Mimi's stories. The deep black bowl of the sky, spangled with light, curved above and around them and dipped into the whispering sea. When the meteors started flaring through the Gemini, they whooped and pointed and gasped at first, then settled into a wowed silence. It was hard not to feel like they were already hanging out in the heavens together.

Day 76

"This is going to be a tough day for you all." Ms. Greenberg folds her hands in her lap and looks around the circle at each of them in turn. She has this unnerving way of making statements and then waiting for them to answer as if she's asked a question. Celeste squirms in her chair. She's wearing a slippery blue velvet jumpsuit—half of the twin costume she shared with Nicky last Halloween—but it fits wrong now, with the weight she's lost, hanging too loose where it once hugged her curves. This morning her mom made it clear that she thought the jumpsuit a bad choice for the school memorial, but Celeste felt an irresistible desire to show up in something tasteless, and the jumpsuit (more of a catsuit, really) fit the bill. She's been finding that even semi-pretend grief is an excellent excuse for antisocial behavior.

One of the freshmen raises her hand without looking up from the cafeteria floor. Celeste knows from the last meeting that this girl, Abby, was close with the kids who died in the rec center fire. Her outfit is spectacularly appropriate, a prim black dress befitting Wednesday Addams. Celeste catches herself thinking snarky thoughts about it and feels immediately guilty. "I just wish I didn't even have to go," Abby says, biting her lip. "I just feel like it's going to make me even sadder." Celeste feels a sudden urge to hug Abby, but weirdly, that seems to be against the code of conduct here. Nobody ever gets up to hug anyone else, nor hugs anyone else before or after the group begins, even though the frequent crying meltdowns would warrant hugs in any normal situation.

"It might," Ms. Greenberg says gently. Celeste does appreciate her honesty, at least. It hasn't been as bad as she thought, coming to these meetings. She told her parents she would join the grief group as penance for blowing up at Carla and Pop. She's been to three sessions in the cafeteria, sitting in the circle of folding chairs with the burrito smell in the air, but she hasn't said a word yet. The group meets twice a week during study hall, a useful way to avoid her friends and the college counselor. It's also useful because her parents and Carla are assuming it means Celeste is ready to stop her detective bullshit and hop on the death-in-absentia train to recovery. She's letting them assume it, too, by pretending she thinks he's dead without ever actually saying it. At first, she walked around in a queasy haze of betrayal, but then it occurred to her: This is probably what Nicky wants. She's pretending *for* him, so that his family can move on. They don't believe her anymore, and she just wants them to feel better, even if it means she keeps looking for him by herself, in secret. Her wall is totally blank now; she moved the transit map with its pins to the inside of her closet. At night she opens the door wide and shoves the clothes aside and stares at the map like before, swinging to sleep in the hammock of lines connecting the twins.

Mostly Celeste uses the grief group meetings as a quiet time to sit and stargaze in her head, thinking about which points are left to visit on the Gemini, trying to figure out what Nicky could possibly have meant by leaving the constellation pattern for her to find. While Abby talks, Celeste thinks about yesterday, when she and Ursa rode the 23 bus all the way east to Castor's left foot. It falls on Heron's Head, a bizarrely pretty little walking trail on a marshy spit of land next to a garbage truck parking lot. Last summer Nicky had a job with the city, cleaning park bathrooms and clearing weeds, and Celeste used to take the 23 to meet him at Heron's Head and walk Ursa after his shift. But the earthquake hit that part of town hard, and everything looks different now. The bus took Celeste and Ursa past the flattened warehouse of the main post office—iron cranes hovering like vultures on a carcass, picking at the debris—and a stretch of abandoned train track dotted with rickety RVs. The Heron's Head trail was deserted except for an actual heron, stalking proudly through the shallows with its slender beak in the air. The only thing Celeste found was an interesting string of graffiti looped around some boulders. It looked a little like math, like the equations in Nicky's Mars book. She snapped a photo, then tried to compare the tags with his writing in the book but came up blank.

"Celeste," Ms. Greenberg is saying, jolting her out of her trance. "Did you not hear me?"

"Sorry, what?" They're the first two words she's ever said out loud in grief group.

"Well, I've heard that you're planning to read something at the ceremony today. I was hoping you'd share with us how you're feeling about that."

Celeste wishes she could disappear. "Um . . . nervous, I guess?"

Ms. Greenberg waits for her to continue. Celeste reaches into the pocket of her jean jacket and finds the folded paper she stuffed in there this morning, the poem she picked out to read at the memorial. They wanted her to write something herself, to give a real eulogy, but of course there was no way in hell she'd be doing that, so she told her mom she was afraid of crying onstage. Bonnie suggested a poem might be easier and started leaving anthologies in strategic places (top of toilet, breakfast table). Yesterday morning Celeste surprised herself by opening one of them over her Cheerios.

> *Do you still remember: falling stars,*
> *how they leapt slantwise through the sky*
> *like horses over suddenly held-out hurdles*
> *of our wishes—did we have so many?—*
> *for stars, innumerable, leapt everywhere;*
> *almost every gaze upward became*
> *wedded to the swift hazard of their play,*
> *and our heart felt like a single thing*
> *beneath that vast disintegration of their brilliance—*
> *and was whole, as if it would survive them!*

Fake Nicky gives her a thumbs-up from his spot in the cafeteria corner. *Solid choice!* Sometimes he likes to hang out over there during grief group, snarking and scoffing and tossing popcorn at Celeste. *Rilke was a genius. Made of goddamn star stuff, like us.*

"If you like," Ms. Greenberg's saying in her cottony voice, "you could read it to us now, just for practice."

Celeste unfolds the paper and smooths it in her lap. The poem almost seemed too perfect when she found it. She had to close the book a couple of times and open it again to make sure she wasn't dreaming it up herself. "Okay," she says, and coughs, clears her throat. "'Do you still remember: falling stars—'"

But the awful yammering of the bell cuts her off. They all start to gather their bags and half-eaten snacks. Ms. Greenberg apologizes to Celeste. "I love that poem," she says. "Rilke was a genius."

"Yeah, that's what Nicky said." She catches herself, covers her mouth, but Ms. Greenberg just squeezes her shoulder, which is the closest thing to a hug Celeste has ever seen in here. They file out to the hallway, where everyone is heading to the memorial. Celeste holds Ursa close and pushes into the crowd, the poem clutched in her fist. The general mood is kind of jolly, probably because classes are canceled for the afternoon, but it seems perverse, all the laughter and fist bumps and collecting friends to sit in chatty groups. It's stuffy in the theater, and hot air is blowing from the vents directly into Celeste's cleavage, making her sweat through the catsuit. Bridget tries to wave her over from the other aisle, but Celeste just gestures vaguely toward the front, where she's been told to sit with the families and speakers. She can see her mom up there already, ensconced in a black poncho, leaning close to Carla's ear. Pop and Nonna are nearby, their wispy white hair glowing in the houselights, and one of the crew dudes is seated behind them, tuning his guitar.

"Bitch, you've been avoiding me." Bridget winds her arm around Celeste's waist, having somehow managed to vault herself over the center seats. "Don't bother denying it." Celeste flinches, suddenly too aware of the way the catsuit hangs on her thin hips and bunches up in the back. She tries to hurry ahead, but Bridget follows. "Seriously, come on, what the fuck is up with you?"

"Seriously, what's up with me? I don't know, Bridge, what do you think is up with me?"

Bridget keeps silent down the next few stairs. "I like your jumpsuit thing."

Celeste sighs. "Thanks. I need to get down there and sit with his mom."

"Hey, I'm having people over Friday night, you know, to celebrate getting our apps in."

Celeste knits her lips together and concentrates on the stairs. Friday is the quake-extended deadline for most schools, including MIT. So far, her application consists of her name, address, and one paragraph of her essay about diabetes, which is honestly the lamest thing she could think to write about—they probably get a million diabetes essays. She doesn't even remember what it felt like to want this thing so intensely for herself. Before the quake, she was starting to forget why she wanted it, and now that Nicky's gone and everything's so fucked up, the thought of college—of figuring out her life in a new place—seems preposterous, like a dream that made perfect sense in her sleep but revealed itself as gibberish in the morning.

"Nothing crazy—just, like, some champagne—Jordan's brother got it for us. But I guess you don't drink anyway. Sorry, I'm dumb."

"You're not dumb. Maybe I'll stop by."

Traffic is stopped in the aisle, where a blob of freshman girls—dwarfed by their giant backpacks, their hair identically flat-ironed—argues about who's going to sit with whom. Celeste uses Ursa to steamroll through them, hoping to lose Bridget in the crowd.

"Did you even know that Jordan's dad is doing better?"

Celeste looks over her shoulder. Bridget's eyes are a little pink and shiny, like she might start crying.

"He's not in the hospital anymore," Bridget says. "Oh, and he doesn't have cancer after all. So yeah, that's great fucking news I think you missed."

"Yeah, great news," Celeste manages to say, sounding to herself like an even less human version of Siri. She decides to add, "Thanks for telling me," and then makes her way down the rest of the aisle, talking softly to Ursa, which is a reliable way to avoid talking to others. She knows she's being an asshole but can't seem to conjure any guilt about it. When she glances up the aisle again, Bridget's back on the other side of the theater next to Jordan, their heads together, talking, eyes narrowed in Celeste's direction. Fake Nicky grabs the collar of her jacket, leaning close to her ear. She expects him to call them a mean name, maybe some choice euphemism for female genitalia. Instead he whispers, *Our heart felt like a single thing / beneath that vast disintegration of their brilliance—*

She whips around, but he's already gone, cloaked under his aura or whatever. Finally she arrives in the third row, feeling like she's walked over coals to get here, and now finds actual fire between her and her seat—in the form of Carla, who hugs Celeste for so long that she thinks she might black out.

"Thank you for today, sweetie," Carla says in a strangled voice.

"You don't have to say that."

"No, I mean it. You're being so brave." Carla releases her at last. The Kleenex she's wiping her face with leaves white specks on her crumpled mouth. Frantically searching for something else to look at, Celeste lands on Nonna. She nudges Ursa into the row behind them and lets Nonna scratch the dog's soft ears.

"How are you doing?" Celeste asks.

Nonna frowns at her over her shoulder. "They told me I had to come here, but I don't understand it."

"Same," Celeste says. She squeezes Nonna's cool hand. Pop offers everybody a Werther's from his pocket, pats Celeste's cheek, and says, "Hiya, kid," which lets her know things are okay between them again. She sinks into a seat next to the super-tall crew dude, Ian, who's got his guitar perched on his knobby giraffe knees. He's quietly practicing "Blackbird," one of Nicky's favorite songs—kind of on the nose, maybe, but it sounds nice, and Celeste tells him so.

She closes her eyes and listens for a minute. Feeling a little dizzy, she opens her phone to check her blood sugar—a little low. Probably she dosed too much at lunch, distracted by the prospect of this shitty afternoon. She reaches in her bag for a granola bar and finds one tucked next to Nicky's bottle of pills. It's stupid to bring the pills to school, of course, but she's been carrying the bottle around the last few days, thinking that if she ran into Neptune boy again, at least she could ask him to give them back to the shady dealer dudes. Who knows if that would settle Nicky's debt, but it might get the boy to leave her alone for a while. She saw him again last week after school, heading across the Panhandle grass to talk to her, and she hurried Ursa onto the wrong bus just to avoid him. Also—he's been showing up, unwelcome, in her fantasies at night. Even picturing him now, sword tattoo drawn along the smooth length of his wrist, makes her body swell in a way that's wrong for this moment on so many levels.

"Hey," she says to Ian, "can I ask you something?" She offers him a piece of her granola bar, which he gratefully munches, dribbling crumbs into the hole in his guitar. "So, this is going to sound kind of weird . . ." She lowers her voice to a whisper. "Did Nicky ever, like, try to sell you anything? Maybe some pills?"

Ian considers this for a moment, thoughtfully chewing.

"It's actually a yes-or-no question, Ian."

"I was just thinking how, you know, when you die—like, unexpectedly?—then people get to know a lot of your secret shit."

"Yeah, well, I knew all of Nicky's secret shit anyway." But as soon as she hears herself saying it, Celeste understands that it really isn't true, not anymore, and the place in her chest where the words came from hardens into a muscly knot.

"See, that's the thing," Ian says. "I feel bad talking about this now, right? Since he's not here to defend himself."

"Look, I don't give a crap if he was dealing, really. I was just . . ." Unfortunately she has no good reason for asking, not if Nicky's supposedly dead. Then she thinks of Lancelot again, goddamn him—but at least he gives her a decent excuse. "I'm just helping figure out how to pay the guy who sold him the pills," she whispers. "You know, so Carla doesn't have to find out."

"Ah, cool. So yeah, he sold some Vikes to a few of us on the team. It was only like a couple weeks before the quake, I think? No big deal. But he asked us not to tell you, so I didn't want to, like, betray his spirit, you know?"

"He said don't tell me?"

Ian shrugs. "I guess he thought you'd be mad or something." He shoves the last bite of granola bar in his mouth and starts to fiddle with the tuning pegs on the guitar. Celeste can only watch him chewing. It feels like his teeth are gnawing at that knot in her chest. Meanwhile, the room is getting louder and more filled with people who smell like their recent lunch. She *is* mad, but not because of the fucking pills. Because Nicky was going around telling giraffe knees here and the other ogre-shouldered rowing dudes his secrets—and *not* her.

She looks around the room. How many of these other gossiping, lunch-smelling idiots did he confide in? *Does one of them know where he's gone?*

The lights begin to dim; the crowd quiets. Celeste hears Carla say, "Here we go," and the silhouette of her head leans on Pop's shoulder. Bonnie looks back at Celeste with a smile that's probably supposed to be supportive, but instead looks kind of menacing, her teeth glowing in the half dark. Some kids from the orchestra patter out onto the stage with their clarinets and cellos. When they launch into "Danny Boy," Celeste blurts out, "Come *on*!" before she can stop herself; luckily only Ian seems to have noticed, and he just kind of awkwardly chuckles. The song choice is almost certainly Oona Dunne's doing, what with her Irish dad and all. At the end of it, when the principal, Dr. Reyes, walks onstage clapping and sniffling, Oona, who's smack in the middle of the first row, her ropy golden French braid unmistakable, stands up to applaud, the additional braided Oona clones following her lead.

Celeste's ears and forehead are hot. The catsuit feels like it's stuck to her skin. While the principal talks about loss and community and resilience, her lips so close to the microphone that you can hear the spit in her voice, Celeste takes out the Rilke poem again and finds that her hands are shaking. The words start to rearrange themselves on the page: *heart disintegration / suddenly wishes hazard / stars would survive.* She asked to be the first reader, hoping to get it over with fast, but now that move seems catastrophically dumb, especially as Reyes starts to talk about Nicky—about the remarkable boy he *was* and the stellar student he *was* and the hilarious jokester he *was*—and every one of those past-tense verbs is a hunk of space junk whizzing straight at Celeste and colliding with her skull.

"We're so pleased that Nicky's best friend, Celeste Muldoon, has offered to share a poem with us today to celebrate his memory."

That's her cue. Celeste gets up. She's about to hand Ursa's leash to her mother and climb the stairs to the stage like they rehearsed, but she can't move. The poem is clutched in one hand and the leash in the other. She's surrounded by a sudden hush, like she's crossed into the actual windless pause at the end of the solar system. Celeste stands there for five seconds, ten, before she realizes that she's going to leave. Her still-careening brain propels her body up the stairs and out of the theater with Ursa, leaving behind a trail of gasps and whispers.

They hurry through the empty school, hoping to lose her mom, who's almost certainly following. Sure enough, her phone pings with a text from Bonnie (*r u okay??*) before she even makes it to the corner, but Celeste just writes back, *needed air, c u at home*, and she keeps going, so relieved to be outside that she actually laughs out loud for maybe the first time in weeks. She shoves her jacket into her backpack and rolls up the catsuit sleeves, even though it's damp and cold.

Jesus, CB, you ditched my fucking funeral!

There he is, perched on a fire hydrant, hugging his knees like little-kid Nicky always used to do when he was sad about losing a board game or something. Celeste blows past him without a glance. She's exhausted from pretending and pissed at Nicky for making this so fucking hard. Why couldn't he run away on a regular day like a normal person? Or better yet, just *not cheat* in the first place? Not keep secrets from her with the dumbass crew dudes? Not ruin everything? It suddenly feels like *his* fault that she hasn't finished her application to MIT or anywhere else, and that she'll probably be living with her parents next year and working at the boba place or some shit while he's off living his brand-new life. Maybe even the fucking earthquake's his fault. She imagines Nicky kneeling next to their stairs, prying the floorboards apart with his hands. Taking a giant cartoon mallet to the library shelves and computers, then flicking a match to flame and tossing it on the heap.

Boba tea actually sounds like a brilliant idea. Celeste feels like treating herself. She can't decide whether it was awful to run out of that theater or ballsy, but either way, she has the recently unfamiliar feeling of accomplishment. The plan for today was to get on a bus to Lands End—the brightest star in the constellation, Castor itself—but Celeste could use a break from Nicky-hunting. Maybe she'll just take her tea to the Booksmith and read magazines, or walk to the Mission to see a matinee at the Alamo.

She leaves Ursa tied up outside the tea shop like always. (In line, she remembers that first little sexy jolt from the Neptune boy, standing right there and watching his hands untying the leash knot—ugh, if only she could banish him from her brain.) The grouchy owner seems even more mystified than usual by her unsweetened boba order, so Celeste dicks around on her phone while she waits forever, reflexively checking Nicky's Insta feed, even though she knows there won't be anything new. His last post is still the same, hanging there on the day before the quake: the swirly peach-colored clouds of Jupiter's Equatorial Belt, a re-gram from the NASA feed. By now Celeste has stared so long at this photo that she's memorized all the whorls and patterns; sometimes she sees them on the backs of her eyelids when she's trying to sleep. Frustrated, she scrolls past the post and spends a few minutes "reading" the comments on the latest video of Blue Ivy Carter. When the grouchy owner calls Celeste's name at last, she thanks him profusely, grabs her tea, and leaves.

She stops dead in the doorway. Everything is wrong. The sky's dark gray; the sidewalk swims under her feet.

Ursa is gone.

She was there, tied to the bench, and now she's gone. The whole massive beast of her, just vanished. Frantically Celeste paces in front of the shop, calling the dog, her breath sharp in her throat. *"Ursa!"* She runs to the corner. Maybe the leash was loose and Ursa wandered into the park? She wouldn't, though, would she? For fuck's sake. *"Ursa!"* Celeste takes off running, cold tears streaming, shouting for the dog, tea sloshing over her hand. She knocks over traffic cones, climbs the orange barriers and webs of caution tape, stumbles on broken concrete. In the park she screams *"Ursa!"* into the trees, and bicyclists skid and stare, and a huge crowd of pigeons erupts into the air. It's starting to rain, everything smelling earthy and brown, and Celeste cries harder because Ursa hates the rain—it flattens her fluffy coat into a sad rag, changing the whole shape of her. None of the dogs in the park are her, so Celeste runs off again, tossing her tea in the trash.

She wanders the neighborhood, yelling, until it starts to approach dark. The rain sticks in her lashes and soaks the catsuit. At some point she becomes too tired to run and almost too tired to yell, her voice frayed, her throat on fire even though she's shivering cold. Her legs start to give out; her vision's a dizzy blur. She isn't even exactly sure where she has ended up, on a street she should probably recognize but doesn't. It occurs to her vaguely that she might be hypoglycemic—she hears the CGM app's muffled buzzing deep in her bag—so she digs out another granola bar, and chokes it down. After a few bites, when the fog in her head begins to lift, Celeste realizes she's standing across the street from where the library used to be. Only now, instead of the mountains of ash and rubble, there's nothing. Just a pit of sludge. A hole.

Her knees are too weak to stand. She leans against a fence,

clutching the chain link. The mist swirls in the orange light from the streetlamps, like the clouds on Jupiter's Equatorial Belt, just the way they look in that stupid fucking amazing photo that's been stuck at the top of Nicky's feed for weeks. For how utterly alone Celeste feels right now, she might as well be standing in those clouds, on the surface of an uninhabited planet, surrounded by seventy-nine empty moons and the even emptier black depths of space.

She fumbles for her phone. *I need you,* she texts, first to Nicky, then to her mom. *Come get me,* she types. *911. Ursa's gone.*

Day 77

When her alarm goes off the next morning, Celeste turns it off and throws her phone across the room, then buries herself deeper in bed. Going to school without Nicky is bad enough, but going to school without Ursa is impossible. Even the thought of it just sucks all the air out of her body, like somebody's flipped open her helmet on the moon.

Celeste and Ursa have been together three years. "Been together"—that's how people talk about service dogs, like it's a marriage. She never wanted a diabetic alert dog in the first place, but her parents insisted: If she wasn't going to wear the pump and let them control her insulin, then she had to get a dog to help maintain her levels. And Celeste hated the thought of wearing a tube stuck in her body and pumping herself full of chemicals constantly, even if it meant staying more even like everyone said.

At the dog training camp, they chose Ursa because they felt bad for her; somebody had decided to train a Newfoundland puppy for the diabetic alerts, and then they dumped her at the camp when she didn't fit in their new apartment. She'd been living there for a year when Celeste spotted her, sprawled in a corner, looking decidedly unloved. "She's the underdog!" Shane joked on the ride home, high-fiving Nicky, with whom he's always shared a love for corny puns. Normally, Celeste would've made a show of gagging, but she was too smitten with Ursa, whose gentle head rested in her lap, her big downy body stretched on the back seat floor. Celeste had never thought of herself as a dog person, but Ursa wasn't like other dogs. She and Celeste understood each other perfectly from the start.

In bed, Celeste presses her face against the blanket, which smells like Ursa, a not-entirely-unpleasant corn-chip kind of smell. She's in her underwear, the wet catsuit balled on the floor, her curls still matted from last night's rain. Her dad is downstairs in the studio already, playing something moody—the score from a History Channel show, one of his freelance gigs—with long, quavering notes that sound like a crying voice.

"Jesus, Dad," she shouts, "I'm sleeping!" But she hasn't really slept at all, paralyzed by visions of the soft lump of Ursa lying dead in a busy street or picked apart by coyotes in the park. Finally, at around three a.m., she decided to dig out those pills from Nicky's closet, assuming they were the Vicodins that Ian had told her about; she stared at one in her palm for a minute before finally choking it down. It didn't help much, just made her feel more achingly sad and tired without ever putting her to sleep. Luckily, her parents let her stay in bed past the alarm and didn't insist on school. Nobody even comes up to bug her about eating or insulin until about eleven, when there's a soft knock on the door.

"Honey?"

"I'm sick," Celeste groans. "Go away." But Bonnie barges in anyway and sits on the edge of the bed. Celeste smells cinnamon and vanilla; it's the magic milk potion her mom used to make in the winters after school. Celeste crawls out from under the covers just enough to accept the mug and take a sip. It's so warm and sweet that it brings tears to her eyes. Her mom strokes her hair away from her face.

"I'm so sorry this is happening," she says.

Celeste shakes her groggy head, holding the mug tight in her hands. "I just . . ." There's an ache so deep in her chest that it's hard to talk. She draws a cinnamon breath and then spits out: "How much more of this bullshit am I supposed to take?"

"I know." Bonnie frowns into her lap. She says, "It doesn't feel like it now, but there will be a time when this is all in the past, Celeste. It won't hurt as much as it does now, and you'll be okay."

"I don't know."

"Well, I do."

Celeste hands her mother the mug and pulls the comforter over her face again. "What are you doing in here, anyway?"

It sounds like Bonnie's shuffling around the room, tidying things. Celeste's hot cinnamon breath warms her under the blanket. "I was thinking," Bonnie says. "It sounds like they finally got 101 fixed and opened up again up north. We should really go and check on Mimi's place."

"What, you mean like now?" Celeste's grandma has been in Haiti for weeks running a Habitat for Humanity project, which she does almost every winter. Bonnie was furious when her mother didn't come straight home after the earthquake, but that isn't Mimi's style; once she found out her house was still standing and Celeste and her parents were okay, she just sent the handyman neighbor over to fix some broken windows and popped her hard hat right back on.

"Sure, why not?" Bonnie says. "Let's drive up, maybe stop for oysters on the way. We could both use a break."

"I can't just *leave*! What if somebody finds Ursa?"

"Dad'll be here. He has to perform tonight. We can keep our phones with us. Play hooky for a couple days. And we'll rush back if we need to. Dad said he'd go out looking again in a little while, put up more fliers." They've already called pretty much every animal shelter in the Bay, with no sign of Ursa at all—so, more fliers. The three of them were up past midnight sticking them everywhere. Celeste even found herself stapling one right alongside a tattered flier of Nicky on a telephone pole on Waller.

It's hard to imagine leaving town without Ursa, but even harder to imagine going to school tomorrow, and Celeste doesn't hate the idea of snuggling up on Mimi's deck and watching the breakers lit by the full cold moon. She just read that this week, for the first time in a decade, the bright orange K5 star Aldebaran is coming into conjunction with the full moon, and it's supposed to be epic. Fake Nicky would tell her she'd be batshit not to go.

She reaches for a big gray sweatshirt and throws it on without a bra. "Okay, I'll pack some stuff."

"Oh yay! A road trip. It'll do us good." Bonnie heads for the door, her arms spilling laundry. "We'll come back in time to give your apps a last pass before Friday. Or I can look them over for you at Mimi's? I know you keep saying no, but I *am* an English teacher, Celeste. I do occasionally have useful things to say. Contrary to popular belief."

Celeste kneels next to a stack of books, running her finger over the titles. She pulls the sweatshirt tighter over her chest. Then she hears herself talking, the sour words just spilling out: "Yeah, actually . . . I already submitted them."

"What? Why didn't you tell me? Honey, that's amazing! Congratulations!" Her mom's face flushes pink, and Celeste feels her whole body tense up with guilt, but Bonnie doesn't seem to notice. "Wow, that's so great! I'll go tell Dad. Now we really have something to celebrate! We'll crack open the blackberry wine."

THE GUILT'S STILL GOT CELESTE IN A STRAITJACKET a few hours later when they're on the highway up the coast. Mostly she keeps silent, afraid she might dig herself deeper into the lie, since Bonnie keeps making comments like "I just wish you'd let me read your essay" and, even worse, "I'm so proud of you for staying strong." After this last one, Celeste says she feels carsick and opens her window all the way, letting the cold air blast her face for punishment. She stares up at the sheer rock face towering over the road. They pass a little girl and a woman hitchhiking, bundled in matching fake fur jackets with leopard print, just as if they were shuttling off to a ballet class or something in the city. All along the way, Celeste has seen groups of drifters, people with frame backpacks and pets, sometimes even dragging suitcases on wheels, sometimes set up in tent camps right on the side of the highway in drainage ditches, under the slanty cypress trees. Celeste has heard about the quake refugees, but this is the first time she's seen them outside the city. When they passed through Petaluma, they could see how burned-up everything was, strip malls and box stores reduced to sooty skeletons. Gas leaks after the quake sparked wildfires up here that burned for weeks. People with retirement condos, people who'd moved out of SF when they couldn't afford it anymore—tons of them lost their homes, so the whole state is filled with these wanderers now.

Bonnie frowns as they leave the little girl and her mom in their leopard coats behind. Celeste rolls up her window, muting the roar of the wind. "It's terrible," Bonnie says. "Where are all these people going to go?"

When it comes to Celeste, her mother can be such a Pollyanna, insisting she believe in things to make them true, and all that crap—but at least when it comes to this earthquake, it's impossible for her to avoid the reality. They talk for a while about what the governor should do—turn the old military barracks in the Presidio into shelters, or let the refugees live in the empty expensive condos down by the Chase Center. "You know those pod apartments they have in Japan," Celeste says, "they're really cheap to build, and they're only like beds and bathrooms, so they can charge really low rent for them. Can't they just put up something like that, you know, for temporary public housing? I feel like they have to do *something*."

Bonnie's face looks drained and gray, blending with the overcast sky above the water. "But so many jobs are gone, too. So you know, if you've lost everything, how do you even begin to build it again? Some people can stay with family until they get on their feet, but some don't have options. We're so lucky, really. It's important to remember that."

Celeste thanks her mother for the lecture, then they're quiet for a few minutes, winding up the coast road, the smells of salt and wet bark seeping into the car. Of course Celeste knows they're lucky, in the same way she knows, like, the date of the Emancipation Proclamation, or the quadratic formula, because it exists in her head as an unequivocal fact. But at the moment, even though it might be selfish, she does not feel lucky. It seems very possible that Ursa might be dead, and Nicky—well, Celeste still doesn't believe he's dead, but she *has* started to wonder if she will ever see him again. Meanwhile, back in her own messed-up Nickyless life, there's a black hole waiting at the end of the summer. An event horizon beyond which nothing seems to exist. So there's that, too.

Bonnie breaks the silence to say, "I hope you know I never wanted to hurt Nicky." With tears in her voice, she adds, "I love him, Celeste. I wanted to do what was best for him. And I couldn't just let it go when I found out what he was doing. It wouldn't have been right. I have a responsibility to the school." She tightens her hands on the wheel, wipes away the tears with her poncho. "I feel so awful. That he was angry with me, I mean—"

Celeste blows a loud sigh. "I guess I should've known."

"What?"

"The point of this trip was to trap me in the car so we could have this little talk you've been planning."

"Oh come on, Celeste, nobody trapped you. For Christ's sake." Bonnie shakes her head, casts a sideways glare. "Anyway, we have to have this talk *sometime*. Eventually."

"Do we?"

They both stare straight ahead, frowning in the same crumple-mouthed way. A deer appears in a turnout, and they gasp collectively as Bonnie swerves to avoid it. "Jesus, that's all we need," she mutters, relaxing back into her lane.

"Yeah, a deer murder would really put the cherry on this shit sundae of a week."

"Gross," Bonnie says, but she's grinning.

Celeste leans her forehead on the window. "I don't think he was actually still angry at you, Mom. For what it's worth."

"Oh," Bonnie says. "Well, that's something."

"There ya go. Good talk." Celeste digs out her phone and opens

Spotify to find a *PodLab* episode, which will get them as far as Fort Bragg without any further need to converse. The newest is about deep-space habitation modules—the Mars huts the astronauts will live in during the mission—magnetically pressurized, with oxygen and water recycling, radiation protection.

"Great," Bonnie murmurs, "but we can't figure out where to put people after this fucking quake. Sorry," she adds with a sigh—nobody bad-mouths NASA around Celeste or Nicky—but this time she doesn't argue. Even the sexy British host mentions the truly insane price tag for the habs, which will be left behind post-mission to be torn to shreds eventually by dust. Celeste leans her head back on the seat and watches the flat sea.

"Nothing is good," she says, and her mom squeezes her hand.

THE LIGHT IS ALREADY WANING WHEN THEY PULL onto Mimi's pebble drive around five. There are a couple of weird things Celeste notices right away, and the first one is that Mimi's fancy red e-bike, her baby, is parked out in the front garden instead of locked in its spot in the shed.

"Maybe Sad Joe was using it?" Bonnie says. Sad Joe is Mimi's handyman neighbor from down the hill—nicknamed because of the massive Droopy Dog bags under his eyes—who takes care of the bees and the house while she's away on her do-gooding trips. But Celeste can't picture Joe riding anything but the caved-in front seat of his ancient VW van.

The bike's beaded with rain, and weeds reach as high as the chain, which is flecked with rust. The weeds are the second weird thing; Mimi would let blackberries and moss swallow her whole house without shedding a tear, but she keeps the ten-foot-square patch of lawn under the front window impeccably trimmed because various pets from over the years are buried there. Sad Joe's supposed to be mowing, but the lawn looks like it hasn't been touched in weeks.

While Bonnie fishes the hidden key out of its driftwood stump, Celeste wanders over to Mimi's "peace platform," a wide rock shelf at the edge of the cliff, with a frothy cascade of ferns tumbling down around it, where she does yoga in the morning and smokes her four o'clock joint. In the summer, Ursa likes to lie here on the warm rock and eyeball the circling gulls, but now the rock is damp and cold when Celeste kneels on it. The wind whips her hair and freezes her ears. The last time she came here, it was for the meteor shower. That night she felt so close to them all—Nicky, Ursa, Mimi—huddled up together high above the crashing waves. Ursa and the Geminids, and who was Mimi? Cassiopeia, they agreed, which pleased her. From down here, Celeste thinks, as the damp seeps into the knees of her jeans, the stars always look huddled up together, too, but of course they're actually trillions of miles apart, burning up in their lonely corners of the galaxy. The constellations are really just lies we tell ourselves about the stars, pretending at a closeness that wasn't ever there.

Bonnie left the door hanging open, and Celeste finds her peering around inside, looking wary. "Someone's been in here."

"Joe?"

"The bed's messy. There's some trash around."

"Wait, what?"

Bonnie calls Sad Joe and puts him on speaker. "Haven't been by in a while," he admits. "Not since right after the quake. I brought the bees over to my place; it's warmer for the winter. Figured the lawn could wait, seeing as Mimi won't be back till May?" He laughs, though, when they ask if he took her bike out for a spin. "Sure," he says, "and then I ran a marathon and swam from here to Oregon."

"We think somebody broke in."

"Oh yeah? Lotta drifters coming through here lately, not the usual surf bums. Foods Co. parking lot's full of people sleeping in their trucks. But hey, I'll keep a closer eye from now on, you can count on it." Bonnie rolls her eyes at Celeste, and he goes on: "How 'bout we don't tell Meems about the weeds? I'll come by next week to get 'em in shape."

They poke around. Despite being a flighty old hippie, Mimi insists on keeping her house in crazy order, never an afghan out of place, so it's obvious to Celeste right away that her mom is right. Somebody *has* been here. It's little things—like the coffee mugs mixed with the wine glasses on the wrong shelf, and the macramé coasters scattered around everywhere instead of piled in their neat stack.

"Pretty courteous burglar that bothers to use a coaster."

"I don't think they took anything," Bonnie says. "The telescope's here, and the bike."

Celeste walks over to the telescope at the window. There's a tingly vibration starting in her chest. She presses her palm over the sun tattoo and can feel the speeding beat of her pulse. "Why's the telescope out here?" she says quietly. "Mimi keeps it put away when we're not using it. Says it fucks up the feng shui."

"Do you have to talk like that?"

Celeste peers into the eyepiece, but the field of sky it reveals to her is dusky and blank; it won't be totally dark out for another couple of hours.

"A stargazing, coaster-using burglar," Bonnie says, flopping into her favorite beat-up papasan chair, massaging her temples. "I guess maybe I should report this to the police? I hate the idea of calling the cops if it's one of the quake refugees. Actually, you know, maybe we should offer this place for quake victims? I heard Airbnb's doing a shelter program. I can email Mimi." Celeste starts stacking the coasters. Only her mother could start a little speech wanting to lock a person up and end it by finding them a house. Bonnie adds, now typing one-fingered on her phone, "At least we can call a locksmith, though. And no more leaving the key outside."

They wipe down and lock up the bike, tidy the place for a while, then make some tea and cut up the cheese and bread they brought. Bonnie does a bad job pretending not to hover while Celeste doses. The locksmith comes and goes. Celeste insists they call Shane to check in about Ursa, but there's nothing new to report. Bridget's been texting all day, offering to help—she saw the fliers with Ursa's sweet face plastered all over the Haight—but Celeste can't manage to write her back. She and her mom start a jigsaw puzzle in silence, then sit out on the deck and read, listening to the waves. Celeste can't concentrate on *Swords of Avalon*, a steamy, ridiculous book she found in the library's romance section when she was looking for stuff about King Arthur; she isn't really reading, just skipping around to the sex parts and failing to avoid thinking about the boy from the Haight. Restlessly she wanders inside to take a shower and gives herself a quick and kind of disappointing orgasm with the showerhead. But the unsettled tingly vibration in her chest still won't go away. She wraps herself in one of Mimi's fluffy robes and stands in the bathroom for a minute breathing the steam.

Bedtime sounds like a solid plan, but then Celeste remembers the telescope, Aldebaran in conjunction with the moon. She goes to the window; as promised by her astronomy apps, the rising moon is incandescent, transforming the sea to molten silver. The fiery bead of the K5 star, trillions of miles away from the moon, appears to hover close enough to burn it. Wanting a closer look, Celeste's about to lift the telescope to carry it outside when something occurs to her. Instead of moving the tripod, she grabs a pad of Post-its and writes down the coordinates where the telescope lens was already trained. Then, on her phone, she finds a star map for tonight and starts looking up some coordinates.

"You okay, hon? Can you grab the wine while you're in there?"

Celeste ignores her mom, busy with the math. If she's right, Gemini—specifically Pollux—should be passing through the field of view a few hours before dawn. Whoever put the telescope here might well have been looking at it. "Actually, I'm tired," she calls to Bonnie, "going to bed."

"Really? There's a Cary Grant marathon on Turner. I think Mimi still pays for cable."

"Night, Mom." She crawls into bed on the futon in Mimi's den, the one they found unmade earlier. They've changed the sheets, but still, when Celeste turns her head to bury her nose in the pillow, she can't help feeling it smells like Nicky's shampoo.

Was he here?

The person who slept here knew where to find the key, even the key to the shed where Mimi keeps the bike, which is stashed in a junk drawer with zillions of other keys. The person who slept here knew how to set up the telescope, how to use it. That person, it seems, might've gazed at the Gemini. Doesn't sound like a random quake refugee to Celeste.

She tries to remember if Nicky knew that Mimi would be away for the winter. In some ways it would've been risky to come up here, with Sad Joe dropping by and Mimi herself being famously unpredictable, but also, it's sort of a perfect place to hide out, cozy and remote, very often shrouded in fog. The closest neighbor lives two miles inland along a forest road. Celeste thinks about the way they found the house and Mimi's stuff. Nicky's pretty neat, polite enough to use coasters, but he wouldn't know about setting everything back in Mimi's careful order, and it would be just like him to forget about the bike outside. They'd found all the wastebaskets empty except for one in the bathroom, which contained an anonymous assortment of trash: wrappers for pretzels and single-serving Advils; key cards from a Best Western and a Super 8, which Bonnie saw as evidence for her refugee theory, since some hotels were used as shelters right after the quake. But Celeste could just as easily imagine Nicky hitchhiking up the coast highway, stopping for snacks at gas stations, splurging for a hotel bed once in a while. Cinched in his hoodie, dirty and tired with just a soaked backpack, arriving here and scooping the key out of the stump, like he'd seen Celeste do so many times before.

The possibility of this makes Celeste feel an almost dizzying mix of resentment and relief. What right does Nicky have to hang out at Mimi's watching the fucking stars while she's choosing his eulogy poem? And also—if he was here, at least he isn't in a tent somewhere on the side of the road, or pulverized in an avalanche of books.

Then again, the shampoo means nothing, really. It's coconut Pantene—even a burglar could get it at Walgreens.

Celeste hears the sliding door to the deck drag open and closed, then her mom's slippered footsteps padding through the house. She slams her eyes shut.

"Still awake?" Bonnie whispers from the doorway. Celeste

pretends to sleep, but her mom comes in anyway, straightens the quilt, and pulls it up to her shoulders. She sits on the edge of the futon, her hair streaked with moonlight slanting through the blinds, and says softly, "I hate that you're suffering." She waits through a few of Celeste's heavy breaths, then goes on: "You'll see, sweetheart. We'll get through this, and then college will be a whole new start for you."

Celeste squeezes her eyes closed, but some tears leak onto the pillow. She can almost feel that black hole at the end of the summer drawing her closer, the heavy pull of antimatter pressing on her spine. "Mom," she mumbles, "I love you, but I'm asleep."

Bonnie kisses her forehead and leaves. The silver streaks are over the whole room now. Celeste lies awake for hours, feeling suspended in the strange not-night. She considers taking another one of those pills to calm her down, but it's stupid for someone like her to mess with that shit, and anyway, she doesn't want to accidentally fall asleep. When the clock finally reads 2:50 a.m., which should be about right according to the app, she crawls out of bed and tiptoes to the telescope, hoping the moonlight hasn't totally obscured the stars. Sure enough, there's Pollux, the fiery golden gem of it, brighter than most other stars we can see from Earth. Installed in the heavens for eternity, that's the story. Of course, Pollux will actually die one of these days, billions of years from now, in an explosion so spectacular that it will send fiery bits of the star hurtling out into the universe—which, Celeste figures, is a kind of immortality after all.

She walks out onto the deck and leans on the rail over the water, drinking the cold salty air. The waves are so loud that they feel like they're crashing inside her skull, tossing and roiling the order of things she is trying to keep straight: the Mars book, the

Gemini map, the crystals, the pills. Hotel keys and snack wrappers and coasters and the bike. Are these the fragments of a supernova, or is Nicky on a path she can actually follow, like a comet? And will it burn out someday, or just keep going, leaving her to grasp at the sparks of its tail?

Day 80

They stay at Mimi's two nights, then Bonnie insists they both need to get back to school on Friday. Still no sign of Ursa at home, so Celeste begs to stay for the weekend alone. She tells her mom she needs quiet time, but really, she's wondering if Nicky might turn up again once their car is gone. Her blood sugar's been a wreck, though, so Bonnie flat-out refuses, sparking a screaming argument that results in an almost totally silent four-hour drive. By the time they get home, it's nearly midnight. Celeste is wiped out, but she barely sleeps; her own bed still feels way too cold and empty and dogless, and the cold and empty and dogless school day looms in the morning, too. Shane drags her out of bed after Bonnie's already left, shuffles her into the bathroom, and pours her a bowl of cereal and even buckles her nearly comatose body into the car and drives her to school, which never happens anymore. He parks behind the building, shuts off his blasting David Byrne, takes her hand, and says, "Listen, kiddo. Sometimes you just have to look a truly shitty day in the face. Go to school now, okay? I'll pick you up later. Maybe take you to a movie."

"Amazing pep talk, Dad."

"Yeah, one of my best. Now get." He leans over to open her door, and she dumps herself out of the car. She runs to the bathroom and hides until five minutes after the bell, vowing to spend all the passing periods there if it means she gets to avoid questions about where Ursa is or why she ditched the memorial. When she sneaks into homeroom late, yet another reason to dread this day asserts itself all over again: the college apps deadline. The classroom's an obnoxious party, everyone hugging, even Ms. Tanaka, who is walking around the room toasting coffee cups with people. Celeste sinks into a desk in the corner and digs out *Swords of Avalon*, but luckily the bell rings for first period before anybody notices her. She moves through the day like this, running to the bathroom between classes, avoiding the senior hallway at all costs, her hood pulled up over her ears, right hand reaching for the leash that isn't there. At study hall she sits silently in grief group, comforted a little by the other students' misery. Crying girl Abby asks about Ursa, but Celeste just says she's home for a vet appointment. She spends the rest of the time unraveling an already giant hole in her favorite gray jeans.

At the end of the day, it's AP Physics. There's a quiz she didn't know about, which would normally send her into a panic, but instead she thinks about how many minutes are left in this building, shifting her paper in and out of a sunbeam, then turning it to see if the questions make any more sense upside down. When her phone buzzes gently in her backpack, she assumes it's one of her parents checking in, or Carla, who's been texting all week with Ursa-related sad emojis, asking to take her out for coffee. She tries to surreptitiously unzip the pocket to look but can't stop herself from gasping loudly when she sees the texts.

I found yr dog.

Meet me outside yr school.

"Ms. Muldoon? Surely you're aware that looking at your phone during a test is a serious no-no."

Celeste grabs her stuff and hurries to Mr. Respini's desk at the front of the room. "I'm sorry, it's an emergency." She sputters that her dog's been missing since Monday, and it looks like somebody found her. Ursa is known and loved at school, so Respini lets her go, a cloud of whispers following her down the hall. She takes it at a sprint, footfalls pounding in her ears, *UrsaUrsaUrsaUrsa*. Even in her frenzy it occurs to her to feel slightly creeped out about the fact that this person with the unknown number knows where she goes to school, so she's a little scared and also frantically relieved as she shoves through the door to Oak Street and looks around for her girl.

They're across the street in the Panhandle: Ursa and the boy with the Neptune eyes. He's sitting cross-legged against the trunk of a huge eucalyptus, and Ursa, unbelievably, is lying down with her head in his lap, which gives Celeste a shudder of pleasure so deep that she wants it back as soon as it stops, even while recognizing just how bizarre it is to be turned on by anything involving your dog. She runs across the street, barely bothering to wait for a gap in traffic. Ursa spots her and barks and strains at the leash, and the boy lets her bound over to the sidewalk, where she slams into Celeste's knees and they both fall over in a heap, Celeste grinning and crying, Ursa slobbering everywhere. Her giant dog heart hammers so hard that Celeste can actually hear it over the static whoosh of the cars. The boy stands nearby with his hands shoved in the pockets of his Carhartts, looking embarrassed. Maybe Celeste should feel embarrassed, too, but she doesn't. Relief spills over her in waves, and she plants her feet in the bracing surf, feeling it lift her and set her down again.

"Oh my god," she cries, "you found her? *You* found her? I can't— I was just so— Thank you!" She hugs him without thinking, carried on the crest of the wave, then lets go as soon as her feet hit the sand, both of them kind of shocked by it, looking everywhere but at each other, the feel of his chest and his flannel shirt still hanging in her arms. She kneels next to Ursa and runs her hands through the dog's fur, examines her face. She's dirty, her coat matted with leaves and burrs, paws crusted with mud, but she doesn't seem hurt.

"Found her in the park," says the boy. "She was just, like, wandering in there." He says he spotted her in the wilder part of the park out by the beach, at least a mile from here, near the fishing pond where he takes his kid cousin sometimes. He recognized Ursa, so he coaxed her into his car and found Celeste's number on her tag.

"Oh my god, really? That's so crazy! She's been missing since Monday! Ursa, where have you been?" She nuzzles the dog, digs out the Ziploc of kibble she carries around, and lets Ursa tear into it with her snout. Poor thing must've been so lost and scared, holed up in the damp forest somewhere, like the bear she really isn't. "Sweet girl, you must be starving!" Celeste wraps her arms around the dog's thick neck. It's been so long since anything was going to be okay that she almost forgot what happiness physically feels like, the looseness in her belly and shoulders, the smile straining her mouth.

The boy crouches next to her, his knee almost touching her arm. Celeste feels the familiar heat in her face. "Really, thanks so much," she says again, very aware that they're both choosing to watch the dog eat, which is pretty gross, instead of looking at each other.

He shrugs. "Not like I was gonna just leave her out there."

"Of course you weren't." Celeste smiles at him sideways. "Lancelot would never." He laughs a little, shoves his hands in his pockets, and performs a little bow. Celeste isn't sure what to do next: Thank him some more? Hug him again? Devour his cute mouth? Take off running into the park? Then suddenly she remembers the blue bottle of pills. She finds it in her bag and holds it out for the boy, but he just shakes his head roughly, backing up against the tree.

"What the fuck?" he says. "You feel like getting arrested?"

"I just thought—I don't know, maybe you could give them to those guys? Instead of the money. Since I don't have it." She feels her cheeks burning, can hear just exactly how stupid this sounds.

There's a weird kind of silence between them for a moment. Traffic whizzes past; the boy picks up a leaf and strips it to its veins. "It might help," he says finally. "Maybe if you give me the pills, I can finally get those guys off my back." He tightens his brow. "I told you, I never mess with this shit. I just know some kids who do."

Frustrated, she says, "Then why didn't you just tell my friend to fuck off or something?"

"He seemed, like, pretty messed up. He seemed desperate for cash. I guess I know how it is." The kid shakes his head again, frowning at the grass. "Look, I told him I'd do it for a little fee, okay? Figured he could spare it, if he was really going to sell those pills."

Celeste looks down at the blue bottle clutched in her fist, the magnitude of her cluelessness expanding in her chest. She zips the bottle into her backpack and shoulders it. "Listen," she says in a small voice, "why don't you just tell me who these assholes are, and I can find them myself."

He looks away across the lawn, his eyes threaded with light, like one of Joan's crystals, an impossibly beautiful lattice of molecules. "Nah, you know what? I'll take care of it. You got enough to worry about. I mean, your boy's dead. You must be— Yeah, fuck, I'm really sorry."

She takes a step back, shoved a little by the shock of the words. This kid keeps surprising her. She wants to surprise him, too, and also to stay here talking to him, somehow, since he saved Ursa. And so she hears herself saying, "Honestly, though? He's . . . not actually dead. I mean—well, he *could* be, I guess. Everyone else thinks so. But I know he's still alive." And then the boy surprises her again: He's still listening. He doesn't respond, except with a patient silence. She wants to speak into his silence. It seems like maybe he could turn out to be a Celeste kind of listener, not a Nicky kind of talker. So she does the talking this time, and without really trying, she goes ahead and tells him everything: Nicky's fuckup, and his plan, and the library and the fliers, and the Mars book and the crystals and the meeting with the governor. Maybe she's breaking Nicky's trust, but that feels broken already. While she talks, they walk, following Ursa into the park, letting her sniff around the edge of the lawn. The dog picks up sticks and acorns in her mouth and drops them again, just contented and fine, as if she'd never gone off on some wild adventure alone.

After a minute Celeste laughs nervously. "I don't know why I'm telling you all this. I don't even know your—"

"Hold up, so—you lied to me, right? What, you didn't want me to keep looking for Pablo?"

"Who?"

"Paolo, whatever."

Celeste feels a chill move through the trees, and she pulls Ursa closer. "That's not his name," she says. "It's Nicky."

He laughs. "I knew that shit sounded fake." A bike speeds down the path toward them, and the boy takes Celeste by the wrist to move her gently out of the way. When he lets go, the spot where he touched her prickles and glows.

"I'm Celeste," she says, "for real."

"Romeo." He lifts his chin. "People call me Meo."

She smiles. "So Lancelot was pretty on point."

"Yeah, go ahead, laugh your ass off, make some Juliet joke." Embarrassed, she does laugh, and he joins her, tipping his head back with an open mouth. His laugh sounds throaty and a little smushed, like there's something trying to keep it down, a toughness or a sadness. He says, "Hey, I can't help it if I'm this legendary lover or whatever," but now he's the one blushing, the tips of his ears turning rosy bronze. He turns up the collar on his flannel to hide it, but Celeste wishes he wouldn't. She wants to touch him again but can't think of an excuse to do it, so they wander quietly for a minute, until she says, "Anyway, sorry I lied. When I find my friend, I'll get him to make it right with you. Taking off like that, he put you in a pretty shitty position."

"You're gonna keep looking for him?"

"I feel like I have to," she says, realizing that it's true. Trying to find Nicky has never felt like a choice. "I told you, everybody else thinks he's dead. So, if *I* don't keep looking, then, you know, he might as well be."

He thinks for a minute, rubbing his knuckles. "There's something else I should tell you. Take a seat, maybe?" He strides ahead to find a bench, and she follows, wary now. The bench is damp under her jeans. She strokes Ursa's head to slow her own heart down. "So—I was with him," Meo says. "The day of the quake. Nicky, that's his real name?" She nods, her chest tight, all the noises around them rising in her ears—a skateboard roaring by, a guy pushing a cart yelling about Jesus—and Meo is saying, "Yeah, I saw him that day, right around here. He had like a hot dog or something? He was eating. He looked pretty fucked up, crying and shit. He said he needed someplace to hide for a while, and could I help him. So I told him about this place I know where street kids stay, out by the beach?"

"The beach?" She pictures the tsunami tide rising to cover the sand. Nicky's aquamarine making a force field around him with its blue glow.

"There's these tunnels at Fort Funston," Meo says. "Kids sleep there. Nobody bothers them; the cops leave it alone. But Nicky asked me to give him a ride to a hotel instead. Said he needed someplace quiet to get his shit together." He looks down at his feet. "I told him to call an Uber or some shit. But he said he'd pay me. His phone was broken, I guess."

"Tell me where you took him."

"Someplace by the airport. When you said he's dead, I was like, shit, maybe it's my fault, like if that hotel—"

"Which one was it? Which hotel?"

"Fuck if I know. They all look the same. I can show you if you want."

THE BACK SEAT OF MEO'S BEAT-UP CAMRY IS PILED with neatly folded clothes, a pillow and a fleece blanket, textbooks and boxes of cereal bars, plastic jugs of water. Hospitably, he moves everything to the trunk to make room for Ursa. While he's piling the stuff back there, Celeste glances in the side mirror to smooth the frizz at her temples and swipe on some lip balm. She hasn't actually bothered to look at herself in days. Usually, she thinks her eyes are pretty—sometimes she wears mascara (to Nicky's delight) if she feels like getting noticed—but today they're red and puffy, so she finds her sunglasses before Meo gets in the car. Once they're on the road, Ursa stretches out on the seat and instantly falls asleep. Celeste starts feeling deliciously close to this boy, enclosed in this space of his own with Ursa safely tucked inside, on their way to maybe figure out some answers, and so she feels brave enough to ask, "So is this, like, where you stay?"

"No, fuck no!" Meo tightens his grip on the wheel, shoots her a narrow look.

Her face burns with a deep blush again. "Sorry, I didn't know."

"Yeah, you don't know a lot."

He's right, of course. Her assumptions about him are turning out to be pretty worthless, which makes her feel pretty worthless, too. She apologizes again, wondering if maybe she ruined the closeness, but after a moment he starts talking quietly.

"I just sleep in here sometimes," he says, "when it gets too crowded in my cousin's place. It's right by your school. There's always a bunch of guys staying there."

"I saw you at my school after the quake, getting some food? So, I guess—I don't know. It just made me wonder. Sorry."

"You've been watching me?" he says, and she says, "No," and for a moment there's a hot current running between their bodies, fizzing her blood and making her want to touch him or touch herself so badly that she needs to look away to make it stop. But then he slams on the brakes to avoid a bike, killing the moment, and Celeste draws a breath of relief. She's trying not to stare at him, at the shifting hollow under his Adam's apple, the faint moon-shaped scar at the corner of his mouth. She doesn't know exactly what's happening here, but it's new. Of course, she has wanted boys (and a couple of girls) before, and she's hooked up with a few, but there's always been something kind of predictable about it, like they were acting from a script. The way she is starting to want Meo feels instead like she's falling from a cliff, and his body's a branch growing out from the rock, and it might break if she grabs it, or it might break her fall.

He's merging into traffic, following the belt of freeway that rises up out of the city. They're repairing this road, and the new part gleams black in the afternoon sun, like it's paved with the marekanite from Joan the crystal lady, the stone that supposedly heals your sorrow. Meo says there was more family staying with them right after the quake, a lot of little kids, so his cousin sent him out for food. "Some Haight kid told me about the stuff at your school." Then he's quiet, drumming his hands on the wheel.

"Everybody was safe, though?" she says. "Your family, I mean. The little kids."

"Our building's okay. Right down the street, this other building, though, on Oak, near the DMV? Like ten people died. This kid I knew from middle school, Jehovah's Witness kid who used to bug me about going to church. He was funny, though. Liked dirty jokes."

"Holy shit," Celeste says, and they sit with it for a minute, the Jehovah's Witness comedian and all the other horrors of that day, too many to name. They talk a little more about what the quake felt like and where they were when it happened. Celeste's made herself so alone recently that she hasn't done very much commiserating like this. She wonders how often her friends still sit around talking about the earthquake, or if they've moved on already—to college apps and prom and somebody's oversharing on Insta.

"My pop, he was so pissed when I didn't call him at first! I was like, chill, my phone doesn't work, what'd you expect?" Meo laughs, shakes his head. "He was a kid in Mexico City when they had this big quake in the eighties, so it's like his worst nightmare, you know? He hated living here." Celeste waits, looking over at him with her head against the seat, and he adds, "They're in Mexico, my parents. They moved back a couple years ago to help my grandparents out." A shadow falls over his face. "My dad wanted me to stay with my cousin, go to college. Work for my uncle at his restaurant. I send home money sometimes to help them out. Maybe they can try and come back, like in another year or two, who knows." Lifting his arm, he flashes his tattoo. "That's why I got the sword. I feel like I'm always fighting." He laughs again, grimly this time. "I've got my DACA papers, but can't do shit for my parents, really. Even a good tips week barely pays my rent. And I'm trying to save for school." Celeste reaches across the seat and pulls back his sleeve until the whole sword shows itself, purple and black, with a thorny vine curled around the hilt, like it would hurt to hold it. At her touch, Meo shifts in his seat, adjusts his grip on the wheel.

"I thought maybe it was Excalibur," Celeste says.

"Nah," he mutters, then laughs a little darkly. "I did get it off a book cover. But I'm no king." After a moment, he reaches into her lap and pulls back the cuff of her sleeve, too. More sparks, this time rising into her throat, so she has to swallow a little gasp.

"What about those cute little matching suns?" He smirks at her. "Are you sure this kid, Nicky Paolo whatever, he's not your boyfriend?"

She refuses too loudly, then chuckles at herself. Her head's starting to hurt—her sugar's probably a little low—but there's no way she can eat right now, not when she's so hyped and buzzing, so close to finding out something like a real clue. "We got the suns because we're like twins," she says. "Same birthday. Like, same year, even. We grew up on the same street. We're basically family. And we read about the sun probably having this twin star, so . . . Also, he's gay."

"Ah," Meo says, "cool." They're quiet for a little while, smiling out the windows, Ursa snoring in the back. Then Meo shakes his head and says, "That's cold as fuck, though, just taking off after the quake, letting everybody think he's dead. You really believe he did that?"

She watches a retaining wall unfurling along the freeway in a blur, matted clumps of trash-scattered ivy creeping up over it and reaching for the road. Sometimes she thinks it might be easier to mourn Nicky's death than to live in this not-knowing place, where he's just ditched her without a word. "If I'm honest, you know, I saw it coming for a while. Like before the whole cheating thing. Even before he told me about any of it. It started to feel like he was on his way somewhere. And maybe I wasn't going there with him, like we always thought."

She glances over her shoulder to check on Ursa, and Fake Nicky is there in his pink sweatshirt, shoved between the dog and the door. He picks up a bottle of some kind of drugstore cologne from the floor of the car and raises his eyebrows. *Shut your judgy mouth,* she warns him silently, and he throws up his hands. *What?*

I said nothing! But Celeste is actually glad to see him again. It seems like a good sign that he's back, like maybe he's okay with her following him just a little ways into his new life.

"Guess he was on his way here," Meo says, taking an exit. He waves at the parade of beige hotel blocks lined up along this frontage road near the airport. "That's the one where I took him. Super 8, shit, yeah, that's right."

Stunned, Celeste fumbles in her wallet for the Super 8 key card they found in the trash at Mimi's. She explains it to Meo, hurrying out of the car almost before he gets it parked in the hotel lot. Still-sleepy Ursa locks her paws to the pavement for a defiant stretch, but Celeste yanks the leash until she follows, hanging her huge head. They hurry through the automatic door with Meo in tow. The lobby smells like disinfectant and fake maple syrup. Plastic plants are scattered around some faceless furniture, with faceless people huddled there gazing into their phones, luggage parked between their knees. It's the perfect place to get lost, the kind of place that's totally past caring who you are or where you're headed. The check-in dude—an extremely pale blond kid in a too-big burgundy blazer with a plastic name tag (JAYCE)—doesn't even seem to notice them or the enormous dog when they get to the desk.

"Excuse me," Celeste says at last. He looks up from his phone. "I'm wondering about a friend of mine who stayed here a while ago?" She fishes the crumpled Nicky flier—hot pink, the color of his favorite hoodie—from the bottom of her backpack and flattens it on the desk. The guy just looks at it blankly.

"Yo, Jayce!" Meo snaps his fingers at the kid. "Look him up or something? What the fuck?"

"I don't think I'm supposed to do that." The kid shrinks into his blazer, but Meo just keeps staring him down. "Fine, okay, you know the date?" When Celeste tells him, he looks at her blankly again. "You mean, like the earthquake day? Yeah, um, that's gonna be hard. I think the records might be messed up."

Meo rolls his eyes and strides around the back of the desk. "Look it up," he says again. Celeste has to bite her lip to stop herself from giggling at this tough guy act. But he grins at her, like, *It's working, right?*

"Sorry." The kid punches a couple of keys on an ancient-looking computer. "Nobody by that name in the system." As soon as he picks up his phone again, Meo takes it out of his hand and tucks it in his own pocket. Jayce cries, "Bro, what?!" but Meo ignores him, leaning closer, squinting at the computer.

"Try Paolo," he says. Celeste glances at him and spells it for Jayce, who sighs heavily and starts to type.

"Last name?"

"We don't know, okay?" Meo says. "Can't you just look for Paolo?"

"Ah, yeah! Here he is! Paolo Reborn? Weird name. He checked in that morning." Jayce starts babbling: "Check-in time's usually four—looks like he came early? They must've made him pay for the extra day. Sometimes people do that, like if they're on a layover? Hey, can I have my phone back now?"

But Celeste has stopped listening. "Okay," she says, "okay. So, he was here." She looks around the lobby, feeling almost frantic, like maybe she should run around flinging doors open—like he might just walk out of the bathroom any second, or show up at the sad buffet, pouring thousands of sugars into a cup of terrible coffee. "What happened here with the quake, anyway? Did you guys have any damage?"

"Nah, nothing major, but people were going apeshit." They

lost power, Jayce explains, and had to evacuate everybody, but the hotel has a generator, so after the fire department cleared the building for safety, most of the guests stayed until the airport was running again.

"What about Paolo?" Meo taps the monitor screen. "Does it show when he checked out?"

Jayce types some more, making a scrunchy puzzled face, then shakes his head. "The records are totally fucked for, like a week after. Probably the system crashed or something when the power went out? It says your friend checked out in 1997."

Meo puts the kid's phone on the desk. "All right, bro, thanks." Celeste thanks him, too, and wanders outside in a giddy daze. Her head's starting to ache because the asteroids are back in her brain, but this time they're all the things she's figured out about Nicky bouncing around, colliding and spinning. He was here, and maybe at Mimi's. The Gemini map. The aquamarine. She starts to chatter to Meo about the asteroids as they cross the parking lot, the sky hanging low and heavy now with billowy clouds.

"You okay?" Meo says. "You sound kind of crazy."

And then from far away she hears her phone beeping, then Ursa's three barks, and the dog's paw come to light, strangely gentle, on her arm. "Oh," she says, "oh no. Can you—my backpack?" And she's stumbling over the blurry words and her feet, falling against the car, Meo catching her waist. He opens the door and helps her sit, crouching beside her with his hand steadying her back. She fumbles with the zipper on her bag, fingers thick and numb, her stuff falling everywhere, books fluttering open on the damp pavement, lip balm rolling under the car. Fog swirls across the screen of her vision. A plane roars overhead, but the roar keeps going after it's gone.

"Hey," Meo seems to be saying softly, close to her face. "It's cool, you're all right." She shakes her head, but he's looking straight at her for the first time all day with his Neptune glow, and he doesn't look even a little bit freaked out, so she closes her eyes and breathes deep and manages to sputter, "F-f-food." In an instant he's gone and back with a cereal bar, his hand somehow never leaving the small of her back. She melts so far into the warmth of it that she forgets what to do with the bar, so he tears it open and feeds it to her bite by bite until the fog begins to clear.

Soon her breath begins to even out, and the trembling in her chest subsides. "More," she whispers, "please," so Meo gathers a pile of snacks from the trunk. Shyly he watches her eat for a minute or two, then he blows a relieved sigh and starts collecting her spilled things to pack them back into her bag, one by one, carefully, even folding her scarf into a neat roll. He moves to get in the driver's seat, but she stops him, curling her fingers around his wrist, and before she can change her mind or totally get her senses back, she pulls him into the back seat next to her. They sit close for a few minutes, recovering in silence. She lowers her head to his shoulder, shifts her arm and leg so that their bodies are touching in one long line.

"It's why I have Ursa," she tells him, her voice still a little gooey in her mouth. "My diabetes." She wipes her lips with the back of her hand and presses the other hand over Meo's at her waist, threading their fingers. She's worried that if she lets go, he might run away—or she'll suddenly switch to feeling ugly and ashamed, like she usually does after an episode, instead of the warm and glowy way she feels right now in this empty parking lot in the gathering rain.

"Oh," he says. "My bad, Celeste. I didn't know." It's the first time he's said her name. She wishes he'd say it a hundred more times.

"Don't apologize," she says. "I can take care of myself." And even though a voice in her head is insisting that's a lie, it sounds so good that it makes her brave, so she leans over and kisses him. Softly at first, then harder, their lips opening—she pulls him close, opens her coat and presses her breasts against him, gathers a fistful of his shirt, and kisses his neck. He winds his hands into her curls, stretches his neck under her mouth. Celeste can't imagine ever wanting this to end, but then it does, suddenly, when it starts to pour outside and Ursa shoves her way into the car, and Celeste and Meo, laughing, have to untangle themselves and wrestle the dog to climb into the front.

"Jesus," Meo says. "What the fuck was that?"

But Celeste doesn't know, either. She laughs again, surprised by the sound of it. They sit, breathless and wordless, the rain on the windows blurring everything else.

THEY DRIVE AROUND IN THE RAIN FOR THE REST OF the afternoon, not really going anywhere, just stopping sometimes in parking lots to make out and talk. She asks about the textbooks, and he says he's taking a couple of classes at City; he graduated from Lincoln last year and is taking chemistry, hoping to transfer to State for pre-med if he can get the loans. He asks about her school, too, but that makes her feel young and spoiled, so she mostly blows off the questions or distracts him with kissing. He also asks what she thinks about Nicky, the hotel—but Celeste, to her own surprise, doesn't feel like talking about that yet. She woke up this morning totally alone, and now she has Ursa back, and she seems to have this boy, too, and she doesn't want to stop touching him. She wants to pretend for just a little while that the rest of it doesn't exist.

At first she ignores the worried texts from her parents, but when she tells Meo why her phone is blowing up, he gets a little pissed: "At least you gotta respect they're worried," he says, staring down the wet road. "If I don't WhatsApp my mom before I go to bed, she's up in my texts all night." With a stab of guilt, Celeste realizes she hasn't even told her parents about Ursa yet, so when they stop for gas, she calls Shane and explains that somebody found the dog. Then there's all the noise of relief, with Bonnie in the background—laughter and some crying, mixed with her parents' favorite rapid-fire interrogation technique: *How's-she-doing-where'd-they-find-her-is-she-sick-should-we-call-the-vet?* Celeste just says she's fine, they're hanging out with a friend, back before curfew. She tosses a "love you" into the stream of stunned questions, then hangs up. Looking around for Meo, she finds him watching her with a distant frown. She smiles, but he startles and looks away, fiddling with the pump.

They get some greasy Chinese food for dinner in a strip mall. This time Celeste, still starving, forces herself to be careful—calculating the carbs for a plate of pot stickers, dosing precisely in the bathroom while Meo orders—but they eat fast and hurry back to the car, which somehow seems to contain their strange new closeness and the warmth of their bodies, like an animal's den. Meo drives to Pacifica, where the waves are tall and angry in the rainy night, whitewater glowing under the still-huge moon. They find an empty parking lot on a cliff over the beach. She's been telling him about *Swords of Avalon*, so she reads to him from a couple of the sexy parts, then sits in his lap in the driver's seat and swirls her crotch against his hard-on, kissing him, until he comes with a shudder that she can feel all the way down to her feet. He's so calm afterward that she starts to climb off, but then he threads his hand into her jeans, waits for her silent, breathless nod, and fingers her until she comes, too—which has never actually happened with a boy before. She leans her head on his chest and curls her body around him. Their breath steams the windows while they listen to the sea and the rain.

At some point they fall asleep, because when she opens her eyes in the dark car, it's already 12:05. Past curfew. A chain of angry texts from her mom and dad. Meo and Ursa are both gently snoring. The car smells like cereal bars and dog breath and vagina, so she opens the door quietly to let the salt air in.

Nicky's out there, standing at the cliff edge. At first her sleepy brain thinks, *It's him!*—but then she sees he's wearing Pumpkin and understands that it's Fake Nicky haunting her again. She pulls her sweater tight and shuffles up next to him in the gravel. She's still a little wet and tender between her legs, her knees wobbly and stiff. The rain's stopped, and the gulls are calling over the waves.

After midnight, Nicky says, wagging his finger. *You missed the deadline.*

Celeste's body goes stiff. The college apps deadline. MIT. She's floated past the event horizon; there is no escaping the black hole now. Stephen Hawking says if you fell into one, its gravity would stretch you out like a noodle, but some other scientists think it would just vaporize you right down to your atoms.

So that's it? Fake Nicky says, stepping closer to the edge, pushing his fists into Pumpkin's pockets. *You just decided to give it up?*

"I didn't *decide*," she tells him angrily. "If anything, *you* decided!" She wants to blow a raspberry at him, or something equally kindergarten-level, but then he takes another step closer to the steep cliff. She gasps and reaches for him, the wind blasting her face, and suddenly he's gone, dissolved into the mist, and Meo is there, draping a blanket over her back. He kisses her ear and whispers, "You're so pretty," but she's still watching the place where Nicky isn't. "Hey, you okay? What's up, you need some food? You need to check your—"

"Don't do that," she says, sounding too snarly. "I mean, please, just don't worry about me, okay? I hate that."

He nods, a little wounded-looking, so she takes his hand and draws him close under the blanket. "It's nothing," she says. "Just curfew. I have to get home." And she holds his hand tightly while they drive, feeling the pull of gravity on the tips of her hair and the soles of her feet, the stretching already underway.

Day 99

"Second-semester seniors are legally *required* to cut school," Celeste explains to her dad, who seems to have been assigned to corner her for a little chat. They're perched in a balcony box at Davies Hall, which is finally open again for symphony rehearsals, a skeleton of scaffold still clambering up to the ceiling. The major repairs are done, but they're working to cover signs of damage with plaster and gold paint. Celeste figures they won't let the audience back in until it looks like the earthquake never even happened. She doesn't get it; three months post-quake and still nobody else seems to understand that things can't ever be the same as before.

"Right, no argument there," Shane says, tipping back in the red velvet seat, hands clasped behind his head. He's looking so much older since the quake, grayer at his temples, the starbursts at the corners of his eyes etched deep and dark. "Still," he says, "your mother's worried it's getting out of hand."

Celeste rolls her eyes, starts packing her books away. She was glad when her dad invited her here to do homework during rehearsal; she and Nicky used to do it all the time when they were in middle school down the street. Sometimes the string section would riff on the *Star Wars* music for them during breaks, and afterward her dad would take them for pizza in Hayes Valley. Today she was hoping to actually get something done—she's late with an essay about Kafka's *The Metamorphosis*, hasn't even finished reading it—but all her homework has felt pretty pointless lately, what with the black hole waiting. Her thoughts and ideas get vaporized into atoms almost as soon as they form in her head. Before her dad came up to the seats to accost her, she'd been reading the same page for probably half an hour. And anyway, now that Shane's hidden agenda has been revealed, Celeste would just as soon get out of here and meet up with Meo.

She texts him: *Come get me?* He's been driving her to check out the rest of the spots on the Gemini map. With his class and work schedule, she's been forced to chip away at her own school days in order to see him, but it seems a small price to pay for having a hot Watson along on her Nicky-sleuthing runs. Even just the buzz of Meo's text in her pocket (*c u in 5*) makes her warm everywhere.

"Listen," Shane says, "the thing is, love—if you really want MIT, you can't let your grades go like the rest of them."

"The rest of them don't have a mom who works at school," she grumbles. "And, like, a cadre of teacher spies scrutinizing their every move." She tugs the leash gently to rouse Ursa and clomps up the aisle with Shane close behind, the whispery practice notes of a flute trailing after them.

"Can't argue there, either," her dad says. "Listen, before you go, just promise you'll sit down with me and look at the financial aid stuff. This weekend, maybe? I told Mom I wouldn't put it off to the last. And I think we better look at all of them, not just MIT, you know, to be safe. Promise, right?"

"Okay, yeah, Dad." Celeste's stomach drops out of her body. She leaves it behind on the red carpet and speeds ahead of Shane down the great curve of the stairs. He snags her by the backpack, raising an eyebrow. She feels a jolt of fear, thinking of the pills rattling underneath her books—Meo hasn't seen the dealer dudes lately, so she's still carrying the pills around, worried about leaving them home, where her parents might look through her shit—but now her dad just gives her a pleading smile.

"Where are you off to in such a hurry, anyhow? Out past curfew, hand glued to that phone. Come on, what's up? I thought we'd get a pizza?"

She kisses him on the cheek and takes the rest of the stairs three at a time, Ursa scrambling to catch up. Celeste hasn't even tried to tell her parents about Meo, but they just seem relieved that her mood's so improved, acting surprised anytime she remembers to acknowledge their presence. Given their history of text snooping and not-so-subtly peeping at her through the blinds when she gets home late, she's pretty sure they suspect there's a boy involved, but this is the first time either of them has actually inquired. In fact, the only place Celeste has talked out loud about Meo is in grief group, because everyone's sworn to secrecy there, and somehow it felt important to tell Ms. Greenberg that something good was going on. Otherwise Celeste's been flying under the radar at school, spending free periods in the library (which is mostly senior-free now that college apps are in) and scribbling in her notebook about (1) Nicky, (2) Meo, and (3) the black hole. There's been some nasty chatter about her on Nicky's Insta feed since she ditched the memorial, but Bridget—who otherwise seems to have given up on her—always promptly shuts it down with profanity. Waiting on the symphony hall steps, Celeste convinces herself to send Bridget a thank-you text, but nothing comes back.

When the Camry pulls up at the curb, Celeste climbs in with Ursa, who already loves Meo madly—it's almost as if she actually understands that he saved her life—or maybe she's just been waiting for someone to take Nicky's place in her heart, but either way, her excitement's too much for the rusty old car, which shudders as she bounds over the gearshift and half into Meo's lap. He coos over her, nuzzling and scratching behind her ears.

"She's just glad we're not on Muni." Celeste smirks at Meo, and he leans over to kiss her hungrily. At first they were shy with each other, but now that it's been a few weeks since that first night in the car, they don't wait for the kissing anymore. Sometimes their tongues are in each other's mouths before she even gets the door closed. Celeste has gotten so used to hating her body; ever since the diagnosis, she's always felt like she's walking around in this uncomfortably delicate bag of blood. But now her body's feeling more like an instrument, honed and sleek and constantly humming. Meo turns her on more than anyone ever has, and he's curious and kind, so that Celeste sometimes finds herself getting caught in a current of pleasure, almost (but not quite) forgetting to notice the cold undertow of grief.

When they finally untangle themselves, Meo turns the radio on and heads for the next stop on the map: Blue Heron Lake, smack in the middle of Golden Gate Park. They've already done fogbound Crissy Field, with no sign, eerily, of the usual picnic mobs nor of Nicky. They drove south to the Cow Palace, too, where Carla used to take the little "twinsies" to *Disney on Ice*.

Now the arena's damaged beyond repair, circled with fencing and FOR SALE signs, patrolled by security guards who don't care for people hooking up in cars in the weedy parking lot.

Celeste knows that Meo's mostly been humoring her—he's along for the kissing, really—he thinks the whole thing with the Gemini map is pretty crazy, and when she showed him the Mars book, he said it looked like a weird serial killer diary from a movie (basically true). But he asks good questions, and he laughs at her Nicky stories, and talking to him about Nicky is a huge relief, anyway, since the rest of the time she has to pretend that Nicky's dead, which means avoiding talking about him altogether. Whenever her parents even so much as drop his name, she finds a reason to leave the room within seconds. Carla texts her daily, sometimes with old photos, but Celeste rarely responds with anything but a heart emoji, which makes her feel like a huge jerk. When Meo's not around, it's like she's wearing one of those suffocating plastic Halloween masks, but when she's with him, she can finally tear it off and breathe.

"Looks like your boy's not here, either." They're standing on the stone bridge over the lake with Ursa, passing a joint back and forth, watching an old man toss chunks of bread at the ducks. "Should we look around the island, too? People sometimes camp in the trees up there."

Celeste shakes her head, takes a drag on the joint. "I don't know," she says. "It's not like I think he's just going to jump out from behind a rock or something."

Meo laughs, coughing smoke. "Then what the fuck are we doing here?"

"I mean, I guess I thought that at first." It's true, she realizes, that she's stopped expecting Nicky himself to actually turn up in one of these places. Still it feels important to follow the Gemini pattern, like the constellation's stars might eventually shed their white-hot light on the truth. "I just feel like, you know, he left this list for me to understand. And maybe if I can figure it out, I'll find him."

"Yeah, and then what?"

Celeste shrugs. Then what. She's asked herself this question but never come up with an answer. "Bring him back, maybe?"

Meo stubs out the joint, snakes an arm around her waist, and they start walking back to the car, Ursa trotting beside them. "But like—did he really leave that list for *you*, though? Didn't that crazy rock shop lady find it? Just saying, the kid I drove to the hotel didn't seem like he was trying to get rescued. Cabrón was on his way *out*."

Celeste frowns at their shoes, climbing down the damp path. "Fine," she says, "maybe you're right. I guess I just don't really care anymore if he *wants* me to find him. It's not really just about what he wants, you know? There's his mom, and his grandparents? They deserve to know he's okay."

"Yeah," he says. "And you're pretty fucked up about it, too."

This stings, but Celeste finds she can't argue with it, so she just leans into him and keeps walking. They follow the path around a little grove of plum trees covered with hopeful blooms. On the other side, there's a group of street kids perched on a couple of boulders, smoking, their backpacks piled in the soggy weeds. They're Haight kids; Celeste recognizes one of their dogs, a sweet-faced golden pit bull on a rope leash. A girl with long blond locs knotted into a lime-colored scarf waves her fingers at them.

"Me-ooooo," she calls.

Celeste wrinkles her nose. "You know her?"

"From the neighborhood. Hey, pass me one of those posters?" She unzips her backpack and hands him one of the pink Nicky fliers. "These kids, they know a lot of people on the street, maybe they've seen him." She starts to follow. "Nah, you stay, I'll be quick. They're not real friendly to kids from your school, you know?"

He tosses her the car keys, and she watches him step into a different costume, his shoulders expanding as he strides down the lawn. Most of the kids just glare at the pink flier, but green-scarf girl points to it and says something Celeste can't hear, something that makes the rest of them laugh. Meo talks to the girl again, but she just shakes her head, fingering a silver spike pierced through her lip. She glances up at Celeste, her mouth twisted with what looks a little like pity. Celeste feels something click open in her chest. She starts walking toward them, but Meo is already hurrying back to her, steering her onto the path just as a park police officer wheels by on a bike. The cop casts a wary glance at the group of kids and slows to a stop, blocking their way to the car. Meo's body goes stiff. He's mentioned a few close calls with the cops before—they're assholes around here, because of the Haight kids—and Celeste knows Meo could lose his DACA status just for looking at this guy the wrong way. It feels like the pills in her backpack must be visible through the nylon, glowing kryptonite green. Thinking fast, her heart hammering, she grabs the flier out of Meo's hand.

"Excuse me," she says, waving to the officer. Meo mutters "What the fuck" under his breath, but she just squeezes his hand and calls to the cop, "Hi, officer? We were wondering if you've seen this kid." She holds the poster out to him while he's still perched on the bike. He lifts his sunglasses to look. "Our friend, he ran away?" she says. "We've been asking the kids around here."

The cop, a skinny white guy with a seventies-style mustache, narrows his eyes at Meo. "That so?" he says, but Celeste just keeps talking, blabbering about Nicky, the cheating and the earthquake, all the true things, because she knows she's bad at lying, plus this cop's probably racist, and she wants to throw up a smokescreen so he'll stop looking at Meo like that. The word *earthquake* makes the cop's shoulders collapse a bit. He takes the poster from Celeste, looks it over, and hands it back with a card from his shirt pocket. Celeste already knows the number on the card—it's the one that would connect her to Merlot, if Nicky's file were still open—but she lets him explain it anyway while Meo shuffles his feet. She can feel him struggling to breathe. Green-scarf girl and her friends, meanwhile, have wandered off into the park with their backpacks and dogs.

"Sorry about your friend. Hope you find him." Glaring at Meo, the cop says, "I'll be seeing you," then pedals off around the lake. When he's out of sight, Meo blows out a long breath and string of Spanish curse words, leaning over his knees. They hurry back to the car on a shortcut through the trees, mud and twigs clinging to their shoes.

"Jesus," he says, pulling her close, and she pours all her wild relief and nervousness into the kiss. Afterward Meo wipes his brow with the cuff of his flannel. "I shouldn't even be talking to those kids. Bunch of druggy white kids, makes me look like their dealer. The last thing I need is the cops to start watching me."

Celeste thinks of the green-scarf girl, her finger on Nicky's face. "The girl with the locs—she recognized Nicky?"

Meo fiddles with the keys. "Not sure. She thought it was him, but like, his hair's different now. Said she saw him a couple weeks ago, in the tunnels at Funston, that place I told you about?" He bites his lip, squinting up at the cottony sky. "This guy was fucked up on something pretty bad," he tells her carefully. "She said he tried to jump the cliff, but somebody pulled him back."

Celeste feels her head shaking no, even as she remembers Fake Nicky on that first night with Meo, melting over the sandy edge of the earth. Her sun smolders on her wrist. "That doesn't sound right," she says. "He had—you know, some money? So why would he . . . And he wasn't into getting super high, not like that."

"Yeah . . ." Meo starts to say, then decides to get in the car instead. Celeste slides into the passenger seat. It used to be true, what she said, that Nicky wasn't into drugs, except weed—but there were times in the past year when he was probably using more than she knew. That time when he almost fell off the fire escape at the party. Those other nights when Carla texted her, wondering where he was, and she lied because she didn't know. Really, though, she didn't want to know where he went. It felt better to pretend that their togetherness was what mattered most.

Meo clucks his tongue, shaking his head. "Yeah, but like, how much cash did he have, for real? Three months, that money goes fast. And it's hard as fuck, living on the street. Maybe he never got high before, but like, for those kids . . . getting high, it makes that life a little easier, you know?" He reaches for her hand, but she pulls away, anger flaring in her chest.

"So what," she says, "you think you were like—*helping* Nicky, or something? By hooking him up with some dealers. Okay, sure, that's what you were doing."

He slouches in the seat, his voice grim and matter-of-fact. "Actually, I was trying to help my family." He starts the car.

"You know what, fuck this," she says. "I want to go home." But her voice sounds as small as she feels, like a kid trying out grown-up words. Meo guns the motor, a hurt look curling his mouth.

Trouble in paradise? Fake Nicky trills from the back seat, where he's cuddled up with Ursa. *Didn't I tell you?* he says. *You can't understand.*

She presses her eyes closed to stop the tears. That day in the kitchen with Bonnie still hangs in her memory in full color and sound—the high-pitched fissure in Nicky's voice when he said those words, *You can't understand. Can't*, not *don't*. Like she'll never be capable. And the way the door hung open, letting in the cold, when he stormed out. She sits up straighter next to Meo. She pushes her curls back from her face. Maybe Nicky's right, or maybe they're both right. She can't understand if she doesn't really try. If she wants to find Nicky, she's got to be real, no matter how much the truth sucks. Maybe if she'd been more real with him this past year, he'd have stuck around. And if she wants Meo to stick around, she can't pretend she understands all the shit he deals with, either.

"Hey," she says after a minute, her voice still small, but Meo scowls at the road, the line of cars and buses winding up the hill through a maze of traffic cones on Ninth Avenue. "Can I tell you something I read about black holes?" He doesn't answer. "So, there are tons of them in the universe. Like maybe even a billion? And the thing is, you can't even see them. Most of them are just, like, out there, and let's say you're a star, you could just end up passing one anytime, and it could basically suck you in and destroy you, like before you know it. Well, not suck you in, I guess—that's not really a thing—it's more like, gravity pulls the star close and starts to tear it apart."

"Yeah, I've heard of black holes."

She hugs her knees to her chest. "Listen, I guess I'm just saying, I'm not that good at, like, getting close with people. I've always been kind of scared . . . of getting pulled in, maybe. And pulled apart."

He shoots her a skeptical look. "What about Nicky?"

Out the window, a bunch of girls her age are waiting to cross the street together, laughing and chatting, surrounded by a kind of buzzing poison-pink energy cloud. It's never been easy like that for Celeste, but at least Nicky was always there, his gravity keeping her comfortably in orbit. "Right, so I had him," she says to Meo. "So that made it okay. But even with him, this past little while? It was like he was on another planet, and I was too scared to go there."

Meo's face is still in shadow. "Yeah, well, it's pretty fuckin' scary on *this* planet, too." There's a long silence, and when he breaks it with a laugh, Celeste feels flooded with relief. "I kinda want to suck you in," he says, "but not destroy you." She punches his arm playfully, her body stretching back to its normal size with breath. Still, the angry words have left a weird haze between them. "So, listen," he says, "I have to work tonight . . ."

She grabs his wrist, the branch that might break her fall. "Do you have time for one more stop?"

HE DRIVES HER OUT TO FORT FUNSTON, TO SHOW her the tunnels where the green-scarf girl might've seen Nicky. Celeste used to bring Ursa here with her parents—it's off-leash dog heaven, a maze of sandy paths and open dunes winding over the bluffs—and by the time they get the car parked, Ursa's practically slamming herself against the door with excitement. When Celeste removes the harness, Ursa bounds through the dunes with the other dogs, sending up sprays of sand, her soft fur flattened by the wind. The sky is a dazzling blue, but with a heavy cloud bank hanging over the ocean, promising rain. Meo leads Celeste off the familiar pavement path and onto a trail that curves into a tunnel of cypress trees. They trudge through the deep sand, Ursa winding her way ahead, sniffing wildly at the ice plant, alert to something sudden. For a breathless moment, Celeste thinks, could it be Nicky? Maybe Ursa's caught his scent . . . but on the other side of the tunnel, there's just a rotting gull carcass near the cliff edge. She leashes the dog to keep her away from it. Meo beckons them around another bend in the trail, which leads to a kind of concrete cavern built into the hillside. There are lots of them up here—the place is an old missile battery—and Celeste has wandered into them before, chasing after Ursa or one of her tennis balls, but this one is hidden, the entrance screened by a huge tangle of fennel with acid-yellow blooms.

They push their way through the weeds into the dark, sour-smelling tunnel. As Celeste's eyes adjust, human shapes begin to form, starlit by lighter flames and the tips of cigarettes. There must be twenty kids in here, bundled in torn sleeping bags spilling wet cotton, some of them fiddling with needles or pipes, others asleep on stained mattresses and pillows made from knotted clothes. Meo moves among them, showing the pink poster, and Celeste follows, holding the leash so tight that Ursa starts to whine.

Nicky's not here. Maybe this should be a relief, but Celeste only feels a deep sadness that seems to have nothing to do with Nicky at all. Somebody yells at them to get the fuck out, and they stumble back through the high weeds and find the path into the dunes.

"Some of those kids looked a lot younger than me."

"Tried to tell you," Meo says. They come out of the trees into the bright day, fighting a sudden swirly wind on their way back to the car. Celeste wonders if the tunnel itself is actually making the wind, its gravity pulling them back toward its dark mouth.

THEY SHUT THEMSELVES IN THE CAR, BUT THE WIND still howls outside. They don't talk or listen to music. He holds her hand while he drives. She assumes he's taking her home, but then he stays on the freeway past her exit, heading for downtown, the skyline glowing golden with the early-spring sun.

"Where are we going?"

"You hungry? Want some dinner?"

"It's like, four o'clock."

"I know a good place."

She rests her head on the seat and lets the car carry her, which feels better than arguing or trying to figure out what to do next. Near city hall, Meo wrestles the car into a tiny parking spot at the end of a pretty little alley. Celeste's never seen this street before, even though they're just a few blocks from her old school. It feels like something out of a storybook: narrow sidewalks scattered with café tables and potted trees, brass lanterns strung overhead between the buildings (a faint pissy smell is the single reminder that, yes, this is SF, after all). A few of the windows are still boarded up, but painted with intricate murals: indecipherably beautiful lettering, California poppies, a tangle of jellyfish.

Celeste follows Meo to an emerald-green storefront with lush vines snaking over the door and around the windows. The word *Quetzal* looks freshly painted in looping gold script on the glass, the tail of the Q long and feathered. "Closed," she says, but Meo rattles his keys. Inside it's warm and spicy-smelling, the small door opening into a long room lined with plush green booths, shelves of gleaming bottles, and a wall of wispy ferns behind a concrete bar. More plants trail down from a floating steel loft, their leaves entwined with tiny lights. There's a turntable playing an old record—Leonard Cohen, which always reminds Celeste of her dad, who used to play guitar for her when she was a baby. All at once she's starving, but also deeply aware of not being cool enough to eat in a place like this. It feels like some adorably down-to-earth movie star—Timothée Chalamet?—is going to stroll inside soon and tuck into his regular table, hiding behind the swoop of his hair.

Gazing around, Celeste feels a shameful sourness in her stomach for how she'd imagined a different kind of place where Meo went to work: neon beer signs, pools of refried beans. Noticing, maybe, the blush of her cheeks, he says, "Not what you had in mind?"

She considers apologizing, then says instead, "It's really magical in here," and Meo grins, calling for his uncle. A small, trim man with a crisp apron and a black bandanna tied around his head skips downstairs from the loft, speaking rapid Spanish into a phone. He wraps Meo in a hug and hands him a rag, then moves the phone away from his mouth and whispers to Celeste, "Finally he brings you around! Probably so I won't fire him for being late." He winks at her, then chatters some more into the phone as he gestures for her to sit at the bar. Celeste feels a giddy surge in her chest. Meo told his family about her?

"Romeo, those candles won't light themselves, por favor!" But Celeste wouldn't really be surprised if they did.

"I'm on it, tío," he says, first dipping a ladle into a ceramic jug behind the bar and handing Celeste a cup of cinnamon-smelling coffee. Her skin still stinging from the wind on the bluffs, she thinks she's never tasted anything better. She kisses him gratefully just as his uncle drops the phone into his apron pocket and starts to applaud.

"Look at this, a nice girl for Meo!" He slides onto the stool beside her and leans in conspiratorially. On the side of his neck, there's a dark tattoo: the silhouette of an exotic bird. "He's much too serious, my nephew, don't you think? Always got his face in a book or working. And now here he is, kissing on the dinner shift!" Celeste's about to apologize—offer to leave, maybe—but he just laughs and says, "I'm Alejandro—call me Ale. Enjoy yourself! I'll send out a plate."

She tries to refuse, but Ale waves her off and strides into the kitchen, shouting orders at a few other servers. For a little while Celeste helps Meo, polishing glasses and spooning pink crystal salt into tiny glass bowls.

"He's nice," she says, "your uncle."

Meo scrubs hard at a stain on the bar. "I owe him a lot." He keeps working silently with the rag, pressing harder, the veins in his arm popping, until there's no trace of purple left on the smooth concrete.

When Ale comes out of the kitchen with Celeste's plate, he cuffs his nephew on the head for letting her work. "You planning to share your paycheck, mi amor? She's our guest!" He arranges the plate carefully before her, as if she were Timothée Chalamet himself, and disappears back into the kitchen. The dish is gorgeous and strange: slices of raw pink fish, so thin they're almost transparent, drizzled with bright green oil and sprinkled with flower petals and threads of lime. A pure white tortilla, crisp with a puff of air in the center, so that when Celeste cracks the top, her face is swallowed by warm steam. At first she eats delicately, but it's so delicious that she's soon devouring it, Meo eyeing her with a smile as he stacks some plates. When she gets back from injecting her insulin in the bathroom, there's a bowl of rich golden broth with perfect, bright cubes of carrot and avocado and the most tender shreds of chicken Celeste has ever tasted.

"He likes you," Meo whispers. "The consomé's off-menu."

After the restaurant opens, Ale sets Celeste up in a booth to do her homework and brings her a plate of mango sprinkled with chili and some kind of rock-candy dust. She pretends to read *The Metamorphosis*, but it's much more interesting to watch Meo move so easily through this exquisite little world. Everybody seems happy to see him—the early customers with their jewel-colored cocktails; the serious, perspiring cooks with bandannas tied neatly over their hair. Two other servers arrive before the dinner rush, a pair of goth-y girls a little older than Celeste, with matching perfect eggplant lipstick and boobs straining the black T-shirts that seem to be their uniform. Celeste's horrified when they both hug Meo a little too long, smushing those boobs on his chest, but then he introduces them as his cousins, and they hug Celeste in the same way, too. The younger one, Marisol, keeps stopping by the booth to chat, despite getting yelled at repeatedly by Ale, who seems to be her dad. Once she sneaks a shot of fancy rum into Celeste's Diet Coke, and Celeste doesn't have the heart to tell her she can't really drink (alcohol sends her blood sugar sky-high).

"You're lucky," Marisol tells her. "Meo's a decent guy. He's not going to fuck you around. I wish I could find a boyfriend like that."

"He's not, exactly, my boyfriend? I mean, I don't think—"

"Marisol, deja de cotorrear, ¿quieres? I need those limes squeezed yesterday." Ale steers her back to the bar, and Meo, balancing a tray across the room, shoots a sweet little eye-rolling smile at Celeste. She isn't sure if chasing after Nicky together and hooking up in the car actually counts as dating, but also, *boyfriend* seems too dumb a word for whatever this is becoming.

MEO DRIVES HER HOME ON HIS BREAK. WHEN HE parks in front of her house, the Daves are sitting on their stoop with their ancient poodle, drinking martinis. They wave to her, exchanging an unsubtle look of scandalized excitement. Hoping to scandalize them further, she makes out with Meo for a few minutes in the idling car. Her parents are out tonight for the first time in months, so she thinks about bringing him inside, climbing the still-broken stairs together—she's never been with a boy in her own bed, and she hasn't seen him without his clothes yet—but there's something about their closeness in the car, the strange and kind of grimy bubble of it, that feels fragile, like she should protect it. They try and fail a few times to pull away from each other; then at last he murmurs, "I gotta get back to work." He kisses her hand, reaches into the back seat to scratch Ursa's belly. Celeste grabs her bag and opens the door, hanging one leg out. At Quetzal, she had almost managed to forget that stinging wind at Funston, the angry faces in the half dark.

"You good?" he asks, pressing her hand between both of his. "Listen, that girl before—maybe she was full of shit, you know, about Nicky? Just messing with me."

Through the front window of her house, dimly, Celeste can see the stairs, all the layers of their guts still exposed—timber, stone, plaster, dust. "This whole time," she says, "I've been thinking, if the quake didn't kill him, then he's okay. But even if— I mean, he really might not be okay, either way. He wasn't okay before."

Meo leans over the seat to kiss her again, this time tender instead of hungry. "It's like you said. Black holes everywhere."

Day 120

When the phone rings, Celeste is sprawled on her bed with Ursa, ignoring Kafka, studying the map in the open closet. It's been four months. There's a new pin color (copper) for places where he may have actually set foot sometime after the quake: Super 8, Mimi's house, Fort Funston. Mimi's and the hotel, outside city limits, are pinned near the top and bottom of the door, on pages printed out from Google Maps. Celeste gets up with a pencil and starts to trace a line between the copper pins, but it's hard to know where to start. The hotel first—but then would he have gone to Mimi's next, when the money ran out? In that case, what would have brought him back to the tunnels? Or did he go to the tunnels, stay there until he couldn't take it anymore, then hitchhike to Mimi's to sober up and make his plan? Celeste knows which version she would prefer to believe. She draws a light line between Funston and Mendocino, a winding road up the coast. Of course, the line's a fantasy, and she's trying hard to be real. He could've made dozens of other stops, really. Could've made it halfway around the world in 120 days.

The phone rattles her brain. Celeste hasn't stopped expecting it to be him when it buzzes, but it's usually one of her parents or

Meo. Still, she answers all the unfamiliar numbers, feels her heart sink every time it's just a robocall. This time, to Celeste's surprise, it's Carla's photo on the screen—a smiling shot of her and Nicky in glitter hats on New Year's Eve. Why would she call now? Does it mean bad news? Happily, the buzzing stops, but Carla calls back right away, and this time Celeste feels like she has to answer.

"Hi, oh, *hi*, honey," Carla says, fumbling loudly with the phone. "I'm so glad you picked up, listen—I'm in the ER."

Celeste bolts up to the edge of the bed and blurts, "Is he okay?" And there's a silence so long and blank that she wonders at first if the call's been dropped. Then she realizes that she's given herself away. "I mean—what I meant was, are *you* okay?"

"My mother had a stroke."

"Oh no!"

"It's bad. They're admitting her. Pop and I have been here since last night."

"Oh no," Celeste says again, "poor Nonna!" She reaches for her old monkey, Palpatine, and clutches him in her lap. It's hard to imagine Nonna in a hospital bed, even now with the dementia; the kitchen on Silver Avenue is her only natural habitat. Celeste tries to think of how her mom talks when people call with this kind of news. "I . . . Can I—do you *need* anything, or—"

"Actually, I was hoping you might come down here and sit with me for a while. Would that be okay? I just—there's something I wanted to show you. Can you come? We're at UC. They're moving us up to a real room now."

Another silence. This time Celeste can hear the incessant song of the hospital in the background, the rhythmic beeping and breathing of all the machinery required to power a body. Unfortunately, she knows that song by heart.

"You're busy, I know—"

"No," Celeste says, "I'll be right there."

AS SOON AS SHE SLIDES OPEN THE HEAVY DOOR OF Nonna's cell in the neuro ward, she wishes she had thought up some excuse. *What's wrong with this picture?*—like the puzzles Celeste always loved in *Highlights* magazine, which she's spent hours reading in the waiting rooms of this very hospital. Here's what's wrong with it:

(a) Nicky should be standing here in the doorway, not her.

(b) Celeste should be the one in the hospital bed, not Nonna, who never had anything worse than the flu, until she started losing her mind. And

(c) Carla's evidently been experimenting with time travel, because she's been replaced with an older version of herself. Gone are the perky ponytail and big hoop earrings, the red nails and lipstick and eggplant streaks in her hair. Celeste hasn't seen Carla since the memorial at school, and she's lost so much weight that her jean jacket hangs on her bony shoulders like she's a mannequin.

Celeste feels guilty at the sight of her, like she should've been checking up on Carla all this time instead of sneaking off with Meo to play Sherlock, so she apologizes right away, without even a hello. Luckily, Carla seems to take it as a standard polite apology, whispering, "Thank you, sweetheart," and wrapping Celeste in one of her overlong hugs. Finally she lets go and waves her into a stiff chair. The reason for the whispering seems to be Pop, who's stretched out in another chair at the bedside, snoring, strangely stubbled on only half his face, as if he dropped everything in the middle of a shave.

"Poor thing—he didn't sleep all night. Won't even leave her to get a bad bagel downstairs." Carla explains how they found Nonna yesterday at the kitchen table like usual, sitting up in her chair, hands wrapped around her favorite NASA coffee mug, but her face was slack, and she wouldn't respond to her name. They brought her here in an ambulance. Nonna's sleeping now, her skin waxy and grayish, the breathing tube taped to her cheek pulling her lips into a saggy frown.

"How is she? I mean, is she going to be okay?"

Carla reaches over to the bed to take her mother's hand. "She's sedated. Now we just have to wait and see. They'll take her for an MRI when they know she's stable."

For a few minutes they sit in silence, the hospital noises clicking and beeping along, the murmurs of the nurses passing in the hall. Celeste wishes that she hadn't left Ursa at home. Somebody cries out somewhere, startling them both, and they exchange a nervous chuckle.

"I really appreciate this," Carla says. "I know you hate hospitals. I mean, who doesn't, but . . . it's been lonely, you know, without him." She finds a wad of tissue in her purse, dabs her wet eyes, and says, "Anyway!" Wiggling her shoulders to sit up straighter, she forces a cheery smile. "Oh, congrats, by the way, sweetie—your mom said you got your applications in! That must feel so good. Fingers crossed. Not that you need it!"

Celeste grips the edge of her chair, worried she might just take off running down the hall, toppling crash carts and orderlies.

"And there's a boy, right? She said you're seeing a boy now? What's his name?"

Celeste raises her eyebrows, coughs loudly into her hand. So her mother knows all about Meo, and she's been spreading it all over town? She glances frantically around the room for a change of subject; then it pops into her head: "Didn't you say you had something to show me?"

Carla's face collapses a little. She hugs her purse, looking suddenly afraid, like she thinks Celeste's going to steal it. "I'm still not totally sure, I guess, if I should show you. But Christ, maybe it's too late now!" She digs into the purse again and takes out an envelope. Under the buzzing fluorescent light, Celeste can see it's addressed to Carla—terrible handwriting, pink ink. But before she can hand it over, the IV starts beeping wildly, and a nurse whirls in to change the bag. Celeste stares at the envelope while Carla talks with the nurse. It's all she can do not to just reach out and snatch it. Approximately a decade later, the nurse finally bustles out. Carla leans in close to whisper to Celeste. "So, you know how the mail was such a mess right after the quake? They lost that whole main building in Hunters Point, the distribution center."

"Yep, yeah, I heard about that." Celeste locks her fingers to keep them from fluttering toward the envelope. She's staring laser beams at it while Carla's going on about the mail.

"But I guess they're actually sorting through all the mail they recovered. Isn't that nuts? I mean, the postal service doesn't have better things to do with my taxes? Anyway, thank God they don't, 'cause we got a whole stack delivered yesterday. Most of it was junk, except this." She lifts the letter delicately between two fingertips, like it's made of ancient parchment, and hands it over to Celeste, whose hands are shaking. First she looks at the postmark: December 18. The day of the earthquake. San Francisco, CA. He must have put it in a mailbox in the morning. After he waved to her through the door at school? Before Meo found him in the park?

Darling, Loveliest, Funniest Mom—

Can you tell I'm buttering you up? Because I'm pretty sure this letter is going to make you mad. I'm so sorry, but I can't figure out another way, so here goes.

I'm leaving. I'm going to disappear. I'm about to be in some huge trouble at school, and I just don't want to hang around for the humiliation—getting expelled, then rejected by MIT and everything else. I want to start over on my own instead, so that's what I'm doing.

I realize I don't even have to tell you what happened, since it doesn't matter now anyway, but I want you to hear it from me.

I cheated. A lot. I wrote papers for other kids, which was actually surprisingly fun. It was like I got to be somebody else, and also learn stuff I didn't even know I was interested in. That part was cool, but it was really tiring, too. I haven't slept very much this whole year, which makes me feel kind of like a crazy person, but I still don't regret writing the papers. I did it because the kids paid me a lot of money, and I'm just sick of seeing you so worried about paying for school. We both know a full ride at MIT is a fucking pipe dream (excuse my French), even for me. So I had to find a way to help. But I fucked it all up on the way.

Stop crying! I know you're crying.

And I know you're disappointed in me.

I really love the stories about Great-Great-Grandpa Paolo, who sounds like he was literally great. I mean, he had this sweet childhood, probably, with the velvet suspenders and everything, and then one day everyone he loved just <u>died</u> all at once, and the city was falling apart, and he was just a little kid, a lot younger than me, and somehow he started it all over again. I mean, the orphanage was probably a shitshow, don't get me wrong, I'm not saying his life was easy. He probably had to eat gruel three meals a day and sleep in a bed with fourteen other kids. Still, I'm just saying, that story gives me hope.

Please don't look for me, Mom. I'll be okay. I have a little money to get on my feet, and I'll send you some when I can. If there's a massive emergency and you need to find me, you can write to PaoloReborn@hotmail.com. But I can't promise I'll write back. I won't check very often, and if you send me fake emergencies or emails begging me to come home or whatever, I'll stop checking it at all—okay? Really not trying to be a dick here. I just have to figure out this new life somehow.

Will you give Nonna hugs and kisses for me, please? And don't let Pop hate me. Oh, and please don't try to waterboard Celeste—promise? She doesn't know where I'm going, and this is going to be hard enough for her as it is.

I love you.

Nicky

Celeste reads the last paragraph over and over until the pink words swim on the page. *She doesn't know where I'm going, and this is going to be hard enough for her as it is.* She knows that last sentence is just Nicky being Nicky, worrying about her, but something about it ties a knot of anger in her belly—the pity in it, maybe, or the way he decided with such certainty to leave her behind.

Finally, Carla sighs, folds the letter, and presses it between her hands. "Did you get one, too?"

Celeste just barely shakes her head. "We didn't get any lost mail."

"Well, they're still digging through it." Carla's frown is tight, the lines etched deep in her chin. "Obviously I emailed frickin' Paolo Reborn about Nonna like, thirty times already. Nothing back yet." She fishes out her phone and flicks at it, checking again, but shakes her head, the frown sinking even deeper. Meanwhile Celeste has wedged her fingers into a painful braid to keep them from grabbing her own phone to email Paolo, too. A few minutes ago, she was desperate to leave this place, but now it feels like she's about to lose her grasp of something slippery and important.

"I really don't know what to think," Carla says, and then, in a voice so quietly broken that Celeste can barely hear: "I was starting to plan my son's funeral, for Christ's sake. I wasn't going to wait anymore for them to find the remains. I had the place picked out." She gazes over at Nonna, whose stillness is total, while the machines all around her bed are whirring and clicking in constant motion. "I showed the letter to Merlot. She said since he mailed it before the quake, it doesn't really prove he's still—"

"Well, it proves I was telling the truth."

Carla looks at her with those sad pools in her eyes. "I never thought you were lying, honey. I just thought you were trying to come up with a way for him to be okay, because the alternative's too goddamn awful."

Celeste's sun tattoo looks blurry and dull under the hospital lights. She touches it but feels nothing.

Carla leans closer, takes one of Celeste's hands, and holds it so tight that her knuckles hurt. "You've been looking for him, haven't you? Still. Even after they said we should stop."

Celeste admits that she has.

"Have you found anything?"

She breathes in and out for a few seconds, in time with the beeping of Nonna's heart. Then, in what feels like a single breath, she just releases it all, telling Carla almost everything she knows about what Nicky did that day and maybe after. The Mars book, the aquamarine, the hotel key, the girl from the park . . . everything but the drugs. She steps around that as softly as she can. By the time she's finished, Carla's crying again, but there's a different shine in her eyes now, a light behind them in place of the dark void. It feels good to have put it there, but also a little scary. "It isn't actually much, I guess," Celeste hurries to say. "I still have no *proof*—and no idea where he is, or where to even look."

"But see," Carla says, her voice a little frantic, "if there's even the most teeny tiny chance he's out there—"

"Yeah," Celeste says eagerly, "that's the thing!"

"Especially with Nonna like this. I just know he would want to see her, no matter what." Carla looks away from her mother's bed. A small woman in a hairnet wordlessly carries in a lunch tray that smells of canned vegetables, deposits it on the rolling table perched over Nonna's legs, and leaves. At the squeal of the door, Pop snorts and coughs a couple of times, but he settles back to sleep, head resting on the khaki wad of his jacket. "I'll walk you out," Carla whispers to Celeste. "You don't need to sit in here."

"I don't mind—"

Carla shakes her head, links their arms tightly, and steers her out into the hall. Celeste can feel Carla's body almost buzzing now, the current of new possibilities coursing through her. They file into the elevator behind a crowd of phone-gazers in various hues of scrubs. The lobby is a construction zone, a maze of caution tape and plastic drapes where the waiting rooms used to be, and when they finally make it out into the windy afternoon, Carla says, "Holy God, do I need a smoke. Just hang with me a minute?"

Nearby there's a depressing little fenced corral of smokers hovered around a couple of stone ashtrays. They find a bench, squeezing close together against the cold, and Carla lights her cigarette with a shaking hand, eyeing the other smokers with disgust. "I shouldn't have asked you to come here, sweetie," she says. "This hospital is the effing pits. I just felt like you had to see the letter in person, you know? It's like I wasn't sure it was real, like maybe some asshole was pranking me. But now, Christ, with the stuff you told me . . ." She digs out her phone again, cigarette perched between her teeth, and checks her email a couple of more times before shoving it back in her purse.

After a minute of silent debate with herself, Celeste ventures to ask, "What did Pop say about it?"

"Oh, I can't show him—are you kidding? He's a mess. I can't tell him about any of this—it'll just make everything worse."

"And . . . my parents?"

Carla shakes her head. "I know they want to help. But I'm not sure they'd understand."

"They want me to move on—"

"They're probably right. This isn't good for you."

"But I *can't*, is the thing. It's like, he left, and everything fell apart—like *literally* everything broke that day—and I just don't get how to put it all back together, unless I can find him."

They're both crying again, snot and tears cold on their cheeks. Celeste is wiping her face with the cuff of her sweater, so Carla hands her a packet of Puffs from her bag, which seems to contain an endless supply. They don't say anything while Carla finishes her smoke, blowing up and away from Celeste, making clouds on the clear blue sky. A constant stream of people is passing in both directions, in and out of the hospital, but nobody seems to notice the two of them weeping. Maybe because they'd rather just pretend the sad little smokers don't exist, or maybe because it's become pretty normal, these days, for people to break down on the street, everybody in town carrying some hidden damage, invisible cracks and fissures to match the ones in the street.

At last Carla stubs out her cigarette and says, "You knew about the cheating?"

Celeste nods carefully.

"And your mom, did she know?"

"She wanted Nicky to tell you himself."

Carla's mouth crumples. She stares at the smushed cigarette between her fingers, the ash blowing back into her face from the wind. "I put too much pressure on him," she says, her voice breaking. "I pushed him away."

Celeste thinks probably she should object to this, but instead finds herself reaching into the pocket of her backpack, looking for the smooth ink-black obsidian from Joan the crystal lady. "Here," she says, "it's supposed to heal your sorrow."

Carla closes it in her fist. "I guess it's worth a shot."

Celeste gets up and lifts her bag. There's a strange fizzy kind of feeling in her limbs; it takes her a second to recognize it as hope. Maybe she can get somewhere with that email. Maybe the letter can lead her to Nicky, a ribbon of pink ink she will follow all the way back to his pen. "I should probably go," she says.

Carla wraps her in another hug, then holds her at arm's length to talk to her straight in the face. "Listen, C, honey." She tucks a curl behind Celeste's ear. "We honestly don't know how long Nonna will hang on. After a stroke this bad, things usually just kind of head downhill. Don't you think he would want to see her now?"

Celeste is pretty sure there's only one right answer to this question. "Maybe I can use the email to track him down?" she says. "I'm not sure, but . . . I'll try."

"Tell me if I can help. But let's keep it between us, for now." Carla hugs her again, whispering, "I'll text you, okay?"

There's a flash of candy pink over Carla's shoulder, and Celeste gasps a little, but it's just Fake Nicky. She sighs at him, rolls her eyes. *Can you, like, get in touch with the real Nicky, please? Is that a thing you can do? We really need him right now.* But he doesn't reply, just stands there huddled in his hoodie, even after Carla says goodbye and goes back inside to Nonna and the smell of her lunch and the endlessly beeping IV.

LATER ON, CELESTE IS WITH MEO, AND THEY'RE talking about being left behind. They're in the back seat, radio on low, legs and fingers intertwined, parked on Twin Peaks with the twinkling city spread out below and a blank sky above, like the starry night's flipped upside down. Meo is telling her about the day he put his parents on a plane to Mexico City. They needed to be with his grandparents but knew it would be a long time before they could make it back. He wanted to go, but they told him to go to school, save some money, and send some. Finally submit the DACA forms and do whatever it takes to get his papers.

"They had no choice, right?" he says to Celeste. "But it still feels so fucked up sometimes, that they just left me here." She kisses the line of his jaw, pulls his hand close, and kisses his knuckles and his wrist. She wants to help him like he's been helping her, but there's no mystery about the way his parents are gone, only a fault line of loneliness stretching down along the length of the continent. Celeste can't pretend to understand what it feels like to stand at one end of it while your parents are at the other, but she does know her own left-behind feeling, the empty ache of it. She's only been waking up with that ache for four months, but for Meo it's been *years* of this, almost three and counting.

Celeste feels an idea taking shape, a dark and inviting blur, like the promise of sleep. It might be a mistake, but she knows she's going to do it anyway, a way to help Meo and Nicky all at once. She leans across Meo's lap, and he moves to kiss her, but instead she reaches into her bag and digs around for the tampon box where she hides Nicky's stash. The dealer guys still haven't turned up again—Meo thinks they left town for a while, with so many cops around after the quake—but he's pretty sure they'll be back. She opens the bottle and starts counting the little white pills.

"What the fuck, Celeste—"

"I bet I can sell them at school." Meo's body tenses, and he untangles his legs from hers, shaking his head, but she goes on, "I can probably get even more than Nicky planned, now that it's prom and graduation soon and everything else. I'll pay those guys back and give you the rest to send to your parents."

"No," he says, frowning, "no way. You don't want to get mixed up in that shit."

"Come on, you've been helping me—I want to help you, too."

"I can take care of myself."

"So can I," she says, and somehow it doesn't feel like a lie. Celeste's been surprising herself a lot lately, saying things before even realizing that she believes them. Sometimes when she glimpses her reflection in a store window, she thinks it's a stranger. Would Nicky even recognize this version of her? "I still like having your help," she says.

"You want to tell me how it helps me if you get arrested for dealing?"

He argues a little longer, but eventually she tucks the bottle back in her bag and says, "Listen, you can't stop me anyway. Why don't you just say thank you before I change my mind about this crazy fucking idea?"

Meo's covering his face, rubbing the bridge of his nose. "What?" she says. "You don't trust me?" She crawls back into his lap, kisses the salty little nook below his Adam's apple.

He holds up his hands to surrender. "Just promise you'll be careful."

"Te lo prometo, Romeo," she says, and wraps her arms around his waist.

Day 125

When the shaking stops, she stumbles outside, arms full of her petticoat, picking over the piles of rubble in her heeled boots. Frightened horses are fleeing, screaming, pulling empty carriages. Billows of gray smoke swallow the sky. A house has lost its face, the entire front of it peeled off, rooms still intact inside. Upstairs, Nicky is standing at a dressing table, adjusting his velvet suspenders in a mirror. Suddenly the floor starts to splinter and buckle below his feet. She shouts his name from the street, but he doesn't hear. A rain of sawdust falls in her hair— she's standing too close—a gloved hand grabs her just in time to pull her clear of the collapse. It's Meo, she knows the shape of his grip—but when the dust clears, that's her own hand in the glove. Her own face staring down at her.

"DID YOU FEEL THAT AFTERSHOCK?" IAN SAYS, MAKing small talk while Celeste counts the money. "It woke me up, bro. Think it was the biggest one yet." Of course Celeste dreamed right through it. Hours later, the dream's still perfectly clear—and the shaking was real. She woke up this morning with grit in her hair.

Ian's money's all there, so she slips three packets of pills into his hand. He tucks them into his guitar case, and that's that. Selling Girl Scout cookies was harder. Maybe she'll be able to get rid of them all in a minute. She imagines handing Meo a fat envelope of cash. "Limited time only," Celeste says. "Tell your friends."

"Stop by the crew party after prom and try them yourself?"

"No thanks."

He waves the guitar at her and heads down the spiral staircase, passing Bridget on the way. How long has she been standing there? Celeste was so preoccupied with looking unsuspicious that she never even heard Bridget's clogs on the metal stairs. She clomps the rest of the way up and emerges onto the roof, where Celeste is camped out on a bench near the empty fishbowl classroom, the cracked glass dome still roped off with caution tape, sparkling in the sun. There's a little Astroturf field up here, some benches where the seniors usually take over at lunch, but today it's deserted (technically still off-limits). Ursa is sprawled on the warm turf, happily panting, and Celeste's got her shoes off. She can see clear across the treetops all the way to the water, where the horizon dissolves in a haze.

She braces herself for a hug, but Bridget just falls onto the opposite end of the bench with a sigh. She's wearing a yellow flowery dress, black fishnets with yellow clogs; the overall effect is reminiscent of a bee, which could of course be either cute or dangerous. "What was that about?" Bridget says.

"What, Ian? He was just—the crew party—"

"Uh-huh. So, why'd you ask me to come up here, Celeste? I'm not going to buy any shit from you."

"What? No, I wasn't—"

"I heard you were dating some dealer kid. What the fuck?"

Celeste sits up straighter, tucks her feet back into her shoes, feeling suddenly too naked. "He's not a dealer," she says. "Nicky was selling them. This is, like, the last of his stash—"

"I couldn't give two shits about the pills. Why didn't you tell me you were dating someone? Instead, I have to hear it from Callie Tran, who saw you get in this Haight kid's car, I guess? And then somebody else saw you guys all over each other in the park." She waits, winding that distractingly shiny hair around her fist. Celeste can't think of anything to say. It never even occurred to her to tell Bridget, or any of their other friends, about Meo. Lately she's been sort of floating in and out of school like a moth, never landing anywhere long enough to get noticed. Even before, she wasn't the type to go around bragging about her few hookups.

"I guess I didn't feel like sharing."

Bridget launches herself off the bench with a frustrated groan. "You know what? I'm really busy, prom committee and shit. I'm gonna go."

"Wait, can you just—"

"I don't get it, Celeste. I sort of fucking thought we were friends, but you've been acting like your only friend is dead. Do you even get that, like, there are other people on the planet who give a crap about you? Oh, and by the way, other people miss him, too." She heads for the stairs, wind whipping the yellow dress. Celeste gets up to follow. It might be so much safer to let Bridget leave, in all the ways, but now that Celeste's hurtling into the black hole anyway, safe doesn't really feel like an option anymore.

"He found Ursa," she calls, and Bridget stops at the stairs. The dog stretches and ambles over to Bridget, who crouches to pet her ears and scruff.

"I saw the posters," Bridget says quietly. "I wanted to help look for her, but you never texted me back."

"I was a mess, I'm sorry. But Meo—he totally rescued her. He saved her! And then, I don't know, it's like we have this crazy connection."

Bridget sighs, relenting, with a sly smile. "I've seen him around. The kid with the eyes? He's hot."

"I know, right?" They laugh a little bit, wandering back to the bench. Ursa rests her heavy head between them on the warm metal. Celeste feels lighter, a froth of relief bubbling up in her chest. She leans in to lower her voice even though they're alone; only Ursa's listening, and she already knows it all. "The thing is," she says, "he's been helping me look for Nicky."

"Wait, what?"

"Just listen for a sec, okay?" She tells Bridget a version of things that ends with Carla's letter. After sending a note about Nonna to PaoloReborn@hotmail.com, Celeste spent the weekend wildly checking her email every four seconds, and in the interim three seconds trying to break into the Paolo account with every conceivable password she could imagine, scouring the Mars book and her memory for ideas.

Bridget rolls her eyes. "That only works in the movies."

"Yeah, so that's why I asked you to meet me. I need to see that Hotmail account, Bridge. I need to know if he ever logged into it after the quake, and maybe where and when."

Bridget narrows her eyes.

"I guess I was hoping you could . . ."

Bridget folds her arms and leans away on the bench. She picks at dandelions in a sad planter box and looks out to the water under the gathering fog. "You know," she says, "this is fucked up, Celeste. I mean, you ditched that dumb memorial, but I sat there and listened to all the speeches and shit, and cried my fuckin' eyes out, and my therapist put me on like, a double dose of my Celexa, and now you're telling me Nicky's actually *not* dead after all? But you don't officially know, like *maybe* he's not dead? And you want me to do something that—oh, by the way, might in fact be kind of *criminal*"—she pauses to throw her arms in the air for a giant air quote—"just in case he's not actually dead. Are you psychotic?"

"Very possibly," Celeste says, trying to sound jokey, but she can also feel this chance slipping away, so she grabs Bridget's hand fiercely, and then a cloud helps her out by passing over the sun, making everything gray and serious. "But if he *isn't* actually dead? Don't you want to at least know for sure?"

Bridget curls her mouth in a skeptical frown but nods. Celeste hugs her without thinking, hanging on too long, but Bridget seems cool with it. She's the kind of person who never lets go first. Afterward, they take turns feeding Ursa treats before they head to class together. On the stairs, Celeste texts the Paolo Reborn email address to Bridget.

"I really don't have time for this," Bridget says. "Stanford interview tomorrow. And the fucking prom committee."

"Wait, so—since when are you on prom committee?"

Bridget rolls her eyes. "Somebody had to stop Oona. She wanted the theme to be an eighties movie, fine, but then she picked *Sixteen Candles*, can you believe that? That movie's racist as fuck. I made her change it."

Celeste laughs. "So, what's the new theme?"

"Actually, it's *Dune*."

Celeste laughs again, but Bridget says, "I'm serious, it's *Dune*. I suggested it. I wanted it to be, like, a tribute to Nicky."

Celeste's a little stunned, stumbling over Ursa as they come downstairs into the dim senior hall, where everybody's filing between classes, passing their phones around and slamming lockers. Nicky always carries *Dune* in his backpack, marked up in pink ink, so warped and worn that it's lost the back cover. He's always reading his favorite parts in the in-between times of day, when they're waiting for the bus or just getting stoned on a weekend with nothing else to do. It took Celeste six months to get through it in eighth grade; when she tried to give up on it, he threatened to break up with her as a friend. Nicky thinks *Star Wars* is a total *Dune* rip-off, and everybody knows if you're dumb enough to try to argue the opposite at a party, you can forget about partying, because he'll hound you for the rest of the night with beery lectures. He even loves the old version of the movie, which nobody else has ever loved; this is a true thing about him, not some flattering bullshit somebody wrote for a memorial. For the first time now, Celeste takes actual notice of the prom banners hanging up and down the senior hall, which do indeed have a *Dune* thing going on, the turquoise moon and an eerie desert sunset, and even the same-ish font as the *Dune* book cover.

"That's really nice," she says to Bridget, trying not to cry.

"Most of these idiots probably don't even get it, but whatever. Will you bring the new boy?"

Last summer Celeste and Nicky made plans to be senior prom dates, one day when they were trying on costumes at the old-timey photo place at the Wharf. "We'll rent this stuff and do like, a whole gold rush look!" Nicky gushed, admiring himself in a hilarious frog-green top hat in the greasy mirror. Celeste picked out a plaid hoop dress with a ruffly corset. When she asked what they would do if one of them had a boyfriend when prom rolled around, Nicky scoffed and said, "We'll share him. Hypothetical love interest can be our servant boy. I bet he'll look cute in short pants." Which is true, Meo would.

"I'm not in the mood," she tells Bridget, who leans her head on Celeste's shoulder.

"I wonder when you're going to come the fuck back to earth," Bridget says softly. They stop in front of chem lab. "This is me. I'll see what I can do about the email. But not till after prom, okay?"

Celeste thanks her, allows another hug, and heads down the hall with Ursa to AP Government, which she's barely attended this semester. She's not even sure what branch they're studying now—judicial, maybe? Instead of figuring it out before walking into class, she checks her email again. A new message pops up, but it's not from Paolo Reborn. The sender is the MIT admissions office. Must be junk, Celeste thinks, or worse, some office intern reaching out at last to ask why her transcripts and scores and FAFSA stuff came in without an actual application to the school. But it's none of those things. It's an interview offer. An MIT alum, somebody called Sarah Varma, is inviting Celeste to her home for an interview next week. Celeste reads the email several times through, but it still neglects to mention that she never, in fact, applied to MIT at all. The hallway empties out, doors slamming shut, silence gathering while she reads it very slowly again, trying to understand. She feels a little nauseous. Sun streams in through the skylights, baking the lockers, intensifying the smell of sneakers and salami.

"Celeste?" It's Ms. Tanaka, munching chocolate pretzels. She has that same look of concerned disappointment that Bonnie's been carrying around—must be contagious. "Are you okay? Shouldn't you be heading to class?"

"What? I . . . Uh, yeah, no, I—" But Celeste can't stop staring at the phone. It's like she's trying to decipher some ancient hieroglyphics; she knows there's a deeper meaning there but can't grasp it yet.

"Celeste, honey, you need to put away the phone and get to class."

"Actually, I'm late for Ackerman." The college counselor? What possessed her? She's been avoiding him for weeks, hurrying to the bathroom whenever he pops up in the hall, ignoring his emails.

"Okay, cool. Can I walk you down there?"

"No thanks!" And she takes off with Ursa through the empty building, downstairs to the counselors' offices. His door is open, as always. At the last moment—already close enough to see that he's shopping for camping gear on his laptop, eating pad Thai from a takeout box—she tries to hurry past, but he calls after her, "Hey, stranger, come on in!" She leans in the doorway, waiting as he wipes his mouth with a bandanna and sets his lunch aside. "How can I help you, Celeste? Actually, I was hoping you'd stop by. I've been getting kinda nervous about what I'm hearing from your teachers. Missed a few tests this semester? I mean, it's normal, okay? But not really for a student like you. Good news is, schools are being *pret-ty* understanding this year with kids from quake-affected areas. So that's a silver lining, right? I mean, not to make light. But at least we can relax a little bit about your grades."

While he's babbling, Celeste keeps herself busy winding Ursa's leash into a coil and glancing around everywhere except at his noodle-greasy mouth. Scruffy Mr. A is kind of cute in a rock-climbing-yogi sort of way, but for somebody with the word *counseling* on his office door, he's a horrendous listener. By the time he gets around to "So anyway, how's it going?" she's almost forgotten why her heart is racing and her forehead's damp with panicky sweat.

"Um, so—I got an interview offer?" she says. "From MIT."

"All right, that's awesome!" He reaches across the desk to give her a high five, but all she can manage is an air fist bump. "Hey, thanks for telling me! That means a lot to me, Celeste, that you took the time to come down here." He presses his palms together and offers a weird little bow. "Seriously, thanks. I usually have to chase people down for updates."

"It's just—I thought there might've been a problem with my application? So, I was just—"

He waves her off with his napkin, burping silently into his fist. "Nah, really, everything must be on track if you got an interview. It means they're serious about you. Definitely no interview offer unless your app's good to go."

"But—"

"Celeste, congrats, this is big! And don't worry, okay? Just show up and be your awesome self. That's all they really wanna see."

He gives her a thumbs-up before turning back to his noodles and sleeping bags. She mutters a thank-you and wanders off, following Ursa slowly upstairs to the skylit science hall, and higher up to the closed-off roof and the cracked fishbowl again. A heavy fog has started to roll over the roof, and the distant ocean Celeste could see so clearly a few minutes ago is now completely obscured. She waits on the bench, momentarily paralyzed by confusion and fear. Then a car alarm below snaps her out of it, and she digs out her laptop to log in to her MIT admissions account.

The last time she remembers doing this was the day when the governor declared Nicky dead. The application then was a single lame paragraph of a diabetes essay and the biographical information. Now her application is somehow complete. Submitted March 9. In process of review. There's a checklist with all the items neatly, impossibly checked off.

She opens the essay questions she doesn't remember answering. Turns out she did actually write these answers, but not for the application; it's her writing, some of it private, some of it from school assignments, all of it edited to fit the questions. An odd but kind of funny little piece she did for government about how world leaders should be forced to go and live together on the International Space Station. A few paragraphs from a comp class essay about playing hide-and-seek in Symphony Hall when she was a kid, listening to her dad's clear-hearted violin from inside a coat closet. And then that lame paragraph of the diabetes essay, rendered a little less lame, she has to admit, by a second paragraph that seems to have mysteriously made its way here from the depths of her Google Docs: a wild-eyed, deeply private rant about the insulin pump and how she's the only person who should get to decide what to do with her body.

What. The. Fuck.

"Am I insane?" she pleads with Ursa, who responds by resting her head in Celeste's lap and closing her eyes. She tries to breathe in time with Ursa to calm her brain. One, two, three breaths . . . When she gets to five, Celeste notices Fake Nicky standing by the fishbowl with his hand on a shattered pane, tracing the jagged cracks with a fingertip. "Don't touch that," she tells him, but he laughs it off. *You think it's gonna hurt me? I'm not exactly corporeal over here.* She covers her face for a moment, rubbing her brow, and when she looks up again, Fake Nicky is sitting right next to her, long legs crossed in front of him. He leans close to her ear and whispers, *I did it, dummy.* And the explanation takes its time to settle in her brain, viscous and toxic-smelling, like a stream of white glue.

It's possible he did it. Filled out all the paperwork. Pasted her writing into the essay questions. She thinks of that time after freshman year when they didn't speak for days—the time he stole her notebook, typed her Mars story, and sent it off to that contest. Faking a whole application was trickier, of course, but nothing Nicky couldn't handle. Celeste's own passwords aren't crafty like Paolo's. He probably could've done it all—busted into her Google Docs and her admissions account, submitted the application to MIT—all on some library computer, God knows where—just by guessing Gemini2007.

It's crazy, but maybe just the right amount of crazy for this fucked-up antigravity version of her life. Suddenly sweaty in spite of the fog, Celeste strips off her sweater and starts pacing around the broken fishbowl. Maybe there's another explanation, some other mysterious application angel who cared and knew enough. But the only candidates she can think of are her parents, and they could never pull off a stunt like this. In a million years it wouldn't even occur to them to try.

It was Nicky. It's got to be Nicky.

A hot swirly nebula is expanding in her core, but everywhere else: empty and numb. What the fuck is she supposed to feel. Fury? Gratitude? None of it makes sense.

Fake Nicky's still lounging on the bench with Ursa. *Did you think I was just gonna let you trash our lifelong dream? Hell no!*

"You trashed it first!"

Touché, Cookie, but still.

"Jesus, shut up and let me think!"

I had a feeling you were going to fall to pieces when I left.

"Shut the fuck *up*!" A bolt of anger, neon hot, shoots out of the nebula and rips down her leg. She swivels and kicks a cracked pane of the fishbowl, shattering it with the toe of her boot, the sound persisting long after the shattering is done. In the hard-breathing silence afterward, she leans on an iron rail and watches the rush of traffic, faceless cars carrying faceless souls to their destinations, people endlessly deciding and deciding, piling their decisions into lives.

And then she realizes what it really means.

Submitted March 9.

If he did this, then he's still alive.

Day 134

Sarah Varma's front door is the color of a blue M&M. When Sarah opens it just a crack to peek out, Celeste can see that her hair is dyed that color, too, from roots to tips, piled in a topknot almost as big as her head itself, with a pair of thick black glasses perched below it, as if there were another actual pair of eyes up there.

"Hi there!" Sarah says with a familiar-sounding British accent, warm and friendly even as she holds the door almost closed. "Look, here's the thing—my cat is a total asshole, and I'd rather avoid the lawsuit that would inevitably result if he were to, I don't know, *maul* or *maim* your highly trained service dog? So I'm just gonna go lock him in the bathroom. Gimme a second."

She shuts the M&M door again, leaving Celeste and Ursa on the stoop. It's an old Victorian building with flowery scrollwork, but everything except the door's been painted the same chalkboard black, a look that has been cropping up all over town in the rebuilds. This is probably supposed to be stylish, but it creeps Celeste out, like the houses themselves are in mourning. It looks like a techie house, but Celeste doesn't actually know if Sarah Varma's a techie. It might've been a good idea to google her before coming here, but Celeste's been busy reeling about the MIT application, driving Meo crazy with her endless speculative babbling. He's been kind and patient, though. He even drove her on a traffic-clogged tour of all the open libraries in town, going on the theory that Nicky might've used public internet to hack her account; Celeste flashed the pink fliers at all the librarians, but no dice. Besides Meo, the only person she's told about the application is Carla, whom she swore to secrecy, dreading the eventual confrontation with her parents. She hadn't planned to tell Carla at all, but then there was bad news about Nonna—a discouraging MRI—and so Celeste couldn't bear to keep it from her, this potential evidence of life. Hiccupping through tears, Carla made Celeste agree to do the interview, to take it as a gift. But up until the moment when she actually rang the doorbell, she had no idea if she would go through with this at all.

The door flings open, Sarah looking winded and relieved as she takes Celeste's hand between both of hers. "God, I'm sorry," she says, "that wasn't a very nice first impression, was it? I should've put Nermal away before I came to the door. I read about your dog in your essays—"

"It's okay," Celeste mumbles. "Ursa's actually trained to ignore cats?"

The woman laughs—a large, unapologetic laugh that spirals out of her like a song. "Yeah, but Nermal's notorious, though. All the neighborhood dogs loathe him. *Such* an embarrassment." She asks to pet the dog and kneels to scratch behind her ears. "No offense, Ursa, but you're no match for Nermal," she says. "Come on, let's get you a treat." She waves Celeste into the front room, then disappears down a narrow hall. "Making us some tea! You like it sweet?"

"Oh, just plain, thanks." Celeste clears her throat—she can't seem to speak above a whisper, which isn't going to work in the face of that laugh—and lowers herself to the edge of a green velvet couch. She finds a tub of lip gloss in the bottom of her bag and hastily smudges it on.

What, Celeste wonders, is she doing here, exactly? She feels guilty, like somebody with a nefarious ulterior motive, but with no idea what that motive might be. She considers leaving but doesn't especially want to. It's nice here, happily cluttered. The room smells a little fruity, like an empty bottle of wine or a jar of applesauce. There are baskets of toddler toys by the fireplace; several pearly-shelled guitars hanging on the wall; a desk at the bay window piled with disheveled papers; and, best of all, in the corner, strung at different heights from the vaulted ceiling, a solar system of glowing glass orbs. The planets—all but Venus, strangely—swirling with color from within, are almost imperceptibly turning in the light breeze from a window.

Sarah comes back from the kitchen with a brass tray and two steaming mugs of chai, kicking a few toys into the fireplace on the way.

"Nice planets," Celeste says, summoning her voice at normal volume.

"Oh yeah, thanks! My wife made them, actually, for a wedding present. We lost Venus in the quake, though."

"She *made* them?"

"Yeah, she's one of those people with like, a thousand really difficult hobbies. Hence the guitars. She's good at all of them, too.

It's exhausting, to be honest." She laughs again, feeds Ursa a dog cookie, and settles into a beat-up leather armchair, tucking her legs beneath her. "So! Starting over now. Celeste! Hello and welcome!" She smiles. "Thanks for coming to talk to me. I know it probably feels really weird to just show up at a stranger's house and put on a command performance. This whole college thing is a bit bonkers, isn't it? Even more bonkers than when I applied forever ago. How are you doing with all of it?"

"Um . . ." Celeste sips the chai, fragrant with spice. "Not that great, I guess?"

A bitter little laugh jumps out of her mouth, but Sarah just says warmly, "I know, it's such a slog. Well, listen, hang in there—it's almost over. We'll just chat for a bit, and then I'll set you free, okay? So let's start with why you want to go to MIT."

Celeste stares at the carpet. Sarah probably thinks she's lobbed a softball, but Celeste can't imagine where to start. With Nicky and NASA and their big old plans, all of which seem so preposterous now? She casts around for a diversion. In the middle of a long and drawn-out drink of tea, she realizes that she has this same orange coffee mug at home; it's a freebie from her favorite science podcast, the one where she and Nicky heard about solar wind and the Golden Record.

"I have this mug, too," she says. "You listen to *PodLab*?"

Sarah laughs again. "Yeah, more than I'd like! I'm actually one of the producers."

"What, you are? For real?"

Sarah goes to the desk and finds a business card with the *PodLab* logo, molecular diagrams arranged into the letters. So that's why she sounds familiar: She's been the voice in Celeste's earbuds on Muni, or walking home from school, or on the little speaker in her warm room, listening with Nicky on a sunny afternoon, lying on the pillows with a galaxy of dust motes swirling over their heads.

"Oh my God, I totally recognize your voice! You're—Europa Varma? But—"

"Yeah, I go by Europa, actually. My middle name. MIT can't seem to get its institutional brain around it, though." She offers a little shrug.

"Oh, okay," Celeste says, feeling inexplicably dumb. "That's so cool! I mean, I love your show."

"Aw, thanks. Okay, MIT, this one's a winner!" Sarah/Europa laughs, spilling a few drops of chai into her lap. *The sun has a wind,* Celeste can remember her saying, *and beyond the reach of the wind, there's a giant pause.* The word *pause* in her accent sounding sort of sultry, with a deep curve in the middle *u*. It's an epic coincidence, really, but Celeste isn't all that shocked. Since the quake, her life's become a mess of these strange connections and flukes, like a pile of tangled wires whose naked ends sometimes happen to find each other and spark. What was it Joan the crystal lady said? *When the faults move, all kinds of energies are released.* Celeste still doesn't really know what that means, but she finds herself believing it anyway. The sun on her wrist begins to prickle and glow. Shyly she pulls back her sleeve to show it to Europa. She tells her the story about the twin tattoos, the podcast episode, and the sounds from the Golden Record.

"Seriously, I'm honored," Europa says. "I don't think I've ever inspired an actual tattoo before. And now you're here for your interview? That's wild!"

Celeste tucks the business card into her phone case. The pissed-off cat starts yowling from the bathroom, but Ursa only lets a single ear perk up.

"They try and match people by their interests now, I think? Which is good," Europa says. "I remember the guy who interviewed me was old, kind of pervy, maybe like a banker or something? *Not* a good fit. But I guess he must've liked me." She laughs again. "Right, that brings me back to *you*, handily. Because you're a writer, aren't you, like me? I mean, Celeste, really, these essays! I can tell you it's rare to find somebody who writes like you and has a great mind for science, too—very impressive."

A terrified little smile pulls at the corners of Celeste's mouth. Her teachers have always liked her writing, but nobody's ever called her a writer before; she doesn't want Europa to get the wrong idea. "Yeah, I don't really write for, like, public consumption? I mean, I had this thing in a magazine once, but my best friend submitted it, the tattoo guy. It's a long story."

"Come on, tell," Europa says. "That's why we're here."

Celeste takes a deep breath, sits on the palms of her hands. "Okay . . . so I used to babysit these twin girls, they were like, six or seven? And one night they were playing house, or that kind of game, but on Mars. And there was a law against boys in their Martian town, which I thought was hilarious, so . . . after they went to sleep, I just kind of took their idea, I guess." She tells Europa about the story, the Martian colony of women and girls, their mail-order XX sperm from Earth, their matriarchal government. "And then my friend Nicky, he just sent it in to this contest without even asking me."

"Wow, sounds really ballsy."

"Yeah, that's kind of how he is."

"Oh, no, actually I was talking about your story. Like a feminist spec-fiction take on the space colony narrative—I love it! Can I read it? Send me a copy later, maybe?"

"Oh—um, okay, sure."

"I loved your piece about the ISS, too, the one in your application. I just think it's great how you have this really fresh, imaginative point of view about space science. You want to talk about that a bit?" She waits, her eyebrows arched expectantly under the blue hair crown, the planets stirring gently over her head. Celeste can't blame her for actually trying to conduct an interview, but answering questions is making her feel increasingly like a fraud; Europa's kindness and compliments sound genuine enough, but Celeste is pretty sure they're intended for somebody else. After a few moments of awkward silence, Europa stage-whispers behind her hand, "Help me out here?"

"I'm sorry, I guess I'm just not much of a talker."

Europa sets her tea down on the brass tray and leans over her lap, sliding her glasses onto her nose to regard Celeste at close range. Surely from there, Celeste thinks, she can see how cheap this disguise really is—the peeling paint and sloppy stitches of it. "That's interesting," Europa says, "because you obviously have *a lot* to say."

"Maybe I should just go." Celeste grabs her backpack, but Europa gently takes it away and sets it down in the pile of toys.

"You want to try something? Follow me." She heads back down the narrow hall, her bangles jingling. Ursa hops up—after all, the cookies came from down that hall before—so Celeste reluctantly follows. They pass the locked bathroom, to Nermal's frenzied dismay, and continue through a messy, onion-smelling kitchen and out the back door, down some rickety steps into a yard overgrown with nasturtium and calla lilies. There's an avocado tree with a tricycle parked beneath it and, all the way at the back of the lot, a red metal shipping container with a door cut in the side. Europa struggles with the lock and finally busts through. Celeste and Ursa follow her out of the sun and into a dim room.

It's a studio, just like the one Celeste's dad spent years building in their basement—the same padded gray walls and thick gray carpet; the same kind of soundboard, a jewel box of dials and buttons—except instead of instruments, there's audio equipment: leggy microphones perched and hanging like rare birds, a canopy of wire vines looped and threaded over the ceiling and walls. Celeste feels the same sense of hushed wonder she always felt walking into Shane's studio when she was little, the sense of a place where mysteries might be coiled in the corners, waiting for you to charm them out into the light.

Europa pulls up a wheelie stool and starts fiddling with the board. "Sometimes I have an interview on the show," she says, "and maybe it's a really brainy scientist, you know, or someone like that? And I'm thinking, *Damn, this person's going to be so shy and scared on mic,* and then when they get in front of it with the headphones on, suddenly it's Howard Stern time. Like all they needed was to really *hear* their own voice." She slides her bangles off and drops them into a felt tray. She explains: "If I move my arm even the most *infinitesimal* bit while we're recording, these'll just obliterate the track."

"Wait, we're recording?"

"Yeah, I thought we might."

"But—I'm not recording. I hate the way my voice sounds, in videos and stuff."

"Everybody does. This is different."

Celeste's still hovering near the door, frowning at her feet.

"All right, look, I can't *make* you do it. But it's really kind of fun. And you're here for an interview, right? So, let's do an interview. I'll delete it after, if you want." She picks up a pair of giant headphones and holds them out to Celeste, who slides them on just because it feels too late to back out of this now. But when she's got the pillowy cups fastened over her ears, she feels an instant calm. The silence is total, except for her own breath and pulse. Europa draws up a chair for her, slides a shining silver microphone across the desk. She speaks into one side of it, and her honeyed voice spills directly into Celeste's brain, her real voice out there making a faint echo.

"Okay, let's see . . . how about you read one of your application essays? You know, just to hear yourself. And then we talk. Does that make it easier? I'll pull one up on my phone. MIT sends us all the stuff." Europa's already scrolling to find the essay in her email. She hands over the phone. "Read this one? It's my favorite."

Tell us about a time when you stood up for your personal values or beliefs, reads the prompt, and then there's Celeste's answer, magically conjured, the curse words deftly replaced with application-friendly alternatives. She remembers writing these furious paragraphs in a hospital bed, in the middle of the night, while her mother slept nearby in a vinyl recliner. Celeste had gotten a bad infection after tearing out her brand-new insulin pump in a fit of stoned defiance, and the doctors and her parents had spent the better part of a day trying to convince her to let them put the pump back in. She continued to refuse, and when they were all gone or asleep, in the lonely hospital half dark, she took out her iPad and wrote. They were deeply private words then, and they still are; she's never knowingly shown them to anyone. When she starts to read into the microphone, it feels like telling herself a secret. She describes what happened that day, the arguments with the doctors, her parents crying and pleading. She tells Europa, too, who listens without looking, gently adjusting the dials on the board. Celeste begins to wonder if the dials are in fact controlling her actual voice, which seems to open wide and grow stronger as she reads.

"I've hated my body, but not for the reasons other girls hate their bodies. For me it's not about being thin or beautiful or different or the same. I've hated my body for being a traitor, a sneak, a two-faced lying asshole. For acting like we're cool and then betraying me five minutes later, just for kicks. Sometimes I scream at myself in the mirror, *You think this is funny?* But my body isn't laughing. If anything, when I shout at her, she looks a little hurt. After all, we're in this together. My body, no matter how much I hate it, is mine. It might be the only thing I'll ever truly own.

"So, when they try to tell me I have no choice—I have to do this thing, to hook myself to a machine that pumps me full of chemicals, to sleep with the machine and have sex with the machine, forever and ever—I tell them no. My fucked-up body is mine." *Messed-up,* says the version on the phone, but Celeste restores the original word, spitting a little on the mic with the force of it. Europa smiles at her sideways, dialing something down. "Maybe they're right. Maybe the pump would make life easier. More convenient. Less dangerous. They're trying to keep me safe, my parents and the doctors. They call themselves my *team,* like we're all trying to win something together. But my body and I know there isn't going to be any winning. We're stuck with this disease. And we aren't going to wear a machine for the rest of our lives."

The last line isn't here on Europa's phone—Nicky must've edited it out, but Celeste remembers it—she remembers typing it just before her mom startled awake and rushed to the side of the hospital bed, frantic from a dream. "I thank my lucky stars for Ursa," she says, and the dog lifts her head sweetly, then cradles it between her paws.

Celeste slumps against the back of the chair with a nervous laugh.

"Right, Celeste, that was brilliant! So honest and powerful. Really great stuff. D'you want to hear it?" But Europa doesn't wait for an answer, just messes around for a moment with her computer and then points to the headphones just as Celeste's own voice begins to radiate through them. She listens in wonder. Europa is right—it's different. She sounds fierce and whole. She sounds like herself, but also like somebody else entirely, somebody she would like to get to know.

"Wow," she says when it's done.

"Yes, I agree!" Europa leans back in the wheelie chair, grinning across the table. She's really beautiful, but not in a way that Celeste is sexually attracted to—in a way that makes her think, *I hope I'm beautiful like that*. She has kind of crooked teeth, but they only make her more beautiful. "Better, then?" Europa says. "You feel like talking now?" Celeste agrees. She almost never feels like talking, but the microphone seems to be a different kind of listener entirely.

"Okay, let's try a question again. Why do you want to go to MIT? Go ahead and tell the mic if you can't tell me."

All at once Celeste understands how she wants to answer, but also, she's afraid. She stares down into the mesh bulb of the microphone, thousands of tiny tunnels waiting to swallow her voice. What happens when she sends the words tumbling down those tunnels? What if one of them is the black hole itself, only a vast emptiness at its core? Nothing left, she guesses, but to hurl herself in.

"Honestly?" she says to Europa. "I don't."

THEY TALK FOR THE REST OF THE AFTERNOON. TIME seems to shrink and stretch in the windowless studio (true to the character of black holes). The story she tells Europa about how her application made its way to MIT loops back in time and forward again so freely that Celeste begins to wonder if her almost eighteen years on this planet did in fact progress in a linear fashion at all. But Europa seems perfectly willing to follow the loops, lingering in the stretches and speeding into the curves along with Celeste, sometimes offering thoughts or questions at just the right times, just when she's about to careen off track.

At first, as usual, she is talking about Nicky. But eventually she starts to talk about herself. Whether it's by her own design or Europa's, she isn't sure. For all Celeste knows, there might've been some kind of truth serum sprinkled into the chai, or maybe like an enchanted gas pumping through the studio vents. But she feels more powerful the more she talks, more in possession of the story than ever before. She admits things to Europa that she hasn't yet admitted to herself. That NASA was really Nicky's dream, never quite hers. That it always felt too scary to try to figure out her own. That she always felt safest letting Nicky be the star, staying comfortably in orbit around him, until he was gone.

"Mixing those metaphors a bit, though, aren't you?" Europa says gently, fiddling with the dials again. "I mean, you're the twin suns—which are binary stars, right? You're not a planet in Nicky's system." Celeste flips her wrist over and draws a circle with her finger around the sun. She's always thought of it as a friendship tattoo, not an expression of herself. Maybe it's both. She wonders if Nicky sees it that way, too.

After a while Europa disappears into the house, promising snacks. Through the half-open studio door, Celeste can see that the garden's gone dusky and pink. She gets up to stretch her legs and can't resist poking around the studio, running her fingertips over the soundboard, lifting the corners of papers, hoping to sneak a glimpse of something *PodLab*-related. There are lots of notes about wind farms, a whole pile of stuff about gene editing in China. But the biggest pile, with the most coffee stains and page flags, has to do with the *Pioneer* launch, now just a few weeks away. There are storyboards and interview notes, printouts of emails from NASA. Tacked on a corkboard, some photos: spectacular shots of the ruddy, storm-tossed Martian landscape where, nine or ten months from now, humans will likely walk. Celeste's still looking through the photos in awe when Europa edges back through the door, cradling a big ceramic bowl of bow-tie pasta sprinkled with curls of parmesan. Celeste slaps the file closed. "Oh sorry, I wasn't—"

"Leftovers!" Europa says. "I'm starved, aren't you starved?"

"I really wasn't snooping, I was just—"

Europa waves her off. "Nothing secret there. What do you think of them? Kind of standard stuff, right? I was hoping for better. I'm telling you, it's like pulling teeth with NASA on this thing. You'd think they'd be falling over themselves to get press right now, after all this time." She folds herself back into the chair. "Everybody's so nervous over there, is the thing. And I get it. My life's going to be insane until the launch. This story's eating us all alive." She nudges the bowl toward Celeste, who shyly stacks a bite on her fork. Pasta is generally a bad idea for her, but she hasn't eaten in a while, and her sugar's probably on the low side; she doesn't want to bother checking, won't risk breaking the dreamy spell of this weird afternoon. The noodles are cold and buttery. Sitting with Europa and sharing from the big bowl makes her feel a longing she can't quite place. For a time, maybe, when she felt close like this with her mom, when they would share a pint of ice cream or eat handfuls of cereal out of the box together in front of the TV. The last time they did that was probably before the diagnosis. Sixth grade? A lifetime ago.

"You okay?" Europa says. "Thinking about Mars?"

Celeste smiles. "Will you be in Florida for the launch?"

"Regrettably, yes."

"Regrettably?!"

"No, I mean, it's *amazing*, obviously, but there's just so much hype, and you know the chances of something going wrong are really wildly high. We could get stuck there waiting for it all to go down for *days*. And my crew's already worn out from quake coverage, and family stuff after the quake and everything. It's been a year. Well, you know."

Celeste takes another bite. "Nicky and I, it's crazy, but we used to talk a lot about going. The launch date's actually our birthday."

Europa laughs. "Oh, this just gets weirder and weirder."

"I know. When they announced the date, we basically didn't stop shrieking for days."

"Well, listen, you should still go, Celeste. Give yourself a birthday gift. It's going to be such a scene. And when it happens . . ." Europa leans back in her chair, presses her hand against her chest and draws a gasp, like she's watching it right now with the rumble of the rockets in her feet. She says, "There's just nothing else like that moment."

Celeste concentrates on stacking more bow ties on her fork. She's never traveled by herself before. There was that one summer when Mimi wanted to send her to Haiti to join a Habitat project; Celeste got sick the night before, alternately throwing up and dozing in her parents' bed. To this day she isn't sure if it was a stomach bug or just her body's way of chickening out. Cape Canaveral isn't Haiti, of course, but the thought of going alone still makes her queasy, and there isn't anyone else she'd want to ask, not even Meo, who puts up with her space talk sometimes but doesn't really give a shit about it. It's only Nicky, really, who would gladly wedge in a tent with her on the crowded beach and wait in line for hours with all the other nerds.

Europa's watching Celeste through her glasses again with that penetrating look. By now Celeste is pretty damn sure those aren't just regular glasses. Europa seems to pop them on whenever she's getting ready to read Celeste's mind. After a moment she leans over the bowl and starts gathering the last of the noodles. "Want to know a cool thing about the sun and its hypothetical twin?" she asks Celeste. "So—they're made of the same stuff, right? Their composition is basically identical. Metal levels, chemical abundance, all of it's going to be the same. So, if the sun really does have a twin out there, it probably has its *own* system of planets, really similar to ours, and there might even be *life* on one of those planets, too."

"Yeah," Celeste says, "I've read that."

"Okay, so maybe you already understand what I'm trying to tell you, then? I'm trying to speak your language here, with the space metaphors, okay? Because, you know—it's not like you asked me, but I'm really good at unsolicited life advice."

Celeste slides to the edge of her stool, leaning as if she might either fall or spring to her feet.

"I'm going to tell MIT to withdraw your application, obviously; you know that. But I think you should also know that you were on your way to getting in, Celeste, and not because of Nicky, not really. Right? So just remember that, when you're thinking about what comes next? Which you should start doing."

Celeste doesn't know whether to burst into tears and throw her arms around Europa or yank those psychic glasses off her face and stomp them to bits. Luckily, she doesn't need to decide, because the door swings open and an adorable knee-high boy in railroad overalls whirls in, screaming "Mummy!" and latches himself onto Europa's legs.

"Hallo, my darling!" She gathers the boy in her lap and kisses his curly head. "Did you have a lovely day?"

"Mama says I can't have a brownie till *after* dinner!"

"Well, that seems reasonable enough." She smiles at Celeste. "Come on, we'll walk you out."

They wind their way back through the yard and the house, Nermal squalling from behind the bathroom door, the little boy hanging on patient Ursa's neck. Europa stops to kiss her wife, who's on the phone, standing over a cutting board in the kitchen, with some kind of Frenchy-sounding jazz in the background; she smiles at Celeste over her shoulder and waves. Celeste follows Europa the rest of the way out, wishing she could somehow tuck herself in the corner to watch their evening unfold, this life of cooking and kissing and talking into a microphone about Mars.

Europa dispatches her son to the pile of toys by the fireplace and hugs Celeste at the door. "Listen," she says, "I'm not saying don't be sad, or don't keep looking for your friend, or whatever. I just think it's time to start thinking of yourself as the most important person in your life. Because, honestly, you might as well get in the habit now. It only gets harder, trust me!"

She laughs again, that giant round bubble of a laugh, which hovers in the air, iridescent and strange, following Celeste down the steps and all the way to the end of the street before it floats off into the sky.

Day 142

All through the next week Celeste feels restlessly giddy, like she's got somewhere fabulous to be, but it's not quite time to leave yet. She wants to tell someone about the interview-not-interview but can't figure out who to tell; Meo's working a bunch of dinner shifts at Quetzal, and Bridget is swamped with prom stuff. In grief group, when Ms. Greenberg asks Celeste how she's doing, she tries to just shrug and keep silent like always, but instead finds herself saying, "I had a college interview, and it was actually so great. But the thing is, the one person I really, really want to tell about it isn't here." The other kids' heads bounce in sympathy around the circle; everybody gets it. Ms. G suggests writing Nicky a letter in her journal, but Celeste goes to the library instead and sits down to write a long email to Paolo Reborn. It's not like the emails she's written before, begging him to write back, but instead just a regular letter, telling him all about what's happened since he left: Ursa and Meo and Nonna getting sick—and finally Europa and the interview. After hitting send, she writes a similar note to her grandma, who won't be back from Haiti for another few weeks. They don't usually email each other, but

Mimi's good at keeping secrets, so Celeste knows she can trust her not to tell Bonnie about MIT.

At some point, of course, Celeste will have to come clean with her parents, but not just yet—not while the strange giddy feeling she carried home from Europa's is still hanging around, sweet and mildly intoxicating, like a cloud of somebody else's pot smoke. Bonnie and Shane are mercifully distracted, anyway, because the staircase is getting fixed at last. It turns out they need to tear up the whole thing to rebuild, which means they're all sleeping downstairs again, Celeste in the music studio and her parents in the living room. The house is choked with white dust, rattling with the noise of drills and saws, doorways and floors tarped like some kind of quarantine ward, all of which gives Celeste an excuse to avoid being home in the evenings. She doesn't exactly have anywhere to go, but it doesn't seem to matter. There's one more stop on the Mars book list—Lands End, which falls on Castor, the brightest star in the Gemini—but Celeste's been putting it off, dreading another place where Nicky will almost definitely fail to turn up. Instead, she takes Ursa to the Japantown mall, one side of which is a boarded-up, singed construction site, the other side still open and buzzing with K-pop and smelling like tea and fried food, like some kind of conjoined twin partying on with its dead sibling still attached. Celeste buys herself a cheap pair of earrings and ramen for dinner, browses the bookstore until closing time. It all feels deliciously pointless, but then she wakes up the next day feeling guilty, staring at the empty spot on the transit map in the far western reach of the city.

She skips last period PE and rides the 38 Geary all the way out to the end of the line. Lands End is foggy and deserted, the visitors' center closed, so nobody's around to frown at the pink flier, which doesn't disappoint Celeste as much as she expected. The misty quiet feels good, so she climbs down the trail to the old ruin of Sutro Baths, picks her way along the broken walls in the fog, Ursa perturbedly stumbling along behind her. They sit on a concrete tower, its pebbled surface sparkling with bits of sea glass and sand. Celeste dangles her legs and wonders where Fake Nicky has been. She hasn't seen him since that day on the roof at school. She wonders, too, if the real Nicky is even still here in SF at all, breathing this same briny air, feeling this same fog in his hair. And if he isn't, does that mean he's lost to her for good? Will she ever be able to stop waiting here, at the end of the continent, for him to come back?

SATURDAY'S PROM NIGHT, AND EVEN THOUGH CEleste has spent the past few weeks actively and profoundly refusing to care, she does feel a little lonely, imagining her used-to-be-kind-of-friends posing for photos together, sharing lipstick and hiding their joints in their cleavage. Missing Meo, too, she decides to show up at Quetzal to help prep for the dinner shift. She hasn't really told Meo much about Europa, the story too big for texting, so she babbles about it while they light the candles at the empty bar. At first, she doesn't notice that he isn't listening; still so wrapped up in the strangeness of the story, the strangeness of Meo's silence doesn't register. Then she asks, "Do you think I was stupid to tell her about the application? I mean, I guess I could've just *not* said anything, and then maybe I would've gotten in?" But he just keeps absently flicking the lighter flame. "Hey," Celeste says, "earth to Meo?"

"What? Sorry. Jesus, I don't know, Celeste." He stacks the

candles on a tray, disappearing briefly behind the bar. "You don't want to go to MIT anyway, right? So why would you lie?"

"Are you okay?" she says. "You seem weird." She tries to pull him into a kiss.

"I'm working," he says. "Got a lot of shit on my mind." Then he softens and kisses her, his fingers warm in the curls on her neck. "Sorry, listen—I'm glad you're not moving to Boston, okay?"

The door flies open, and Marisol strides in on shiny black platform heels, her dress a twist of black fishnet, her hair pulled into a stiff bun. She's trailed by some other girls teetering in heels—surprisingly not all goth-ified, just wearing a rainbow of skintight dresses, the boys in tuxes. Marisol throws her arms around Celeste, catching the corsage in her hair, leaving bits of baby's breath behind. "Jaime got a hilarious limo!" she cries. "Dad's going to make us dinner first. When's *your* prom? Meo, get her a fucking limo!"

Meo laughs deep in his throat and says, "Maybe a pumpkin." He finds a lime on the prep station and presents it to Celeste with a flourish and a bow. "Your chariot awaits."

"Oh come on," Marisol says, "let's see a pic of your dress, at least!"

"Ours is tonight, too," Celeste says. "I'm not going. Not my scene."

"What, no way!" Marisol shrieks. "Meo, you *have* to take her!"

Meo actually looks a little hurt. "You didn't tell me," he says. "What, you don't want me to go?"

"I don't want *myself* to go. I hate that kind of shit."

He's wiping down the bar, even though it's already so clean that Celeste can see the reflection of his frown in it. "Hey," she says, about to do some explaining—it's not him, she genuinely doesn't give a shit about prom—and then she thinks of the bubble in the sky over Europa's, and the way she's felt a little bit floaty ever since, like the wind might carry her somewhere amazing if she lets it, and so instead she says, "I mean, should we just crash it? I guess we could."

"Nah, look, if you don't want me—"

"Shut up and take her!" Marisol's already dragging him to the back to talk to Ale, and the rest of it happens in a laughing blur: borrowed clothes from Ale and Marisol (who live next door), sneaky shots of expensive tequila with Ale's fancy yuzu margarita syrup, and a corsage for Ursa's collar made from roses meant for the tables. Meo wears his uncle's ancient wedding tux, and Celeste a slinky black one-shoulder dress that's so perfectly un-Celeste that she never wants to take it off. She doesn't usually go sleeveless, but nobody asks about the CGM on her arm, and for once, she doesn't seem to give a shit if they do. By the time they're squeezed into their clothes, Meo's over his bad mood, even acting a little giddy like Celeste, like it's catching. They dance down the hall outside the bathrooms, Celeste tripping over the dress in her boots (she had to draw the line at Marisol's stilettos). They eat with Marisol and her friends at the family table in the kitchen and even catch a ride in their limo, packing themselves in with four other couples and Ursa sprawled on the floor. They pass around a flask in the neon limo glow, and Celeste lets herself take a few swigs. She sits on Meo's lap, arms looped around his neck, and they kiss all the way to downtown while everyone else takes turns hanging out of the sunroof for selfies. They climb Nob Hill, where the two remaining hotels stretch tall, starry-eyed, with the purpling sky behind them where there once were other buildings. The car drops them off at the Fairmont and speeds away to Marisol's prom, trailing laughter and music.

The dance started a while ago, and nobody's in the lobby, so they stumble into the elevator, hands all over each other, Celeste a little dizzy from the margarita shots. It was more than she'd meant to drink, but she'd quickly dosed before they left, needle stuck right through the flimsy skin of the dress—so maybe the dizziness is just desire, just lusting for Meo so badly that she's wondering how much of her savings it would cost to get a room in this place.

On the top floor, Rihanna's blasting out from the end of the hall, and somebody's laughing nearby who might be Oona 3.0. Celeste feels suddenly out of breath, her heart racing. So far, she's managed not to think about what it'll actually be like to go to this thing without Nicky. She whispers to Meo, "Let's not go in yet," and leads him away from the music, finger through his belt loop, catching the thick toes of her boots on the tongue-colored carpet. They find an unlocked door and push into a darkened conference room, abandoned tables and chairs and floor-to-ceiling windows looking down on the city glitter. Celeste drops her diabetes bag and Ursa's leash and pulls Meo to the window. She presses her back against the glass and draws him close with both hands, tugging his lip in her teeth. From up here, with the bridge spanning the sky and the carpet of lights rolling down to the bay, you can almost imagine that things are just the same as before the quake, so Celeste lets herself do it, heady with forgetting, opening the slit in her skirt and guiding his hand between her thighs.

"Let's have sex tonight," she whispers, and laughs in his ear. "Prom night, it's hilarious!" He kisses her hard, wets two of his fingers, and curls them inside her in that way that almost makes her cry. "I haven't—with a guy," she says, and he kisses her hair and her neck, softening, tender. She's never told him this before. He takes his fingers out and rests both hands on her waist gently, runs them behind her back and pulls her close, tucks his face into her shoulder and draws a deep breath. "It's okay," she says, "I really want to," but he's shaking his head against her skin. He pulls away and looks at her and says, "I have to tell you something."

"What?" she says, still smiling, fumbling at the waist of his pants. Then she sees there's a frown on his face so deep it looks like a seam. His eyes are black and gleaming like an animal's in the half dark. "Hey, it's okay," she says, but he takes her hand and leads her to one of the conference chairs. She tries to fall into his lap, but he pulls up another chair and sits on the edge of it, crossing his arms in a knot. In the too-tight tux, with his shoulders hunched, she can see what he probably looked like as a little kid.

"Is this about the pills?" Celeste says. He tried to get her to leave them behind, but she insisted, thinking of the eager crew dudes; now she feels a pang of anxious guilt.

"Nah, come on," Meo says. "It's not about that."

Celeste can feel the slick ribbon of the evening's promise slipping away from her, the beautiful maybe-filled balloon floating out of her reach. Ursa wanders over and leans on her legs. She picks up the leash again and grasps it, waiting. A deep bass beat from down the hall thuds in her chest. She wishes she'd just dragged Meo into the dance instead, kissed him in front of her friends, made Bridget laugh with a big drunk surprise hug.

"What the hell, Meo," she says, talking to his reflection, the city lights shining a mask over that terrible frown. "Just tell me."

He covers his eyes. "I took Ursa."

Celeste doesn't understand. Her hand is on the dog now, curled around her soft ear. "She's right here."

"Jesus," he says, "this is *fucked*." Celeste can feel a hardening in her body, a spreading heaviness threaded with cracks, like somebody in a fairy tale turning to stone. "I had her," he finally says. "When she was missing. I saw her tied up at that place in the Haight, and I took her."

Celeste stands, toppling the chair. "What the fuck," she says. "What the *fuck* are you saying to me right now." She's stumbling over Ursa and the leash until they're backed against the window again.

"Just let me explain."

"Explain?"

"I stole from Ale, okay? Like a year ago. I fucked with his books and stole from him, okay? I was just, like, fucking tired of always being broke. At first it was just once, but then—a bunch of times, like I don't even know how many. And I couldn't pay him back, and then the quake made it worse, the restaurant closing down for a while, nobody coming in, and I couldn't take it, Celeste, I felt so fucking guilty, after everything my uncle did for me . . . and I thought, maybe, Ursa . . ." The words keep spilling into the oily dark, and Celeste is pressing her hands and body back on the glass, feeling already like she might be falling through it, plunging into the ruin of a pricey hotel, the brick and glass and ash of velvet curtains. "I saw her just sitting out there, you know? And I thought, like, maybe I could . . . maybe I could, I don't know, get a reward or some shit? It was stupid, I don't know. I felt so fucked up, I didn't know what I was doing, but it was too late, I had her, and you put up those posters, and I thought, yeah, the reward . . . but then when you and me started, like, whatever this is—"

"Stop it," she says, shouting now, "stop saying this shit!"

"Listen—"

"No."

"Celeste, I'm sorry, Jesus, I'm *really* fucking sorry."

"Fuck you, Meo!" She turns away, drops her forehead onto the window. Her breath makes a gray haze over the broken city. The bass from down the hall pounds through the cold glass, rattling her skull. Distantly she understands that Meo's still talking, but he's just saying the same shit, he's sorry, he never, he wouldn't, and all of it's covered with static and grime, *footsteps heartbeat mud pots thunder,* as worthless as those recordings on the *Voyager* will probably sound to whatever unfathomable being might actually hear them. Ursa barks a few times, and the CGM alarm shouts beneath the pounding beat, and Celeste tightens her grip on the leash. Suddenly she wants to be out of Meo's sight and never ever be near him again. She grabs her bag and runs out to the hall, crying now, stumbling to the elevator in the stupid dress, wiping tears and snot on the side of her hand.

"Celeste, you came!" It's Bridget, huddled there in the hall with Jordan and some other girls, checking their makeup in a mirror. "What the fuck, are you okay? Celeste!"

She falls into Bridget's hug and lets the girls gather around—girls she hasn't talked to in months, girls who are probably pissed at her—they're digging Kleenex out of their sparkly little purses and putting their hands on her bare back.

"What the fuck did you do?" Bridget shouts over her shoulder, her voice a little drunk, but it's Meo she's yelling at—Celeste can hear him swearing, jabbing the elevator button—*fuck this,* then a bunch of Spanish, and the elevator doors slide open and shut somewhere under the static in her ears, and then he's gone.

Celeste presses her face into Bridget's sequin shoulder. "Hey, you're all right," Bridget says softly. "You don't need him." Ursa barks again, three short clips. "Holy shit, isn't that the code or whatever? Crap, Jordan, can you get some food?" And then it's like they're carrying her somewhere, the girls, the hands, the sequin and silk, they're moving her down the hall in a rustling blur, and into the dark, hot ballroom with the music clattering. They pour her into a chair. Bridget's holding her hand and talking, but the only voice Celeste can hear is Meo's, telling her the worst possible story, telling her how dumb she was to trust him, to trust anyone at all—telling her how far away one star really is from another—so far that it takes centuries for light to move between them. *So incredibly fucking dumb,* she thinks just as somebody presses a strawberry into her hand and helps her carry it to her mouth. She eats it, then a couple of crackers, and slowly the dizzy veil begins to lift. There's a dim jumble of kids starting to gather nearby, the rest of them scattered and dancing under a pinkish flickering light, under giant banners painted kind of beautifully, with watercolor sand dunes—maybe even sprinkled with actual sand, it's hard to tell from here—but it really is just like Arrakis in *Dune*, that dry and lonely planet from Nicky's favorite book. *What a weird prom theme,* Celeste hears herself thinking, and then—fuck, the prom, she's at the *prom* . . . sitting here slumped and sweaty in a sexy dress getting fed crackers and fruit like a toddler. Bridget snaps at a few people to mind their own business.

"Bathroom," Celeste whispers, her dry mouth full of crumbs.

"Let's go," says Bridget, taking her hand, but Celeste struggles to stand and pulls away. She's still crying; she just needs to get someplace where no one can see her. She tries to smile at Bridget, but her mouth feels stuck. "Thanks," she mutters, staggering off with Ursa into the crowd. Bridget calls after her, but Celeste hurries with her head down, jostling past some juniors stabbing at their phones, past a gaggle of Oona clones and another bored teacher. She spots the open double doors glowing with hallway light and stops short with a gasp caught in her chest. There's a table there by the exit loaded with candles and flowers and many, many photos of Nicky. Nicky rowing on the lake. Nicky's face zipped tight in the pink cocoon of his hoodie. Nicky laughing with Celeste outside the fishbowl in the fog. Nicky at a desk, pen poised in his hand. Jesus, even Nicky as a tiny kid, wearing his favorite Cheerios T-shirt and pushing the little doll stroller they used to roll up and down their street. Celeste feels herself weeping now, the tears clogging her throat. She flees into the bright hall, lurches around a corner, and stumbles into a huddle of crew dudes.

"Yo, Celeste, you came!" Ian shouts. "Hey, you got any more of those Vikes? Whoa, fuck, are you okay?" She shoves him away, pushing through the laughing blur of boys until she spots the bathroom, runs for it, and slams herself inside. She sinks into a squat and buries her face in Ursa's neck, the tears silently streaming now through choking sobs. She squeezes her eyes shut and spins in the black hole for a minute, gasping for air. Ursa barks again, and Celeste is fumbling for her bag in the dark—then somehow she remembers that she can choose to open her eyes. She squints at the zipper until her fingers find it and reach inside. Instead of her insulin pen, she finds the little bottle of pills. Angrily she manages to struggle up to her feet. She dumps the pills into her cupped hand and stands over the toilet. Fuck him—she'll flush them all.

Oh, my holy Christ on a coffee cup, don't you even dare! Fake Nicky's dolled up in a sleek black tux, perched on the sink counter with his legs crossed. *Jesus, Cookie, you're a mess.* He wavers in and out of her teary vision, and yet she can hear him clear as day saying, *Like I said, you can't understand. You're really gonna flush those? Instead of helping out poor lover boy? Come the fuck on, CB. People do crazy shit when they're desperate, amiright?*

And then he's gone. The shuddering bass still pounds in her ears.

She swallows some pills. Three, five, hard to be sure. Presses them between her lips and chokes them down her dry throat.

Somebody's calling her name, banging on the door. She fumbles over to the sink, tries with clumsy numbing hands to spill the other pills back into the bottle.

The door swings open. Ms. Tanaka. She might be talking, shouting even, but the words are stretched as thin as they'll go, pulled into infinitesimal strands that bend along the beams of light and spool around Celeste, spinning her toward the blackness, the vast dark nothing at the center.

Day 146

Bowl of cherries on the table. Dark and gleaming in the pale place. Still wet from when somebody washed them.

Cherry pie, plastic plate, two candles burning. Blow them out, together breath.

Lifted on a ladder, picking the reddest. Metal so hot. First the bucket tumbling, then Nicky. Cast spangled with math.

Another birthday, at Mimi's, spitting pits into the sea.

Somebody wanders in, a nurse. Summons the cherries into her hands. Pale place again with the red glow gone.

This is the place.

This is the place she always ends.

Why is this the place.

What she's wearing may be made of leaves or paper. Twined in some tubes. Like the tea trees in the park, twisty trunks they used to climb.

Smell of pencils, mother smell. She's at the window, face in her hands. Passing in and out of the light.

WHEN THE CHERRIES ARE BACK, CELESTE'S GRANDmother is there behind them. It's several minutes before Celeste can figure out if she's real. The lines of her face keep blurring out of focus. What's focused are the cherries, the smooth mound of them. Celeste isn't hungry.

"They took away the first bowl," Mimi says. "I guess they don't let you bring food to diabetics." And then Celeste realizes that Mimi is holding her hand. "Can you believe that? Fucking fascists."

Celeste's throat is as papery as the bedsheets, as the gown. "Mimi," she rasps. "Water."

"Of course, sweet pea." Mimi pours some into a waxy little cup and hands it over. Celeste is surprised to find her own body functioning, her hand taking the cup and lifting it to her mouth.

The cherries. Her favorite, Nicky's too. Cherry season always means their birthday. Very soon they will turn eighteen.

Somebody's coughing behind a curtain. They are not alone in the room. There's a lot of noise in the hallway. Maybe this is still the ER. Celeste doesn't know how long she's been here. She turns to look out the window. The corner of a building on a clay-white sky. "Mom . . ." she starts to say.

"I sent her home," Mimi says, "to get some sleep. Told her I would bust you out of here myself, when you're ready."

Celeste lets her eyes drift closed, although it seems possible they will stay that way for a long time. Mimi's talking to somebody else now, so Celeste just listens to the slow hum of the words, soft sounds cradling her into a daze. Still not sure if Mimi's really here or in Haiti. The frayed threads of prom night begin to trail in and out of sleep. An ambulance, the smell of it, metal-sharp, like a knife. Tanaka strapped in a red seat belt. Cold burn of the IV. By now Celeste knows to look away.

"Come on, they discharged you," Mimi's suddenly saying. "Let's blow this joint." She is peeling back the blanket, lifting the papery gown. Celeste doesn't know what happened to Marisol's black dress. Mimi's got a hoodie and some jeans for her to wear, but they're an old pair she hates now—Bonnie must've brought them. Celeste fumbles with the button fly while her grandmother kneels on the hospital floor and works her feet gently into the clunky boots. Ties the laces for her, too, like she used to do when Celeste was little, when Mimi's long braid was brown.

"You're back," Celeste says, the words sounding slower in her brain than in her ears.

"Yeah, well," Mimi says. "You know me, I go where I'm needed."

IN THE CAR, CELESTE SLEEPS. FLICKERING SUN AND the lull of the road. *Tick, tick* of tires on the bridge. Mimi's station wagon, Joni Mitchell and Nina Simone, and a lemony smell from her hand cream. Drifting in and out of the dark. Meo's words hanging there in her sleep, sticky and grim, like a tangle of bats. Once she wakes up on the winding road, stomach tumbling, and Mimi gives her a sip of ginger ale. Squinting through the bright window, it's Nicky there on the shoulder, stooped under a heavy pack. Stepping into a sunbeam, and he's gone. Just like that. Celeste goes back to sleep.

SHE DOESN'T REMEMBER THE USUAL THINGS ABOUT getting to Mimi's house, like the briny air or the driveway pebbles crunching under her shoes, but somehow she's on the futon now, sweaty in her jeans, the pink cast of evening coming through the blinds. Ursa's stretched at her side, huge and snoring, but Celeste doesn't remember picking up the dog. She must've slept in the car while Mimi went inside to get Ursa at home. Celeste wonders if her parents even came out to see her. She pictures them peering through the window in their bathrobes, disappointed and pale.

Her forehead throbs. She has to pee, even though her entire body feels parched, dust caked in her veins. She forces herself to stand and Ursa follows, thumping her forelegs heavily off the bed to curve herself into a stretch. In the mirror, Celeste is a fucking wreck, her eyes milky and ringed with gray, her hair a ratty cloud. She pees and splashes some water on her face, so shocking that she gasps. Ursa stands there looking a little bit fed up. Celeste kisses her head, apologizes in a whisper.

They find Mimi outside on the peace platform, standing in warrior pose in her usual uniform, some silky batik pants and a men's white undershirt. At her feet there's a smoldering joint in a molded clay dish that Celeste is pretty sure contains her own baby footprint. Mimi doesn't break her concentration. The sunset is offensively beautiful behind her. Celeste lies down on her belly. The hard rock is warm from the day and feels strangely comfortable. She rests her chin in her hands and stares directly into the copper heart of the sun. Is this what its twin looks like right now, setting over the edge of some distant planet, breaking alien hearts with its gorgeousness? Ursa isn't buying it. She sits on her haunches and frowns at some passing pelicans.

"Good morning," Mimi says, folding herself into downward dog, with a pause to drag off the joint. The smell of it makes Celeste's stomach turn.

"How long did I sleep?" Her lips are dry and cracked at the corners. She presses her sweatshirt against them. "What day is it?"

"Monday."

Celeste squints at the sun. "I think I have a test tomorrow."

Mimi rolls up to standing and gazes out at the sky herself for a moment, leathery tan hands braced on the small of her back. Then she picks up the ashtray and sits down next to Celeste. "You've been suspended, sweet pea. A week, while they review this mess. You need to go in and see the principal next Tuesday with your mom and dad. For the decision."

Celeste's brain still feels kind of swollen and wadded up, and the pounding waves don't help. At first, she isn't sure exactly what Mimi's talking about. Then—the pills in her hand at the dance. Tanaka at the door. An elevator thuds to a close behind Celeste's ribs.

"They say you were dealing at school," Mimi tells her. "Some narc teacher overheard—"

"Not *dealing*," Celeste says. "Helping a friend."

Mimi smirks. She reaches over to rub Celeste's back, spreading a gentle calm over her skin. Celeste lowers her head onto the rock, looking away from the sun at last.

"I got off the phone with your father a little while ago. He called MIT, wanted to talk to somebody about all this before they heard it from the school. I think he was going to explain about Nicky, how tough you were taking it."

"Oh . . ." Celeste says. "Oh no." She knows the shape of her dad's face when he's disappointed in her, the crumpled mask of it. She presses her own cheek into the stone until it stings.

Mimi picks up the joint. Smoke from her mouth pours over the edge of the rock, like the fog can sometimes do. "You still need rest," she says. "Check your sugar and go back to sleep. We'll talk in the morning."

Celeste pushes herself to her knees. The disc of the sun is half gone now, melted into the mirror-slick sea. She turns her back on it and trudges toward the house, letting Ursa stay behind. The lawn's been sheared down to stubble. She turns to Mimi, who is watching her from the rock, her eyes creased with love, her white braid dyed candy pink in the evening light.

"Was he here?" Celeste calls to her. "Nicky."

Mimi's thin shoulders lift with a sigh. She watches Ursa watch the pelicans. Something dangles from the mouth of one of the birds, a dripping carcass. "Could've been . . ." she says. "But you know I've given my keys to a lot of wayward souls."

Celeste can't absorb this, her brain already a heavy sponge. She wanders inside. She guzzles a glass of water, checks her blood sugar in a daze, and forces herself to eat a banana and dose. Her diabetes kit and a tote full of her stuff are under the futon, but she doesn't know how they got there. When Celeste was little, Mimi used to pretend she could move things with her mind, slipping coins or candies or polished stones soundlessly into Celeste's pockets. Sometimes they were things that had been missing for weeks. Mimi was always magic like that.

Celeste's phone is in the bag, mercifully dead. She doesn't plug it in. Her tattered monkey, Palpatine, is in there, too. Her mother is the only one who would've thought to pack it. She tucks it back in the bag and lies down in the lowering dark.

CELESTE WAKES UP WHEN THE AIR IN THE ROOM IS utterly black, storm-tossed, waves crashing on the walls, like she's trapped in the hold of a ship. Ursa's lying next to her, so she buries her hands in the dog's fur and holds on until sleep. Then just before dawn she peels her eyes open again. A little bit of murky light filters in to reveal the room, the bloody IV gauze she left on a table, the basket of Mimi's laundry. Celeste pulls a pillow over her head. She hated the terrifying night but wishes the day would never come. When it finally does, she's asleep again, this time thick in a dream. Gazing into a canyon on a desert planet, Nicky and Meo both striding along the distant ridge. Their bare feet so terribly close to the edge. Her voice lost in the wind.

IT IS AFTERNOON WHEN CELESTE FINALLY WAKES with a clearer head. The pounding static is gone, but the dread has stuck around, humming under her skin. There's no sign of Ursa, but Mimi is noisily tinkering in the kitchen, rattling some silverware, running the sink. Celeste climbs off the futon at last.

She finds her grandmother surrounded by cartoonishly tall stacks of wheat bread sandwiches, wielding a mustardy knife. Bob Dylan is singing to Isis on a cassette in Mimi's little old pink boom box, which always travels with her, around the cottage and on the back of her bike and even to Haiti. Celeste heaves herself onto a stool at the counter and says, "I'm sorry I slept so long."

Mimi reaches over the counter to cup her cheek for a second. Then she fixes Celeste a giant ice water and hands her a box of aluminum foil. "Give me a hand?"

Celeste drinks half the water in one gulp. The cold hurts her ears. "Who are you feeding today?"

"There's a tent camp at the Foods Co. under 101. The place burned, so folks are sleeping there now."

Celeste can picture it. They used to stop there for picnic stuff sometimes on their way to Mimi's. While her parents went inside, she would play in the little creek that ran below the parking lot, sometimes with Nicky, too. Once they found a lizard there with a sky-blue tail. Her body still aches all over, but she stretches a piece of foil and starts to wrap the sandwiches. There is the sound of Dylan's crooning—*What drives me to you is what drives me insane*—and the crinkle of the foil and the waves outside, but much louder is the silence. Mimi has always had a way of filling a room with it. It occurs to Celeste that she could ask again about Nicky—did he come here, did he know about the key—but she doesn't have the energy right now. Eventually, she decides to say, "I don't really know what happened in the hospital."

Mimi flops another sandwich onto the stack. "Not much. They said the medics gave you Narcan at the dance. They wanted to keep an eye on you; sometimes it causes seizures. And they wouldn't let you go home until your sugar was stable. So."

"Narcan? I only took a few pills."

"That's not what your teacher told them."

Celeste wraps the sandwiches into careful shiny packets. After a minute she says, "Nicky was selling them, at school. That's how I got—" But Mimi stops her, waving the mustard knife.

"Nope," she says. "You know you never have to justify yourself to me. I'm a grandma, so I get to opt out of that crap now. It's one of the perks." She tosses the knife in the sink and braces her hands on the counter. The harmonica wails from inside the boom box. Celeste feels the sun from the skylight on her neck. Mimi's braid is pinned on top of her head today, which makes her face look more like Bonnie's. Wispy silver hairs catch the light around her ears. "Come on," she says, "let's finish wrapping these up and go hand them out."

Celeste sinks on her stool. She can't even imagine scraping herself out of these jeans, wrangling with her hair. "Mimi, I feel awful. I was in the *hospital*—"

"But you're not now, are you?" Mimi washes her hands, wipes them on her overalls, clicks off the music. "Listen, sweet pea," she says, "I get it. You're so goddamn sad right now. I get what that feels like, truly. I've been on my own a long time. On my own—hell, *lonely*—for a really long time." Celeste is struck even quieter than before. Of course, she knows about her grandfather, who died of a heart attack when Bonnie was just a baby. He wasn't such a nice guy, evidently, and they lived on the commune at the time, surrounded by lots of other parent-type folks. Celeste's heard all about how they nursed each other's babies and slept with each other's husbands and strung the laundry lines on the ancient redwoods. And then one day when Bonnie was ten, Mimi just up and left, moved them to the city, and sent Bonnie to real school for the first time. *Our life needed to be about her, for once,* she has said to Celeste (Bonnie refusing to comment, her nostrils silently flaring at the mouth of a glass of wine). The story has always loomed large for Celeste, but maybe in the wrong way. She hasn't ever thought much about what Mimi gave up.

"Being so sad, it's heavy," Mimi says, "right?" Celeste nods, her eyes swelling with hot tears. Mimi squeezes her hands. "For me, when it's so heavy I can't take it anymore, you know what I do? I figure out where I'm needed. I figure out who's suffering worse than me, and that's where I go. It's the only thing that helps."

Celeste leans into her chest, the thin warm arms enfolding her. She stays there a little while, breathing the lemon verbena, crying on Mimi's T-shirt. Then finally she says, "I'll go change," her mouth still dry and sour. But back in the den it takes her fifteen minutes to get out of her clothes. She sits on the futon in her underwear. It is perfectly cool in her room, and she feels the sea breeze from the window on her sweaty neck. She closes her eyes and tries to imagine herself weightless, an old trick from a therapist that hasn't worked in a long time. She looks around in the darkness of her own mind and tries to see the inside of a space station, the panels of slick cool buttons she can run her hands across, the handles and rungs she can grab when she feels herself flailing. And it works—eventually she manages to float into her clothes and out to the car, where Mimi is waiting and singing along to the boom box as if no time at all has passed.

WHERE THE FOODS CO. USED TO BE, THERE'S NOW A blackened cage of rebar and concrete glinting with flecks of yellow tape. In the creek below the parking lot, where Celeste played as a kid, people are washing their socks and jeans. Somebody wrings out a Warriors T-shirt over the rocks. A little boy is bathing his doll in a mossy puddle. When the boy spots Ursa, he scrambles up the bank and drops to his knees to nuzzle her. Celeste gives him three sandwiches because Mimi isn't looking (the rule being one per person, so there's plenty to go around).

Together they knock at the doors of rusted-out RVs, cars, and pickups with garbage bags taped over the windows. They leave the sandwiches in the tidy vestibules of tents and offer them to people waiting in line for the first aid station and the porta-potties. People like to talk to Mimi, as they've always liked to talk to Celeste, but Mimi's better at answering. She doesn't worry about saying the wrong thing. She tells people she loves them, which Celeste knows is true, even though these are perfect strangers. One lady tells them how she'd just put new carpet in her trailer when the quake brought a mudslide down on top of it. "Fawn, that was the carpet color," she says sadly, and Mimi hugs her, writes her own phone number on a paper towel, and says, "Call if you need me, okay?"

Everyone looks so tired, their faces etched with worry and pain. A man with a ropy rust-colored scar running the length of his jaw walks up to them slowly. Celeste's hand trembles when she offers him a sandwich. Thanking her, he crouches down to pet Ursa, who snorts happily and starts licking away at his scar. Celeste's horrified, but the man just laughs. He takes a minute to untie his own yellow bandanna and knot it around Ursa's neck. Celeste tries to politely refuse the gift, but he waves her off and says, "She's a very special creature," which reminds Celeste of Joan the crystal lady, who called Ursa an ancient warrior queen. *Nobody really survives an earthquake . . .* Joan also said. *We're all forever altered*—and Celeste thinks she was right. For a moment Celeste can understand the smallness of her own pain, which doesn't seem to make it hurt less.

They are almost out of sandwiches when the ground begins to

tremble under the tents. There's a wave of cries and cursing, people grasping hands and dropping to their knees in the gravel. Celeste and Mimi cling to each other, Ursa wildly barking, a fog of dust rising around them, but after only a few more seconds, it is over. Coughs and laughter and relief as the dust clears. It wasn't a bad one. People are climbing up the creek bed, soaked and smiling. "Good gravy, enough already!" Mimi says, wiping the dust away from Celeste's face with her sleeve.

On the way back to the car, Celeste is thinking how she'd like to write something down: the yellow bandanna, the way that man folded it corner to corner and smoothed it on his knee. She sees the phrasing arrive in her mind and doesn't want to forget it. It occurs to her that she hasn't been writing much lately. She knows where Mimi keeps some notepads and sharpened pencils in a drawer.

MIMI MAKES THEM POTATO OMELETS FOR DINNER. Some old boyfriend from Spain taught her how, and she always makes them when Celeste comes to stay. Thin gold disks with blistered peppers on the side, and honey bread with mint tea for dessert. Celeste can't remember the last time she actually ate. She devours it all.

Later they're out on the deck, the sunset finished, sky leaning just past a deep blue dusk. Celeste has set up the telescope to look for Mars—only one week now until the *Pioneer* launch—but it's not quite dark enough yet. The breeze is calm, so they've lit a couple of Mimi's ancient candle lanterns, rainbow layers of wax melted over empty wine jugs. Mimi has a slim joint and a fat mystery novel, and Celeste's got a legal pad propped on her knees, writing things down from the day. The bandanna, the thin film of dust settling on the tents. The way people seemed to find it laughable, that baby quake. When Celeste gets to the end of a page, her chest is loose, her breath easier. She stands to stretch and deeply swallows the salt air, sending it all the way down to her feet.

"New plan," she says. "I'll just stay here forever. Cool?"

"Not cool, I'm afraid," Mimi says without looking up. "I really love you, though." Celeste pulls the cuffs of her sweater over her hands and leans on the rail of the deck to gaze down into the velvet sea. There's one rock down there that just gets pounded all day long, drenched with salt and kelp and wild pearly explosions every time a new wave set comes in. Celeste feels a little bit like that rock right now. When they got home from the Foods Co., she made the mistake of plugging in her phone. It woke up and proceeded to vomit dozens of texts. Meo, Bridget, Meo, Meo (many times Meo), Ian, Carla, then tons in a row from her parents, asking her to call. Celeste felt newly scoured out, as if she'd been the one doing the vomiting, which she supposed she probably had—at some point in that gray blur of hours after the prom.

"Think I'm going back to bed," she says. "I'll put the telescope away." But now Mimi is watching her closely, smoking, the mystery book closed on the table.

"Hang on," Mimi says. "First come sit by me." Celeste obliges, curling up at the end of Mimi's lounger. She doesn't expect a lecture—that's not Mimi's style—but something about this moment makes her nervous, maybe the way Mimi seems to be steeling herself for it.

"Listen, sweet pea, I need to come clean about something," she says at last. "The thing is, I *do* think Nicky came here. I knew he was having a rough time, back in the fall, and I told him he had a bed here if he ever needed to get away."

Celeste feels herself shrug. Distantly she's aware of Fake Nicky standing nearby at the telescope, gazing at—what? The almost dark.

Mimi draws a big breath and goes on: "You can't tell your mother this—she would murder me. But I told him where he could find some cash, too, just in case. And, sweet pea—the cash is gone."

Celeste is strangely numb to this news. Nicky's never really been dead to her, after all. And yet the feeling that he might be hiding somewhere close at hand, the old panicky hide-and-seek feeling, is gone, replaced by the certainty of his having drifted very far away. She remembers Europa Varma's voice describing the *Voyager* on its journey through the pause, and then on the other side, in the deep beyond, dropping contact with Earth forever. Celeste closes her palm over the sun on her wrist. "Still," she says quietly. "Somebody else could've taken it. One of your wayward souls, or—"

Mimi shakes her head and reaches for her novel, slips a bookmark out from between the warped pages. Only it turns out not to be a bookmark at all. It's a sealed envelope with Celeste's name written across the front. Even in candlelight, the pink ink is unmistakable.

Celeste takes the envelope and tears it open. There's a plane ticket inside, a weird paper one. SFO to Orlando.

Her heart slams in her ears. Another wave plunges into that same tortured rock. She can hear it from way up here, the sound of a giant hourglass shattering, releasing its flood of sand.

"Florida?" Mimi says distantly, but Celeste is already walking away, the ticket crushed in her hand. She's at the telescope, shaky fingers fumbling with the dials. It takes a minute to steady herself enough to get a look.

Mars. It's bright tonight, visible in clear detail. The stormy red deserts. Vast silty craters. So close it feels like she could reach out and run her fingers through the dust. But so spectacularly far away, too.

Day 154

It is the day before their eighteenth birthday—153 days since the planet split open and swallowed Nicky—when Celeste steps out of a Gray Line bus and into the loamy hot swamp air of Cape Canaveral, Florida. Shag-carpeted Ursa, built for the north winds, looks faint, her tongue dragging on the pavement, but for Celeste, it's a relief just to be outside at all after so many hours of refrigerated, fluorescent-lit caverns: from airport to airport to bus and bus again. They arrived in Orlando close to one a.m. and spent the night loitering around the terminal, alternately dozing and trying to appear distractedly annoyed, as if they were just waiting out a flight delay. Celeste was half asleep with her head on the Gray Line desk when it opened at nine. Flashing Ursa's service dog credentials, she bought a ticket for the first bus to the Kennedy Space Center, where she now finds herself roasting in the late-morning sun, squinting around at the tour guides in their sweaty button-downs, looking for her name on their little printed signs, as if one of them might turn out to be Nicky himself.

And then she sees it. Rising up tall in the distance, towering over the huddled visors and panama hats, shimmering in the heat:

Pioneer. The shuttle is just now emerging out of the massive Lego block of the VAB, beginning its painstaking journey to the launchpad on a giant rolling platform they call a crawler. Celeste has only ever seen this happen on YouTube, but now she's watching it with her own eyes, the graceful slender shuttle set against the piercing blue sky—and for a good five minutes while she stands there taking it in, nobody else even seems to notice. *Jesus,* Fake Nicky says, reaching for her hand, *isn't that the most beautiful fucking hard-on you've ever seen in your LIFE?* At which point the hats of the tour guides and bus passengers (maybe they can hear him, too?) whip around in a wave to look. The cries of amazement cause a smear of distortion in the humidity over their heads.

Celeste snaps a photo of the distant, lovely *Pioneer* and texts it to Real Nicky, tacking it to the endless scroll of unanswered texts that stretches back so many weeks into the past. By now she's pretty sure he no longer has his old phone, but she adds this anyway: *Where are u?? We're actually HERE!* And then drags Ursa to beat the crowd to the ticket booth.

Space Disney, that's what they used to call it, back when they were first researching the birthday trip, giddy with plans. They spent hours reading idiotic travel blogs and scouring space-nerd message boards, watching videos of other nerds touring the Kennedy Space Center (KSC, as it's affectionately known), gawking at the astronauts, and eating "rocket dogs" at places like the Orbit Cafe and posing with Snoopy, who was some kind of space-travel mascot. Celeste made up Space Disney songs and filmed Nicky singing them: *It's a small, smaaaall—infinitesimally small world— only one tiny world out of trillions of worlds—after aaaall . . .* They both understood why NASA had to stoop so very low—those rockets aren't cheap—but Celeste and Nicky swore *they* would take their visit seriously, celebrating their twin birthday while simultaneously celebrating the awesome scientific triumphs of the space program.

And yet—the trip they actually planned was going to be so much stupid fun.

It's all there in the Mars book. Three pages of notes from all that research, along with a running budget tally (way more than either of them had managed to save, or so Celeste used to believe). They stopped even mentioning the trip so long ago, probably right around when Carla and Nicky got kicked out of their house. The dream of the trip had slipped from Celeste's mind, kind of like an actual dream, but it came trickling back as she read through the notes and remembered squealing over the photos and videos with Nicky in her attic. She could hear the squeals in his pink exclamation points peppered over the pages:

- *Jetty Park Campground (dolphins!! sea turtles!!)*
- *Starlite Inn: cheap, dog-friendly—looks shitty, but @launchratblog says it's super clean—fresh cookies on pillow!!*
- *Bioluminescent lagoon tour!! prob too expensive:(*
- *Rock shrimp tacos*
- *Shuttle-shaped pancakes!!!!!*

Celeste counted 107 exclamation points. She'd read through the notes again at Mimi's, marking them up with her own black pen as she planned her trip. The campgrounds were all full for the week of the launch, but the Starlite Inn, which had no website and took five calls to get through, had had a cancellation. Celeste can just barely afford two nights, which will get her to her flight the day after the launch. The lagoon tour and the rock shrimp are totally not going to happen; she's already spent half her savings on the Gray Line bus and two days of tickets to the KSC. There aren't any tickets left to watch tomorrow evening's launch from a real NASA viewing spot, but Celeste bets that Nicky already bought two bleacher seats at the LC-39 Observation Gantry (best and closest view!!!), like they'd always planned. He'll be waiting in here somewhere, waving the tickets at her with a shit-eating grin.

Mimi wanted Celeste to take some money, but she refused. Then, at the Orlando airport, she found an envelope in her backpack with $150 cash inside and a Post-it note: *This was supposed to be your graduation money, so don't blow it all in one place. I love you. Be safe.* It hadn't been hard to get Mimi, who after all had run off to the woods and thrown her bras in the bonfire at age sixteen, to agree to this plan; she even drove Celeste down to SFO to catch her flight yesterday afternoon. But in the idling car outside the terminal, Mimi said she needed to know that Celeste was going to take better care of herself. She made Celeste promise to text a blood sugar report every four hours. "I'm not trying to control you here, sweet pea," she said. "I'm trusting you to get some control of yourself. You understand that? It's past time." Celeste wrapped Ursa's leash tight around her hand. She watched the other travelers resolutely shoving their bulky baggage through the revolving doors, where Celeste could see her own reflection slicing in and out of view. She almost asked Mimi to drive her home instead. But she went ahead and promised, gave Mimi a long hug on the sidewalk, and set a four-hour timer on her phone. The alarm is buzzing again just as she's about to get to the front of the KSC ticket line, so she steps aside and dutifully checks the app in the paltry shade of a palmetto.

Her phone says it's eleven thirty a.m., eight thirty at home, time to do the other thing she promised Mimi, too: call her parents. Except she's going to break this promise, just a teensy bit. There's an email draft waiting to send to them instead, with a cc to Carla. Celeste worked on it late last night, bleary-eyed in the airport, and finished it on the bus this morning, angling the screen of her phone away from the nosy lady from Cleveland (Hawaiian shirt, dyed blond perm) who kept baby-talking to Ursa. Trashing and retyping drafts until her fingers hurt, Celeste eventually figured out how to explain about the ticket from Nicky, the birthday trip they'd planned. She promised to take care of herself and told them she needed to see this through on her own. She didn't mention the disciplinary meeting that's supposed to begin in half an hour in Dr. Reyes's office. Her parents might already be there, sipping their coffee on a bench in the school courtyard. Bonnie's probably fussing with her topknot, Shane nervously twisting his watch. They think Celeste is on her way to meet them right now in Mimi's car, to find out if they're going to let her come back to school and graduate. She takes a deep breath and hits send, and the email flies off to meet them instead. There's an anxious flutter in her heart, like a real letter getting snatched and tossed around by a breeze, which instantly makes her feel lighter. She blows through the turnstiles on a dizzy current, her mind awake for what feels like the first time in weeks, utterly certain that this is exactly where she needs to be.

"Come on, girl, we got this," she says to poor bedraggled Ursa, who gazes longingly at the plumes of water spewing from a fountain. And so, the Nicky-seeking begins again. Celeste takes a grinning selfie with the old launch countdown clock, thinking, *Ready or not, here we come*—and then she jogs into the park, pulling Ursa at her heel.

They stop at an information kiosk to get a service dog badge and a KSC map. There's a "Lost Kids" bench, where Fake Nicky is sitting, licking a rocket Popsicle with a smirk. Celeste rolls her eyes at him. This would all be so much easier, she thinks, if Real Nicky would just give her a fucking call, but after all the sneaking around and Paolo Reborn and the Mars book and the hidden ticket at Mimi's, a simple text from a burner phone seems highly improbable now. At this point it feels like her best bet is to wander around the park until she finds him. She doesn't want to really *appreciate* any of it alone, but she can't help herself. This is space-nerd mecca, after all. Even the big blue retro-fabulous NASA globe gives Celeste the happy shivers. The whole place smells like cotton candy and the black grease that she could never quite manage to wash off her fingers back when she was into model rockets. Being here makes her think about another lost kid, her small and unsuspecting self, the one who could actually eat stuff like cotton candy. In the Rocket Garden, she circles the towering giants for over an hour, wading through the melting, disorienting heat. Mercury-Redstone, Delta, Atlas-Agena. She once built models of them all; now the models are lost, too, packed or given away, and she can't believe she's standing here among the glorious rockets themselves.

Standing by Gemini–Titan II, there's a tall kid in a white cap with wide flat shoulders. Nicky shoulders. Celeste's pulse is suddenly peppered with pink exclamation points. The Gemini pattern from the Mars book, *of course*, meant to lead her here, to Florida, to the launch—the constellation a reminder of their twin birthday, when Mars hangs in Gemini! But when the kid in the cap turns and laughs, it is very clearly *not him*. This guy is Florida frat boy head to toe (Nicky would never be caught dead in cargo shorts, even in disguise). Celeste realizes she's got to get out of this heat. Thankfully the sea of sweaty nerds and patriots parts itself for Ursa, and they find their way swiftly into the nearest building. In the chill air of the vestibule, Celeste shakes the humid fuzz out of her skull, downs half a bottle of water, and pours the other half into a little bowl for the dog. She spreads some peanut butter on a tortilla while an usher in a blazer gives her the stink eye. Then, with a clearer head, she spends the rest of the afternoon wandering the blissfully cool indoor exhibits, looking for Nicky.

She bathes in the glowy hologram light of the astronaut heads in the Hall of Fame, forces Ursa to pose for a couple of photos with Mae Jemison and Sally Ride. They scour the Apollo building and the *Journey to Mars* exhibit. Every time Celeste steps into a new gallery, she catches a shallow breath and darts her eyes around the room in search of Nicky's silhouette. All the nerves in her skin and chest are prickly with sparks. She gapes, teary-eyed, at the massive space-beaten *Atlantis* hanging in its black dome, lit with a clear gold wash of light. Nicky's been obsessed with seeing *Atlantis* forever, but Celeste doesn't find him anywhere—just Fake Nicky messing around with the pilot simulator.

By the time the alarm on her phone buzzes again, they've made their way through the whole complex three times over. Celeste's feet are sore, Ursa is thoroughly pissed, and the KSC is closing in twenty minutes. Celeste checks her sugar, texts the number and some heart emojis to Mimi. She writes, *I assume Mom's furious with both of us?* and Mimi replies, *She'll get over it.* Celeste buys herself some fries and finds a table under a misty sprinkler where she can take her insulin and eat. There are twelve missed calls from her parents and a thread of incredulous texts from Carla—and Meo, again, with the same plea: *Please talk to me.* Celeste eats her fries instead of responding to any of them.

Where could Nicky be? The only place Celeste didn't look for him was on the bus tour of the actual NASA grounds. He wasn't in line for the bus any of the five times she checked, and aside from the launch itself, the tour is the one thing she's most excited about doing together with him. She digs out the Mars book and looks over Nicky's notes again. He could be waiting somewhere outside the park, at one of these other spots they planned to visit? Cocoa Beach, maybe, where all the space tourist shops and restaurants are? She isn't going to put it past him to turn up somewhere unlikely.

Trailing the mopey Ursa, Celeste finds her way out to the parking lot. The asphalt is baked so hot she can feel it through her sneaker soles. In lieu of a bazillion-dollar Uber, she sneaks onto a free shuttle to a Cocoa Beach resort by letting a couple of sweaty little boys play with the dog while they wait. "My brothers," she tells the driver when the bickering parents are already on the bus, but he just waves her on anyway. The trip along the causeway is short, and the bus is cool; Celeste is considering a quick nap when the little boys' dad, unaware that she's used his family for nefarious purposes, strikes up a conversation, asking Celeste where she's from. He gasps at her answer, solemnly removes his camo sun hat, and says, "You've been in our prayers. Such a tragedy. How's it going over there now?" She's not sure what to say (*Actually, my best friend's been missing for months, I'm here looking for him, and the whole thing's basically turned my life upside down, thanks for fucking asking?*), but before she can say a word, the dad has turned away to break up a fight over a pouch of astronaut ice cream. Celeste pops her earbuds in and closes her eyes until the bus lurches to a stop. The resort where it lets them off is enticing, all palm trees and plush chairs in an open-air lobby with a view straight through to the beach. Briefly she wonders if that family might adopt her after all, take the little earthquake runaway swimming and feed her some rock shrimp—but instead she scuttles away down the boardwalk.

It's almost dusk now, and the air is still heavy with damp heat. Celeste can feel blisters burning on both her heels. Somehow, she had the idea that Cocoa Beach was a little seaside town where it wouldn't be hard to find the places she was looking for, but actually it's sprawling and cheesy, a seemingly endless chain of identical hotels. There's a boardwalk where she finds some of the spots in the Mars book notes: a couple of restaurants she and Nicky read about, and a sweet old museum with space memorabilia, and a place where you can get your name embroidered on a NASA hat. All the places are there, just like the internet promised, but Nicky is not.

Celeste has made a vow to Mimi about eating regular meals, so she doses in a gas station bathroom, then gets a couple of fish tacos from a truck and feeds Ursa, too, in the vacant lot behind it, sitting on her jean jacket in the probably snake-infested weeds. The guacamole's okay, but it's not as good as Ale's. The taste of it floods Celeste with grief and longing, a thickly spreading emptiness in her chest and behind her eyes. Meo betrayed her in such a ridiculous terrible way, and he betrayed Ale, who trusted and looked out for him—but still she seems to really want to see and touch him right now. If she closes her eyes, she can feel Meo's hands on her back. She opens her phone and scrolls his texts for a few minutes, the screen glowing in the orange twilight. Under the rumble of the taco truck's generator, the night bugs are starting to sing. She types a text to Meo—*I went away for a while, maybe we'll talk when I get back*—and doesn't send it.

Jetty Park Campground is on the way to the Starlite Inn, less than half a mile away according to Google Maps. Celeste walks in a drainage ditch with trucks honking at her, tires spitting gravel into her shoes, the dog miserably hanging her head. By the time they get to the campground, Celeste is drenched with sweat and Ursa with slobber. She can feel the gravel dust inside her socks, between her toes. It's gotten so dark that she has to creep around shining her phone light at campfire circles to look for Nicky, apologizing and trying to act a little drunk, like she got lost on her way to the bathroom.

Eventually she gives up and follows the wave sounds to a wide beach. She kneels and puts her hands in the sand, which is fine and white and sparkly as salt. There isn't much of a moon, so all the light in the air seems to come from the sand itself. It smells so different here from the beach at home. Celeste misses Mimi. She takes off her backpack and sits for a while, raking the sand and Ursa's fur with her fingers. Offshore there's a barge twinkling with red and white lights, motoring slowly to the south. It takes Celeste a minute to realize those are dolphins playing in its wake, their slick backs slicing through the black water. As promised in the Mars book. She watches them for a while. She takes out her phone and dials Nicky. It goes to his voicemail, as always. He's still on Carla's phone plan, just in case. "I'm here in Florida," she says. "I'm starting to wonder why. I'm pretty sick of this game now. Come out, come out, wherever you are—okay?" And then she winds her way back to the road on the lush dark paths.

Another long roadside walk in the humid night, shadow palms

slicing the air above her head in the hot breeze. Celeste's backpack and her dress are soaked and crusty with sand and sweat. Her water bottle's empty, and the taste of the tacos lingers in her throat. Eventually the neon sign for the Starlite Inn appears in the distance, and she makes a run for it, desperate for the AC. A water cooler shines blue in the dim lobby. Celeste gulps down four tiny paper cones of water, deliciously cold and almost sweet, before even noticing the desk, where a slender man about Mimi's age is fussing with the top button of his cardigan. He's got a little TV on where it sounds like he's watching launch coverage on the local news.

"May I help you?"

"Sorry, yeah! I have a reservation."

She gives him her name, and he types it into a bulky old computer. "So you do, Ms. Muldoon. How many in your party?" He looks around the empty room, so Celeste does too, but they're alone.

"Just one. Just—me. I guess."

The man hands her a key card. He reaches into a desk drawer, opens a bag of Chips Ahoy, and places a single cookie on a plastic plate.

"Actually," she says, "I'm meeting a friend. Maybe he's been here already?" She finds a photo of Nicky on her phone, but the man shakes his head.

"If I see him, I will call your room. Okay?" She thanks him and shoulders her gross damp bag. She's dying for a shower. She is almost out the door when the man calls after her, "You're here to watch the launch? With your friend? It's a long way to come for a young person like yourself. All the way from California!" And while he's probably just being friendly—no bells sounding on her creep radar—she feels the need to explain herself, somehow, in a way that makes sense, so she tries the cover story she concocted on the plane: "I'm actually, like, an intern? For a podcast. You know, like a radio show."

He laughs. "Yes, I know what a podcast is, my dear. Very interesting. So, you're a space geek, too?" He swivels around in his chair and pushes open the flimsy door to another little office. Inside it is bright with lamplight, and the walls are completely plastered with newspaper clippings about NASA. There's a silver model rocket in process on a desk and another dozen or so displayed on shelves above it. There's that smell again, the model grease, laced with black licorice. "I've seen hundreds of launches," the man says proudly, leaning back in his wheelie chair to gaze up at the wall. "I watched Apollo 11 from the beach! I was your age. I had only been in this country two weeks."

"That's so cool," Celeste says, squinting into the office, her eyes so tired she can barely make out the bold headlines.

"I know," he says. "I have a plan, okay? Someday I will sell this place to a developer and use the money to buy a SpaceX ticket." He laughs again and reverently, gently closes the office door. "But I need to live long enough for the ticket price to go down. Nobody is going to pay fifty million for this dump."

"It's not a dump," she says. "It's very nice."

He eyes her again for a moment, one eyebrow raised, then reaches for two more cookies and puts them on the plate. He bends over creakily, opens a mini fridge with a sucking sound, and adds a tiny carton of milk to the plate, too.

"There you go," he says. "Enjoy your evening, Ms. Muldoon."

Celeste's eyes sting with tears. The man's kindness and the cold water and the cookies. She knows she needs sleep and doesn't want to cry. She thanks him and takes the cookies, although she will not eat them, and leaves the lobby to walk to her room at the end of the parking lot. In between the blinds she can see into other people's rooms, where they're watching TV in the blue light and eating fast food on their beds and buttoning up their kids' pajamas. Inside Celeste's own room it is frigid, the window unit turned to max, rattling and coughing. She stumbles into the shower and stands there unmoving for ten minutes in the spray. She thinks about Meo, about a time when they were lying on the beach and he made a pattern with hot stones on her flat belly, and when she sat up carefully she saw that it was a heart.

In bed, with her wet hair wrapped in a towel, she texts her parents and Mimi to let them know she's alive. Ursa cuddles up next to her, and Celeste turns out the lights. The neon from the Starlite sign filters through the blinds. Celeste moves her wrist into the pink beam to light up her tattoo. Tomorrow she and Nicky will turn eighteen. Tomorrow humans will depart this planet for Mars. Thinking about the launch, Celeste has a desperate kind of feeling. Half in a dream, she imagines Nicky on the shuttle, the way they always pictured it when they were kids: huddled under somebody's bunk bed, the perfect hiding place, ready to blast off into space—unless she finds him first. The launch clock flickers in the dark behind her eyes as she finally drifts asleep.

Day 155

On their birthday, for the first time in Celeste's memory, there's no crack-of-dawn text from morning-person Nicky. Usually he sends a string of birthday memes on his way to crew practice, and the phone buzz wakes her up when the sky's still pink. Today—nothing. In the motel somebody's TV is blasting the Mars mission news at an absurd volume. She lies there for a minute with the pillow pressed on her face. Eighteen. Supposed to be a big birthday, the one that launches you. But Celeste still feels like she's fighting the black hole, spinning in the dark. The only way out is on that rocket, as far as Celeste can tell; she has to find Nicky.

After a cold croissant and coffee in the lobby, it's back to the KSC. She springs for an expensive cab with Mimi's "graduation" cash but still doesn't get there early enough to avoid an hour-long wait. By the time she gets in, her cute tank dress with the green stripes (packed in case of a birthday dinner) is plastered wet to her back and pits. With the launch scheduled for six p.m., the crowd is even thicker today, more lines everywhere, her blisters raw and throbbing. Yesterday everyone was high with space fever, wowing at things with a collective spirit of awe, but today it's just sniping moms and sticky, cranky kids and beefy dudes in flag hats. How's she going to find Nicky in this mess? Waiting in line feels like a waste of time, but that's the only way to get in. She checks her phone incessantly, in case he decides to text or call, which makes it painfully harder to ignore her parents and Meo—and especially Carla, who's the first person Celeste would call if she had anything real to report. Which she does not, even as the morning stretches to afternoon.

The exhibits that delighted her yesterday are starting to feel corny and lame. In the Hall of Fame, the astronaut holograms look like sci-fi clones, so many white guys with smooth hair. Mercury mission control looks like the set of a bad seventies movie. Grandiose orchestra music blares over the speakers in every last corner, even the bathrooms. Yesterday the music was a perfect playlist for Celeste's own super-exciting mission—but now it's just stuck in her ears, drowning out rational thought. Ursa barks to warn her—it's one thirty—she waited too long to eat, and the CGM says her sugar's dropped to 70. By some miracle they find an empty patch of shade, where Celeste makes herself eat an apple even though she's not hungry.

In ten minutes she checks the app again and texts Mimi the better number. *Still no Nicky,* she writes, and Mimi says: *Take a break. Sometimes things turn up when you stop looking for them.* But Celeste doesn't want to take a break. The launch is four hours away. There must be something she's missing, some piece of the puzzle she hasn't figured out. She pours a little water over her head to clear the hot funk out of her brain, then stands and squints at *Pioneer* in the distance. It's arrived at the launchpad now, flanked by the full stack of boosters, dwarfing a parade of army jeeps circled around its base.

The orchestra music cuts out and an announcement blasts over the speaker: The day's final NASA tour will depart in five minutes. Suddenly Celeste understands that this is her last chance for a closer look at the shuttle. Unless she somehow manages this big reunion with Nicky in the next hour, she's going to end up watching the launch from the parking lot of the Starlite or, if she's lucky, on the beach, alone in a massive crowd, so she has to get on that bus if she wants to get anywhere near the rocket itself. Dog treats in hand, she hurries Ursa down the little slope of lawn to the buses, using the bulk of the dog to push through the crowd. Celeste is the last person to join the tour line before they cut it off. "My hero," she whispers to Ursa, crouching to give her a sweaty hug.

On the cool, humming bus, a nice lady offers Celeste her window seat so Ursa can squeeze in. As the bus lumbers out of the lot, Celeste rests her forehead on the glass. She tries to let the driver's deep drawl and the flat green marsh out the window calm her down. They pass the old launchpads, which Celeste has always been desperate to see; she used to be able to name all the shuttles that launched from here in chronological order. Once in a while the driver pulls to a stop for a dramatic view of *Pioneer*. At the LC-39 Observation Gantry, the bleachers are already loaded with people gazing through binoculars and fanning themselves with their hats. Everyone in the bus hops up to aim their phones, but Celeste stays in her seat, snuggled up with Ursa. She feels a sinking confusion in the pit of her belly. Just yesterday, she'd been so sure that she and Nicky would be on those bleachers together, listening to the countdown, feeling that different, better kind of rumble under their feet, like they'd always planned.

"Now coming up on your left, ladies and gentlemen, the very spot where Walter Cronkite himself watched the Apollo 11 launch in 1969, the CBS building, and beyond it here we have the press tents, lots of folks very busy here today, as you can see, getting ready for another historic moment coming up in just a few hours. Up on your left, once again that's the NASA press site, folks; take a look, and then we'll be on our way."

There's a corral of video cameras and more bleachers, some tents with tables set up underneath, and lots of frantic people milling around with phones. Celeste is watching them sulkily through the window when she spots a bright blue head of hair hunched over a laptop. She sits up straighter, a jolt of energy kicking breath into her chest. Europa had tried to convince Celeste to show up for the launch, even without Nicky. *Give yourself a birthday gift.* Celeste takes out her phone. Her dad is texting: *Please call. At least let us wish you a happy birthday.* Instead, she digs around and finds Europa's business card. Closing her eyes, Celeste can smell the chai, even hear Europa's laugh. She can feel the swell of light in her chest as she read her own words into the mic.

She starts a text: *Hi Europa, this is Celeste Muldoon, from the MIT interview.* And then she lets it hang there while the bus driver talks more about the mission, about how many months it will take to reach Mars, and how long it will be before the astronauts return to Earth, splashing down at last. *I actually came to Florida for the launch after all! Just thought I'd say hi.* She adds a couple of rocket emojis and deletes them, makes a tight fist for a few seconds, then sends. Probably stupid—Europa won't remember her. But then the three dots, and: *Hi Celeste, so glad you came!! Hope you have so much fun!* Celeste blurts a happy noise, startling Ursa. Bolder, she writes *No launch tickets left*—and adds a sad cat face. Then

Europa: *Playalinda Beach is a great spot for viewing! Send me some pics.*

Celeste feels a stab of rejection. What did she expect, some grand invitation? The bus grinds over some gravel, roiling her mostly empty stomach. Sweat beads on her throat, where she can feel the acid thump of her heart. Soon they'll be back at the complex, which is about to close. If she can't find Nicky—what the fuck is next?

Her phone buzzes in her lap. She checks it with a little leap of her heart, but it's Bridget. Celeste lets it ring through, waits for the voicemail. The bus pulls back into the KSC lot, *Pioneer* presiding in the distance, casting off ribbons of heat.

Celeste, listen, we really need to talk at some point, or maybe we don't; I don't know. I really don't know what the fuck is going on with you, but whatever—the real reason I called is about that Hotmail account, Paolo Reborn? I hacked it, finally—it was kind of a pain in my ass—but the thing is, nobody's logged in to it for months. Like, not since March, here in SF, I don't know exactly where, so . . . fuck, I have no idea what it means—I just thought you'd want to know.

The bus lurches to a stop. Celeste closes her eyes and listens again, watching the words implode one by one in the darkness, blue supernovas in a dazzling fiery show. She stumbles down the stairs, out into the baking sun, whirling, dizzy, as the crowd spins around her, the exodus to the parking lot. Brilliant Ursa finds a little shaded fire hydrant where Celeste can sit down. The word debris swirls in her brain: *Paolo/garbled/March/Reborn*. There's a sputtering in her chest, a molten fury rising in her throat. She writes him a text: *HAPPY FUCKING BIRTHDAY. I'm in Florida. Where are you??* But she can't hit send. She clutches the stupid tiny computer that doesn't have any real fucking answers and only makes everything worse.

"What the fuck am I doing here?" she says out loud, and then Fake Nicky is there, scared and small, zipped into Pumpkin in spite of the heat. Hands crossed flat on his chest, like when they got in trouble when they were kids. *You really need to ask?* He turns to gaze at the rocket. It's painted a rusty red, like Mars dust, like the Golden Gate Bridge. They're playing that big cheesy music again, all impassioned strings. People are everywhere, swarming and sweating and laughing, but none of them is Nicky.

Lost/gone/missing. Now even Fake Nicky has vanished into the crowd. Celeste's eyes swell with tears. The fury in her chest is starting to cool into a jagged quartz of resolve. She thinks of Joan, the cloaked aura: *You won't find him unless he wants to be found.* Celeste presses her palm on the sun tattoo, but the only thing she can feel there now is her own pulse.

"Attention, explorers: The Kennedy Space Center visitor complex is closing. Please make your way to the exits. Come see us again soon!"

The music resumes, knocking Celeste back into her brain with a clash of cymbals: *Nicky is gone.* She's not going to find him today, maybe not ever. She came here to find her friend—her twin, her other half—but she has the feeling there's something else she's been looking for, too. Something else she was meant to find all along. And if she gives up now, she might never figure out what it is.

WIPING AWAY HOT TEARS, CELESTE GULPS HER WATER and pours Ursa a drink, splashing with shaky hands. She takes a minute to steady herself, then climbs up onto the fire hydrant for a better view of the rocket. Above the crowd, she can breathe a little easier. *Pioneer* is poised in the distance, trembling in the humid air. Closer, by the main gate, there's the old launch countdown clock ticking away: one hour and fifty-nine minutes.

She hops down and packs up Ursa's bowl. Buses are boarding lines of hot, impatient ticket holders headed for the observation platforms, shuffling their flip-flops and wrangling their kids. Celeste is wondering if she could find a way to scam a ticket—maybe use Ursa to play the sympathy card?—when she spots a bus with no line idling on the far side of the lot. A sign in the window reads PRESS SITE. The driver is settling behind the wheel.

A ludicrous idea begins to arrive in Celeste's mind, letter by letter, as if someone is typing it there. Time seems to hesitate, all the other tourists and ushers and tired kids floating in a pause that lasts just long enough for the bus driver to close the door. Celeste grips Ursa's leash and runs.

"Wait, hi, sorry!" She knocks on the glass and waves, out of breath. The driver opens the door halfway. He reaches into a bag of peanuts in his lap. "Badge," he says, and she freezes with a dumb grin on her face. This is about as far as she got with this crazy plan.

"Press badge," he says again.

"Oh no . . ." she says, failing to steady a tremor in her voice. "Um, you know what? Oh my god, I think I lost my badge!" She rummages in her backpack, trying to get a little frantic without drawing the attention of the passengers, who all seem absorbed in their phones anyway. "I had it right here, but . . . Shoot, what am I going to do?"

The driver crunches peevishly on his peanuts. "Can't let you on without a badge."

She glances into the bus and lowers her voice. "I'm only an

intern, at *PodLab*? The podcast? I don't want to get in trouble. So, like, do you think you could just maybe let me on?"

He shakes his head. "Step aside, please."

"No, wait—the thing is . . ." She lowers her face. It isn't hard to muster some desperate tears; it's actually a relief to let them spill over her cheeks and run out her nose. The driver says, "Christ almighty," and hands her a Kleenex. "Listen," he says, "I don't make the rules here, okay? Wish I could help you—"

"It's just—" She pauses to blow her nose, casting around for some excuse until the perfect one presents itself on a platter: "The thing is, my *insulin's* in my other bag, at the site? I'm diabetic—that's why I have the dog. And I really need my insulin, I need to take it soon, so I can't, like, *wait* to get a new badge, or whatever—"

"Jesus!" the driver says. He checks his watch, wipes his bald brow with his floppy NASA cap. "Fine, get on. Sit right here behind me, and don't go passing out on my bus. Better find somebody to vouch for you at the site, hear?"

"Totally, yes, thank you!" She slides into the front seat, still sniffling, and tries to make herself as small as possible as the bus pulls out of the lot. Her heartbeat's in a manic sprint. There's the insipid orchestra music, now some blaring trumpets; Celeste does her best to think of it like a soundtrack for this ballsy but very possibly suicidal move. She sneaks a glance behind her, where everyone seems enraptured by their devices. (Makes sense, since they're all here to cover the launch in one hour and fifty-two minutes.) Celeste pretends to care about her own phone, even as she's desperately trying to figure out what comes next. But there's a text from Meo—*Miss you, mi estrella*—and so with the brave soundtrack behind her and her heart already swollen with stupid courage, she sends off the text that's been hanging there since yesterday:

I went away for a while, maybe we'll talk when I get back. Then she turns off the phone and zips it out of sight.

"Press site," the driver announces, pulling off the causeway into a weedy lot. Out here the marsh grass is long and fragrant, and a cloud of muggy air billows into the bus when the door opens. Celeste spots Europa's blue M&M hair again under the tents, maybe just thirty feet away now, in a little cluster of people standing around a table picking at a fruit platter. Celeste waits for the other passengers to file off. "There's my boss," she tells the driver. "I'll go talk to her, okay? She can vouch for me. Thanks again, really, so much!"

He grunts and waves her out. She grips her backpack and the leash, draws a big wobbly breath, and holds it all the way down the bus stairs, into the pressing heat, and across the long grass. Ursa makes it pretty much impossible to arrive anywhere unnoticed; people in the tents are starting to stare, giving them the weird, not exactly unkind smiles they always get in places where dogs aren't allowed. One of the guys standing with Europa says something that makes her turn and look. With a startled sort of smile, Europa laughs—that distinctive golden coil of sound—and waves uncertainly. "Hey, I think I know her!"

Celeste's whole body is shaking, but somehow she manages to wave back. Her legs carry her over to the little group of reporters. Up close Europa's smile looks wooden and confused, her eyebrows stretched high. "Wow, Celeste, what a surprise! Listen, excuse us for a minute, guys, okay?" She links her arm with Celeste's and walks her out from under the tent, back toward the bus, where the driver is sitting on the stairs, eating his peanuts and eyeing his watch. Europa's grip tightens. "Please," she says, "tell me you have an uncle or cousin or something who got you a press badge."

"Not exactly."

"Shit," Europa hisses. "What did you do?" They stand close together in the baking sun, voices lowered. Europa's face is zipped in anger, her glasses kind of fogged, obscuring her eyes. She's dressed differently today, in a prim black shirtdress with sweaty pits, a tightly twisted blue bun in place of the wild topknot.

"I just— It sort of just came *out*. I wasn't trying—"

"Goddamn it," Europa says, "I *really* don't have time for this today." Celeste can feel the pissed-off heat from Europa's face and the guilty scalding flush of her own. She wants to step away, but there's something else holding her feet to the grass, a magnetism she doesn't recognize or understand, which seems to come from deep in her chest.

"Look," Europa says, "I thought you and I were going to be friends, but now I'm starting to think you're not a very honest person. You came to my house for what was basically a fake interview, right? Under false pretense, which I forgave, because I liked you. You snooped through my stuff, which I totally ignored. And now you're showing up here—"

"But that's the thing," Celeste pleads, the magnet pull deepening in her chest, spreading into her throat and back. "I never really *do* this kind of stuff! This is all just . . . I mean, since the quake—"

"Celeste, you can't keep blaming everything on the bloody earthquake!" Europa shakes her head, presses her forehead with the heel of her hand. "We're moving on now, okay? The earthquake happened to us, and now everybody's moving on to Mars, whether we goddamn like it or not, okay? And I have a job to do here. So come on, you have to go. I'll ask Archie to take you back to the complex."

"Wait, please!"

Europa stands with her fists on her hips. Celeste can feel people glancing up from their phones and coffees. The words are hanging there behind her teeth, birds at the cage door. If she lets them out, they might attack her, or they might flee to the open sky. She lets them go in spurts: "I was just going to say . . . it's just, ever since the quake—I'm like this different *person*, you know? And I don't totally get it, and it really *really* freaks me out, because I keep doing stupid things, but also—they're kind of *brave* things? I feel like. So I just . . . keep letting myself do them." She looks away, at the rocket standing ready in the distant haze, and adds, "I guess I'm not making any sense." But then Europa pushes the steamy glasses up to rest on her head, and her eyes are kind underneath.

"I do understand, okay?" she says. "It's just so crazy here today—"

"I could be an intern or something? Just for the day."

Europa laughs, and the familiar looping ring of it fills Celeste with jittery hope. "We already have those," Europa says, "and they more or less had to spill blood to get the gig. They probably wouldn't appreciate me pulling you in off the street."

"I can be *their* intern! Get them coffee and stuff."

Europa takes off her glasses to clean them with her sleeve, rubs her eyes with the back of her wrist. She laughs again and says, "Oh my god, I'm so tired!" Then she puts the glasses on with a sigh. She blinks at Celeste through the clear lenses. "I just remembered—it's your birthday."

"Yeah," Celeste says, although she'd actually forgotten for a little while. The magnet pull that's stopping her from fleeing seems to throb inside her sun tattoo and in the other wrist, too, where there's just a fork of veins. The two of them stand there paused in a cloud of heat and Ursa's heavy breath, murmurs drifting from the tents, the rocket looming over it all. Then Europa says, "Wait here," and walks over to the bus. She talks for a minute to the driver while Celeste looks on, the magnet pull combined now with a kind of glorious lightness. She wonders if this is what zero gravity feels like, the thrill of doing something utterly new and powerful.

Europa gives the bus driver a hug (somehow this doesn't surprise Celeste, that Europa is a hugger) and watches him gather his peanut shells and climb behind the wheel. She waves to him with a huge smile, then returns to Celeste and says, "You're lucky Archie's a fan of mine." In her shock, Celeste somehow finds a way to shout "Thank you!" at the bus as it recedes. "I mean thank *you*," she tells Europa breathlessly. "Thank you so much!"

"If anyone asks, you're my wife's cousin, okay? You're interested in an internship, so I invited you here to watch the launch with us."

Celeste feels just as lucky and honored as if it were actually true. She follows Europa to the tents.

"I beg you, do *not* do anything to make me regret being nice to you. I can't hang out with you at all. Too much going on. You're on your own, okay?"

Yes, Celeste thinks, that has probably never been truer.

UNDER THE TENTS, *PODLAB* HAS A TABLE LITTERED with water bottles and recording equipment, some folding chairs, and a paper sign with their logo, all of which feels like just the perfect amount of shabby glamour, like some kind of ink-smelling newsroom from a noir movie. Europa introduces Celeste to the real interns—Sam, Kamiesha, and Soli—who are crammed around the table, hunched at their laptops. They sling their headphones around their necks to say hello.

"It's okay," Celeste says, "you don't have to, like, *entertain* me or anything—" but they insist on taking her along to raid the cookies and fill up their waters while Europa goes back to her own workstation to take a call. The interns seem to buy the story that Celeste is some kind of relative who showed up out of the blue, or at least they're too busy and caffeinated and hyped about the launch to care. But they're all friendly, wishing her happy birthday, piling her plate with cookies—"Smart money's on oatmeal raisin," Soli tells her slyly—and cooing over Ursa. Within five minutes it's clear that they are all spectacularly smart, too. They're working on a bonus episode about the launch; the plan is to drop the episode late tonight, so they're on a crazy deadline with less than four hours' sleep.

"It's inhu*mane*," Kamiesha groans, but when she tells Celeste about the segment she's editing—an interview with Jessica Watkins, the *Pioneer* geologist—her eyes get huge and bright, and she goes on about Watkins for five minutes while the other interns drift back to work. Then she gives Celeste a pair of headphones and a job flagging some tape for interference and ambient noise.

"You sure it's okay? Should we ask Europa, or one of the other producers?"

"Hell no," Kamiesha laughs, "half the time I need to tell them what to do." So Celeste settles happily into one of the plastic chairs, closes the foam cups over her ears, and spends a few peaceful minutes in the quiet, listening. Kamiesha shows her how to add a red flag in the software when there's a disruption, however faint: distant voices, the exhale of a bus's brakes. It's strange to be sitting here surrounded by this historic commotion—reporters shouting into their phones and loudspeaker announcements from NASA and more buses grumbling up to drop off more reporters—but hearing none of it, only Europa's voice and the astronaut's. At 5:13 there's a burst of somebody's faraway laughter on the track, and Celeste marks it with a flag. At 7:37 some insistent beeps are muffled deep in the background, like a truck backing up in a distant neighborhood, and she flags those, too. Cocooned in the quiet, Celeste thinks of that afternoon listening to the Golden Record in her little attic with Nicky, *footsteps heartbeat mud pots thunder*, which seems so long ago that she can't be sure whether it's memory or dream.

"Celeste, hey." It's Soli, tugging the cord of Celeste's headphones. "They're calling us, come on." She joins the interns, coaxing a reluctant Ursa out from under the shade of the table. They follow the crowd to the grandstand and find seats with Europa and two other producers whom Celeste hasn't met, but she doesn't ask—it's enough that Europa catches her eye and tosses her a little wave. The interns pass around a bag of pretzels and talk about how they can't believe it'll really go ahead as planned. Yesterday, apparently, there was talk that they might scrub the launch because of some minor electrical problem, but NASA's press team has been insisting all day that it's fixed, and everyone should prepare. "Not buying it," says one of the producer guys, "not till that baby's up in the sky." And they all gaze at the shimmering rocket with sweat in their eyes. Celeste is thinking about how, if she's figured out anything in the long months since the earthquake, it's that crazy shit can happen, so you might as well expect that it will.

The countdown clock says thirty-four minutes when a woman with a sleek black braid trailing out of a NASA cap steps onto a plywood stage and waves her arms for the crowd's attention. "All right, y'all, settle down now and listen up." Sam and one of the producer dudes hoist some giant overhead mics onto their backs and join the camera operators at the foot of the grandstand. When it's finally quiet, the braid woman (Soli says she's the NASA media chief) announces that preflight checks are complete, and the shuttle's been cleared for launch. The crowd explodes with whoops and whistles and applause, causing a flock of small white birds to erupt from the grass and flood the sky in a beautiful swirl, which seems itself to pull Celeste and the rest of the crowd to their feet. The ovation lasts a long minute while the media chief grins, pretending to try to quiet them down. Eventually they sit, but Celeste still feels aloft with those birds, who, like her, are accidental witnesses here.

The birds are still winging overhead a moment later when the *Pioneer* crew appears on the giant screen behind the stage, and everyone goes nuts all over again. It's a live feed from inside the rocket, where the astronauts are strapped in and ready for launch. Kamiesha cheers wildly when Dr. Jessica Watkins smiles and waves—looking a little bit nervous, Celeste thinks, which is kind of awesome, really—how could she not be? Even those gilded holograms in the Hall of Fame yesterday, no more human than the glowing rocks in the glass case at Crystal Visions, are stand-ins for very real people. They lay flat in those old rockets and probably worried they'd get diarrhea at takeoff or start sobbing during their interviews on this very spot the day before they went to space. Celeste can see in Dr. Watkins's eyes that she's afraid, and she thinks of Nicky and Meo and Carla and even Bonnie, who looks at Celeste with those eyes pretty much whenever she leaves the house. The fear connects them all, and maybe so does the hope; Celeste can almost feel it in her wings.

There's a video briefing from one of the deputy mission commanders—Celeste thrills to all the NASA jargon spilling from the stiff jaw of this military guy, fluid and easy as a poem—then the media chief quiets everyone down again and announces a forty-five-minute hold. The countdown clock stops at T minus nine minutes exactly.

"I don't get what's wrong?" Celeste says to Soli, who tells her kindly, "It's a planned pause; they do it every time. They're polling the crew and the ground teams to check all the systems, look at the weather again, all that. It's a safeguard. We just wait."

Celeste looks over at the rocket, thinks of Dr. Watkins strapped flat and scared. "That must suck for the astronauts," she says, and Soli agrees. Europa has gone to the tent and returned with a little cooler full of blissfully icy drinks; she hands Celeste a can as if she were just unremarkably part of the team. The producers all open their laptops, but the interns get to take a break, so Celeste sits with them, sipping her Diet Coke and kind of blissing out with the ease of it while they chat about the launch and the bonus episode and how Kamiesha's obsessed with Jess Watkins and Sam is stalking the media chief on Insta ("Want to know how many fucks she gives about me? Zero"). They talk a little about the quake, too. Soli's building in the Richmond has structural damage they still can't seem to fix, so she's been living with her parents. "How's *that* going?" Kamiesha asks, and Soli groans: "The fuckin' *worst*. I gotta find a new place." She turns to Celeste. "How about you, Celeste—what's your deal? Are you a student?"

Europa casts a sideways glance but keeps typing. It should be an easy question, but Celeste's been vigorously avoiding it for days. She doesn't know if they are going to let her graduate, but this doesn't seem to terrify her as much as it should. At school this is the time of year when the senior hallway turns into a big party, complete with balloons and Silly String, when they all parade around in college sweatshirts and skip class to leave sappy notes in each other's lockers. Everyone else complains about this during finals time, but Celeste and Nicky always secretly loved it, detouring through the senior hall so they could spy. Celeste always assumed the reason she didn't belong was that she hadn't arrived yet; it wasn't her time.

"Not exactly," she says to Soli. "I'm . . . kind of, like—in a *pause.*"

Soli nods matter-of-factly. "I get that."

Celeste risks a glance at Europa, who's still wrapped up in her work, but there's a tiny smile at the corner of her mouth. "I'm interested in the internship," Celeste adds clumsily, because that's the story, but then she realizes that it's true.

"Cool," Soli says, and then the countdown clock resumes with a loud alarm, causing another brief chaos among the reporters and birds. The media chief climbs onstage and announces, "Go time, folks! We're bringing you direct shuttle and ground control audio, so keep it down and listen up. We're fixin' to make some history here."

"God, I love this woman," Sam says.

"Talk later," Soli whispers to Celeste, just as the speakers begin to crackle and echo. At first the *PodLab* team quietly grumbles about the audio quality, but soon they're just as captivated as everyone else, surrendered to listening, pens and tablets neglected in their laps. The voices seem to come from very far away, as if already soaring above the atmosphere. In the grandstand every last pair of eyes is trained on the rocket, trembling perceptibly in the distance.

"T minus seven minutes thirty seconds and counting. Retract orbiter access arm." Somebody passes Celeste a pair of binoculars

so she can see the arm pulling back from its position. She remembers holding this tiny piece of the model rocket in her palm. She remembers Nicky narrating the launch into the mic of his fist, the whole grand dream poised in their small hands, just waiting for them to claim it. Somewhere along the way, Celeste realizes now, she stopped believing in it. When she got sick, it got harder to dream about the future. She'd been thinking it was the quake, Nicky's disappearance, that had cracked open her world, but really it had started happening with the diagnosis: a spreading web of painful fissures, so when the quake arrived with its massive jolt, she fell apart. *I had a feeling you were going to fall to pieces,* that's what Fake Nicky said, and she suddenly knows what he meant. She guesses she'd been waiting for it to happen, too. Now it's up to her to sweep the shards, to weld them into something new and strange.

"*T minus five minutes and counting. Start auxiliary power units.*" The crowd rises to their feet. Nobody chats or laughs now; there's only the ghostly back-and-forth between shuttle and mission control, sometimes the papery fuss of the white birds unsettling themselves. Celeste listens, her eyes on the rocket. Underneath the sounds, deep in her memory, there's Nicky's voice—*Come in, Ground Control, this is Major Toniolo*—and she wonders, as she has so many times in recent months, what he is doing right now. Is he watching the countdown, too? Is he reinvented somewhere, Paolo Reborn living a new life? Or truly lost, strung out in a dark tunnel, or worse? She might never know the answer. She understands now that Nicky never wanted her to know. It hurts so much, but also it feels, finally, like the truth. The "clues" Celeste found were never supposed to lead her to *him*. The dream from last night comes back to her: playing hide-and-seek in the shuttle. But was it

Nicky stowed away, or Celeste herself? She closes her eyes to remember, but the details of the face flicker and fade.

"*T minus two minutes and counting. Crew members close and lock your visors.*" The crowd is lifted onto their toes, caught in a stillness so taut you can almost hear it.

"*T minus thirty-one seconds and counting. Ground launch sequencer is go for auto sequence start.*" This time she knows that the ground is about to shake. Searching for something to hold on to, she finds only her own hands.

"*T minus . . . ten . . . nine . . . eight . . . seven . . . six . . . five . . . four . . . three . . . two . . . one—*"

A crackling roar, a swift cloud billowing over the island for miles. A rumble not only in the earth, but in the air.

There will be a time in the almost-near future when Celeste is tasked to write about this moment. She will wait until shortly before deadline—it turns out she works best this way, for better or worse—and then she'll find herself struggling with how to describe the strange before-and-after feeling: standing there on the grandstand watching the rocket fly, nothing ever so impossibly bright as its fiery tail, and also standing somewhere else entirely, watching it happen from a distant moment, at the other end of an unknown span of time. She is in her body, in the arms of strangers, drowned in the shuttle roar and in the roar of the applause, but also in another body, thicker and sturdier, rooted through the soles of her feet. In the actual future, Celeste will remember the fire, the smoke, the tremor in the ground; there was a kind of violence in it, and she will wonder—was it just like that when the library fell? One moment an end, one a beginning, every moment both beginning and end.

Day 657

Nobody will ever believe Celeste when she tells them, so much later, that she was thinking about earthquakes at the very moment when she finally found Nicky.

Specifically, she's thinking about seismic activity on the moon. She is sitting at LAX, folded into a terrible plastic chair with her laptop perched on her knees, taking some research notes to submit to Europa. Evidently, the moon's quakes last much longer than ours, some of them rising up from deep inside the lunar core, and others inexplicably forming just beneath the silver crust, these shallow quakes much stronger than the deep ones. Some of the quakes are signs of thaw: morning sun hitting the frigid moon at the end of a two-week night. It's almost been long enough now that Celeste has stopped thinking *gotta tell Nicky* every time something cool comes up—and yet, when she lifts her screen-tired eyes and wanders them over the terminal, stretching her arms and thinking of moonquakes, that is when she sees him. Tall, wide-shouldered, dressed in military fatigues. Sitting at a sports bar, his forehead propped in his hands. Legions of people are rushing over the wide corridor between them, a blast of sun from a huge skylight casting everything in a harsh white glow, but still she can tell it's him; she knows his profile like her own, and that is *Dune* lying open on the bar, the same bloated copy he's carried around for years.

Among the many feelings swirling hotly in her chest as she fumbles with her suitcase, she doesn't seem to feel at all surprised. She stopped looking for him long ago, but objects in close orbit are bound to eventually collide.

"It's him," she whispers to Ursa, who knows something is up, her nose twitching in the air. Together they wade into the stream of travelers. They're half across the walkway when Celeste feels herself stop. What if he still doesn't want to see her? He's staring into his book. He picks up a glass of water, a flash of the sun tattoo. Annoyed people drag their rolling bags in a huff to avoid the dog, but Ursa's figured it out; she lifts her head and barks straight through the crowd at Nicky. Everyone turns to look. His face is different—shaved clean, too thin. But when he sees them, a blaze in his eyes brightens everything nearby: the bar, the dog, his skin. He calls her name with a question mark. "Oh my god," he says, and then again, shouting, "Oh my god!"

He jumps off the stool and runs to her and grabs her in a hug, both of them laughing, crying, stunned. The shape of the hug is so familiar and also utterly strange. Celeste feels a surge of deep relief, an undertow that lifts her off her feet. Ursa is barking wildly, which could probably get them in airport trouble, but who cares. Nicky nuzzles the dog's neck and lets her slobber all over his ear. "Ursa my love, your breath is still so foul," he laughs, wrapping her in his long arms. And somehow when he stands again to face Celeste, the moment is changed, his face cast in shade, the laughter giving way to a long and wordless pause. Everything seems floaty and hollow, made of transparent color, like a projection. Celeste has that strange before-and-after feeling again, just like at the *Pioneer* launch—not exactly déjà vu, more like the feeling that something already happened, and this is just the memory of it.

After a minute Nicky opens his hands. He says, "So . . . time for a drink? Or if you have to go—"

"No, yeah, I can stay for a bit."

"Cool."

Their words seem to restore the substance of things, re-engage the gears of time. Nicky takes her laptop bag—weirdly chivalrous, not his style—and they find their way back to his spot at the bar. On his neck there's a scar from jumping off a rope swing once at the river near Mimi's. There's a bruise, too, but Celeste doesn't know how it got there.

"You want, like, a bubbly water, or—"

"Maybe coffee." He orders it for her, weird again, like they're on some kind of a date. She thanks him but can't really look at him. Her heart is frantically pounding, but the rest of her is frozen stiff. She eyes the clock behind the bar—two hours until her plane boards. They're sitting so close that she can smell the coconut shampoo and see the careful way Nicky has trimmed and cleaned his fingernails; the last time she saw him, they were speckled with chips of purple polish. A guy in a rumpled suit a few stools away laughs loudly into his phone, startling them both.

"Jesus," Nicky says. They giggle nervously, and for just a minute Celeste feels a lift in the strange weight between them. On the TV behind the bar, there is silent news of the Mars mission crew. They're home at last, after one hundred days on Mars and more than a year of travel, out of medical quarantine now and starting to talk to the press. Celeste's connecting flight will take her back to Orlando, where she will assist with the Jess Watkins interview. Europa has given the segment to Kamiesha, her first big story as a real producer; last night on a Zoom call, they all celebrated with too much champagne. Celeste packed her clothes a little bit hungover, forgetting the Florida heat, and probably threw in three too many pairs of jeans.

"Did you see it?" Nicky says, watching the TV. "Like, in person?"

"Thanks to you, yeah, I did."

"Aw yes! That's awesome."

"It was, it was awesome." Her coffee arrives, and she studies the film of oil on its surface. "What about you?"

"Nah, I wasn't really in a great place then."

They both take a drink. There are so many questions, but Celeste has carried them around for so long that they're part of her body now, and voicing them feels like vomiting. Nicky drains his soda to the ice, then kind of slams it loudly on the bar. Is he going to get angry, or storm away? She can't predict him anymore, which nauseates her, too. But when he turns to face her, the old Nicky-light is there on his skin, pale and faintly sparking. "Fuck it, Cookie," he says. "Let's cut to the chase. You're better off without me, right? I can tell, you look amazing. Come on, fuckin' spill it."

She reaches out to touch the elbow of his camo sleeve. As far as Celeste knows, there is only one photo around of Nicky's father, buried in an album in Nonna and Pop's house, and in it he is wearing head-to-toe fatigues, just like the ones Nicky is wearing now. As kids, the two of them used to wonder at the photo, leaving fingerprints on the plastic page, shoving it back onto the shelf before Carla could see.

"You first," she says.

THEY WALK. THE BAR'S TOO DIM AND CONFINING, Ursa jammed between the stools, so Celeste rolls her suitcase and Nicky shoulders his duffel and they set out into the terminal, which is quieting as the day wanes. She wants him to start at the beginning, with the earthquake, but he goes backward instead. He's on his way to Texas—San Antonio, he tells her. There's a spot waiting for him in the Air Force Academy prep school. At first, after basic training, they stuck him with a shit job, hauling crates of engine parts at Vandenberg, because he had a GED instead of a diploma; then a teacher at tech school noticed his margin doodles and fast-tracked him for the academy. Celeste listens for her friend underneath this story, tries to imagine him marching in a line of stiff recruits. She calls to mind their dream of college in Cambridge—empty wine bottles piling up in a cheap apartment, Nicky rowing on the Charles—but that seems to make even less sense now than this weird reality. At first, she thinks maybe it has something to do with his dad, some longing she never knew was there, but then she searches his voice and begins to understand: This is how he will get to outer space.

"I kind of dazzled them, I guess," he says, and she says, "Of course you did," but there's a little snag in her voice that she can't seem to hide. Nicky in the military? How's that going to work, exactly?

"Gay flyboys are definitely a thing," he says, "in case you're wondering."

"Good to know." There's a faint ache in her wrist, underneath the sun, as they pass a couple of crowded gates, people slumped together in this most mundane of pauses. "Will they make you get rid of the tattoo?"

"Over my dead body!" He stops to roll back the sleeve on his other arm, to show her a new one. It's black, looks homemade, maybe India ink. Just dots and lines. She squints at it and realizes after a minute: the Gemini.

"Oh my god," she says, tears welling in her eyes. "So beautiful!"

He laughs again and crows, "It's a hack job! Some kid did it for me—I was really high, I guess. Lucky I didn't get fucking sepsis." He smiles out the window, only with his mouth, gazing at a plane's wings glinting copper in the dusk. After a moment Celeste kneels to unzip her backpack and takes out the Mars book, which she still seems to bring along everywhere. She tries to hand it over, but he just stares. "You found it?"

"You knew I would."

Without taking the book, he starts walking again. For a minute they're quiet, heading down a long empty arm of the building full of plaster and paint smells, scaffold hiding a construction site, *please excuse our mess*. Only a few other travelers are listlessly hanging out here, looking lost or weary, tethered to the walls by their skinny charging cords. Finally, Nicky says, "I knew you'd try to look for me . . . I guess I figured knowing where you'd look would make it easier to hide. Like hide-and-seek at Nonna's. I always knew you'd check the best places first."

She balls her fists, fights the urge to start crying again. She didn't realize the wound was still so tender. "You kind of tricked me, though."

His mouth crumples, a face she remembers from when they were very small, whenever he couldn't make her understand. "I needed you to let me go," he says. "I didn't know how to convince you. And anyway, I thought, like, what's wrong with a good mystery. Maybe she'll find something else worth looking for." He's rubbing the Gemini tattoo with the heel of his hand, like it's still sore. "Constellations," he says vaguely, then after a minute: "They're completely arbitrary, you know? Just humans making up stories. You can find any shape you want up there. But also, they had a purpose once, for the ancients, right? Navigation. They used the stars to find their way."

She glances at the new tattoo, the splotchy stars, before he covers it again with his sleeve. Her skin feels hot. The old anger still simmers in the pit of her belly. He ditched her, sent her on a wild-goose chase. After *Pioneer*, she stopped looking for him, but it took her months, maybe a year, to stop feeling pissed at him all the time. He should apologize now, right? Get on his knees and beg her forgiveness?

Maybe—but also, she knows he isn't wrong. At first, after the quake, she didn't understand how to let him go. Failing to find him taught her how.

Celeste's phone rings loudly, shattering the silence. She almost forgot there was a world apart from this airport at this moment. Before she can shut it down, they both see it's Meo, a selfie flashing on the screen, his lips smashed on her cheek. With a little smirk Nicky says, "I'll get it!" but she darts out of reach. "The fuck you will!" For a moment things are easy again, both of them laughing as he tries to snatch the phone. She runs a few steps ahead and checks the screen. A text from Meo: *Miss you too much*. They'd promised to wait a while before calling, but it's only been three days since she helped him pack the car and said goodbye.

"Oh, I know all about your star-crossed lover boy," Nicky says, catching up to her. She shoots him a puzzled look. "Uh, you two are all over Bridget's Insta? And anyway, I read your emails,

Cookie! At least for a while. I had to stop, eventually. Too hard not to write back."

She wants to ask more about the emails—when he read them, where he read them, why he read them—but it feels like she shouldn't push. It feels like he's coming to all of that, and still she's worried that he might vanish again before he gets there, suddenly running off for his flight or slipping away at a crowded gate.

"That kid always had a thing for you," he says slyly. She smiles a little—he wants the scoop—but she isn't sure where to start. Nobody in her life really knows the whole truth about what Meo did—except Mimi, for whom forgiveness is a state of being, as natural as breath. It was Mimi who paid off the debt for Nicky's pills, and Mimi who helped Celeste figure out how to forgive Meo, once she realized that's what she really wanted to do. Mimi helped her work through what she'd already started to understand: that people don't have to be defined by their mistakes, especially mistakes they make when they're scared and helpless and broke. Ale forgave Meo eventually, too, and let him work off the money he took. Celeste even worked at Quetzal for a while herself, waiting tables. Ale loved her, insisted Meo bring her along to family meals, taught her to make hand-churned cinnamon ice cream and avocado mousse. When she got hired at *PodLab*, they threw her a surprise dinner at the restaurant, invited her parents and Carla, Soli and Bridget. The time when things were bad with Meo seems so long ago now that Celeste feels weirdly protective of it. It's strange not to want to just spill it all to Nicky, like she's done every other time she so much as kissed anyone. But this isn't the same Nicky, after all. She doesn't even know if he's still going by that name. She'll have to figure out if Paolo is someone she can trust.

She texts Meo: *Something crazy happened. Crazy good, I think! Call you when I get to FL*, and then she turns the ringer off and tucks the phone in her bag.

"He just moved away," she tells Nicky. "San Diego. To be closer to his parents."

"Aw, that sucks," he says, leaning a little closer, as if he might sling an arm around her neck, but he doesn't. "I'm sorry."

"It's okay. We'll figure something out. Or not, I don't know." On the good days, when she's busy working and feeling the forward movement of her life, Celeste remembers that Meo didn't vanish or abandon her; he just left, like people do. She can visit him. The water's so much warmer down there.

She says to Nicky, "I think he helped me feel less mad at you."

"He helped me, too, you know. When I was really messed up."

"I know." She hasn't thought about this in a while: Nicky in Meo's car, the two of them setting out on the wide freeway, heading toward a Super 8 while the vast cracked shell of the earth was getting ready to shift. It comforts her now to think of them together. She takes a deep breath. "How long did you stay there, at the hotel?"

He stops walking, adjusts his duffel, rubs his shoulder under the strap. "I guess we're really doing this," he says, looking away. "Let's sit again. Okay?"

THEY FIND SEATS BY A WINDOW AT AN EMPTY COR-ner gate, the low pink sun streaming in to warm their skin and the vinyl chairs. It's strange, sitting so close. She wants to touch him, just to convince herself he's real.

"I had it all planned," Nicky says, his voice muffled and small, like somebody talking too far from the mic. Celeste scoots closer on the sticky seat. "I took Mimi's money and left the ticket there, that last time we went together—remember? For the Geminids." He's kneading his hands together, staring into the knot of them. "I was gonna take some months to get my shit in order, you know, and then meet you at the launch, like *ta-da*! It's the new me! But that day in the hotel I got nervous, cold feet. Decided to put it all off and come back home. I went looking for you at the library."

Celeste feels a chill. The acrid smell of the ravaged library burns her nose, as it always does when that memory comes to mind, standing there with her dad, the ash in their hair. "Holy shit," she says.

He nods. When he got there, she was already gone. He hid out for a while in the sci-fi section, hunched on one of those little rolling stools, hugging his knees, breathing the book smell. Then he wandered outside, stood for a minute on the wide stone stairs. A strange stillness in the air. Then the shaking, some kind of explosion. He managed to run into the street but saw the building come down.

"The sound of it, that was the worst thing. The sound, and the dust. It just like . . . *swallowed* everything. I couldn't see for so long. Everything was just, you know, *gray*, like a fucking thick gray cloud everywhere, and you'd be wandering, and then somebody would come out of the smoke screaming or bleeding, or whatever, worse—it was just . . ." He keeps shaking his head, refusing it all. "It fucked me up," he says. "I was okay, but like, by a hair."

She touches his arm, without thinking or worrying, and pulls him into a hug. He's crying; she didn't realize, because he's silent. He buries his face in the shoulder of her shirt, a hoodie they bought together years ago, vintage Rolling Stones with the giant tongue, black cotton worn so thin it's almost transparent. They used to share the shirt before Nicky got so tall and started rowing crew. His tears soak through to her skin. They stay this way for a while. One of the things Celeste has figured out lately is that her inclination to silence is actually a talent—a power, even. It doesn't make her feel small anymore, the way it did when she was always next to Nicky. She understands, better than most people, when to speak up and when to listen. She's okay with letting long minutes go by, as they do now in the vacant gate, the distant sounds of the busy terminal making a steady hum.

Eventually Nicky keeps going. His head was spinning, he tells her, full of sirens and smoke. He couldn't breathe well; it's possible he blacked out. Couldn't put two thoughts together, kept getting lost in the streets they've been walking for years, making the same turns again and again.

At some point later, almost in total darkness, the power out at the edge of that deep night, he found himself wandering near their school. By then it was deserted, yellow caution tape stretched over the door. "I couldn't really think straight, but I was thinking about the field, that night with Ursa, remember?"

She does. Summer before junior year, they snuck onto the cramped little soccer field late one night when they were stoned. Climbed over the chain-link fence at the side of the building. Nicky even managed to boost Ursa over—such a triumph that they whooped at the moon too loudly, and somehow without consequence. Then the dog (lumbering massive Ursa!) was running circles around the silvered grass at top speed—Celeste had never seen her move like that—like a wild bear in a clearing. They watched her in awe. It was one of those nights that didn't seem real when you looked back on it. But Nicky managed to climb that fence after the quake in the same spot, where the chain link had a few little dents they'd made with their boots.

He lay down on the damp field. Smelled the dirt. Maybe fell asleep for a while. At some point he tried the back doors and found one unlocked. "Nobody there," he tells her. "Maybe the building wasn't safe, but I didn't really think about that. These blue emergency lights were on in the hallways, like the spaceship in *Alien* or something! My phone was dead—figured I'd walk home in the morning. I went up to the fishbowl, which was all broken and fucked up. Slept on the turf up there." He laughs darkly, crosses his arms tight on his chest. "It was stupid. I was sick from the smoke. Should've walked my ass to the hospital."

Celeste thinks about what she was doing just then, while he wandered around the empty school. Maybe she was with the Daves, warming herself at their hibachi, waiting for her parents and Nicky to find her. "You must've been really scared," she says.

"I don't know. I think I was just, like, delirious or something. In the morning I got scared, because I didn't remember getting there. The rest of it came back to me later."

The morning rose on the roof with a strange yellow haze. Celeste remembers this from waking up in the Daves' yard that day: hard to tell if it was dawn or dusk. Nicky woke up utterly parched, all the way down his throat and into his chest. He stumbled back into the building to a bathroom and drank from the tap, washed his face, cleaned the grit out of his eyes. "Let me tell you, Cookie, it wasn't the last time I had to actually *bathe* with that fuckin' gross bubble-gum hand soap." He shudders, a sweet glimmer of vintage Nicky, and cries, "The horror!" But it revived him. He looked at himself in the mirror, caught a flash of an older man he never wanted to be: stubble flecked with ash, dark pits under his eyes. He wandered out into a building filled with ghosts. It was like he could hear them laughing. The emptiness in the senior hall was so total that every tiny movement was loud—his breath, the broken glass crunching under his shoes, the corners of college posters rippling when he walked by. Nicky remembered that he no longer belonged in that place. He walked out onto the soccer field, the yellow sky swirling with sirens.

And then it occurred to him: *I could leave now, after all, and make it easier on everyone. They'll assume I'm dead.* A clean break.

He climbed over the fence and jumped down into a different life.

THE WAY HE TELLS THE REST IS IN A RELUCTANT KIND of haze, the details misarranged or eraser-smudged, the timeline tangled in knots. He bounced around for a while, slept in the sand dunes sometimes, once in a while in a motel for a day or two to recover some rest, his cash dwindling. Twice up to Mimi's, where he watched the stars and tried to make some plans. He tells Celeste he went up there the second time to get clean before he could enlist. Otherwise, he doesn't talk about the drugs, and she doesn't ask.

He stands at the airport window, presses his palms on the glass. A plane takes off to the west, rising over the water. The roar of it builds and fades. Celeste's phone alarm rings, rupturing the silence.

"Lover boy again?"

"Nah, it's just my pancreas." She lifts the hem of her hoodie to show him the insulin pump—so small, sometimes she even forgets that it's there.

"Well, I'll be!" he says, putting on a syrupy *Gone with the Wind* accent. She checks the app, turns away to fix a kink in the tube—blushing hotly, for some reason kind of embarrassed. This device has literally saved her life—just like her parents and Nicky always insisted it would—but it also feels weirdly like selling out.

The old Nicky was a big fan of I-told-you-so moments, but this one—Paolo?—doesn't go there. "Holy crap, Celeste," he says admiringly. He leans over his lap to scratch the soft down behind Ursa's ears. "Poor baby. You're a relic now, huh?"

Celeste laughs. "Just, like, semi-retired. Still wears the harness so I can take her everywhere."

Nicky smiles at Ursa, her black eyes watching him, full of wonder and sweetness. "I was right," he says quietly, "you're better without me," and Celeste feels a flare of anger, such a white-hot bolt that it kicks her out of the chair, her fists sweaty and coiled.

"Jesus, Nicky," she sputters, "really?"

"It's true," he says. "You're all better off."

"Fuck that, Nicky, okay? This is not about you. *This*"—she shows him the pump at her waist, too pissed to be embarrassed now—"is not about you. Believe it or not, I'm starting to figure out my own shit. Things are good. And I really just wish you were around." He sighs, covers his face. She glares out the window onto the sparkling tarmac, feeling the force of the next words on her lips like a weapon: "That's bullshit: We're 'better off'? I don't think you really believe that anyway. Your mom, 'better off'? *Bullshit*, Nicky. You're just trying to let yourself off the hook."

He's silent, so she waits, a little stunned, a little disgusted by how good it feels to hurt him. She stares at the palms of her hands like they're bloody. Of course, she could go on; she could punish him, tell him more about Carla's suffering, or her own. But he already knows. She thinks about Mimi, about Meo. She thinks about the sea at Mimi's house, the relentlessness of the waves on the rocks, the deep blue calm that hovers in the distance. She sits back down beside him, touches his wrist. A little bit of the pain drains from his face.

"There was, like, this ghost of you?" she says. ". . . Or something. I kept seeing him everywhere, when you were gone. But it wasn't you, I guess—that's the thing I figured out. It was actually just me."

They're both crying a little again. Celeste reaches up and wipes his cheek with the cuff of her hoodie. He grabs her sleeve and pretends to blow his nose on it, making them both laugh. Then he says, "Nothing *just* about you, Cookie," and she smiles into her lap. He digs a bottle of water out of his duffel and glugs from it like a runner. After a minute he says, "You didn't go," and then, a little warily: "MIT."

She tosses him a smirk. "What are you, a cyberstalker now?"

"Yeah, basically. It's a hobby of mine these days."

"A creepy hobby."

"I shouldn't have interfered."

"Very true."

"I just felt like—" He turns away from her again, squinting, like he's looking down a long road. "You deserved MIT. And it wasn't fair for my shit to mess up your shit, you know? I couldn't let that happen."

She takes out a pack of tissues so they can wipe away the last of the tears. She starts to tell him her own story—bits of it, anyway—about Europa and the interview and the door that Nicky's meddling actually opened for her. She tells him she has a GED, and some credits at City, and now a for-real job at *PodLab*, and in the fall she'll be moving into an open room in Bridget's Berkeley apartment with three other roommates. Nicky is shocked that she didn't graduate with their class; he makes a big show, fake fainting onto the airport carpet, which has the ironic effect of making Celeste not want to explain.

"Long story," she tells him, deciding not to correct the guilty look on his face.

"Fuck, how did Bonnie take it? Murderous rampage? Good ol' nervous breakdown?"

"Yeah, she wasn't thrilled." There were months, in fact, when Celeste hardly spoke to her parents. After Florida she stayed with Mimi for the summer, then crashed on Soli's couch while she figured things out with Bonnie and Shane. But of this time, all she says to Nicky is "I bounced around for a while, too."

There is so much more she could tell him, but it's hard to choose. She thinks about their beloved, troubled city and its scars, so many neighborhoods still scraped raw, clumsy rebuilds sandwiched between the stoic survivors, other neighborhoods fully repaired with the pristine gleam of wealth. She thinks about her own clumsy rebuild: the past few months living back home again, helping her dad install a beautiful old rug down the slope of the brand-new stairs. And of course, she thinks about Nonna, too—about how you could always tell, by the fan of wrinkles at the corner of her eye, whether she liked the soup for lunch or the sweater you picked out for her to wear. Finally, Celeste decides to say, "I actually stayed with your mom, just for a few months. She needed help with Nonna, and my parents were cool with it. They knew Carla and Pop would keep an eye on me."

Nicky's face collapses a bit. She was going to tell him the rest—how Nonna died a month ago in her room at the top of the house, with a distant view of the silvering sea—but now Celeste can see that he already knows. Carla never stopped writing to him at Paolo Reborn, just in case; he must be reading the emails again after all.

"I'm really sorry," Celeste says, but Nicky only leans away and starts to dig through his duffel. She waits, holding her breath, feels the moment beginning to swerve, the ground uncertain under the soles of her shoes, the faraway announcement that her flight will soon begin to board. Then Nicky draws something slowly out of his bag, something supple and purple and alive, like a rare bird emerging from a magician's hat. He dangles it between them. Paolo's tiny suspenders. The little brass clips glinting in the window light.

"She said I should take them. When I left that morning, I told her I wouldn't come back. I actually think she understood. She told me where to find them, super clear, like she had a whole fucking map of the basement in her head." He hands them to Celeste, who spreads them over her palms, feels the velvet under her thumbs. Nicky laughs. "They're a little snug. I've been working out."

"Nicky," Celeste says, "my flight's leaving soon."

He takes the suspenders and tucks them gently back in the bag. He stands and offers her an arm, just as if they were playing one of their old pretend games, dressed as a king and queen wrapped in a thousand scarves, or posing for a gold rush photo at the Wharf, buttoned up in petticoat and tails. They always loved to try on different lives that wouldn't ever be theirs. They'd kept on doing it long after other kids had stopped. It feels strange to be standing here in new costumes, still wondering if they fit. Celeste takes his elbow and leans her head lightly on his arm. They walk a little in silence, heading to her gate, the numbers scrolling down with their steps. After a minute she says, "You could call her."

Nicky doesn't reply. The airport seethes around them, but they move through it with a kind of calm that Celeste had not expected to feel in his presence again, their linked arms forming a bonded molecule. There is so much more to ask and tell, but the silence is strangely lovely, cushioned by their shared relief. Eventually he says, "I can't talk to my mom yet. I think I need to just keep going right now, alone. But I'll write to her," he says, "and you, too."

They've reached the gate where Celeste's flight to Orlando is boarding. The people who will sit beside her in boredom for the next six hours have no idea what just happened: the quake that nobody noticed, the sparkling lace of thaw that's only just begun to form on the frozen crust of the moon.

Nicky says goodbye to Ursa, kissing the soft crown of her head. Then Celeste throws her arms around him. "See you up there," she whispers into his ear, and a moment later she can't find him through the crowd. He is gone again as swiftly as he came. She doesn't know if he'll actually write—but she will call Carla herself and tell her everything. She'll keep the story. This is the role she has chosen.

In a few days, when she's listening to the astronauts talk about walking on Mars, the lightness of it—more like flying than walking, really—on the surface of a lonely world, Celeste will close her eyes and see Nicky's footprints in the silt, and her own, coiling endlessly together and away.

ACKNOWLEDGMENTS

I'm a librarian, so I touch a lot of books every day, and the fact that each one of them contains thousands of hours of work by creative, passionate people who just want to bring beautiful stories into the world gives me a deep feeling of wonder. My agent, Molly Ker Hawn, and my editor, Andrew Karre, are two of these people: exceptionally talented, crazy intelligent book nerds who've made it their mission to launch stories into orbit. I'm so lucky to be working with these two!

My gratitude for the inimitable Molly starts with the fact that she plucked my manuscript out of her mountainous pile of queries, mostly because the first chapter happens to mention her childhood dentist (thank you, Dr. Plack!). Molly believed in me and this book when I was almost ready to give up. She's a lovely, savvy, indefatigable person and the best agent on either side of the pond. Thank you also to the rest of the team at the Bent Agency, US and UK, for your behind-the-scenes support and guidance.

Andrew, the depth of your insight, sensitivity, and kindness has made this whole process feel like such a magical collaboration. I can't imagine an editor more in tune with my vision for this project or more astute and careful with each revision, no matter how small. I can't wait to show you the next one!

It's a magical, humbling experience when someone creates art inspired by your art; I was blown away when I saw Hokyoung Kim's gorgeous cover illustration and all of Kelley Brady's stunning design details. I can't envision a more perfect package for this story. Thank you both! And thanks also to the rest of the Penguin team, especially Kaitlin Kneafsey, for all the work you're doing to put this book in readers' hands.

To the librarians and booksellers who devote their lives to connecting young people with the stories they need and want and love, you're my people – I'm so grateful to you for finding this one and passing it along.

In some ways it feels like I've been writing this book my whole life, ever since the 1989 earthquake rocked my teenage world. But in fact I started writing it in 2018, when I had the astounding good fortune to be included in the first group of authors at the Brown Handler Residency at Friends of the San Francisco Public Library. Lisa Brown and Daniel Handler, I can't thank you enough for that gift of time and space, without which this book would definitely not exist. What a cool idea, to surround writers with people who love books and libraries and let that community of inspiration grow. Thanks also to the fabulous humans at Friends of SFPL (now and former) who shared their space and cheered us on, especially Marie Ciepiela and Michael-Vincent D'Anella.

So many miles of thanks to Katharine Mitchell Zamarra, whose story sense, ear for language, and powers of human observation are peerless, and Laura Scholes Baedeker, who always drops the best "don't hate me, but what if . . ." comments on a draft, the kind that make you go *Daaaang, she's good!* These two have been my ride-or-die readers since the turn of the millennium, and I'm so grateful for them.

Thank you also to Susy Jeng and Caleb Blumenfeld, who sprinkled their wisdom on early drafts, and to these teachers and book wizards for their guidance and encouragement over the many years that I've been trying to do this crazy thing: Dee McNamer, Kevin Canty, Rob McQuilkin, Aaron Wehner, and Susan Faust.

My friends fill my life with the joy and conversation that a person needs in order to get up in the morning and do the work. Denise, Jason, Sarah (Songer!), Eileen, Amy, David, Anne, Alex, Rachel(s), Katy, Kerber, Maggie, Elena, Allison, Sarah (Cole!), Brooke, Bianca, Vanessa, Virginia – I love you all so much.

My family-in-law are the best cheerleaders. Thank you, Nadlers, for your love and support from near and far!

I'm also incredibly lucky to come from the Coatar family, which is lousy with amazing storytellers. We can tell stories all night long and into the next day. These stories are the food that I grew up on, and I'd be lost without the hilarious, loving humans who tell them. Special thanks to my Aunt Joan, who told me once years ago with utter certainty that I would make this happen. And as we all know, she's the boss.

I'm so grateful for my parents and my brother, Dan, whose love has always made me brave. My mother's unwavering belief that I could do this convinced me to believe it, too. If you know her, you know what I mean. She makes you want to be the incredible person she thinks you are. I wish my late father were still here, too, because he always loved to read my stories, and he taught me so much about living with illness, which helped me write Celeste. I'd like to know whether he thought I got it right.

Saul, my gratitude for you is as deep as the sky. Your partnership and love quite literally made this dream come true.

My kids won't forgive me if I forget to thank our dog. But she can't read (at least, I'm pretty sure she can't?), so I'll thank them instead. Iris and Jonah, watching you be yourselves in the world inspires me every day and makes me want to create beautiful things. This book is for you.